PRAISE FOR STEPHANIE KUEHNERT'S EDGY AND EMOTIONAL
DEBUT, *I WANNA BE YOUR JOEY RAMONE*
A *Chicago Tribune* "Hot Summer Read"

"Kuehnert's smart gal, punk-rock narrator is irresistible, and her harrowing sexual initiations, tragic family predicament, and struggle to stay close to her best friend and secure respect as a rock musician will enthrall."

—*Booklist*

"As a fictive artifact of an aggressive, didactic genre in which shades of gray are often obliterated by black and white beats of rage, Kuehnert emerges as a true subversive—retaining her cred while expanding the form."

—*Los Angeles Times*

"Car won't start? Don't call AAA. Just grab a copy of *I Wanna Be Your Joey Ramone,* hook it up to a pair of jumper cables, connect the other end to the car battery—and stand back. The power surge emanating from Kuehnert's first novel will be more than enough to get the engine going."

—*Chicago Tribune*

"A manifesto for defiant high school girls, as well as a refresher course for the goddesses they turn into."

—*Venus Zine*

"Allusive, real, and honest. . . . It makes no difference if you're a punk-rock chick or a glam princess, I would recommend this book."

—*Elle Girl*

"Raw and gritty."

—*Publishers Weekly*

"Kuehnert's language is slick. The punk references bite with genuine angst and hunger, and Emily's tough, sardonic attitude, as revealed through chunky, poetic language, is feverishly tempting."

—*Kirkus Reviews*

"A rich muscular story."

—*BUST Magazine*

"This book could be any real band's *Behind the Music*. . . . Solid writing."

—*Racket Magazine*

"A powerful story. . . . I could almost believe that Emily was a real musician, not a character created by the author. I was sad to come to the last page, wanting the story of Emily to go on forever."

—TeensReadToo.com

"Unputdownable. . . . Kuehnert is an unbelievably talented writer. Her debut is a smart, touching, intense and emotional novel that readers will absolutely love."

—Teen Book Review

"Heartbreaking, hilarious, touching, exciting, upsetting, elating and exhilarating. I loved this book fifteen pages in, and that feeling continued to grow the more I read. In fact, the end was one of the best endings I've read in a very long time. It was a perfect close."

—Plenty of Paper Reviews

"I promise you won't regret picking up this unforgettable novel. I definitely look forward to more amazing novels from Stephanie Kuehnert."

—The Book Muncher

"A wonderfully written and evocative story of a mother and daughter parted by circumstance and joined by music. I heartily recommend it."

—Irvine Welsh, internationally bestselling author of *Trainspotting*

"Teeth. Punk. Combat boots. Attitude. Feminism. Family. Girls with guitars. Relationships that jack you up. Sharp things of the not-good kind. Friendships. Love. . . . It's all here; it's all pure and real. I loved it."

—Melissa Marr, *New York Times* bestselling author of *Wicked Lovely* and *Ink Exchange*

Don't miss Stephanie Kuehnert's first stunning coming-of-age tale

I WANNA BE YOUR JOEY RAMONE

Now available from MTV Books

BALLADS OF

STEPHANIE KUEHNERT

POCKET BOOKS   MTV BOOKS
New York   London   Toronto   Sydney

MTV BOOKS

Pocket Books
A Division of Sim
1230 Avenue of
New York, NY 10

3 1357 00042 4090

First MTV Books/Pocket Books trade paperback edition July 2009

POCKET and colophon are registered trademarks of Simon & Schuster, Inc.

For information about special discounts for bulk purchases, please contact Simon & Schuster Special Sales at 1-800-456-6798 or business@simonandschuster.com

The Simon & Schuster Speakers Bureau can bring authors to your live event. For more information or to book an event contact the Simon & Schuster Speakers Bureau at 866-248-3049 or visit our website at www.simonspeakers.com.

Manufactured in the United States of America

10 9 8 7 6 5 4 3 2 1

Library of Congress Cataloging-in-Publication Data

Kuehnert, Stephanie
    Ballads of suburbia / Stephanie Kuehnert.—1st MTV Books/Pocket Books trade pbk. ed.
        p. cm.
    Summary: An aspiring film writer tells about her troubled teen years in the Chicago suburbs when she and her friends tried to escape the pain of their lives through rock music and drugs.
    [1. Emotional problems—Fiction. 2. Drug abuse—Fiction. 3. Rock music—Fiction. 4. Punk culture—Fiction. 5. Chicago (Ill.)—Fiction.] I. Title.
    PZ7.K94873Bal 2009
    [Fic]—dc22   2009008658

ISBN 978-1-4391-0282-4
ISBN 978-1-4391-2685-1 (ebook)

*For my best friend, Katie, who helped me
through my own high school experience.*

*In loving memory of Marcel Fremont, who helped
us all survive high school and become better,
wiser people. We miss you so much.*

ACKNOWLEDGMENTS

Thanks to:

Everyone at MTV Books, especially Jen Heddle, the best damn editor on the planet, for pushing me to do my best. Also to Erica Feldon, publicist extraordinaire, and to Jane Elias, copyedit queen. I can't send you guys enough cupcakes to repay you.

Caren Johnson Estesen, darling agent.

Sheryl Johnston, for all the guidance, both professional and personal.

Scott, sweet husband-to-be, who talked me off the ledge numerous times while I was writing this and just generally makes me happy.

Vanessa Barneveld, Katie Corboy, Jenny Seay, and Aaron Golding, the best critique partners a writer could ask for.

Jenny Hassler, goddess of the interwebs, and Elise Coleman, mistress of graphic design.

The Columbia College Chicago Fiction Writing Department. Special shout-out to Joe Meno, who taught class with Johnny Cash songs one day, inspiring the concept behind this book.

My family, including my future in-laws.

BFF Katie and all my amazing friends. Polly and Thea, I'm especially glad we've reconnected.

Everyone at the Beacon Pub—bartending is my favorite job besides writing.

My street team; you guys seriously rock.

All the authors who have offered wisdom, especially those I've had the privilege to read with, and all the incredible folks at bookstores, libraries, taverns, record stores, and schools who have graciously hosted me.

Special thanks to Alexa Young, my partner-in-crime for Rock 'n' Read. Also to Irvine Welsh and Joe Shanahan for making my rock-star fantasies come true by inviting me to read onstage at the Metro.

And of course, the biggest thanks of all go to my wonderful readers. Read on.

"If you made a book of what really happened,
it'd be a really upsetting book."
—*Angela Chase on* My So-Called Life

EPILOGUE

THE BALLAD OF A HOMECOMING

"And the embers never fade in your city by the lake
The place where you were born."

—*The Smashing Pumpkins*

December 1999

SIRENS AND LIGHTS WELCOMED ME BACK TO the suburbs of Chicago. It seemed fitting considering they'd also heralded my exit. And it couldn't have happened anywhere else: only a Berwyn cop would pull Stacey over for rolling a stop sign and cash in on her total lack of insurance, but not notice the underlying stench of pot smoke on us. It clung to Stacey's auburn ponytail, my freshly dyed black hair, and the clothing beneath both of our winter coats. I'll never know how he missed it. A rare stroke of good luck? The karma I was owed for agreeing to come home in the first place?

I'd been gone for over four years. Around the holidays Stacey always tried to guilt me into visiting. She'd remind me that my mom missed me or point out that there was no chance for a white Christmas in Los Angeles. She knew I never intended to set foot in the Chicago area again after everything that had happened at the end of junior year, but the girl wouldn't give it up. Finally, she resorted to playing dirty, name-dropping her daughter: "Lina wants you to be there for her fourth birthday. She wants to know why she's never met Mama's best friend."

It was an underhanded tactic, but it worked.

"I don't know why I didn't think of it earlier," Stacey congratulated herself.

"Because using your kid to get what you want is low even for you," I joked.

"No, it's not!" Stacey laughed a hoarse, smoker's laugh. She gestured to the car seat in the back, bragging, "Do you know how many times I've used that thing to get out of a ticket?"

On cue, the whoop of a siren behind us.

"Shit!" Stacey slapped the steering wheel hard with the heel of her hand. "Don't the goddamn Berwyn cops have anything else to do?"

I gazed at the flashing red and blue behind us. I couldn't take my eyes off the colors, remembering how they looked reflected in my friend Cass's wide brown eyes the night I came to surrounded by paramedics in Scoville Park.

I'd said "Adrian," and when Cass heard me over the commotion, her jaw clenched.

"He left you here to die and saved his own ass."

"Good," I cackled. "Good for him."

The tears streaking down Cass's full cheeks turned to rainbows in the red and blue light. I closed my eyes, silently begging the heroin to drag me all the way under.

That was one of my last memories of home.

Stacey eased the car to the side of the road and turned down the radio. Old reflexes kicking in, I lit a cigarette in what I felt certain would be a failed attempt to cover the pot stink.

Stacey's litany of excuses began the moment she rolled down her window and smiled flirtatiously at the frowning officer. "I was at Midway picking her up—my best friend who I haven't seen in over four years—and my husband paged me. Our daughter's sick." She indicated the empty car seat.

Great, I thought, tuning out her diatribe, *I'm in town for an hour and I'm already in trouble.* I did not want to spend my first night back at the Berwyn police station. Why had I agreed to Stacey's suggestion of taking "the long route" from the airport? I'd known it was code for stopping by her mother's basement apartment and getting stoned. Stacey's mom, Beth, had been smoking us up since freshman year of high school. Apparently Stacey had forgotten that I didn't indulge in those activities anymore.

Sure enough, Beth had answered the door with a bong in her hand, screeching, "Kara-leeeena! Kara-leeeena! You're finally home!" Both she and Stacey called me that even though I wasn't a Carolyn or a Caroline, just Kara. In naming her daughter Lina, Stacey had effectively named her after me.

The last time I'd been at Beth's was a mild June evening the summer after junior year. That was when Stacey told me she was pregnant and planned to keep the baby. She'd be moving out of her mom's house into prematurely married life. I worried about her, but I had serious problems of my own. Like heroin addiction. After I left Stacey's that night, I OD'd in Scoville Park.

My parents and I collectively decided that it would be best for me to live with my dad in Wisconsin until I finished high school. I hadn't come back for Christmas or birthdays or Stacey's wedding or Lina's birth. I stayed in Madison and held my breath that my poor grades from junior year wouldn't keep me out of USC's film program. After high school graduation, I went straight to L.A. and hadn't touched down on midwestern soil since.

Beth's house was still the same. After she gave me a long, bone-crushing hug, we followed her through the kitchen—the sink filled with dirty dishes as usual—down the short hallway—the floor strewn with clothes and junk mail—to the living room. Beth swept pillows and blankets off a futon mattress on the floor in the middle of the room. We plopped down and Beth handed me the bong.

When I declined, passing it to Stacey, Beth offered me a glass of wine. "You still drink at least, don't you? We should toast to your homecoming!"

"I don't drink much, actually," I replied, adding, "but we're celebrating, right?" before Beth's grin could turn into a pout.

"Exactly!" Beth enthusiastically poured nearly half a bottle of wine into a large plastic cup. "Sorry I don't have proper glasses, but the wine's good. My boyfriend works at Whole Foods. He got it there."

The wine was good and I drank it a little faster than I should have, but I wasn't used to being around Beth and Stacey without a buzz.

Beth, in particular, could be intense. She played with her hennaed curls and asked incessant questions about "la-la land." What famous people had I seen? Had I really given up writing screenplays to work on movie soundtracks? Was there money in that? Didn't I know I was supposed to be writing a big blockbuster so I could move her, Stacey, and Lina out to my mansion in the hills? Beth breathed only when she inhaled pot and hardly gave me time to respond to one question before throwing another at me.

And this had gone on until Stacey declared, "We gotta get home before Jason gets pissed." She grabbed her coat and I followed, waving to Beth.

"Now we can finally talk," Stacey said, swinging her long legs into the car.

Back in grade school, Stacey and I had plenty of time to talk. It was just the two of us and we'd spend all afternoon chattering about silly kid stuff. Things changed when we reached high school. Stacey discovered boys and weed, so she was always busy and soon I was, too. We made small talk when we crossed paths at parties, but that was about it. We started to have more meaningful phone conversations after I moved away, but they often got cut short by Lina or Jason. So, Stacey learned to talk rapid-fire like her mother and mostly I just listened.

In the car, Stacey launched into the tale of her latest argument with Jason as she wove through Berwyn, past the greasy spoons that lit up Ogden, and then down the quieter East Avenue, peppered with brick bungalows and tall apartment buildings. Stacey's fights with Jason were generally minor—considering the odds against their teenage marriage of convenience and Stacey's feisty nature, they were doing quite well—but Stacey liked to dramatize things. Since both of us were absorbed in her tale, neither of us noticed her poor driving.

Then, of course, that stupid cop pulled us over.

I smoked two cigarettes while Stacey turned on the charm. But the worried-mother routine failed to impress.

"Do you have proof of insurance?" the cop asked, dark eyes unwavering.

"No . . ." Stacey replied meekly.

He went off to his car to do his cop thing. Stacey was so irritated, she didn't even talk. We chain-smoked in silence for ten minutes until he came back. She fished for compassion once more. "I don't know how we're going to afford this and my daughter's prescriptions. We don't have health insurance either, you know."

The cop shrugged unsympathetically.

Stacey repressed her rage until he slammed his car door. "Jason is going to be so pissed!" she moaned, staring at the five-hundred-dollar ticket for driving uninsured.

"At least he didn't smell the pot. We totally reek." I rolled down my window to toss out my cigarette butt. A cold wind grazed my cheeks. I shivered but enjoyed the novelty of it, since I hadn't experienced real winter for years.

"True." Stacey wrinkled her nose and asked, "Do you have some gum?" As if that would make her smell any less like a stoner.

I fumbled through the pockets of my hoodie and offered her my last piece. After she took it, she stared at me, her aqua eyes burning into mine.

"What?" I self-consciously smoothed my short hair and tongued my lip ring to make sure it wasn't turned some weird way. My eyes darted from her finely plucked eyebrows to the freckled bridge of her nose and down to the familiar crescent-shaped scar indented on her chin—from a bike accident when she was six, a year before we met.

She shook her head soberly. "I fucking missed you."

I smiled. "I missed you, too."

Then she changed the topic again. That was Stacey; her thoughts moved at warp speed. "Soundtracks? What exactly is it that you do again?"

"I'm interning with a music supervisor who works for Warner Brothers. It's nothing glamorous. I don't hang out with rock stars. I just do the grunt work, but that's what most internships are, after all."

She studied me quizzically. "And you like this?"

I nodded. I liked it better than my writing internship. I'd worked fourteen-hour days assisting the writers of a TV medical drama. The intensity of the job had almost led to a nervous breakdown.

"And now you want to be a music supervisor even though you've been going to school for screenwriting?"

I shrugged.

Concern flooded Stacey's eyes. "Why aren't you writing?" she implored. "You loved writing. You wrote screenplays in high school all the time."

I worked on one screenplay junior year. With Adrian. And I talked about it once with Stacey at a party; her memory was a steel trap. Sure, I'd fallen in love with screenwriting that year, which had spawned the idea to go to USC, but it wasn't like I'd been aspiring to it for years. "I've always loved music, though. Besides, I realized I don't have any stories to tell."

Stacey's facial expression changed paths like a hurricane. "You?" She choked back laughter, holding her gut. "You don't have any stories? Growing up here? Hanging out with the people you hung out with?"

"I don't have any stories." I clenched my jaw hard and watched the cop pull out from behind us. He turned right onto Fourteenth Street without signaling.

Stacey got back on the road. "Okay, fine. Here's a song for your sound-track, then." She flashed me a grin and reached for the volume knob, turning up "Back in Black" by AC/DC. She rolled another stop sign and we both laughed.

We cruised across Roosevelt Road into our hometown, Oak Park. Stacey meandered this way and that toward her apartment, narrating the changes that had occurred in the past few years. There weren't many. Remodeled Walgreens. Condo conversion. Condo conversion. Condo conversion. We passed houses we'd gone to parties in—both the innocent kind with birthday cake and parentally supervised games, and the kind where parents were nowhere in sight and I left blasted with my underwear on inside out. We reminisced about getting high on that playground or making out with what's-his-name in front of that 7-Eleven.

These were all memories that felt good. Stacey swerved away from the ones that wouldn't, like my ex-boyfriend Christian's house and Scoville Park. If I looked in the direction of those places, she distracted me with "Remember when we were eight . . ."

Before the last chorus of "Back in Black" ended, Stacey punched buttons on the radio in search of another good song to keep the buzz going. She practically blew out the speakers when she found Social Distortion. Our gazes collided as we shouted, "High school seemed like such a blur . . ."

Yeah, "Story of My Life," Stacey knew it was my type of song. It's the ballads I like best, and I'm not talking about the clichéd ones where a diva hits her highest note or a rock band tones it down a couple of notches for the ladies. I mean a *true* ballad. Dictionary definition: a song that tells a story in short stanzas and simple words, with repetition, refrain, etc. My definition: the punk rocker or the country crooner telling the story of his life in three minutes, reminding us of the numerous ways to screw up.

As we zigzagged around Oak Park to Social D, memories of the wild times seduced me. I wanted to spend the whole week stoned. I wanted to call old boyfriends. I wanted to go to a punk show at the Fireside to meet new boys. I wanted to ride in Adrian's car, him taking the curves of Lake Shore Drive way too fast. I wanted to drink coffee at Punk Rock Denny's until dawn. I wanted to snort a line in Scoville Park as the sun rose.

It would be so easy to be the person I used to be. My life was like a song. L.A., working my ass off to do well in college and be a "healthy person," just a verse, and the chorus was coming up again, the part where I fucked up the same way I always did.

The spell was broken when Stacey screeched to a stop behind her apartment building, the radio cutting out abruptly as she killed the engine.

"I can't stay," I reminded myself curtly.

"What?" Stacey's brow knit in confusion. Apparently I said that aloud.

"I mean, after New Year's. I'm going back to school, back to L.A."

"I know that." She shook her head, shooting me a "you're insane" look before popping the trunk and getting out to grab my bags.

The heady combination of a little wine and a lot of nostalgia had me feeling dazed, so I stopped in the kitchen for a glass of water while Stacey dragged my suitcase into the living room. I heard her greet Jason, but before "Hi" made it all the way out of her mouth, she asked sharply, "What the hell is he still doing here? I told you he needed to leave before we got back."

Jason drawled "Staaaaace" like a stoned hippie surfer. "He just got out of jail yesterday. He's got nowhere to go. Six months in County for some coke that wasn't even his, give the guy a break."

I knew who *he* was before *his* voice rumbled. "I just wanted to say hi to Kara."

Adrian. I hadn't seen him since we did heroin beneath the metal stage they used for summer concerts in Scoville Park. Then, we lay entwined on the hilltop, nodding in and out. At one point, I noticed that the sky looked sickly gray. Our skin looked gray. The grass looked gray. I ran my fingers through the dying gray grass, wondering if that was what Adrian's hair would be like when he was old. I crawled back toward the stage, puking and crying because I knew that neither of us would grow old. Especially me, I was going to die right then and there. I screamed for Adrian's help and got no response.

I guess he'd nodded out and when he came to, he found me. He'd slapped my face, trying to bring me around, and when I didn't wake, he ran to the pay phone to call Cass. Apparently her suggestion of calling 911 conjured images of the cops he'd been avoiding, so he dropped the phone and ran. Cass and Stacey hated him for it, but honestly, I hadn't expected anything more from him, even though that night, strung out and groping on the grass, he'd told me he loved me for the first time.

"Kara doesn't want to see you. Get out of my house!" Stacey snapped.

I didn't want to see him. I did, but I didn't. I shouldn't. I wanted to see Lina, though. I crept warily down the hallway toward the living room and caught my first glimpse of her: sprawled out across Jason, her head in the crook of his arm, little feet dangling over his knees, right hand loosely gripping an empty sippy cup. Lina looked nothing like Jason, with his ginger hair and green eyes. Instead, she had blackish brown curls, a pale face that would freckle in the sunlight, and heavily fringed blue eyes—a miniature clone of Stacey and Beth.

I wandered into the living room, needing to be closer to her. I knelt by Jason's legs and carefully took the cup from Lina's hand, stroking her silky skin. I couldn't believe I'd been so selfish and stayed away from her so long just because I was afraid to confront my past.

"Kara," Adrian whispered.

I stared at the sleeping baby a moment longer to steel myself before I faced him.

He was a relic of the early nineties, of our crazy youth: same leather jacket, same strong shoulders, same thick waves of tawny hair stretching to the middle of his back, same sharp jawline covered with the same stubble, same searching brown eyes.

When his gaze locked on mine, I mentally chanted my mantra of *I can't stay,* and then I let him embrace me. His scent had always reminded me of a muskier version of the air off Lake Michigan, and as soon as it reached my nostrils, it shattered the icy indifference that I'd tried to force myself to feel about him. As I melted into his familiar arms, I could no longer deny it: I'd missed him and I'd missed home and I'd gone too long without facing all of my bad memories and old ghosts.

Suddenly, I envisioned my high school best friend, Maya, standing behind Adrian. Her red hair glistened (although it wasn't red the last time I saw her, that's the way it remains in my memory) and her gray eyes had an ethereal glow to them. Right hip cocked, hand firmly clamped to it, she made that mischievous I-told-you-so face like she did when citing her grandmother's clichés.

She told me, "Kara, it's like my grandma always said, 'You're gonna have to face the music.'"

AUGUST 1992–JUNE 1994

(FRESHMAN AND SOPHOMORE YEARS)

"When I got the music,
I gotta place to go."
—*Rancid*

1.

THE SUMMER BEFORE I ENTERED SECOND grade and my brother Liam started kindergarten, Dad got the promotion he'd been after for two years and my parents had enough money to move us from the South Side of Chicago to its suburb, Oak Park.

When I say "suburb," you might envision subdivisions that center on a strip mall or a man-made lake and "ticky-tacky box houses," as Maya's grandmother would call them. You know, where the only thing that varies from one house to the next is the color of the paint job. But Oak Park is not one of those suburbs.

Separated from the West Side of Chicago by an imaginary line down the middle of Austin Boulevard, Oak Park still looks like part of the city. The houses were built in the same era and are of the same style. The east-west streets have the same names. You can catch the "L" in Oak Park and be downtown in fifteen minutes.

The big difference is the feel: more of a small-town vibe, less of the hustle and bustle. My parents talked up Oak Park like it was a fairy-tale kingdom. Middle-class but diverse. An excellent number of parks, trees, "good" schools, and libraries per capita. Chic, independently run shops populating the main streets and the pedestrian mall in the center of town. Houses of the Frank Lloyd Wright ilk sprawling like midwestern miniplantations across two or three normal-size lots on the north side. Classic

Victorian "painted ladies" speckling the entire town. My parents couldn't dream of owning those houses, but our four-bedroom had an enclosed sun porch at the front, a deck out back, and a living room with a real working fireplace. It was a huge step up from the bottom half of the two-flat we occupied in the city.

My parents claimed suburbia was safer than Chicago, but I certainly didn't find it kinder and gentler. On my first day of school, I was approached by Maggie Young during recess. Maggie had a face like JonBenét Ramsey's, but with big brown eyes and perfect ringlets of chestnut hair framing her features. She was always trailed by an entourage of five or six girls. Two of them were her best friends; the rest acted as servants in hopes of winning her favor.

When they came up to me, I smiled, mistakenly thinking I would be welcomed to join them on the playground. Instead, I was given a bizarre test of my coolness. Maggie asked if my jacket had a YKK zipper. When I checked and responded that it didn't, she scoffed, "Does your family shop at Kmart or something? I bet those aren't even real Keds."

Her minions giggled like chirping birds. I stared down at my dirty white sneakers, both ashamed and confused. I hardly had a clue what she was talking about. We were seven, for Christ's sake, and fashion hadn't been a big deal at my old school. But my faux pas meant my automatic exclusion from the upper echelons of second grade.

Later that afternoon, when it came time to pick partners for a science project, every girl I sought out with my gaze refused to meet it except for Stacey O'Connor. She came running over, gushing, "Wanna be my partner?" Her bright blue eyes danced. "I already have an idea for the project."

Later we would use two empty two-liter bottles, some green food coloring, and a little plastic device Stacey'd seen on some PBS show to demonstrate the workings of a tornado.

Since Stacey already had the project figured out and discussing her plan took five minutes of the thirty the teacher allotted, Stacey launched into getting-to-know-you talk: "Where did you move from?" she asked, smiling so wide her freckled cheeks dimpled.

"The city," I boasted, having already decided Chicago was superior to Oak Park. It had taller buildings, the lakefront, and far friendlier kids.

"I lived on the South Side until I was four," Stacey told me. "My dad still lives there." She seemed equally as proud of her Chicago roots, but then she frowned, becoming defensive. "My mom and dad aren't married and never were. If you're gonna be mean about it . . ." She glared in the direction of Maggie Young.

I shook my head so vigorously that auburn strands of hair slapped me across the face. "I'm not gonna be mean to you! You're the first kid who's been nice to me."

With that out of the way, we moved on to our favorite cartoon (*ThunderCats*), color (blue), and food (peanut butter), marveling that we shared all of these common interests along with our non–Oak Park origin and ethnicity (Irish).

Stacey also said, "Wow, you have cool eyes. Are they orange in the middle?"

"They're hazel. Mostly green and brown, but they change colors sometimes."

"Oooh, like a mood ring!"

I nodded, beaming. Her words melted the feeling of insecurity that had been lodged in my gut since Maggie mocked my clothes.

Maybe if I'd begged my mom for a new wardrobe and a perm, I could've joined Maggie Young's elite crowd of Keds-sneakered, Gap-cardigan-wearing, boy-crazy girls with perfectly coiffed bangs. But once I aligned myself with Stacey, I was branded uncool for life and I didn't care. Stacey was a genuinely nice person; I was relieved to have a real friend, and so was she.

Stacey's low position on the social totem pole at school—just above the girl who smelled like pee and tried to blame it on her cats—stemmed from her undesirable family situation. She lived in a tiny apartment, not the prime locale for elaborate sleepovers, and all the other parents looked down on her mom. Beth had Stacey at sixteen and Stacey's dad had been thirty. Beth had scrimped and saved to move Stacey to the 'burbs for that mythic "better life." After that, Stacey rarely saw her dad.

Two years into our friendship, in fourth grade, I went with Stacey to visit him. We waited anxiously in the backseat while Beth went in to talk to him first. Five minutes later, Beth stormed out, red-cheeked, and started the car again, announcing, "He can't pay child support, he can't see his kid."

On the drive back to Oak Park, I stared out my window, feeling sick to my stomach for Stacey, who chewed on the ends of her dark hair, trying not to cry. Beth played the radio as loud as it could go, Led Zeppelin making the windows rattle, Stacey and I learning to find solace in a blaring rock song.

My friendship with Stacey was never supposed to change. It was supposed to stay frozen in time like the photograph on the mantel in my living room: me and Stacey, ten years old, eyes bright, our forefingers pulling our mouths into goofy, jack-o'-lantern grins. It would be okay if our hair and clothes changed with the times, but we were supposed to be standing side by side with wacky smiles on our faces until the day we died.

A week after eighth grade graduation, Beth broke the news that she and Stacey were moving to the neighboring town—and different school district—of Berwyn.

She tried to butter us up first, ordering pizza for dinner. We ate in front of the TV as usual, but after *The Real World* ended, Beth turned it off.

"We need to talk about something." Beth took a deep breath before blurting, "We're moving in August when the lease is up. I can't afford Oak Park rent anymore."

Stacey and I both sobbed and begged and pleaded, but it had no effect on Beth. She scowled, one hand on her hip, the other palm outstretched, sliding back and forth between us. "You girls wanna get jobs? Wanna see if I can get you dishwashing positions at the restaurant?" She jerked her hand away. "Didn't think so."

I wrapped my arms around myself and cried harder. Stacey screeched until she was blue in the face, calling Beth things she'd never dared, like "motherfucking bitch."

Finally, Beth roared, "Get to your room before I ground your ass for the entire summer!"

Stacey grabbed my hand and yanked me down the hall. She slammed her door and blasted a Black Sabbath album. Beth shouted at her to play it louder. Stacey changed the music to Nine Inch Nails, but Beth said she could turn that up, too.

After fifty similar arguments, Stacey didn't want to talk about it anymore. But I kept scheming to keep us from being separated. I even tried to convince my parents that we should move to Berwyn, too.

I accosted them in the kitchen one night while Mom prepared dinner and Dad thumbed through the files in his briefcase. I contended that we could find a cheaper house in Berwyn and the taxes would be lower. Feeling desperate, I also asserted, "Berwyn has the car spindle that was in *Wayne's World*. Oak Park doesn't have cool public art like that."

Dad snorted. "Kara, that thing is beyond tacky. And we're staying in Oak Park for the schools. That's why I work so hard to pay those high taxes."

"Doesn't Stacey deserve to go to school here, too? Maybe she could live with us or at least use our address—"

Dad cut me off with his patented "Absolutely not!" signaling end of discussion.

Mom chased me upstairs to my bedroom, where I threw myself

on my bed, shouting, "Dad's so unfair! He didn't even listen to me. He doesn't care about anything but his stupid job and he doesn't understand . . ." I buried my face in a pillow, sobbing.

Mom gently stroked my hair. "I understand," she murmured. I turned my head to look at her. She brushed away the ginger strands that clung to my damp cheeks before explaining, "My best friend's parents sent her to an all-girls Catholic high school. I begged my parents to send me, too, even though we couldn't afford it."

"You do understand. Will you talk to Dad?" I asked with a hiccup.

Mom smiled in that patronizing parental way. "Sweetie, Jane and I stayed friends even though we went to different schools. We hung out after school almost every day. That's what you and Stacey'll do. She'll only be a couple miles away. And you'll meet new friends like I did. It'll be okay."

"No, it won't!" I spat, feeling betrayed. Mom tried to hug me, but I flopped over on my stomach, growling, "Get out of my room!"

Mom spent the summer trying to reassure me that everything would be fine, but I couldn't shake the feeling that our annual trip to my aunt's cabin in Door County would be the last of the good times for me and Stacey.

My family always spent the second-to-last week of August at the cabin and Stacey had been joining us since fourth grade. Stacey's move was scheduled for the weekend after we returned, but we tried to enjoy our vacation.

On our last night, we snuck out after everyone went to bed. We crept through the backyard, down the dirt path to the lake. We did this every year, settling on the edge of the small pier just past where the motorboat was moored to talk and look at the stars. But this time we had a mission: to smoke pot for the first time. We thought getting stoned would help us forget the move and laugh and have fun like we used to.

We sat on the pier in silence at first, listening to make sure none of the adults had woken. Then Stacey fumbled in the pocket of her flannel shirt for the joint she'd carefully wrapped in a plastic bag. She hadn't shown it to me yet and I'd wondered if she'd actually been able to swipe some pot from Beth like she'd been promising.

Stacey extracted the joint and placed it in my palm. I studied the rolling job. It looked like a regular cigarette, but with the paper neatly twisted at both ends. "Whoa," I breathed upon examining the craftsmanship. "Did Beth give this to you?"

"No, she's not that cool. I took the pot and the papers from her dresser drawer while she was at work."

"*You* rolled this?"

Stacey nodded, obviously proud of her accomplishment. "Learned from watching the best." She smirked and handed me her lighter.

We'd started stealing Beth's cigarettes that summer, but they hadn't prepared my lungs for the burn of the first inhale. I coughed, tucking my chin toward my chest to mute the sound. Stacey took the joint and her first drag yielded the same result.

"Pretty cool, huh?" I managed to say in a scratchy voice.

"Yeah." Stacey squeezed her watering eyes shut.

After a few more drags, I stared up at the sky slightly light-headed, wondering if soon I'd feel happy or at least hungry with the munchies like Beth talked about.

Stacey looked up at the stars, too, and started laughing.

"What?" I asked excitedly, knowing her laughter meant the pot was kicking in.

She wiggled her fingers and imitated her mother's new-agey best friend, Lydia. "Our *fuuuuu*-ture is in those stars, Kara." Stacey sounded very stoned.

The only thing I saw in my future was torturous days at high school without her. "The future is going to suck."

Stacey kept the impression going, attempting to cheer me up. "The distance between our homes does not matter. The physical world does not bind us. We are linked *sooooo-uls.*" She giggled hysterically, but my frown remained.

I raked my hand through my hair and turned to Stacey. "You have to promise me that no matter what happens, you and I will always be best friends, exactly like we are now."

Stacey inhaled from the joint, cupped her open fist to her mouth, and pulled my face toward hers, my lips connecting with the other side of her hand. She blew smoke through her circled fingers into my mouth. "Smoke sisters," she pronounced with a grin, handing me the joint.

I smiled, but decided to one-up her. Pulling a Swiss Army knife from the pocket of my frayed cutoffs and flicking open the tiny blade, I suggested, "Blood sisters?"

Stacey blinked hesitantly. She hated pain. "Okay," she finally agreed, extending her forearm.

I traced a thin line in the smooth space between her wrist and her elbow. It was a tiny scratch, barely splitting her skin, and producing only a few droplets of red that dried almost immediately.

The one I gave myself in the identical spot went deeper, making Stacey shudder, but the twinge of pain ignited the rush I'd been expecting from the pot. A strange warmth crackled through me, leaving me with a sense of tranquillity I hadn't felt since Beth announced the move. The blood oozed out and formed one fat drop that lazily rolled down my skinny arm. I marveled at it momentarily before pressing my forearm to Stacey's.

"Blood sisters," I pronounced, admiring the sticky smear that stained my skin when I pulled away.

2.

I CUT MYSELF AGAIN AFTER MY FIRST day of high school.

There'd been so much to adjust to: trying to find my way around the building that was literally a block long, figuring out when I could stop at my locker to change out the fifty-pound textbooks I had for each class, not being one of the most brilliant people in the room.

I'd been recommended for and taken all honors-level classes. I'd never been a genius by any means, but I was smart and had always been able to keep up effortlessly. Stacey and I both were like that. We didn't consider ourselves "nerds" (though we'd been called that along with a slew of other inapplicable names, like "lesbians," throughout the years). We didn't kiss up to teachers. We sat in the back of the classroom and passed notes. We even smoked cigarettes in the bathroom once. Basically we acted like bad-asses, but got straight A's. However, I could tell that in high school, I was going to have to work hard, especially without Stacey, who usually tutored me in science while I helped her in history.

That day I thought about Stacey every few minutes. I wanted to ask her where we should sit when I got to class. I kept looking for her in the labyrinth of hallways. The school teemed with a few thousand students. Sure, they didn't *all* know one another, but they all had friends who greeted them when they entered a room. I had acquaintances, people I could sit next to and ask about their summer, but when the small talk ended I was alone.

After school, I raced home to wait for Stacey's call. We'd agreed she would take the bus to my house that day and the next day I'd take it to hers. When my phone rang, I didn't even say hello, just asked, "When are you coming over?"

"I don't know. I'm really tired." She sighed into the phone.

"Yeah, it was hard, wasn't it? I have so much homework."

"No, it wasn't hard. I just didn't sleep last night because I was nervous. It was anticlimactic, really."

I wanted to tell her that I missed her, but I wanted her to say it first. Maybe she was just tired, but she sounded a lot more nonchalant about the situation than I felt. "Do you have a lot of homework?" I asked. "Maybe you could bring it over. We could see if it's similar."

"I don't have a lot of homework and it won't be the same. I didn't take any honors classes."

This was news to me. "Why not?"

She sighed again. It seemed every sentence began or ended with a sigh. "I don't know. To try to get a social life, I guess."

"Oh."

I felt like she'd pointed to something shiny in the distance and then punched me in the gut; her revelation caught me *that* off guard. Could you just decide to have a life? Was she doing some sort of "new town, new school, new me" thing like kids on TV who move always do? And how did she plan to incorporate *me* into this new life?

Stacey exhaled noisily into the phone again. "I'm tired, Kara, I think I'm gonna zone out and watch TV. We'll hang out tomorrow, okay?"

I managed to hang up before bursting into tears. Her not coming over was a bad omen. Especially on top of all the other bullshit. The school that was too big. The classes that were too hard. And now Stacey wanted to add parties and football games and stuff to the mix? I just wanted it to be me and her, like it always had been.

I found myself flicking the scab on my arm from our blood-sisters oath. The little twinges of pain were oddly soothing. I progressed to picking at it and was disappointed when it didn't bleed. Somehow I knew that blood plus pain would make me calm, like it had the night Stacey and I became blood sisters.

After locating my Swiss Army knife in my nightstand drawer, I sliced two more tiny lines next to my scab. The pain rippled through me, awakening me like it was caffeine. The blood that dripped down my arm released all the stress of the day, all the sadness over Stacey. I stopped crying. Blood felt more purifying than tears, more numbing.

One more cut would give me strength. It would drain the bad feelings. I would daub it up with Kleenex. I would ride the ache and turn it into energy to get my schoolwork done.

I could cope.

I knew it wasn't a good thing, but I could cope.

The Ballad of Kid's Kid:
Stacey O'Connor

"It's up to me now
My daddy has gone away."

—Jane's Addiction

May 1995

I WAS A BABY'S BABY. A KID'S KID. My ma was sixteen when she had me. I gained a year on her. I'm pregnant and I'm seventeen. When I have the baby I'll be almost eighteen. Almost an adult, but not really. Eighteen's still too young. They say if you're too young it stunts you. Developmentally, emotionally, or whatever. In your head you're stuck at the age you were when you had the baby.

My ma got stuck, that's for sure. Before she had me she was a stoner waitress, always listening to the latest rock bands and always at the best parties. After she had me, she remained a stoner waitress, but one who brought her baby to the not-quite-as-cool parties. She kept that up until I got old enough to ask questions like "What's in that Kool-Aid, Mommy?" Then, she blamed me for the demise of her social life and her musical taste. Once I got to be school-age, she spent all her money on suburban rent instead of records so I could go to the "good" schools and not screw up like her. I guess she didn't realize the example she set for me was just as important as the education I got.

So am I gonna be stunted? Stuck at seventeen forever in my mind? I don't know. I don't think I ever acted my age in the first place. I grew up fast. I was a latchkey kid starting in third grade. Maybe some people would find that kind of freedom cool, but it gets old. All I really wanted was someone to take care of me.

Everyone thinks of women as the primary caretakers, but since caretaking didn't come too naturally to my ma, I decided that stereotype was wrong. I wanted a guy to take care of me, and my first, most logical choice was my own father. My parents broke up before my ma had me, but when I was little I spent more time with my dad. Usually I was at his place on weekends, and sometimes I stayed for weeks at a time. Those, I realized later, were his unemployed periods. But I saw him less and less after we moved out to the 'burbs. It was a long drive south and Beth wasn't willing to make it unless she got compensated with child support.

The summer before I started high school, when Beth decided to move us to Berwyn, I embarked on a last-ditch mission to involve my dad in my life. It was top-secret. I didn't even tell Kara, mostly because if plan A, "Give Ma some money so she can stay in Oak Park," failed, plan B would upset Kara worse than me moving to Berwyn. It meant I'd move even farther away. Plan B was "Please, Dad, take me to live with you."

I met my dad at the food court of North Riverside Mall. Weird and pathetic, I know, but it was my only idea and he didn't have any other suggestions. He was caught off guard when I called him. He sounded gruff, like I'd woken him up. He coughed a phlegmy smoker's cough during his hello, but his voice warmed up when I said, "This is Stacey, your kid."

He immediately agreed to meet me at the mall, which I chose because I knew how to get there on the bus. I didn't want to chance Beth seeing him if he came to pick me up. It turned out he didn't even have a car. He took a train and two buses to get to the crappy North Riverside Mall and eat at the sticky food-court table, surrounded by screaming kids and teenagers and dead-eyed moms, just to see me. I guess that's touching if you ignore the fact that he hadn't tried to visit in over four years.

I didn't know how we'd recognize each other, so not only did we plan what we'd be wearing (him: Chicago Bears T-shirt, me: Metallica T-shirt), but I gave him an exact table to meet me at (southwest corner, near the bathrooms, third table in, across from the cookie place).

He was waiting for me. I knew he was older than Ma by like fifteen years, but, man, he *really* looked old. He had huge bags under his eyes and crevices around them, across his forehead, and at the corners of his mouth. He'd probably been one of those guys that always looked old, but in a good, rough-and-tumble, Clint Eastwood way. I bet that's what Ma went for about him. Now it was pretty plain that he just had a lousy life.

He hugged me limply and told me how much I looked like my mother, which everyone always said. Then he offered to buy me lunch. "My little girl can have anything she wants." He smiled awkwardly and opened his arms, presenting the mall food court like it was a four-star restaurant. I hoped that this would remain true when I pleaded my case later. When he ordered the cheapest thing on the McDonald's menu for himself, I should have lowered my expectations.

While we ate, we made awkward small talk. I told him all about the past couple years, the great times Kara and I had, and what I was looking forward to in high school. I didn't mention the move. I changed the subject and asked him, "How's work?"

He nodded nonchalantly and said, "Fine."

I took a long, final slurp from my Coke. "What do you do now?"

"Oh." He crumpled his burger wrapper. "Solo cup factory."

I didn't know what to say. I thought about joking that his house was probably stocked with plastic cups, but he looked worn out, so I figured that his job was no laughing matter.

My silence brought an end to our lunch. Dad capped it off with a head jerk toward the cookie counter. "You, uh, want something? Uh, dessert?"

I knew it was time. Now or never. Cut to the chase or he'd get back on his two buses and a train and I'd lose my chance.

"Yeah, I want something. But not a cookie." I took a deep breath. I'd prepared an argument, a full case. Before I could launch into it, the waterworks cued up without me even summoning them. I gulped pathetically. "I need you, Daddy. I need you to help me and Ma. We've gotta move out of Oak Park 'cause she can't afford it anymore. And I would have to leave Kara and I really don't want to. So maybe if you could give Ma some child support . . ."

Dad's pudgy cheeks reddened. He looked like an angry, overripe tomato. "Did Beth put you up to this? Did she send you?"

"No!" I hadn't expected that accusation. The tears that had been welling up overflowed. "If you can't do that, if you can't help her that way . . . if I have to move . . . I wanna live with you."

His skin faded to the color of cigarette ash and his eyes got watery, too. "Stacey," he murmured. "Stace . . ." He seemed amazed, and I thought for sure the answer was going to be yes, but then he started shaking his head the wrong way. "I wish, baby, but I don't even have a job," he choked. "I got fired from the factory over a year ago. I don't even get unemployment anymore. I got cockroaches in my apartment and it ain't even a one-bedroom, it's a studio . . ." He kept blathering on, but I'd heard all I needed to hear. He offered me a cookie again, but I didn't need that crap.

"I don't want to take your last dollar." I knew it was mean and I automatically felt bad. I mumbled "I'm sorry" before rushing out of the food court, leaving him with my tray and greasy pizza plate.

He was pathetic. My mother was pathetic. I came from pathetic. Pathetic that couldn't take care of me. I went back and forth between sad and angry about it for over a month. But when I noticed the boys with cars in the parking lot at my new high school, I developed an alternate plan. I would find one of them to take care of me.

I thought it would be like TV, all free dinner and dates to the movies. They would get me away from my mother. And I guess eventually one of them did, right? But only because I'm headed straight into taking care of his kid.

I'm gonna try to do things better than my parents did, though. I'm sure everyone says that, and the odds are against me, but I'm sure as hell gonna try.

3.

HIGH SCHOOL WASN'T HOW I IMAGINED it at all. I mean, I didn't expect my life to turn into *Beverly Hills, 90210* overnight or anything, but I didn't think I'd be spending most of my afternoons alone with my twelve-year-old brother, Liam, either.

At the time Liam and I hated each other, but it hadn't always been that way. When we lived in the city, we spent hours playing together, Liam providing a constant soundtrack. He sang songs from *Sesame Street*, belted out commercial jingles—"Dial 588-2300, Empiiiiiiiire!"—like they were opera, and brightened my days with his off-color compositions, like "Don't Flush an Alligator Down the Toilet, It Will Bite Your Butt."

Then we moved to Oak Park, I met Stacey, and Liam was relegated to tagalong or worse. Stacey and I enslaved him, made him over into a girl, and ditched him places when we didn't feeling like "babysitting." Liam grew tired of the torture by the time he was in fifth grade and started avoiding us. I'd never tried to patch things up. Why bother? I had Stacey; I didn't need my lame little brother to like me. But then Stacey moved, and despite all the plotting and researching of bus routes, she and I weren't together as often as planned.

In her quest for a social life, Stacey'd discovered boys. Her first boyfriend was Jim. He was really proud of the weight set in his basement and his facial hair, even though he had scrawny arms with knobby biceps and the fuzz above his lip couldn't justifiably be called a mustache. Stacey bragged about him because he was a junior and had a car.

While Jim scraped bird crap off the windows of his rusty Pontiac Firebird, Stacey twisted herself around in the front seat and said, "I know we promised to hang out every day, but Jim mentioned he'd like some alone time with me. Maybe if I spent one afternoon a week alone with him . . ."

And I agreed to it, even though my time with Stacey had already been limited to a couple days a week since she was always "too tired." When we did hang out, we had fun because Beth had started smoking pot with us—she'd caught Stacey and initiated the cool-parent, "you can only do it with me" rule—but every day I was separated from my best friend I felt miserable. I consoled myself with MTV.

I'm sure Liam's resentment of me grew when he came home and found me occupying his former territory in front of the television. High school got out earlier than junior high, and by the time Liam rushed through the door, skateboard and backpack in hand, I'd already claimed the cozy living room as my domain. I'd be stretched out on the La-Z-Boy with the remote firmly in my grip, controlling the big, colorful TV stocked with over forty cable channels. Since no one was home to force us to share, Liam was exiled to the sun porch to sit on a poorly stuffed armchair surrounded by boxes of our old toys and our parents' junk to watch the ancient, black-and-white TV that got only five channels.

By October, the sun porch had grown frigid, the windows that enclosed it rattling with the slightest puff of wind. One day, Liam approached the living room tentatively, a bag of chips in hand, his strawberry blond head bowed. His hair was just growing out of the summer buzz cut he'd gotten at Mom's insistence. Tufts of it stuck up every which way, and when he questioned,

"*Tiny Toons*?" he looked as childish as his plea for cartoons sounded.

"Music videos," I replied firmly.

He sighed and sank back against the couch, rolling his green eyes. That attitude reminded me he was nearly a teenager, nearly on my level, and I decided to bring him there by teaching him about rock 'n' roll.

"Liam, you're too old for cartoons. This is really good," I told him, indicating the scene on the TV: a gymnasium overrun by a mosh pit. "This is Nirvana."

He shrugged. "I don't really care about music."

"You used to," I objected, pointing at a photo on the mantel above the fireplace: Liam at four, gripping the guitar I'd helped him make out of a potato chip box and some rubber bands. His hair was slicked back and shiny and he wore a black dress shirt, pants, and even a little black tie because he'd idolized Johnny Cash. An odd choice for a preschooler, but I'd loved him for it. He'd dressed like a mini-Man in Black until third grade, when he'd abruptly come home from school one day begging Mom to take him to the mall for "regular clothes."

My finger swung back to the music video. "Dave Grohl's a good drummer. You play drums in the school band."

"Only because Dad made me. This year I quit band."

"Why'd you quit?" I asked, concerned. When had my brother become such a sour little kid? He'd always been a bit weird and introverted, but he'd seemed happy.

"Being a band geek wasn't exactly making me popular, Kara. I decided to drop it, start fresh in junior high, and see if I could make some friends."

His words struck a nerve, reminding me of Stacey's comment about trying to get a social life and how I'd lost her in the process. I told Liam what I wished I could tell her: "You shouldn't change who you are just to get popular, and you definitely shouldn't give up things that you love."

"I never loved playing the drums," Liam retorted. "I wanted guitar lessons, but Dad insisted we pick orchestra instruments. Good for college applications or whatever."

It was true. There was an oboe in my closet, but I'd quit playing in fifth grade. Dad had gotten too busy to come to my concerts, and the only real enjoyment I'd gotten from them was seeing him cheer me on. Shaking off that memory, I suggested, "How about asking Mom for guitar lessons? You could start a band. When you used to dress up like Johnny Cash it was so cute—"

Liam's face flushed crimson and he exploded. "You totally don't get it! I didn't have any friends 'cause everyone thought I was a huge freak because of the Johnny Cash thing. I thought when I got to junior high things would be different, but I still don't have any friends. And I have no idea why you think I should take advice from you. Where's Stacey? She still lives close enough to hang out. Did she *ditch* you?" he taunted. "Sorry if I'm not sympathetic, but after the way you ditched me when we moved here . . ."

Sniffing back angry tears, I threw the remote at him. "Here, watch your stupid cartoons."

I stormed upstairs to my room and forced myself to delve into my homework. Six o'clock passed and then six thirty and Stacey didn't call and my biology assignment felt increasingly impossible and I needed to ask her about it and I was hungry and wondered why the hell my family wasn't inviting me down to dinner. Was I being shunned by everyone? Overwhelmed by stress, anger, and self-pity, I grabbed my knife from the drawer of my nightstand; I'd upgraded from the Swiss Army to a sharper X-ACTO blade I'd found in Dad's toolbox.

Since I'd been cutting a few times a week for the past month, I had a whole routine: I rolled up my sleeve, ran my fingers over the raised pink scars, and then picked at my most recent scabs. Sometimes that slight twinge of pain gave me the adrenaline I needed to conquer a lesser problem like biology homework, but when I was really feeling sorry for myself, I wanted to see blood.

I never cut along veins; I wasn't suicidal, just in need of stress relief. When the blood bloomed to the surface of my skin, the warmth of it soothed like a hot bath. After I finished cutting, I felt like I'd cleansed myself in the ultimate way, draining all the anger and sadness directly from my veins.

Liam barged into my room while I was still admiring the blood.

"Knock!" I screeched, jerking down my sleeve.

"I did!"

"It doesn't count if you knock while you're opening the door."

"Sorry to interrupt your top secret homework," he scoffed. "Dad's finally home. Mom said come down for dinner."

He slammed the door after himself and I frantically cleaned my arm. I worried throughout dinner that Liam had noticed. I waited for him to bring it up to our parents, mentally rehearsing my retort—"Well, he quit band"—so obsessively that I barely paid attention to what was happening at the table. Not that anything new ever happened.

My dad had remodeled the kitchen two years before and it looked like a set for homey supper scenes on a sitcom: the perfectly arranged table with the glossy red plates, shining silverware, and place mats of thatched yellow fabric that matched the cushions of the chairs, a slightly deeper shade than the butter-colored walls. At dinner, the setting sun shone in through the windows behind the table and blended with the red accents and yellow hues to make the room glow with warmth.

In stark contrast to the setting was our chilly exchange:

Dad kissed Mom on the cheek.

Mom told Dad that he was late.

Dad mumbled something about a grant. Then he asked, under his breath, if this wasn't the same meal we'd had two days ago.

Mom replied under her breath that he of all people should be familiar with how work consumed so much energy.

Dad ignored Mom and asked me and Liam about school.

Liam said school sucked.

Mom told Liam that she didn't like that word.

I shrugged in response to Dad's question and pulled my knees up to my chest, leaning over them to stab at the food on my plate.

Dad studied me with mild irritation and told me not to do that.

I let my feet fall to the floor with a thud and acted angry for the rest of the meal.

Everyone stopped talking until Mom reminded Dad that he needed to help Liam with his algebra. Before Dad could complain about how busy he was and Liam could object that he didn't want help, Mom disappeared to bed to read.

I put my plate in the dishwasher and went to my room to listen to music with my headphones on because I'd been reprimanded by Dad for being too loud too many times. Every time, I'd hoped that when I turned the music down, he'd stay and talk with me, but he always rushed off.

Dad and Liam remained at the dinner table, struggling with algebra until they both got frustrated with each other.

That was our routine.

My forcing Liam to watch MTV instead of cartoons after school became routine, too. He sat there with his arms crossed for the first week, but didn't ask me to change the channel or try to provoke me into leaving the room. By the middle of the next week, he was quietly singing along to "Smells Like Teen Spirit" when the video came on.

I turned to him and declared triumphantly, "You like it, don't you!"

"Yeah," he admitted with a shrug, "I guess."

But then he flashed me a smile and I grinned back.

4.

"**God!**" Liam gagged as he hit mute on Whitney Houston's "I Will Always Love You" video. "They call this crap one of the greatest ballads of all time?" he asked, mocking the VJ's introduction. "Have they ever heard a Johnny Cash song? Ballads aren't all sappy love songs. The truly *good* ones tell a story about real life."

I vigorously nodded my head in agreement. My brother had become quite the music critic in six months' time. I definitely preferred discovering new bands and bashing crappy ones with him to talking boys with Stacey. She was preparing to break up with boyfriend number five. Luke, I think. All of them had monosyllabic names that would easily fit on the McDonald's name badges they were destined to wear. Stacey'd invited me to go to the mall that day, but I'd declined. Hanging with Liam was a lot more enjoyable than watching Stacey strut around in a short skirt and too much makeup in pursuit of Neanderthals.

"Switch it back to MTV," I told my brother. He did, but since it was spring break, we were assaulted with images of overbaked sorority girls in skimpy bikinis dancing like fools for the camera. I rolled my eyes. "Put it back to Whitney on mute."

Liam did as instructed, but he also smirked at me. "You're just jealous."

"Of a bunch of airhead bimbos on a beach? I don't think so."

"Seriously, you wouldn't rather be in Florida with a ton of friends than in our living room?" Liam asked without a trace of his usual flippant sarcasm. "I'd rather be anywhere in the world than here. Admit it, our home life sucks."

He said those words with such intensity, implying that our house was an awful place. Our parents were busy, sure, but we were a happy family, goddammit. And why was he talking about this? I thought we had an unspoken rule: lighthearted music-video banter only.

"Our lives aren't *that* bad. Look at everything we have," I objected, rubbing my slashed-up arm through my ratty blue cardigan, as I'd taken to doing when uncomfortable.

Liam's eyes drilled into me in such a way that my gaze drifted to my blanketed feet. Then he slowly looked around the room. It had been redone the year before when Dad had gotten sick of "living in a pigsty." The creamy walls had been repainted to conceal the smudged handprints near the light switch. The wooden floors were kept neatly swept, and the area rugs were no longer stained by Kool-Aid and muddy shoes. All the furniture actually matched (spring green) and so did the vases (earth tones) and the picture frames that lined the mantel (silver).

Liam focused on the center photo, my parents' wedding picture, and said coldly, "Dad redecorated this house so he can pretend he has the life he wants. He's miserable. Mom's miserable. It's only a matter of time before the whole thing falls apart. I bet they'll be divorced within a year."

My jaw dropped so low my internal organs could have tumbled from my mouth. "You're fucking crazy! Where would you get an idea like that?"

Liam glared at me. "I pay attention. They've been fighting in silence for two years now, ever since Mom said she wouldn't consider moving us to Texas for that job Dad wanted to take. She tried to make it up to him by going back to work to finance this home-makeover crap, but they haven't been happy since. They hardly talk or touch each other. It's *so* obvious."

As much as Liam wanted to convince, I wanted to deny. I didn't want to think about the dinners we'd had since the kitchen had been remodeled, how we barely spoke, Dad's graying head bowed, Mom's jade eyes focused on some invisible yet incredibly absorbing thing outside the kitchen window . . .

"Mom and Dad are fine! Everything's fine!" I insisted, tugging the blanket up to my chin like I could hide behind it the way I did when watching scary movies.

"Whatever! I've been stuck in this house with them while you had Stacey. I can't ignore it like you do by sitting in your bedroom with your headphones on, slicing your wrists or whatever!"

My skin went cold. *He knew.* The little sneak *had* noticed. Feelings of betrayal replaced the concern I had about my parents' marriage. This was worse than Stacey ditching me for boys. Liam had violated my most private act. And I'd been treating him like an equal, like a friend.

"Fuck you." I flung the afghan to the floor.

I didn't even make it out of the living room before Liam shouted, "No, fuck you! You're gonna face it. You're not gonna abandon me like you did when we moved."

I felt a slight twinge of guilt, but then the remote hit me in the shoulder blade. I whipped around in a blind rage, found the remote, and hurled it back at Liam. It would have cracked him in the cheek if he hadn't caught it.

The La-Z-Boy rocked violently as he leapt up and lunged across the room, trying to slap me with the remote. I knocked it out of his hand and it skidded across the floor, bouncing off the metal grate in front of the fireplace. His hands flew for my throat and I attempted to knee him in the groin. He deflected my knee with his own, but it threw us both off balance and we went tumbling to the floor.

We wrestled like we had as kids arguing over the same toy. Well, it was kind of like that. We didn't actually want what the other had. We hated our silent house, our empty, friendless lives, and the reflection of that we saw in each other's eyes. We slapped and scratched those feelings out. Liam's long legs—he was taller than me now, I realized midbattle—sent the coffee table careening into the La-Z-Boy, spilling my Coke onto a book of *National Geographic* photos. My flailing arms upset an end table, ejecting a lamp onto the couch. We rolled dangerously close to the fireplace and Liam's shoulder slammed into the wall, shaking the mantel.

Picture frames crashed to the floor, glass shattering around us. I instinctually covered my brother's body with mine as if a bomb had gone off. My elbow hit the remote and a roar erupted from the TV: the Nirvana video was on for the millionth time. I almost screamed, but ended up joining Liam in an uncontrollable fit of laughter.

He sputtered, hiccupping and trying to regain control of himself. I turned down the volume on the TV as he sifted through broken glass to retrieve a posed family photo that had been taken at Sears the Christmas before we moved to Oak Park. He smirked, handing it to me. "Maybe someone will actually yell tonight. Wouldn't that be a relief?"

I nodded, staring at another photo—one of my father with a wild beard and hair that hadn't yet grayed, grinning as he stood in front of a tent, squeezing Liam and me on either side of him. I reached for the picture, but Liam blocked me.

"Don't cut yourself," he said gruffly, frowning again. His eyes drifted away like our mother's always did nowadays. I followed his gaze to the TV, to the mosh pit in the music video I'd used to educate him. We'd seen it so many times, but it still managed to strike inspiration in me.

"We should see some of these bands live," I proposed. "You know, after we're done being grounded for this mess."

"Pffft, grounded." I expected another rant, but apparently my suggestion—or our wrestling match—had diffused some of Liam's bitterness. He wandered back to his chair, remote in hand, turning up the volume as the Red Hot Chili Peppers came on. "I wonder who's touring," he mused, smiling. "You come up with good ideas sometimes, sis."

5.

LIAM AND I SNUCK OUT TO concerts on a weekly basis. We went to the Metro, the Aragon, the Riv, anything on an "L" line because we didn't want to deal with getting permission and rides from our parents—though we did help ourselves to their wallets when allowance money ran out. We saw famous bands, local bands, whoever happened to be playing an all-ages show whenever we happened to need to get the hell out of the house. That was the ballad of suburbia: give me loud to drown out the silence.

The summer after my freshman year, we saw our biggest show of all: Lollapalooza. We had to tell our parents about that one because we needed a ride; the venue was way out in the southern suburbs. Dad tried to say no. He was still frustrated at Liam for having to retake algebra in summer school and at me because I'd announced I wouldn't be taking any more honors-level science or math classes. Mom overruled him.

I got some pot from Stacey to ensure that we had the ultimate outdoor music experience. Shrouded in late evening shadows, we smoked up at the top of the hill at the New World Music Theatre. My brother nodded and smiled his way through his first joint, blissfully stoned. I liked pot, but I liked anything that gave me a buzz: beer, cigarettes, razor blades. Pot would become Liam's escape of choice, and even the first time he got high, it made him introspective, not silly like it had me and Stacey.

He squinted at the dyed, pierced, and tattooed masses milling around the lawn and concluded, "If these people went to my school, I'd have friends."

I played with a hole in the worn canvas of my sneaker. "Some of these people probably do go to my school and I still don't have friends."

"Why?"

"It's not like I haven't tried. I go places with Stacey, but you know . . ."

I trailed off, thinking about a party that Stacey had dragged me to on the north side of Oak Park. I'd followed her and her metalhead boyfriend into some stranger's basement toward a keg of cheap beer. It was a hot evening and the room so packed that everyone dripped with sweat even though the air conditioner ran full-blast. Guitars screeched from stereo speakers mounted on the wall, but a blue-haired boy's voice was audible over everything. He shoved through the crowd, screaming "Penile augmentation!" like some cracked-out town crier. Stacey giggled, reaching for him, telling him she loved him, because of course she knew him. He probably went to *my* school, but *she* knew him. The combination of beer, humidity, and the loud strangers who all knew one another—who, in fact, knew so many people that they didn't need to know me—made me sick to my stomach and I went home after half an hour.

"I have all these leftover insecurities from grade school, I guess," I told my brother. "I automatically assume people won't like me, so I don't talk to them unless they approach me first. I can't become a part of a crowd because I can't get past that feeling that I don't belong."

Liam nodded sympathetically, but before he could say anything, the people around us rose to their feet, signaling that the band was about to come on. We followed suit, but couldn't even see the giant screens that flanked the stage, we were so far back. Over the deafening roar around us, Liam bent down and shouted in my ear. "You need to conquer this crowd thing. Literally. Crowd surf with me!"

"No way!" I shouted back. At the shows we'd been to, I'd hung out in the balcony while he braved the mosh pit.

"I'm gonna do it and I don't know how I'll find you later."

Though I was unnerved by his threat, I continued to shake my head.

Then he said what I, as the older sibling, should have said to him back when we first moved to Oak Park, and later on in life, too: "Come with me. I'll protect you."

Reassured by his simple words, I let him take my hand and we waded into the writhing masses. Liam tapped a big dude on the shoulder and said, "Help me lift my sister."

They hoisted me into the waiting hands of others. At first I was tense, afraid I might be dropped, but eventually I realized that passing me around was part of the fun for everyone else. I relaxed and let myself enjoy the experience. It was exhilarating, like riding a roller coaster made of people. I gazed up at the starry sky and sang along with the crowd. Liam followed my path, weaving through the audience so that he could be there at the end of my ride.

I shouted, "I wanna go again!"

Liam laughed. "See, you fit in here just fine."

6.

FITTING IN AT CONCERTS WAS COOL, but when the music ended, so did the camaraderie. You'd see familiar faces at the next show, maybe even say hello, but you wouldn't hang out every day or form a permanent circle of friends. And though I liked going to shows with Liam and was pretty content just sitting on the couch watching TV with him, part of me still wanted a group. That's why I went with Stacey to Scoville Park when she asked me to at the beginning of sophomore year.

Scoville was a few short blocks from my high school. It was *the* hangout for anyone who didn't play sports or join clubs or fit in with the popular crowd. Metalheads, stoners, hippies, punks, ravers, indie rockers, skaters, and those really weird kids who seemed to elude all categorization—those were the people you found at Scoville.

When school got out, they all met up at the main entrance of the park, a small concrete plaza with a couple of benches, an ornamental water fountain that no one used, and a much more popular pay phone—one of the few in town that could still receive incoming calls. (No one had cell phones back then, but all the dealers and wannabe dealers had pagers.) After lingering for fifteen minutes, everyone wandered into the park, dividing into small groups, generally according to subculture.

The hippies played Hacky Sack in the sun. The punks chain-smoked near the bushes by the entrance. The stoners retreated into the deep shade in the southwest corner and smoked pot on top of a shit-brown wooden sculpture that had probably passed for some version of modern art in the late sixties.

The skaters trekked up the hill to a huge statue, its base blackened from years of skateboards grinding against it. This abused monument divided the grassy part of the park from the tennis courts and playground. It consisted of three soldiers—one dressed in navy uniform, one army, one air force—and an angel who looked out over their heads, as if keeping watch over the rest of the world, but ignoring the park at her feet.

The first time Stacey and I went to Scoville, we accompanied her drug-dealing boyfriend on business. We returned twice more when Stacey was trolling for new guys. She migrated toward the stoners and the metalheads. It wasn't really my scene, but Stacey wasn't up on the punk and indie bands I listened to. Boys had taken priority over music for her.

Even though I hung back the way I always did when I tagged along with Stacey, I knew that Scoville was supposed to be my place. The key was finding the right person to go with, and halfway through sophomore year I finally found her.

7.

CHEMISTRY CLASS, TWO DAYS AFTER CHRISTMAS break: I zoned out in my usual spot in the back row by the cabinet of beakers, chemicals, and lab equipment. Like everyone else, I was thoroughly disinterested in the long chemical equations that Ms. Bartolth scrawled across the blackboard, her flabby arms jiggling with each stroke of chalk. Instead, I watched Maggie Young and Alexandra Kennedy play with their hair. They repeatedly let it down and twisted it back up into a stylishly disheveled bun, which somehow stayed in place with the aid of a mere pencil.

I wondered if my hair would've been capable of that if I hadn't recently given myself a jagged bob with the kitchen scissors. Stacey had reluctantly helped me bleach the front of it white-blond and dye the rest black. The whole time she muttered that it would look a lot prettier if I got highlights and let her even out my cut. No one appreciated my new look as much as I did. Maggie and Alexandra nicknamed me "Skunk Girl," so I spent chemistry fantasizing about experiments gone awry that would leave them bald.

Suddenly a voice drifted into the classroom like cigarette smoke, interrupting Ms. Bartolth's drone: "Hey, is this chemistry with Ms. Bar-tolllll-th?"

Everyone turned to look at the waifish girl in the doorway.

She only stood a couple inches over five feet, but her flame-colored hair made her appear bold and big enough to challenge even Ms. Bartolth.

After a moment of infuriated silence, Ms. Bartolth responded, "Yes, can I help you?"

The girl stuck a crumpled schedule in the back pocket of torn jeans covered with black ink sketches. The holes in the knees were so big that they exposed her legs from lower thigh to mid-shin. She wore black fishnet tights beneath them and a faded Ramones T-shirt. "I'm Maya Danner. Just moved from Florida and assigned to your class."

"Take a seat," Ms. Bartolth replied, her mustached lip pulling tightly around her teeth in a fake smile. "Talk to me after class, so I can catch you up."

Maya waltzed to the back of the classroom, slouching into the seat beside me. As she approached, I saw that she was as stunning as her fiery hair. She had perfect china-doll features that Alexandra and Maggie would envy, but she wore her makeup like mine, eyeliner smudged across her thunderstorm gray eyes. Maya smiled at me, indicating my purple-and-black-striped tights and giving me the thumbs-up.

When Ms. Bartolth finished explaining the lesson of the day and told us to pair up for lab, Maya turned to me and asked, "Wanna be my lab partner?"

"Sure," I agreed quickly. Pairing up for lab was often as humiliating as gym class. I always got picked last. "My name's Kara," I added as we carried our equipment to an open lab table.

"Lucky for you, Kara, I'm a whiz at chemistry," Maya informed me.

It proved to be true. She chatted away while effortlessly mixing chemicals. "Your hair is fucking awesome. And I love your tights. If you let me borrow them, I'll bring you some Manic Panic to color your bangs. I have purple, blue, and red, of course."

"Cool, I'd love to try the blue."

"I'll bring you the jar tomorrow." Maya put a few more drops of something into our beaker and it began to smoke like it was supposed to.

"Good job, girls," Ms. Bartolth said approvingly. "Now you can start on your homework."

Maya rolled her eyes as our teacher trotted off. "Pfft, that's what study hall's for. So," she asked me, "do you like the Ramones? They're my favorite band."

"Definitely, and PJ Harvey's my favorite." I pointed to the sketch on the left leg of her pants, where she'd written "50ft Queenie" in pretty lettering beneath a sketch of the songstress wearing a crown. "Those jeans are a work of art."

"Wanna see my sketchbook?" Maya asked enthusiastically, pulling it out of her backpack before I could reply. We flipped through pages of lizards and sorrowful mermaids and beach scenes, Maya pointing out the ones she was most proud of.

Then Maggie and Alexandra approached our lab table. "Oh, look, Skunk Girl made a friend," Maggie taunted. Turning to Alexandra, she added, "Do you think we should warn New Girl that Kara's, like, the biggest loser in school?"

My face flushed as red as Maya's hair and I rubbed my scabby arm through my sweater. I wished that for once I could think of a witty retort to put Maggie in her place.

Maya came up with something for me. "My grandmother has a saying for girls like you." Her lips curled into her signature smirk. "No brains, no headaches."

"Yeah, that's the truth." I laughed.

Maggie huffed and muttered "bitch" before flouncing away.

As the bell rang and Maya walked to Ms. Bartolth's desk, she promised, "I'll bring the dye tomorrow."

"Can't wait!" I replied, and practically skipped to my next class.

When I got up the next morning and tucked a few pairs of

tights that I thought Maya might like into my backpack, I was excited to go to school for the first time since Stacey'd moved. I wished that Maya and I had more classes together or shared a lunch, but at least chemistry was a double period.

Over the next few months, Maya and I acted as not only lab partners but partners in crime. She brought out my mischievous, goofy side the way Stacey once had. But while Stacey and I had always avoided Maggie and her friends, Maya and I antagonized them: "Is that mixture supposed to be turning pink?" Maya had asked Maggie, interrupting the story Maggie was relating to Alexandra about some kegger in Thatcher Woods. "Let me go get Ms. Bartolth for you."

Before Maggie and Alexandra could screech a synchronized "No!" Maya and I shouted "Ms. Bartolth!" and relished the dirty looks we got as the teacher hovered over them for the rest of the period.

But as much fun as we had, we didn't actually hang out outside of the classroom. I had no idea how to broach the subject. Should I invite Maya to my house? What would we do there, watch MTV with my brother? I quickly concluded that I was too socially awkward to have a real friend and forced myself to forget about it, but apparently it simply hadn't dawned on Maya yet.

One afternoon in mid-April as we were sneaking a cigarette between classes, Maya slapped her knee and declared, "Oh my god, Kara! Why haven't we hung out? Why don't we even call each other? I mean, we have so much fun in class, don't we?" A look of doubt darkened her perfect features.

"Yeah, we do." I grinned, as surprised by her insecurity as I was by her outburst.

"Let's do stuff, then. You want to come over after school?"

"Okay." I rubbed at some ash that drifted onto my gray corduroys, trying not to act too exuberant. I didn't want her to know I had no life.

"I live at the Write Inn. Do you know the place?"

I nodded, a little confused because the Write Inn was a hotel. Not like a Marriott; they didn't have those kinds of hotels in Oak Park. The rooms at the Write had kitchenettes and the feel of a studio apartment, but still, it was a weird place to live.

"It's only temporary," Maya explained. "My dad's searching for the perfect house, but his job started in January and I guess he thought it would be easier to stay at a hotel than rent a place. I've got my own room, so it's almost like living alone, which has its perks." She flashed me her patented troublemaking grin. "Like we could go there, smoke a bowl, and then meet up with Harlan, this kid from my art class. He's always talking about the park down the street from me."

"Scoville?"

"Yeah," she said. "Does that sound fun?"

"Sure," I told her, because if there were good times to be had at Scoville, Maya would be the person to have them with.

8.

MAYA AND I CUT THROUGH THE tennis courts at the north end of Scoville Park. There were quite a few people on the other side of the hill, but Maya easily spotted her friend Harlan near the main entrance.

"There he is, with the purple hair." She pointed to a kid in an orange jumpsuit, not unlike something a prisoner would wear.

Even though he now had violet liberty spikes instead of shaggy blue hair, I recognized him as the "Penile augmentation!" guy from the party Stacey had dragged me to. This made me slightly nervous, but that evaporated once we were properly introduced.

Harlan threw his arms around Maya like they had known each other for years. Then Maya pushed me forward. "This is Kara. Kara, Harlan."

I waved hello, but that wasn't Harlan's style. He screamed, "Kara, welcome to the park! Maya talks about you *all* the time," and enveloped me in a big bear hug. Harlan's personality was overwhelming but endearing. I appreciated the way he immediately accepted me. He kept one arm around my shoulder, confiding, "Okay, the main reason I've been trying to get Maya to hang out with me is because I want to introduce her to my friend Christian. I think they'd make the most adorable couple."

Maya sighed, shaking her head, and a blond girl standing beside Harlan rolled her eyes. "You and your matchmaking. I wouldn't send any girl near Christian. Mary wants him. She and Jessica will destroy anyone who gets in her way."

Harlan dismissed the girl's concern. "Pfft, she's been trying to hook up with him all year. He's not interested."

Harlan's friend extended her hand to Maya. "Hi, I'm Shelly. Excuse him, he's crazy." Shelly's blue eyes shone with laughter as she turned to me. She studied me quizzically. "Weren't you at one of my parties last summer? I live on Kenilworth."

"Maybe."

She had to be talking about the party Stacey had taken me to, but I didn't remember seeing her there. Normally a girl like Shelly would stand out—she was drop-dead gorgeous, with dirty-blond curls that spilled out of a purple bandanna—but her house had been packed with at least sixty kids. I'd been stuck with Stacey and her metalhead friends. Shelly and Harlan definitely weren't part of that crowd. I'd only noticed Harlan because—well, he made sure he was the center of attention.

He threw his other arm around Maya and pleaded, "Come on, won't you at least meet the guy?"

Maya patted his spiky head. "I'll let you introduce us because it means so much to you, but like I've told you a million times, I don't want a boyfriend."

"We'll see what you think after you meet him. Or maybe Kara will like him." Harlan gave me an exaggerated wink. I just shrugged as he led us over to a circle of kids sitting on the dead grass near the bushes. But when Harlan said "That's him," gesturing to a boy wearing a ratty thrift-store cardigan, my stomach flip-flopped.

I'd seen him before on one of my trips to Scoville with Stacey. We'd stopped at the Amoco station along the way because the clerk there didn't card for cigarettes. Christian stood in line behind us, noticeable immediately with his scruffy, apple-red dye job, which stuck up around big, black headphones. While the clerk had his back turned to get Stacey's Marlboros, Christian grabbed a carton of Winstons that someone had forgotten to finish stocking. He grinned at me as he stuck it inside his leather coat and tossed me a pack before running to catch up with his friends.

"He likes you!" Stacey teased.

My cheeks grew hot. "Shut up, I don't even know him."

"Christian Garrickson. We had history together in eighth grade. According to his T-shirt collection, his likes include Nirvana, Sonic Youth, and the Cubs. According to his performance in class, his dislikes include history and homework."

"I hate the Cubs" was all I told her, though I mentally dissected the way Christian looked at me for days.

Much to Harlan's disappointment, Christian barely nodded at Maya and me, though this could have been because Mary was hanging all over him, trying to distract him. When Christian looked up at us, she sullenly crossed her arms over the enormous boobs that dominated her bony frame and scowled in such a way that it emphasized her underbite. Meanness spoiled all of her features. She didn't even fake a smile when Harlan introduced us to her.

Mary's best friend, Jessica, looked disinterested in everyone. She stared around the park, continually fussing with her dyed black pixie cut. She was cheerleader pretty, but wore a hipster uniform of Converse sneakers, faded jeans, and a thrift-store-chic Smurfette T-shirt. She did flash a big smile that dimpled her cheeks and wrinkled her cute-as-a-button nose, but her green eyes were stamped with the same judgmental expression as Mary's and she didn't deign to speak to us either.

Craig sat on the other side of Christian. When Harlan introduced him as Mary's older brother I did a double take. They didn't look related. Craig was on the pudgy side, had much lighter hair, and his plump cheeks were spotted with freckles. Upon closer examination, I noticed that Mary covered her freckles with a thick layer of makeup and Craig bleached his hair. His dark brown roots matched his sister's shade. Craig had a bit of an attitude, but at least he spoke, flicking his chin in the air and mumbling, "What's up?"

The last in their circle was Quentin. His skin and blue eyes were so pale, he seemed albino, but his hair was inky black and braided into the teeniest braids, which hung down to his chin. He hardly spoke, and when he did it came out in a near whisper, but he was the only one who kept smiling at us genuinely.

Within fifteen minutes, I really wished he would talk, because everyone else cracked inside jokes, chatted about band rehearsal, and ignored Maya and me. I felt just as left out as I had on the other side of the park with Stacey's metalhead friends. I even squinted in their direction, thinking that if Stacey was there, I'd take Maya over and introduce them. I figured Maya could overlook Stacey's embarrassing boy-craziness since they shared the same sense of humor. But I didn't see Stacey.

I was relieved when Maya announced, "Kara and I are going to take a walk."

Harlan and Shelly were the only ones who said good-bye.

We wandered up the hill and sat down. Gazing out at the entire park, Maya remarked, "I don't know about Harlan's friends. Besides Shelly and the kid who didn't talk, they weren't very friendly."

I studied Christian. His apple-red hair color was washed out, almost pinkish with crimson streaks. Cute, sure. Cute as I remembered, except his face was set on permanent glare. The more Mary touched him, the more irritated he grew. Even though she didn't seem like the nicest person, I felt kind of bad for her. I told Maya, "I can't believe Harlan wanted to get one of us mixed up in that drama."

"I know."

We lit cigarettes and watched as Christian stood abruptly and stalked over to a bench. Mary trailed him. Observing the heated argument that ensued and ended with Mary fleeing the park, Maya cocked her head and smiled. "I guess it's as good as TV."

There were footsteps in the brittle grass behind us. Maya and I turned slowly to find a teenage girl dressed in a heavily starched white blouse and a long, itchy-looking gray skirt. She said, "I'd like to talk to you about Jesus."

I stifled laughter and Maya raised her eyebrows, asking, "Who? Does he hang out here? 'Cause I don't think I've met him."

The girl remained composed. She fluttered her eyelashes and smiled. "That's why we've come today, because we've noticed that Jesus does not *hang out* here." She said "hang out" carefully, as if translating it from a foreign language. "This park seems to be a place of . . ." She paused as if to measure her words, but apparently decided to be firm. "A place of sin."

"Sin?" Maya snorted. "Are you a sinner, Kara? 'Cause Ah come from a fine family of Flor-dah Baptists, so Ah know Ah ain't no sin-nah," she continued, conjuring up a southern drawl.

This was going to be even better than screwing with the kids in chemistry class. I focused on the white bra strap that I could see through the girl's blouse and dramatically pulled my lipstick-stained cigarette from my mouth. "I'm really more interested in learning about Satan than Jesus."

The girl's cheeks flushed. "Your mockery is foolish, but Jesus will forgive you and only He can save you on Judgment Day."

Maya got to her feet and dropped the exaggerated accent. "Listen, lady, I heard about you people coming by busload every month to try to convert the heathen kids at the park and I've been looking forward to it 'cause I want you to explain something to me. The Ark. I mean, come *on*. How the hell did that work? Two of every animal in the world and just some old guy and his wife taking care of them?"

While Maya ranted, I glanced down the hill and noticed at least fifteen more people dressed similarly to our proselytizer roaming the park.

Ours struggled to keep her voice pleasant. "I'm not here to debate with you. I'm here to explain the joys of Jesus. If you let Him into your life—"

"Okay! But before we get to that, tell me how big the damned boat was!"

The girl pulled two tracts from a cardboard box and shook them in front of us. "If you read these, you'll learn about faith. Faith will settle all of your doubts."

"Gimme those!" Maya grabbed the box and sprinted down the hill, her shoulder-length scarlet hair streaking through the air behind her. The stunned girl backed away, dropping the two tracts she had in her hand. I picked them up, laughing at the title, "Rock and Roll: A Tool of the Devil," and tore down the hill after Maya.

She stood in the center of Scoville, dumping the box of tracts into a messy pile. I tossed the two I had on top. We stared at the pile, trying to figure out what to do next. In a flash of inspiration, I picked up a handful of booklets and lit them on fire.

"Yes!" Maya exclaimed, and began to flick lit matches at my growing inferno.

The sparks caught everyone's attention. Harlan snatched the box from the hands of the man who was lecturing him and Shelly, and ran over to add more fuel. Others quickly joined suit. A metalhead who Stacey had thought was "soooo cute" doused the fire with Zippo fluid, and the flames leapt high, sucking down the soaked paper like a fourteen-year-old with a stolen bottle of booze. Soon there were twenty of us whooping and cackling and joyfully slamming into one another as we danced around the flames like a pagan tribe, or maybe more like a circle pit at a punk show.

The God freaks ran toward one another for safety from what surely was a sign of Armageddon. When their bus sped away, a cheer arose, but the celebration was short-lived. The bus had been blocking the ever-present eye of Youth Officer Robbins, stationed in a squad car across the street. He dropped his coffee out the window and screamed into his radio.

Since we were all caught up in the destruction, hardly anyone noticed the cop's approach, but Maya did. She grabbed my hand, and we retreated back up the hill. As sirens wailed, we strolled innocently into the Write Inn, and then hurried upstairs to Maya's room.

Collapsing on Maya's bed, out of breath, I asked her, "Aren't you afraid someone will tell the cops we started it?"

A dark grin spread across her doll face. "Nah, they had way too much fun. No one will ever forget the day you came to the park, Kara."

"But you're the one who started it by taking the tracts from that girl—" I began, ready to add that it wasn't the first day I'd been to the park.

"No," Maya interrupted. "I grabbed the box, but you started the fire. Everyone's going to love you tomorrow, girl. We *are* gonna go back, right?" Her eyes gleamed, and I could still see those flickering flames reflected in them.

Feeling as exhilarated as I had the first time Liam helped me to crowd surf, I matched Maya's twisted smile, my dark red lipstick giving it my own signature. "Sure, we'll go back tomorrow. It's better than TV."

9.

THE DAY AFTER THE FIRE, MAYA sauntered into Scoville like she owned the place. I followed, not feeling nearly as self-assured. We joined the same people from the day before. Harlan gave us both bear hugs, and Shelly smiled widely, but that was to be expected. I was certain the others would continue to ignore us. I couldn't have been more shocked when moody Christian welcomed us into the fold.

"Hey, Firestarter," he said, tossing a wicked grin my way. "Thanks for the giant ashtray." He flicked his cigarette butt into the bald patch hemmed in by scorched grass. Beneath a few cigarette butts, the ashes of the tracts mingled with the dirt. I proudly realized that they'd moved into the center of the park to sit around the remnants of my fire.

Craig reached across the fire pit to hand Maya and me some flyers. "You should come see our band Symbiotic next weekend. Our old frontman is gonna be back in town. It should be pretty cool. Maybe you could provide us with some pyrotechnics to give Shelly's basement that genuine arena-rock feel." He chuckled at his own joke.

On the flyer, Symbiotic was drawn as a late-eighties cock-rock supergroup, their names even written across their pictures as Christian aka Slash, Quentin aka Nikki Sixx, and Craig aka

Rikki Rockett. In bold letters, it also touted the return of Wes aka Sebastian Bach.

"I love Symbiotic, but Wes is not going to be happy when I tell him that his band has started doing Skid Row covers," Maya remarked with a smirk.

A chorus of voices responded to her statement. Craig, who didn't get Maya's sense of humor, explained that the flyer was a joke. Christian, thinking his band had gained notoriety all the way down in Florida, wanted to know how Maya'd heard Symbiotic. But Harlan shouted over everyone else, "Whoa! Maya, how do you know Wes? He left Oak Park before you moved here."

"Oh," Maya answered simply, "he and Cassie are my cousins."

This quieted everyone. Finally I asked, "Why didn't you ever mention that?"

Maya shrugged and gave the response I should have expected, given her tendency to antagonize religious zealots and our fellow chemistry students: "I love social experiments. I wanted to see who was friendly to strangers"—she smiled at Harlan and me—"who wasn't"—she honed in on Jessica and Mary and kept her focus on them as she finished—"and how that all changed once everyone found out who my cousins are."

Quentin, the one with the shy smile and the black braids, softly admitted, "I knew. Cass talks about you all the time and I see the resemblance, very similar eyes. Not the color, but—"

"Are you kidding?" Jessica interrupted. "They don't look alike at all. Maya's obviously playing some weird game. Hello? Cass and Wes are black."

"Cassie and Wes are biracial," Maya corrected. "Our moms are sisters. I'm not playing any game. Why would I?"

Jessica looked to Mary to back her up. I'd noticed that Mary was sitting as far from Christian as possible that day and her expression was even more dour than before. Mary shrugged and told Jessica, "Cass does have a cousin named Maya. Remember that picture on her dresser from when she went to Florida in second grade?"

Jessica grimaced at Mary. "No. But if you recognized her, why didn't you say anything yesterday?"

"Yeah, Mary, isn't it your job to keep Jessica up on all the latest gossip?" Maya mimicked snapping a whip.

Everyone laughed except Jessica and Mary. Mary crossed her arms over her chest, ignored Maya's remark, and replied to Jessica, "I didn't recognize her. She was a cute little blond kid in the picture. Besides, why wouldn't Cass tell *us* about her cousin moving here? We've been best friends since kindergarten."

Jessica nodded, sitting up straighter. Clearly this was the defense she expected from Mary.

"'Best friends'?" Maya questioned coldly. Her gray eyes shone like freshly sharpened knives. She forced her mouth into a straight line and said no more.

An awkward silence descended until Christian filled it, asking Maya, "Did Wes send you the Symbiotic demo? What do you think of my band?"

"Of *your* band?" Maya laughed. "I thought Symbiotic was *Wes's* band."

Christian shrugged. "When he comes home and visits, sure, but when he left I stepped up. I play lead guitar and sing now."

"Ah, *you're* the cocky sophomore he told me about." Maya watched Christian's face flush. Then she smirked and added, "He says you're pretty damn good."

Shelly nudged me and whispered, "Maybe Harlan's right about those two. I see some potential sparks." Speaking at a normal volume, she asked, "Are you coming to my party on Friday? It'll be Wes's big homecoming."

"I didn't know about it."

"Well, consider yourself invited. Every Friday night from now on, come to my house. I get a keg, everyone comes over."

I thought about the last party I'd been to at Shelly's, and the uncertainty I felt must have shown on my face, because Harlan threw his arm around me and implored, "You *have* to come, Kara. It won't be any fun without you."

"It won't be any fun if Harlan takes over the stereo again with his terrible techno," Craig interjected.

Harlan turned to me for support. "Sorry, not a techno fan," I told him.

Craig gave me the thumbs-up. "What bands are you into?"

And a conversation about music started up. Soon we were on to movies, then books, and by the time evening crept in, we all seemed like old friends—at least Maya, Shelly, the guys, and I did. Mary and Jessica managed not to speak directly to me or Maya and went home an hour before the rest of us. But I didn't care about them. I was too pleased that suddenly things were happening for me. I had new friends. I had plans for Friday night. I had a life.

10.

ON FRIDAY I TOLD MY PARENTS I was sleeping over at Maya's so I could do whatever I wanted that evening. Maya and I hung out at the park for a few hours before returning to her hotel room to get ready for the party. The plan was to walk to her cousins' house and catch a ride with them.

We walked a few blocks northwest, the houses getting bigger and bigger the farther we went. Maya murmured, "Wide lawns and narrow minds. That's what my grandma said about this town when my dad told her we were moving here. My grandma speaks mostly in clichés."

I chuckled and told her, "Your grandmother was actually quoting Ernest Hemingway's opinion of Oak Park."

"Hmm, if it's really like that, no wonder Wes is so happy to have gotten away."

"So, is he coming home from college on spring break or something?"

"College?" Maya laughed so loudly that someone in a house across the street flicked a light on and peered out the window at us. "Wes got expelled in November for setting off a smoke bomb in the caf."

"Holy shit, *that* was your cousin? They evacuated the school for half an hour!"

Maya smirked. "Yep, that was Wes. Between that and his drug dealing, my aunt and uncle were fed up. They sent him to California. He's working on my uncle's friend's farm and getting his GED. I guess he actually likes it out there, but Cassie misses him. She's going to be so happy . . ." Maya trailed off, squinting at a shadowy figure crouched in a driveway two houses down. "Cassie!" she shouted, but the girl didn't look up. She sat with her head in her hands.

Maya rushed to her cousin, kneeling behind her and embracing her in a Harlan-style bear hug. Not wanting to intrude, I approached slowly. Cass's tears glittered in the light that shone down from above her garage. She swallowed back sobs, stuttering, "He's not coming home . . . Mom's flipping out again . . . she has been all week . . . that's why I haven't been at school or the park . . . but I hoped he would still come home. I'm sick of dealing with this alone." Then Cass noticed me. She blinked, summoning her strength, and said, "Oh, hi."

"Hi," I replied awkwardly, shifting my weight from one foot to the other.

Cass rose and wandered down the driveway toward me, Maya following. Dabbing at her darkly lined eyes, Cass allowed a tentative smile, asking softly, "I met you before, right? At North Riverside Mall?" She furrowed her brow. "Kara?"

"Yeah," I said, studying her.

Cass was a willowy, caramel-skinned girl with dreadlocks in shades of brown, red, and blond spilling from a black bandanna down to her waist. Three years ago she'd been a good six inches shorter, slightly pudgy, and those dreadlocks—all her natural coffee shade—had hung just past her shoulders. Regardless, Cass was unforgettable. Etched in my mind as part of a rare cool moment Stacey and I had had in junior high.

"I still have the necklace you stole for me." I pulled a metal pot leaf from the mass of black cords, silver chains, and beads that decorated my neck.

"How do you guys know each other?" Maya demanded. Even though she thrived on being secretive about her life, she didn't like being kept in the dark.

"We shoplifted together once," Cass told her, asking me, "When was that? The summer between seventh and eighth grade?"

"Yeah."

That summer Stacey and I had taken the bus to the mall practically every day to bum around the food court and steal crap because we were bored. We kept seeing Cass there with two other girls—Mary and Jessica, I realized. Stacey liked Cass's skull-and-crossbones bandanna, so she decided we should introduce ourselves. She'd always been the more social one. She walked right up to Cass and said, "Nice bandanna."

Cass replied, "Nice hair wraps," reaching out to touch one of the many braids wound in colorful string that Stacey wore in the undermost layer of her hair.

Cass and I exchanged smiles, but didn't actually speak for half an hour. Not because I was being snotty like Cass's friends, who ignored us. I was just shy as usual. The first thing I said to Cass was "Thanks," after she handed me the stolen pot leaf on a black leather cord. She gave Stacey a bandanna, but didn't give her friends anything. Even though I didn't smoke pot yet, I added the necklace to the growing menagerie of jewelry that made undressing preshower quite a ritual.

Stacey and I looked forward to seeing Cass the next time we went to the mall, but we never saw her again.

Cass explained the reason for her disappearance to Maya: "It was the day before Jessica got caught stealing from Claire's. She refused to go back to the mall after that." Cass turned to me. "Hey, do you still hang out with that girl, what was her name . . . Tracy?"

"Stacey," I said, privately pleased that Cass had remembered my name but not hers. "I don't see her that often anymore. She moved to Berwyn."

"Right, Stacey . . ." Cass's smile faltered and she nervously played with her hair. "Sorry, I'm a little . . . flustered tonight. My mom's nuts and she freaks out like once a week . . . and my brother was supposed to come home, but he decided— My parents decided," she quickly corrected, "that he couldn't given Mom's state."

"It's okay."

Maya and I followed Cass's gaze up to a bedroom window. The silhouette of a woman's figure was visible, her fingers prying apart the slats in the blinds to stare down at us. Maya's face grew stony.

Catching sight of Maya's expression, Cass decided, "Let's go. Shelly's is only a six-block walk. I need to get over there and break the news to everyone."

— —=◄ ►=— —

Shelly lived in a huge Victorian house set back from the street on a double lot. Her neighbors either didn't notice or didn't care about the parties she hosted every Friday night, and her parental situation allowed for big, teen-movie-style bashes. Shelly's dad was a big-time attorney in the city who went straight from work to his girlfriend's Gold Coast condo on Friday nights. He provided his daughter with a hefty chunk of change to amuse herself with on the weekends, which Shelly, in turn, used to amuse the rest of us.

Shelly's mom was MIA. Her parents had met back in the sixties when Shelly's dad still had "ideals," and when he'd sold out, her mom bailed—apparently her "ideals" didn't involve taking her kid along to the commune in Oregon she'd joined.

"That's why hippies suck," Shelly told Maya and me as she

led us upstairs on the grand tour of her house. I could imagine her mom, though. Except for her raver wardrobe of huge Jnco jeans and sparkly shirts, Shelly embodied my mental image of a hippie with her insanely long, sunshine-colored curls.

Shelly showed us her room first. It had pale blue carpet and lilac walls—a lot more pastel than I'd expected. "Dad's girlfriend thinks she's an interior decorator," Shelly explained. "Wait till you see the bathroom."

"Ugh!" Maya and I groaned in unison upon poking our heads in. The walls, toilet, sink, and tub were all pink.

"My dad insisted on earth tones for his bedroom, though." Shelly led us farther down the hall, but when she pushed the next door open, she shut it again immediately, calling, "Sorry, Adrian!"

Maya and I hadn't glimpsed what was going on, but Shelly herded us back to her room, giggling. "Lesson number one about parties at my house: if a door is closed, knock." She reached under her bed for a bottle of Absolut Citron. "If you do happen to see too much of Adrian Matthews—the person you are most likely to find behind a closed door—this is where the secret hard liquor supply is kept. Shots?" she offered.

"Yes!" Maya and I answered.

Maya was probably drowning her disappointment about Wes. Everyone we encountered bemoaned the fact that his parents had kept him from coming home, acting like he was a war hero whose tour of duty had been extended.

Personally, I needed a drink to loosen up. As soon as we'd entered Shelly's and I'd found it just as packed as it had been the last time, I got a bit queasy. I didn't normally like parties. When I went to them with Stacey, I stayed glued to her side, and when she inevitably ditched me, I retreated into a dark corner until it was time to go. I was determined to be part of this crowd, though. I swilled three shots of liquid courage in quick succession before Shelly put the bottle away and said, "Let's continue the tour."

The first floor was mostly empty. There were a couple people, including Cass and Quentin, sitting on the back porch, but Shelly's basement was the epicenter of her parties. Down there, the beer held a central location across from the foot of the stairs, dividing the long, rectangular room into two sections. To the left of the keg, people shot pool on an expensive-looking pool table. Behind that, a polished wooden bar lined the entire wall. In the farthest corner, there was a large booth like something you'd see at Denny's, except the table had storage for poker chips and cards built into the center of it. I would have suggested that we sit there, but Mary and Jessica had already laid claim. Jessica fawned over a skater boy while Mary glowered across the room at Christian.

He sat on the other side of the basement. Over there, all the couches and chairs were pushed against the walls. A rug had been rolled up to reveal shiny black ceramic tiles: the dance floor. Shelly'd put a card table with a stereo in front of the big-screen TV in the corner of the room.

Shelly left Maya and me by the keg and went to settle an argument between Craig and Harlan about the music. Maya introduced me to Gonzo, a guy she'd met in her Spanish class. He was a big dude who looked like a lumberjack, with hair so unwashed it actually matted together.

"Gonzo knows everyone at the park," Maya shouted over the throbbing techno. Harlan was winning the music war.

"Of course I do," Gonzo replied. He had a booming baritone and didn't need to shout. "This is my second senior year," he told me before signaling that Maya and I should follow him to the bar. "Let's go where it's quieter. Maya promised to share her sociological cigarette research with me."

"Another social experiment?" I asked Maya.

"More of a social theory." She sat down on a bar stool, Gonzo and I standing on either side of her. Maya lit a Winston and studied it. "I've been collecting data for a while and these are my findings. Punks and indie rockers smoke Winstons. Ravers smoke Newports. Skaters smoke Camels. Hippies roll their own or smoke American Spirits. Metalheads smoke Marlboro Reds. There have been anomalies, but let me tell you, only bitches smoke Marlboro Lights."

A shrill giggle rung out above the music and I glanced at Jessica and Mary's table. Jessica sat on the skater boy's lap. She habitually smoothed her black hair, laughing at whatever he'd said. "I bet Jessica secretly smokes Marlboro Lights," Maya concluded.

Gonzo tapped his pack of Parliaments. "What about me?"

Maya didn't even flinch. "You're like Switzerland. You're friends with everyone. Cassie's like that, too, and she smokes Parliaments. They're the neutral cigarette."

"I like this sociological cigarette research." Gonzo nodded, impressed.

I finished my beer in two gulps and headed to the keg alone, since Maya and Gonzo weren't ready for a refill yet. After I filled up, Craig and Christian waved me over.

"Harlan adores you, can you please sweet-talk him into putting some good music on?" Christian begged.

With a beer and three shots under my belt, I was feeling pretty persuasive, so I went over and asked Harlan to put some Social Distortion on. He agreed as long as I'd dance with him. I told him that would require more alcohol. Christian and Craig high-fived me on my way back to the keg. I beamed; I was part of the gang.

The last time I was at Shelly's, the cheap beer made me nauseous, but this time it was good. Really good. I swallowed three beers almost as quickly as I'd thrown back the shots upstairs.

And the more I drank, the more social I became. I felt like I knew everyone. Even though I'd only talked to about ten of the fifty people in Shelly's house, I'd seen them all at the park.

I flitted from group to group like a butterfly. Quentin had joined Maya and Gonzo and I philosophized with the three of them. I picked out music with Craig and Christian. I danced with Harlan and Shelly. I hung out with people I wouldn't later remember until they'd point out, "We met at Shelly's party," and even then I'd usually fake recollection.

Around one in the morning the crowd began to thin. I went looking for Maya so we could head back to her place. Before I found her, I came across Cass sitting alone on the back porch.

I lowered myself beside her. "Have you been out here all night?"

Cass quickly closed the notebook she'd been writing in. Ransom-note-style lettering spelled out "Stories of Suburbia" across the ragged red cover. Clearly, I'd interrupted something private.

I rose again, apologizing. "I didn't mean to bother you. I thought you might know where Maya is."

"You're not bothering me. Sit."

So I did and I waited for her to answer me about Maya. Instead, she absently traced the letters on the cover of her notebook. "That's a cool journal you've got," I said, trying to make conversation.

"It's not mine. It's Adrian and Quentin's. No . . ." She paused, carefully considering her words. "It's everybody's. It's for when you have a secret or a story you feel like you can't tell anyone. You write it in here. Quentin saw that I was upset tonight and thought the notebook would help. It did a little bit, but I don't know . . ."

"Maybe you need to talk to someone," I suggested. "I know we don't know each other very well, but if you want you can talk to me."

Cass's eyes met mine. Her pupils were huge, practically filling her brown irises, and it felt like she was looking deep inside of me. After staring at me for a minute, she said, "I don't know if it's the acid, but for some reason you seem like the most trustworthy person in the world."

"You're on acid?" I asked with naive excitement, my drug repertoire being limited to pot.

Cass shrugged. "Acid's what I do to escape."

From the little bit I'd gathered about her family earlier, I knew she had a lot to escape. "I'm really sorry your brother couldn't come home."

"That's the thing. My brother could've come home. He *chose* not to," Cass stated icily.

"Wait . . ." Alcohol had impaired my thought process. I gripped the edge of the stair I sat on in hopes that the world would stop spinning so I could focus. "I thought you said that your parents decided—"

"Do you know why my brother left?"

"Maya told me that after he got expelled your parents sent him to California."

Cass nodded with her whole body, rocking back and forth on the step. "That's what Maya and everybody else thinks. That's what Wes told them. But my parents didn't send Wes away. He chose to leave."

"Why?" I scooted closer to Cass even though watching her rock made me dizzy.

"Wes doesn't deal well with our family. Our mom in particular. She has manic depression. And she's been way worse since my aunt . . . I can't really talk about that." Cass cut herself off with a sharp drag from her smoke and stopped rocking for a second.

Then she continued, the flow of her words and the movement of her body quickly picking up speed. "After Wes got expelled, he was stuck home alone with Mom during the day. After a week, he freaked out. He begged our dad to send him away so he could get his life together. Said he needed a fresh start, to get away from Oak Park and drugs and everyone and their problems. Dad agreed. When Wes asked me what I thought, I wanted to scream at him, '*Please* don't fucking leave me.'" Cass rolled her eyes upward, swallowing hard.

"But I agreed. He's my big brother. I've always wanted what's best for him. I even let him lie about being sent away so he could protect his rep or whatever. He promised he'd visit, though. This is the second time he's broken that promise."

Cass dropped her head into her hands like she had in the driveway when Maya and I had found her earlier. My heart ached for her. I imagined she felt a million times worse than I had when Stacey moved and broke all her promises to me. I wished I had some sort of advice for Cass, but I coped by cutting, which wasn't any better than dropping acid. Even if I'd known what to say, I was so drunk I probably would have screwed it up. But at least the alcohol helped me do one thing right. With my inhibitions lowered, I had no qualms about hugging a stranger, even someone like Cass, who acted like one of those tough girls who didn't like to be touched.

She cried in my arms for five minutes and then she started laughing. "Acid," she explained between giggles. "I can't help it. It makes the tears tickle."

"That's so weird!"

Maya stumbled outside, looking for me. "What are you guys doing out here?"

"Talking about acid," Cass said. She hugged me one last time and whispered in my ear, "Please don't tell Maya. She can't handle the family stuff, either."

I promised that I wouldn't.

The Ballad of a Hallucinating Guardian Angel: Cassandra Channing

> "She's been everybody else's girl
> Maybe one day she'll be her own."
>
> —*Tori Amos*

April 1994

CRAZY RUNS IN MY FAMILY, MATRILINEALLY AT least. My grandmother had a psychotic break back when my mom and aunt were in high school. She moved every electronic item in the house into the kitchen and blocked it off entirely to "protect the family from radiation." My grandfather sat in the living room staring at the spot where the TV had been, incapable of dealing with his wife—kind of like how my dad is now. My mom, the oldest child by two years, dialed 911 and had her mother committed to an institution.

I wonder what that's like, watching your mom get strapped into a strait-jacket. I wonder with half dread, when will I learn firsthand? Because I'll be the one to deal with it. My dad's always away—having an affair with his work or maybe another woman, who knows? And Wes can't deal with Mom. I've been running interference between them since I was five, which is my first memory of one of my mother's episodes. It might be my first memory, period.

It was spring, planting season. I wasn't in kindergarten yet so I spent all afternoon with Mom. She took me to pick out the annuals—marigolds, petunias, that stuff. When we got home she decided to dig up the entire garden. Every plant was carefully unearthed, ready to be rearranged, when suddenly she got overwhelmed. She paced from the front yard to the back for five minutes, repeating, "I can't do this!" She went to lie down and left me standing in a yard that looked like it had been descended on by a thousand dogs searching for bones.

Then Wes came home.

At seven, he immediately recognized signs of our mother's mental illness. Stomping two of the uprooted hostas with his sneakers, he exclaimed, "This is my fault! She's upset with me about school."

Wes always blamed himself for triggering Mom's "sick days," and I hated it. A week earlier he'd been told he would have to repeat the first grade because he had so much trouble reading. He was given a battery of learning disability tests before it was determined that he "just couldn't concentrate," and was prescribed Ritalin, like too many of the other boys I've grown up with. Take a drug, problem solved. We're taught that from a young age.

Even as a kid, I innately knew that my brother already felt bad enough about himself and didn't need to be upset by Mom's weird behavior, so I stepped up, pushing Wes with my conveniently dirty hands off the plants he was trampling. "No, I did this. I wanted to surprise Mama. Help me fix them, Wes. Before she wakes up."

We flung dirt at each other as we put the plants back into the ground. We rushed to get it done before our dad got home or before dark, whichever came first. And when we finished—fingernails so caked with mud that they wouldn't be clean for a week—Wes was so amused and exhausted that he forgot entirely about our mother, who was still locked in her room.

That's when I became Wes's family protector. I can't count how many similar situations I've defused.

But with our friends, Wes was the kingpin, the boss, the father figure. Everyone went to him with their problems. He'd cuff them on the cheek to get them in line when they needed it, or fight an entire army for them when someone had done them wrong. I'd say he was a shoulder to cry on, but no one cried that often. Our friends didn't deal that way. You cheered them up with drugs and parties. Wes always had the best drugs and he threw the best parties at our house when Mom went into one of her Valium coma phases and Dad took one of his fishing trips to avoid it.

The party I remember most fondly took place the summer before my freshman year. I was sitting on the kitchen countertop, slightly drunk, when Adrian shoved a strip of paper in my face, crowing, "Look what I got!"

"A litmus test?" That's what it looked like, except it had tiny pictures on it, clowns and circus animals. "What do you wanna test with it?"

Adrian rolled his eyes. "It's acid, dumb-ass!"

"Oh! What do you wanna do with *that*?"

Adrian set the ten-strip on the counter, reached for a knife, and—*wham!*—hacked into it. He gave me the slightly smaller half and instructed, "Let it dissolve for as long as you can, then swallow."

I spent the next twenty minutes whining to him that nothing was happening. Right when he told me for the millionth time, "You're gonna feel it, Cass," I saw the wall wiggle a little bit, like Jell-O.

I ran over to poke the wall and it rippled *exactly* like Jell-O. Adrian and I wandered my house poking the walls and burrowing our feet in the carpet, which felt like freshly cut grass.

Eventually we went outside to smoke on my front porch, but I never got around to smoking. I jumped up and planted both feet on the porch railing, no hands. "I'm perching!" I exclaimed. "Like a bird! Perching is awesome, you should try it."

So Adrian did. We hopped down and up again for who knows how long. Eventually, Adrian got sick of perching and sat on the steps.

My brother suddenly appeared. He stared at me without blinking, his huge pupils revealing that he'd dropped acid himself. I told him brightly, "I'm perching."

"She looks like a pigeon," Adrian added with a chuckle.

Wes stared at me and said, "No, like a guardian angel." And we had a silent moment. Then he shook it off and asked, shocked, "Holy shit, Cassie, are you tripping?"

"Yeah."

"Oh my god," he panicked, turning to Adrian. "You gave the acid I sold you to my little sister?"

"I'm okay," I reassured him. "I'm great, actually."

Wes shook his head." Just wait for the comedown."

And he was right. The comedown was awful. It happened in the very early morning when everybody had finally staggered out of our house. Wes, who'd mostly sobered up by then, tried to convince me to go to bed.

"But when I close my eyes I see snow, like the static kind on a TV with no reception. I'll never sleep again," I informed him, bug-eyed. "I'm scared."

"Let's go someplace you'll feel safe, then."

He led me to our parents' bedroom. Mom was so zonked on her meds that she didn't even notice when we climbed into bed beside her.

My parents had a California-king-size bed, probably inspired by John and Yoko's whole bed-in thing in the sixties. They'd been hippies after all, met during the civil rights movement, protested together, fell in love, and got married when it was still kind of a big deal for a white woman and a black man to do that. In Oak Park, I didn't really have to think about my race as much as I might have in other places. Children raised by PC parents didn't tease too often, but I was well aware that I was different. I stood out among my mostly white friends and I didn't look like either of my parents. Deep down, I didn't really feel like I fit anywhere or with anyone.

For some reason, being on acid and seeing my ghostly pale mother, whose skin was nothing like mine, intensified my usual feelings. I looked at my brother and pressed my hand to his. Our skin tone—like milk with just enough chocolate syrup to make it taste good but not so much that it's overly sweet—seemed identical. I reached up to touch his wool-thick dreadlocks, a shorter version of mine.

"You are the only one in the world who matches me," I told him. "You are the only one who understands."

"I know," he whispered sleepily. "I will always match and I will always know how you feel."

We communicated on some higher level. We talked without words about our mother. But as he drifted off, my panic renewed.

"Wes?" I shook him slightly. "I'm still scared."

His toffee eyes fluttered open. "How can you be scared? You're the guardian angel. You take care of everyone. Especially me." He squeezed my hand. "Don't be scared. I'm here. I promise I'll always be here and one day I'll take care of you like you take care of me. I love you, Cassie."

I was able to close my eyes without being fear-stricken. His gratitude, his promise, were all I needed to feel safe.

When we woke up midafternoon, a miraculous thing had happened: our mother was out of bed. She cheerfully cleaned up the party mess, chiding, "You kids need to learn to pick up after yourselves." She offered to make us breakfast and called the old folks' home where she volunteers when she has it together.

Acid, I decided, equaled good things. It was fun plus it made my brother tell me that he loved me and it made my mom better. Like maybe I'd taken her craziness and channeled it into my trip somehow. I could do that. I could do that forever.

Of course it was just a coincidence. A month later Mom had another episode.

They got worse and worse every time. But at least now I had a way to escape into my own head when Mom retreated into hers and Dad and Wes disappeared. I tripped a lot, but usually no one noticed. I guess I'm that good at covering up insanity. It's like I was born to do it. Or I was born to be crazy. Sometimes I lie in bed with Mom for hours. We both stare at the ceiling and I wonder if we're seeing the same thing. Every once in a while I ask her, but she never answers.

At least she never lies to me the way Wes did. I really thought that he meant it, that one day he'd step up and take care of me for a change. Instead, he left and everything really went wrong after that.

Right before Christmas, I tried to throw a party at my house like Wes used to. Dad was gone on business and Mom had been in bed for two days. Nobody had any acid, but I was okay with that. Quentin and I had started spending a lot of time together. He'd been really sweet, consoling me after my brother left. When I was with Quentin, I didn't need acid or even pot or beer to have a good time. I just needed him.

The party was going well at first. I'd taken the opportunity to spread the word that Wes would be home for the holidays, so everyone was in a good mood. Everyone but Jessica. I'd noticed her stomping around scowling that night, but figured she wasn't getting enough attention from whichever boy she'd been flirting with lately.

Apparently, she had a problem with who *I* was flirting with.

I was talking with Quentin and Adrian in a corner of the living room. Quentin reached over and took my hand. I didn't think too much of it because he did it a lot when we were alone. But I guess it was the first time he'd done it in public and as soon as it happened, Jessica swooped in, dragging me into the dining room.

Pink-faced, she ranted, "When Mary told me that she thought you *liked him* liked him, I told her, 'Cass would never do that to me. We've been friends for too long and there's a code.'"

"Whoa," I interrupted, putting my hand up between us. "What the hell are you babbling about?"

"Quentin! You can't go out with him. He was my first boyfriend!"

I brought my hand to my mouth, attempting to conceal my laughter. "You can't be serious. You were in seventh grade. You went out for like five minutes."

"We went out for a month. He was the first guy to tell me I was beautiful. He said I looked like Winona Ryder." Her eyes grew wistful and she tugged at her Winona Ryder haircut.

I laughed openly. Quentin and I had recently discussed this. I'd told him, "You know you upset the whole balance of our friendship by telling her that. Suddenly, she was the skinny starlet, and Mary and I were the chubby girls who wore baggy clothes because we hated our big boobs. She made us feel like shit and ordered us around."

Quentin smiled at me and said, "I don't think anyone could order you around."

He was right.

I told Jessica, "This is ridiculous. You broke up with Quentin. It's not like he broke your heart or anything. You've dated a bunch of guys since. And it's not like I'm mad at Mary for going after Christian. He was *my* first boyfriend, remember?"

"That's your business. I don't want you with Quentin."

I softened for a moment. "Do you still have feelings for him? If you really do, I'll back off."

"No." Jessica wrinkled her nose. "He's too short for me. I just don't want *you* with him."

"Jessica . . ." I took a deep breath, preparing to reason with her.

Then I heard my mother call out for me.

She'd never left her room during our parties before—even if there was a band playing and kids all over the house. No one had known she was there until that night when she stumbled into the living room like a zombie, moaning, "Cassandra! Wesley!"

Jessica craned her neck to look through the doorway at Mom in her stained blue nightgown and tangled blond hair sticking up every which way. "Oh my god," Jessica snorted, stifling a giggle.

I wanted to tell her to shut up. I wanted to slap her. Instead, I raced into the living room, telling myself: *Get the situation under control. And don't cry. Whatever you do, don't let them see you cry.*

Everyone had backed up, giving my crazy mother a wide berth, like she was an animal who might attack. I put my arms around her skinny body and tried to steer her toward the hallway that she'd come from, saying, "Mom, let me get you back to bed."

She refused to move. She reached up to pet my hair and said, "Cassie, get your brother. I took too many pills. He needs to drive me to the hospital."

When it came to my mother, I'd dealt with a lot, but nothing that bad. I froze, stammering, "Mama, Wes isn't here."

Confusion filled her gray eyes. "Get Wes. We need Wes!" she insisted loudly.

We really fucking did need Wes, but he wasn't there. I had to handle it.

"Adrian, I need you to give me a ride. Everybody else needs to get out of here now!" I barked.

No one needed to be told twice. The house cleared and Adrian and Quentin helped me lead my dazed mother to Adrian's car. I stayed calm. I didn't even cry when the doctors told me they'd have to pump Mom's stomach.

I didn't cry until I called Wes to tell him about it and he told me that he wasn't going to come home for the holidays.

"No," I bawled. "You have to. I need you. Everything is falling apart." And I went on to explain about Quentin and me and how Jessica insisted I break it off.

"Jessica's just jealous," he assured me. "She'll get over it. I'm glad you're with Quentin. You keep an eye on him and Adrian because they need it. You watch over everyone for me until I come home, Cassie. Be the guardian angel."

Every time I talk to him he says that, "Take care of everyone for me, Guardian Angel." And I'm trying, but I really don't know if I can do it. I really wish that he'd just come home and I'd have someone to watch over me for a change.

11.

"**ARE YOU GOING OUT AGAIN?**" **LIAM** asked as we microwaved leftovers in the kitchen together on Saturday evening. Our parents were out on a date for the first time in ages. "Didn't you say that there was a concert tonight and I could come?"

I'd shown Liam the Symbiotic flyer when I'd first gotten it and promised to take him to the show to make up for ditching him after school for the past two weeks. I'd been so busy that I'd forgotten to update him. "Sorry, Liam, the show got canceled. That guy Wes, who used to be the frontman, didn't come home like he was supposed to last weekend and the rest of the band didn't want to do it without him. I'm just going over to Maya's. I'd invite you, but I don't think you want to sit around with three sixteen-year-old girls."

"Not really," Liam grumbled. He opened the microwave and tested the warmth of the pasta with his fingers. "Get a plate. It's ready."

We ate our dinner in silence in front of the TV. I could tell Liam was disappointed, but I didn't realize how upset he was until I rose to leave.

"I won't be out too late," I told him.

"Oh, you're sleeping at home for once?" he replied coldly.

"For once? I've only slept over at Maya's three times—"

"You spent all of last weekend over there. Sorry if I'm having Stacey flashbacks and feel like I'm getting ditched all over again."

"Liam!" I objected, but quickly apologized after seeing the hurt in his eyes. "I'm sorry. I won't be out too late. I'll watch the end of *Saturday Night Live* with you, okay?" He shrugged, so I gave him a big, melodramatic, Harlan-style bear hug.

"Okay!" he huffed, pushing me off of him, but at least he was smiling.

———=≍)⊱=━—

I found Maya and Cass having a cigarette on a bench outside of the Write Inn. Maya'd dyed her hair a darker red and in the faint street light, it looked almost purple. "Do you think Symbiotic should have played tonight?" she asked me as I sat beside her. "Christian really wanted to, but the other guys still look at it as Wes's band."

"It *is* Wes's band. He started it in eighth grade," Cass interjected.

"Clearly Cassie sides with them, but I don't know. Wes is gone. He can play with them when he's around, but they can do shows without him. Christian's a good frontman, too. Even Wes says so."

I shrugged. "I don't know the history and I've never seen the band."

"Maya hasn't either, but she likes Christian, so . . ." Cass teased her cousin straight-faced, her amusement evident only in her brown eyes.

Maya dropped her head into her hands and groaned. "Not this again."

I exchanged a glance with Cass and joined in on the torment, joking, "That's who you ditched me to be with last night! You've disappeared on me at Shelly's two Fridays in a row now."

Maya looked up quickly, concerned. "You didn't really think I'd ditched you, did you? I would *not* ditch you for a guy."

"Don't worry. I was so drunk I didn't notice you were gone," I reassured her with a smile. It was nice to know she wouldn't pull a Stacey on me.

"Good. And yes, I was hanging out with Christian. He's cool, but I couldn't go out with him. He and Cassie have a history."

Cass choked on the smoke she'd just inhaled. "'A history'? We dated briefly the summer after eighth grade and I think he was just using me so he could hang around Wes and get into Symbiotic. I'm over it. When it comes to pursuing Christian, the girl you should be concerned about is Mary."

Maya brushed that off. "She and Jessica can't spread rumors about my sex life. I'm from out of town, they don't know me."

"They'll make stuff up. That's what they did to me. According to them I've slept with Adrian, Christian, half the skater boys . . ." Cass ground out her cigarette with the toe of her boot.

"They said all that about you?" I asked, horrified. "I thought they were your best friends." Then I remembered the way Maya had scoffed at Mary's claim. "Or used to be."

"Used to be, I guess." Cass stared out at the traffic speeding down Oak Park Avenue instead of facing me and Maya. "And they claim they had nothing to do with those rumors. But it all started after Jessica warned me not to go out with Quentin and I ignored her."

"Well," Maya asserted, "at least Mary got hers."

Cass lit another cigarette. "What are you talking about?"

"Kara and I saw Christian freak out on her at the park last week. She ran away crying. And Christian told me last night that he told her to stay the fuck away from him because he'd never go out with someone who treated her friends like she treated you." Maya grinned at her cousin. "You should've seen it."

Cass shook her head. "I'm glad I didn't. I would have felt bad for Mary."

"What? After all she's done to you?"

"I don't blame her. She's always been Jessica's pawn. They've been friends since birth and Jessica's been ordering Mary around since she could talk. Jessica's a bossy only child whose parents don't pay any attention to her. I kind of feel sorry for her, too." Cass sighed. "We were friends for a long time. As shitty as they've been to me lately, I miss them. It sucked to lose my brother and my best friends in the same month."

"Cassie . . ." Maya put her arm around her cousin's shoulders and squeezed her.

Cass accepted the hug for a second before squirming out of it and standing up. "Can we get out of here and talk about something else?"

We instinctively headed in the direction of Scoville in awkward silence.

"Someone say something," Cass insisted as we approached the tennis courts.

"O-kaaay." Maya turned to me wearing that smirk of hers. "Kara, if Cassie's got Quentin and I've got Christian, you need someone. Do you think Craig's cute?"

"Are you Harlan now or something?" I groaned. "And no, I don't think Craig's cute. Subject change, please!"

Maya pointed at her cousin. "At least Cassie's smiling again."

Cass flicked her cigarette to the ground. "I'm smiling because I'm gonna beat you to Tasty Dog and then you're gonna have to buy me a milk shake!" She ruffled Maya's hair and took off running down the hill.

"Cheater!" Maya called after her, telling me, "I'm not chasing her."

"I feel really bad for her about Jessica and Mary," I said seriously.

"Yeah, it sucks when friends turn on you—"

"Oh, Jesus Christ!" Cass shouted. She'd halted at the bushes near Scoville's main entrance and we ran to catch up with her.

Two kids rolled out of the shadows and into a circle of mulch illuminated by one of the tall lampposts that stood around the edge of the park. I recognized Quentin's pale face and dark braids, which were matted with twigs. Cass quickly sat him up and brushed the dirt from his hair.

The other boy, whom I didn't recognize, retched violently. Cass shifted Quentin into Maya's arms and went to the guy I didn't know. He tried to push his dark brown hair out of his face, so Cass pulled it into a ponytail at the nape of his neck; it hung halfway down his back. After he finished spewing vomit and wiped his stubbled chin, I realized he was gorgeous.

His pale skin glowed in the moonlight, making the dark ink on his inner arms prominent. "Thrown" was tattooed down his right forearm in Old English–style lettering, and "Away" completed the phrase on the left. He tried to focus his bloodshot brown eyes on me. I should have been disgusted by him, but I'd never felt so instantly drawn to someone. It wasn't just the tattoos that fascinated me. I liked that he looked pure punk with the Misfits T-shirt and the chain wallet and the leather jacket painted with Social Distortion's skeleton logo on the ground beside him, but he rebelled against the stereotypical image with his long, almost hippieish hair. All the other nonconformists still conformed to their subculture of choice. This kid immediately struck me as someone who was completely comfortable in his own skin. I desperately wanted to feel that way.

"Jesus, Adrian, what happened?" Hearing Cass speak his name erased the names of any other boys I'd ever thought about from my mind. I couldn't have scripted a better entrance for my first love, as ripe with impending disaster as the beginning of Mickey and Mallory's romance in *Natural Born Killers*.

"Whiskey," Adrian moaned. Two empty fifths lay in the bushes.

"I know that. You guys showed up half drunk around six, right as I was leaving. Do you remember that?" Cass questioned calmly. She forced Adrian to lean against her instead of lying down in a vomit-drenched spot and looked over at Quentin, asking, "Do you remember that, Quentin?" He slumped against Maya, his eyes closed. "Quentin!"

His eyelids fluttered, but he made no effort to talk. Maya lightly slapped his cheeks. I glanced at Cass, who seemed like she'd handled this type of situation before. She instructed, "Take Adrian." So I knelt beside him, putting my arms around him for support as Cass had.

Cass leaned over Quentin and shouted his name at the top of her lungs. His eyes opened with a jolt. "Where did Jessica go? Where's everybody else?" Cass demanded.

"Left," Quentin stated, his eyelids drooping.

Adrian stirred in my arms and said, "I have my car."

"What? They expected you guys to sober up and drive home!" Cass's skin flushed with fury. She rifled through the pockets of Adrian's coat and pulled out his keys. "You guys keep them talking," she told Maya and me. "I'll get Adrian's car and we'll drive them to my house."

She rose and found herself facing Jessica and Mary. Craig stumbled up behind them, just slightly less drunk than the two boys on the ground. Cass tried to shoulder past Jessica, but Jessica grabbed her by the wrist. "Where ya going, Cassie?"

Cass squared herself and raised her fist.

"Go ahead! You know my parents are both lawyers," Jessica quipped.

Cass emitted a sharp cackle and wrenched her arm away from Jessica. "Do *not* call me Cassie. Only family calls me that. You're not even a friend anymore." Her tone was low at first, but then she screeched in Jessica's face, "You left them here to die!"

Jessica closed her eyes to the sound and wrinkled her petite nose. "We did not! We were hungry, they were too drunk to come, and we told them we'd be back."

Cass pointed at Craig. "And he drove? Between the three of them they drank two bottles of whiskey!"

Craig interrupted, laughing hysterically as he rushed toward Adrian and Quentin. "They're still so wasted!" He collapsed beside Adrian and tugged him out of my arms. "Dude, what did you do?"

Adrian moaned the same response he'd given Cass, "Whiskey," even though Craig clearly knew, having indulged himself. Adrian turned and attempted to meet my gaze again. One eye pointed in one direction, one in another, like a broken doll's. "Who is she?" He reached for me with a limp hand.

"That's Kara. Kara and Maya." Craig gestured to my right, where Maya still cradled Quentin.

Adrian slurred at me, "Maya, you're beautiful."

"No, dude, that's *Kara*." Then Adrian puked again and Craig almost dropped him, exclaiming, "Sick!"

Cass glared at Craig, reprimanding, "Jesus, sober up!" She shook her head and said, "Fuck this. I'm driving them to my house."

"No!" Jessica objected. "We're taking them back to my house."

In a whirlwind of dreadlocks, Cass lunged toward Jessica so violently that Mary took a step back. "And what are you going to do with them there? Let them choke on their own vomit while you guys hang out in the rec room? My mom was a nurse, she'll know what to do."

Jessica scowled. "Your mom's a psycho. She'll just feed them an entire bottle of aspirin. Isn't that what she took at your party a few months ago?"

My jaw dropped. I expected Cass's well-posed fist to meet with Jessica's pretty face. Instead, Cass blinked twice and started walking toward the hill. Mary dodged out of her path.

But Maya wasn't nearly as collected. She set Quentin down and grabbed Jessica by the shoulders, working her fingers close to Jessica's throat. "You say one more word about Cassie, I'll smash your face so bad your jaw will have to be permanently wired shut. I doubt your lawyer mama'll give a shit 'cause she'll be so glad that someone finally shut you up." Maya shoved Jessica into the bushes, breaking branches with a loud crack, before stalking off in the same direction as her cousin.

I took one last look at Adrian, the boy who I'd come to think of as my soul mate, his face resting beside a puddle of puke, and went after my friends. I found them on the playground. Cass sat on a swing, blowing smoke rings into the night, and a few feet away, Maya leaned against the building that housed the bathrooms. She muttered, "Sheep in wolves' clothing. That's what my grandma would call them."

"Is she okay?" I nodded in Cass's direction.

"Give her a few minutes. She'll go back to check on them. Unlike Jessica, who only cares about herself, Cass treats her friends like family."

I thought of Liam when she mentioned family. I couldn't believe I'd ditched him for this. Aside from Maya and Cass, the kids at Scoville Park suddenly seemed just like everyone else at high school. Maybe they looked different, but like Maggie Young's crowd, they backstabbed their friends for petty reasons and drank too much on the weekends for the hell of it. Why had I wanted to be a part of that?

I told Maya, "It's kinda late, I'm gonna go home now. Tell Cass . . ." I trailed off, having no idea what I actually wanted her to tell Cass.

"I'll tell her you'll see her here on Monday," Maya finished for me.
"I don't know about that. But I'll see you in class at least."

—— ==≺ ⊨= ==

I mentally composed my apology to Liam as I walked home. Most
of the houses I passed were dark or lit only by the flickering of
a television. I expected to find the lights on at my house since
it was only ten, but from the street it looked pitch black inside.
Thinking my brother had fallen asleep in front of the TV and my
parents had turned it off, I tiptoed to the living room, expecting to see Liam snoozing in the La-Z-Boy. Instead, I found Mom
asleep on the couch with the pillows and blankets that belonged
upstairs on her bed. Mom had never slept on the couch before
and the sight of it made me so queasy that I could have puked
the way Adrian had.

I hurried upstairs. The familiar click of keystrokes sounded
from behind the tightly closed door of Dad's office. Liam's door
was shut as well. He didn't respond when I knocked, but I decided to enter.

The reading lamp beside Liam's bed was on and Liam lay
on his side under the covers, wearing headphones. He didn't
respond when I called his name so I walked closer. An open
notebook sat next to him. I couldn't read his tiny handwriting
except for the words scrawled in capital letters at the bottom of
the page: "Fuck this house!"

I heard the quiet strains of a Johnny Cash song as my brother
removed his headphones. Liam closed his notebook and rolled
over to face me in one fluid motion. "What are you doing in my
room?" His throat sounded thick with mucus and his red cheeks
and bloodshot eyes gave away that he'd been crying.

"I knocked but you didn't answer. Mom . . . she's sleeping on
the couch. What happened?" I stammered, rubbing the scabs on
my left arm through my blue cardigan.

Liam coldly stated the obvious. "Mom and Dad had a fight."
The tinny sound of applause leaked out from his headphones as
Johnny finished singing "I Got Stripes."

"But what about the date?" I asked urgently.

Liam answered in a monotone, squeezing the foamy earpieces
of his headphones. "She wanted to have coffee and talk. He
wanted to see a movie. She gave in. He fell asleep at the movie.
They had a fight. You weren't here. I was. Same old story."

Instead of being a bystander for the stupid drama at the park,
I should have been protecting my brother. "Liam, I'm really sorry.
Do you want to talk about it?"

Liam angrily punched the stop button on his Walkman and
tugged his covers up to his neck. "No, I want to go to sleep and
fuckin' forget it. I was almost asleep when you barged in."

"I'm sorry," I murmured again.

"Good night, Kara." Liam snapped off the light on his nightstand, plunging the room into darkness.

Tears spilled down my cheeks as I stumbled over Liam's
books and dirty laundry on my way to his door. I stood in the
hallway, looking helplessly in the three directions my family had
split into. I considered waking Mom, but imagined that she'd
cried herself to sleep and didn't want her to have to do that all
over again. My gaze landed on Dad's office door. I walked past
my bedroom toward it.

Our two rooms sat catty-corner from each other, precisely
three steps apart, but the distance between us had grown so
vast. It started when I was in fourth grade. He'd helped create
a program for terminally ill children and worked long hours to
get it off the ground. I wrote a paper about him being my hero
and said that even though I missed him tucking me in at night, I
knew he was helping so many sick kids.

I put my hand on his door, listening to him type faster and
louder than ever before. I wanted to bridge that gap between us.

I wanted to walk in and ask, "Daddy, are you okay?" But then I thought about how he'd never come to my room to ask me that. He'd only come to lecture me about studying harder or to tell me that I couldn't do something even though my mother had said I could: "No. Absolutely not. Turn that music down and study."

My parents most likely hadn't noticed I wasn't home when they'd returned from their doomed date. But if I made Dad aware of it, I'd probably get chastised for going out without permission instead of reassured that he and Mom would be okay.

So I retreated to my room and got out my knife. I drew blood for my mother, sleeping alone and angry on the couch. I drew blood for Liam, who'd had to seek shelter in his room alone and angry yet again. I drew blood because I was the one who'd abandoned him. I drew blood because my father didn't care about any of us. I drew blood because I hated myself for cutting. It didn't fix anything or make me feel any less guilty.

I fell asleep bleeding and had to throw my sheets away.

12.

THE NEXT MORNING I AWOKE TO the smell of eggs frying. When I was little, breakfast smells roused me every Saturday morning. Dad would be in the kitchen making pancakes, scrambled eggs, and bacon. Well, he'd be trying. Mom would have to rescue the food before he burnt it. Then we'd all sit down in front of the TV and eat together while watching cartoons. I hoped my dad had woken up feeling guilty and gone downstairs to cook for Mom.

I dressed quickly, but carefully concealed my injured arm under a long-sleeved shirt and my cardigan. On my way downstairs, I noticed Dad's closed office door, but since I didn't hear any typing I hoped he wasn't inside. Passing the living room, I was glad to see that the couch was no longer made up as a bed, but grew disheartened at the sight of Liam watching music videos alone, an empty plate in his lap. My fantasy was completely shattered when I reached the kitchen and found Mom making omelets by herself. She offered me one, her voice oozing with fake cheer.

"I was hoping for pancakes," I complained. "Why'd you make omelets? Only Dad likes them and it's not like he appreciates you making breakfast for him."

Mom blinked several times. I saw a couple tears fall and felt kind of bad, but hoped it would force her to talk to me about what had happened. Instead, she scooped food onto my plate and told me, "I used plenty of cheese for you. Why don't you go watch TV with your brother?"

I did as told. Liam glanced over at me when I entered the room, but said nothing. We watched videos in silence while Mom cleaned, filling the house with a Lysol stench. When she started to vacuum the dining room, I sighed and asked Liam to turn up the volume.

"You do it. I'm out of here. I can't fuckin' take this." He tossed the remote at me and headed to the front door, grabbing his skateboard.

I followed him outside without putting my shoes on, worried he was about to take off. He'd stopped on the first step and stood there, board hanging limply at his side. "Where are you going?" I asked softly.

Liam spun around, glaring, and spat, "Nowhere. I wish I could skate till I ran out of concrete, but there's fucking nowhere to go."

"Yes, there is," I told him.

———◄※►———

Since it was a dreary Sunday morning, no one was at Scoville Park. I sat on a bench and watched Liam circle the statue, grinding his sadness and frustration into the steps that led up to it.

He skated for an hour before rolling over to me and bumming a cigarette. We smoked in silence for a few minutes, staring up at the angel part of the statue.

"Is this where you hang out now?" Liam asked. I shrugged, not sure how much I liked Scoville after what had taken place there the night before, but Liam pressed, "Tell me about it?"

Seeing as how I'd ditched him for two weeks, I owed him that much. So I sighed and told him about Maya and how much fun she made everything, and about hilarious Harlan, and about Cass, who was the kind of person I wished I could be: tough, honest, and fair to everyone, even the people who didn't deserve it. Then I explained the cliques. Liam smiled when I mentioned the skaters, but grew somber when I told him about tattooed Adrian in a puddle of his own puke and Jessica lashing out at Cass instead of caring for her drunk friends.

"I don't know if I'm coming back here," I concluded. "If I wanted backstabbing friends and drunken drama, I would have joined the cheerleading squad."

Liam shook his head in disagreement, his shaggy bangs flopping in his eyes. "But that's high school. You're gonna have to put up with that shit no matter who you hang out with. Maya and Cass sound really cool. Just hang out with them and ignore the rest."

"But I can see them in class and hang out with you after school, go back to our simple, drama-free life of watching MTV."

"Until Mom and Dad come home screaming at each other." Liam flicked his cigarette butt at the base of the statue. "Life at home isn't simple and I'm sick of being there." He took a deep breath and asked, "Do you know what I wanted last night, Kara?"

I rubbed the new scabs through the sleeve of my sweater and hung my head like a shamed child. "Me to be there and I wasn't."

"No, I wanted you to take me away." Liam's voice squeaked, causing me to look up and see the tears clinging to his long eyelashes. "Every day for the past two weeks I hoped that you would invite me to come with you."

Blinded by my own tears, I threw my arm around his shoulders. "Liam, I want you to meet me here after school tomorrow. I'm not coming back for Maya and Cass. I'm coming back for your sake."

He hugged me, pressing his head to my chest like he had done when he was a little kid, smaller than me. "Thanks, Kara," he whispered.

13.

On Tuesday, June seventh, Mom left a note on the kitchen counter instructing Liam and me to be home by six for a family meeting.

Liam had been coming to Scoville with me for over a month. I also took him to Shelly's parties on Friday nights and we'd snuck in drunk after curfew on more than one occasion. Mom and Dad must have finally noticed.

"Crap," I told my brother. "Get ready for the crackdown."

Liam dismissed my concerns. "Nah, they probably just want to talk about family vacation."

We met in the living room, where Dad claimed the La-Z-Boy, relegating Liam and me to the couch. Mom sat in her rocking chair, staring blankly at the photographs on the mantel.

Dad cleared his throat and began with, "Your mother and I have something to tell you . . . Rachel, do you want to start?"

This was when I let myself realize what was happening. Some tiny part of me had known all along, had been waiting for this conversation since Liam had first mentioned the D-word in relation to my parents, but I'd worked slavishly to deny it. Sure, Mom had slept on the couch, but only once. Things had gone back to normal after that. Of course, "normal" consisted of my parents barely speaking . . .

The icy front Mom had maintained for months finally shattered. Her face went fuchsia and she said with a sob, "No, Jack, I will not tell them. It's your decision and you will tell them."

"Rachel, we agreed to do this together." There was a slight waver to Dad's voice, but that was all. He didn't yell. He didn't break down. He never did.

Mom, on the other hand, clawed at the air hysterically. "Well, I'm here, aren't I?"

"Rachel—"

"Tell them, Jack. Tell them!" she spat through gritted teeth.

My father removed his wire-framed glasses and daubed at his hazel eyes. "Uhhh . . ." His voice cracked. Finally, evidence of pain. "Your mother and I . . . we're separating."

Memories played out like home movies, but not the good ones, not the times when Dad helped Liam and me pitch a tent in the backyard and stayed out there all night with us. No, those times were long gone.

I visualized Dad's closed office door and heard that clicking keyboard. I imagined Mom alone in her room, wishing her husband would talk to her. I imagined Liam at the table, struggling with his homework, wishing his father could help him without yelling. I imagined me in my room slashing at my arm with the X-ACTO blade that had belonged to Dad, wishing he would come in, rip it out of my hands, and hug me. But instead he'd sat in that office typing, raising money for needy families while ignoring his own.

I kicked the pop can that I'd carefully placed on a coaster per Dad's rules. Coke splashed across the coffee table as I shouted at my father, "This is your fault!"

"No . . . no one's to blame," he stammered.

Angry tears blinded me. "You're moving out, though, right? I hope so because I want to stay here, but I don't want to be near you!"

Dad closed his eyes, long and hard, like my words were a knife slowly severing his muscle from bone. "Yes. I got an apartment—"

"You got an apartment? You planned this?" I screeched.

He blinked in slow motion again, but kept talking over my objection. "I got a two-bedroom apartment near the high school . . ."

Mom blew her nose and cried harder.

"I hoped you and Liam will visit."

I faced Mom. "Why are you letting him do this?"

"Honey, it wasn't my—"

"You can't tell them that! It was *our* decision!" Dad protested.

And then Liam, who had said nothing, who had been utterly invisible since the meeting started, suddenly shouted, "Fuck all of you!" He pointed at my parents. "Fuck you two for not even trying." And then he turned to me. "And fuck you because you'll be out of here in two years when you graduate. You'll leave me like always! Every one of you is selfish! Fuck this family!"

I reached out to him, but he jumped up and kicked the coffee table over with a magnificent crash. My mother grabbed for him, too, but he dodged her and went for the mantel, sweeping down all the photographs. Glass flew everywhere and Liam grabbed his skateboard and ran out the front door.

Dad immediately started in on Mom. "If you had just gone about this like we discussed—"

"Like we discussed? You discussed, Jack! You begrudgingly went to one counseling session and made it your divorce planning session instead!"

"We've been miserable for years."

"But I wanted to *fix* things."

They entirely forgot me as they yelled at each other. And more important, they forgot about Liam.

"Hey!" I stomped on a vase that had toppled to the floor during Liam's dramatic exit. "Are you going to go after him or do I have to? Can you do one last thing together?"

Dad said, "I didn't expect him to—"

"Shut up and get your keys, Jack. I can't drive like this!" Mom's face was a wreck of mascara and snot.

So they left me there alone with the worst pain I'd ever felt in my life. I picked up one of the ceramic vase shards, rolled up my sleeve, and desperately slashed at my scarred arm. The result was scrapes, not the smooth, easy slices that brought me the usual wave of relief. I barely bled from the ragged, disconnected lines. Tears blurring my vision, I swiped at my forearm a few more times before tossing the shard to the floor in frustration. I stumbled upstairs to my room, seeking my faithful knife, and used it to cut deeper than ever before.

The blood wooshed to the surface like a geyser. I felt light-headed and scrambled for a dirty towel on the floor of my bedroom. I was still trying to stop the bleeding when the pounding at my door began.

"Kara, please, you gotta help us find him. We drove around the block, but he's gone and I have no idea where he went!" Mom sobbed through the heavy wood.

I threw on a flannel shirt, not caring if the blood seeped through and they saw that I'd been cutting. It was their fault. They ought to feel bad about it. Besides, I knew no one would notice. I knew that as soon as we found Liam, Mom would cry herself to sleep and Dad would straighten up the living room. Actually, since he was selfish and the cleanliness of the living room was no longer his problem, he would probably begin to pack his things.

When I opened my bedroom door, Mom nearly toppled into the room. Dad stood a few feet down the hall, rubbing his temples like he did right before a proposal was due. I considered holding out my hand and demanding the car keys. I'd gotten my license a few months ago, and Liam would be more likely to come along with me than with either of them. But I knew Mom wouldn't go for it, fearful that she wouldn't see either of us again. So I informed her, "I'll take you to find Liam. *He*"—I glared at Dad—"can stay behind."

Mom was still too messed up to drive, so I drove us to Scoville Park. "I think I know where he is, but you should wait in the car so he doesn't run off again," I told her when we got there.

She didn't have the energy to object. She remained in the passenger's seat and watched me get out and walk toward the statue.

At first, when I didn't hear the whir of skateboard wheels, I thought I was wrong, but then I spotted him, skateboard propped against a bench, sitting with Christian of all people. I hung back for a moment, watching them.

"I just don't know what to do," Liam was saying.

"At least you have your sister, man. When my dad got divorced, my stepmom took my little sister, Naomi. I only see her like twice a month. She's eleven years younger, but having her around would've made it easier. The two years that my dad and stepmom were married were the only stable years of my life. You and your sister should stick together. Get each other through this."

Christian's eyes met mine over the top of Liam's spiky ginger hair. He flicked his chin upward at me, indicating that I should come to them. I walked slowly, feeling a little sheepish since he was aware of my eavesdropping.

My brother—his back to me, eyes on his ratty Vans—didn't notice my approach or Christian's gesture. "I want to . . . I mean, Kara and I are close, but there's always been a gap between us. She has her own issues and sometimes she forgets about everything else around her. Not that I blame her or anything."

"Liam," I whispered, trying not to spook him, but he turned with that expression an animal gets when it's about to bolt.

Christian murmured, "It's okay," not to either of us in particular, but it seemed to settle both Liam and me. Liam stayed where he was and I kept talking, my eyes leaking tears. I don't know if I'd been crying the whole time or if Liam's words did me in.

"It is my fault. The gap, I mean. But there's nothing bigger than this. And I'll be there for you. Just please come home with me. Don't leave me alone with them."

My brother cried, too—I hadn't seen his eyes that red since the summer he'd practically lived at the pool, refusing to wear goggles. Liam didn't usually cry. When Stacey and I messed with him or the kids at school teased him relentlessly about his Johnny Cash act, he hadn't cried. But this . . . this was different. This was more painful than either of us wanted to admit.

Liam bit his lip. I could tell from the way it trembled that he was glad to see me, but he was still pissed. "Who's with you?" He half growled the words, sounding like a dog tired of barking.

"Just Mom. I wouldn't let Dad come."

He gave me a sharp nod of approval, but scanned the car in the distance warily.

"I won't let either of them bother you, I promise. And I won't bother you either, but whenever you want you can come to my room. We'll listen to music. We can even get high and cover up the smell with my incense."

"I don't know."

Worried, I dug my fingernails into my palm and asked in a small voice, "Where else are you gonna go?" Cass's brother had left her, but mine couldn't possibly, right? He'd just graduated from eighth grade last week.

Liam shrugged. "I guess I don't really have a choice."

"You just have to sleep there, man," Christian encouraged. "I'm sure you'll be able to get away with almost anything now. At least that's how it was with my dad after the divorce."

"And I'll be there," I added.

Liam finally looked at me instead of my mom's parked car and bit his lip again. "I guess I'll come home. For you." He turned to face Christian. "Thanks, man."

They did a halfhearted skater-boy handshake—a cross between a low five, a handshake, and a finger snap all at once. "No problem," Christian told him. "If you ever need anything, you know where to find me." He extended his arms as if Scoville was some great prize he was presenting, a living room set on the Showcase Showdown of *The Price Is Right.*

My brother cracked a smile. Then he put his board down on the cement, opting to take the path instead of cutting through the grass like I had.

Left with Christian, I felt awkward. We suddenly knew way too much about each other. "Thanks for looking out for Liam." I leaned in the direction Liam had exited in, tugging on my frayed sleeves.

"No problem. I was just here skating, waiting for Maya. Liam showed up, he was upset, and I've been there."

"Well, thanks. I better go. Tell Maya I said hi."

But as I turned, he stuck his hand out, grazing the inside of my forearm, fingers lingering over the flannel. The sticky, bloody flannel. "If you ever need to talk sometime . . . well, you know where to find me, too."

Had he noticed the blood? Was that what jarred his speech? I couldn't look at him, my face hot with embarrassment. "Yeah, thanks. Bye." I waved lamely over my shoulder.

"Bye." I could feel his concerned eyes on me as I scurried off.

Liam waited for me where the grass met the sidewalk, still hesitant to face Mom. I got in beside her, but that didn't prevent her from sliding between the two front seats and grabbing for Liam.

Through her tears, Mom apologized for things she couldn't change or make up for in any way. "I'm so sorry," she choked. "I tried . . . he's just so unhappy . . . I wanted us to be a family . . . I want to fix it."

"Mama, we don't blame you," Liam assured her.

And with that, we chose a side. We took care of our mother and refused to speak to our dad. He moved out just three days after announcing the divorce. Even though I hated malls, I went shopping with Mom all over the place—Oak Brook, Yorktown, and Woodfield—to buy crap to fill the holes where Dad's books and knickknacks had been. But Mom still cried herself to sleep that night, like she had been doing every night since the family meeting, so Liam and I went to one of Shelly's parties and stayed out until two in the morning.

Like Christian said it would, the divorce gave us a free pass to do what we wanted. There was no talk of curfews. I only got lectured halfheartedly when I started smoking in my bedroom. Liam's sudden use of incense wasn't commented on at all, even though it barely veiled the reek of pot smoke. Maybe we were taking advantage of Mom's depression, but we didn't think about that. We did what we needed to get through the loss of our family. By the time Mom had the strength to try to rein us in we ignored her, no longer used to rules.

There are so many ballads about divorce. Achy-breaky country. songs about the cheaters. Mournful pop songs about the heartbroken. Then there's the rare punk song that tells it from the view of the kids. Feelings aren't laid bare in those particular ballads. There's no crying and moaning. Divorce is shrugged off like it's no big deal, just a messy part of so many kids' life stories.

That's how I treated it. When my friends asked if I was doing okay, I waved off their concern and said, "Whose family isn't fucked-up, right?" I didn't admit to anyone that the divorce totally, irreversibly changed me.

Before my parents split, I got high sometimes, partied a little bit, but was still basically a good kid. After my family disinte-grated, I lived my life as loud, fast, and angry as the music I listened to. The songs I adored warned me about addiction and love that was no good. But I didn't care about what happened in the long run. I focused on escaping the pain one night at a time.

Back then, I didn't tell anyone what I was running from, but now I want to make it clear: my self-destruction started with the divorce, not with Adrian Matthews like everyone thought.

CHORUS

JUNE–SEPTEMBER 1994

(SUMMER BEFORE JUNIOR YEAR)

"That legendary divorce is such a bore."
—*Nirvana*

1.

I HADN'T EXPECTED ADRIAN TO REMEMBER ME, since he'd been so wasted the first time we met. A week after that incident, we'd crossed paths at one of Shelly's parties.

It was a warm May night, about a month before my parents split. Adrian sat on the back porch with Quentin and Craig. I went out there looking for Liam, but when Adrian called out to me—even getting my name right—I immediately forgot about everything else.

"Kara, want to smoke with us?" He offered me a joint.

My insides did somersaults as I lowered myself into a cross-legged position beside him, trying to maintain a facade of cool. The long inhale I took from the joint helped. After passing it to Quentin, I pointed to an open notebook resting on Adrian's lap. "What's that?"

"Oh, this?" Adrian grinned lazily and detangled the top of the notebook's spiral binding from the strings surrounding the hole in the knee of his jeans. He looked particularly good that night in a faded Operation Ivy T-shirt, his free-flowing dark waves hanging down his back. "Quentin and I have been working on this since junior high. It's kind of like a scrapbook."

He plunked the heavy five-subject onto my lap. I traced the ransom-note-style lettering on the cover; it was the "Stories of Suburbia" notebook Cass had been writing in. I opened it, skimming the contents in the weak light that shone through the kitchen window onto the porch. The pages were filled with newspaper clippings about crimes and unsavory incidents from suburbs around the country. Prominent doctors murdered their wives, prominent attorneys were killed by their children, suicides were committed by seemingly happy high school seniors, and then there were a few lighthearted things in between.

Adrian indicated a police blotter from our local paper, the *Oak Leaves*. It reported sightings of three teenage boys vandalizing cars with rotten fruit. "Drive-by fruitings," he said, laughing. "That's me, Quentin, and Wes."

Adrian's fingers graced mine as he flipped through the articles, and I reached for the joint again to keep from visibly swooning at his electric touch. He flicked past a handwritten page that had "The Confession of a Ritalin Zombie: Quentin Hawthorne" written in tiny print in the margin. Quentin cited Bad Religion lyrics before launching into his tale. Several pages beyond that I recognized Cass's meticulous writing beneath a Tori Amos quote. I started to read it, but finished only the first sentence—*Crazy runs in my family, matrilineally at least*—before Adrian turned the page.

"I don't like rules, but I did make one for this book," he informed me, face uncharacteristically stern. "You have to write your confession before you can read anyone else's."

"What do you have to confess to?"

Adrian tapped one of the doctor-turned-wife-killer stories. "In these articles, they act like people just go crazy, do terrible shit, and it's a big anomaly, but everybody in suburbia has a fucked-up secret, an event or series of events that made you who you are. That's what you're confessing to here."

"So, it's like your ballad," I murmured.

"What, like a Whitney Houston song or some crap?" Adrian snorted.

"No," I said quickly, not wanting him to think I was an idiot. I was well versed in this subject thanks to Liam, the Johnny Cash fanatic. I quoted my brother: "'A true ballad tells a story about real life.'" Then I elaborated, giving it my own spin: "I'm sure you know the Rancid song 'The Ballad of Jimmy and Johnny,' about two friends who fight because they have different ideas about what being a skinhead means."

Adrian nodded. His wary expression vanished and he leaned in, interested.

"It's stupid for them to fight, but they do anyway," I continued. "A lot of ballads are about the mistakes we inevitably make while trying to figure out how to live our lives. Some of those newspaper articles remind me of 'Cocaine Blues' by Johnny Cash. You know, 'I took a shot of cocaine and I shot my woman down,'" I sung softly, watching Adrian's lips curl into a smile. Blushing, I shook my finger at him. "Don't make fun of my singing."

"I'm not! You're good. And I know the song." Adrian had a voice deep enough to mimic Johnny's baritone, but he made no attempt to sing. He recited the rest of the first verse and concluded, "Gotta love songs about outlaws."

"Yeah," I said with a grin. "There's something more genuine about Johnny Cash singing about going to prison than those articles, though. Those are so sensationalized. They don't get inside people's heads like Johnny does. Tim Armstrong, Mike Ness, all those punk singers, they do that. *You guys* are doing that by writing firsthand accounts of the things that changed you and the mistakes you made." My voice rose, growing more passionate with each example, but then my insecurity returned. Even though the three boys listened intently, not laughing or looking at me like I was nuts, I concluded quietly, "That's why I instantly thought of them as ballads. Sorry if it's totally stupid . . ."

But Adrian shook his head in awe. "That's not stupid. It's fucking brilliant." He paged through the notebook and crossed out "confession" wherever it was written, replacing it with "ballad." When he finished, he offered the notebook to me. "Since you understand this so well, you wanna write one?"

I shook my head, mumbling, "I don't know what mine is about yet."

"Really?" I could tell Adrian was preparing to interrogate me, but fortunately Liam poked his head outside, shouting, "Kara, we should get going."

"My brother." I shrugged sheepishly, though secretly I was relieved to exit while everyone still thought I was cool.

As I walked away, I heard Adrian declare, "We gotta hang out with Kara more often."

A hopeless crush had never made me feel so good before.

———≈{ }≈———

Of course, it never made me feel so miserable either. Things with Adrian did not go nearly as well a month later.

The weekend my father moved out, Christian made it his mission to get me and Liam wasted. He'd filled a two-liter with a concoction of everything in his dad's liquor cabinet plus some 7UP and lemonade. It looked like piss and tasted like cough syrup, but he, Maya, Liam, and I sat at the booth in the farthest corner of Shelly's basement, gulping it down like water.

I got drunker than I'd ever been before and even though depressing thoughts about my parents still nagged at me, I tried to push them away, focusing on more pleasant things. "Where's Adrian?" I slurred. "I like him a lot. We should offer him a drink."

My friends shrugged, but Jessica, who stood nearby, irritated that we wouldn't relinquish her usual table or share our booze, rolled her eyes and laughed. "Adrian's rather busy." She gestured to a couch across the room where Adrian lay, stretched out on top of some purple-haired girl and doing extremely vampiric things to her neck.

My stomach turned. I swallowed the rest of my drink and stumbled up, announcing, "I have to pee."

Actually, I went out on Shelly's back porch and puked over the railing. I puked and cried, hating myself for thinking that when Adrian called me brilliant, it meant something. When I heard footsteps on the porch, I assumed it was Liam coming to check on me. Without turning around, I whimpered, "I want to go home."

Adrian's husky voice replied, "Oh? Jessica said you wanted to talk to me."

"That stupid bitch," I muttered, spinning to face Adrian. It looked like there were five of him standing in front of me.

"What?"

"Nothing. You should go back to your girlfriend."

"Viv's not my girlfriend. She's just . . . a girl."

This statement confused me and I wobbled slightly.

"You look like you need to sit down." Adrian took my hand and led me over to the steps. He put his arms around my shoulders and carefully lowered me into a seated position. His touch still felt electric even though the thought of him touching that Viv girl made my stomach churn again.

"Can you get my brother?" I pleaded.

"Sure, but tell me what you wanted to talk about first." He sat down on the step beside me, his knee brushing mine.

Damn Jessica. I'm sure she'd hoped that I would drunkenly confess to Adrian that I had a huge crush on him and he'd laugh at me and I'd puke on him. I was determined not to embarrass myself that way.

"Uhh . . ." I stalled before remembering the last time I'd talked to him on the porch. "I was thinking about writing my ballad. My parents announced they're getting divorced this week. That's why I'm drunk. Too drunk to write about it like I was going to. Besides, I'm not really sure if that's my ballad."

Adrian chuckled. "Yeah, you're definitely too drunk. And I think you're right. You're an interesting girl. I'm sure there's more to your story. Now I'll go get Liam."

And then he did it. As he rose to leave he kissed the top of my head. But he kissed it with those lips that had just kissed another girl. I dropped my face into my hands, not sure if I should smile or cry or puke some more.

I really, really hated liking Adrian.

2.

SPENT SATURDAY NURSING MY HANGOVER AND anguishing about Adrian. I'd mentally replay him kissing Viv and grow queasy. Then I'd relive him kissing me on the head and get butterflies in my stomach. By Sunday, I just wanted to blot it out with more booze. Fortunately, Maya invited me over for an afternoon of wine drinking while Liam and Christian skated at Scoville. Christian had a stockpile of wine from a party his dad had thrown and he'd given it to Maya.

Maya still lived at the hotel. Her father had finally found a house, but now he was remodeling it and their move-in date kept getting pushed back. I enjoyed the novelty of her living situation, though. We pretended to be on vacation whenever we hung out in her room, a mind-set that lent itself nicely to our wine buzz.

Even after we'd knocked back a bottle apiece, I still hadn't managed to get Adrian out of my mind. I gave in and decided to share my dilemma with Maya.

"Adrian's definitely cute," Maya said through gritted teeth as she struggled to open a fresh bottle of wine. "Yes!" She held the cork aloft and took a celebratory swig. Passing it to me, she warned, "But Adrian doesn't do serious."

"How do you know?"

"He and Cass have been good friends for years. They decided to lose their virginity together at a party during her freshman year 'cause they were bored. He's been sleeping around ever since."

"What?" I exclaimed, choking on the wine.

"You didn't know that? I thought everyone knew thanks to Jessica and Mary. It wasn't a big deal or anything. There's never been anything serious between them."

"Sex kind of is a big deal, though. Maybe I'm totally old-fashioned," I mumbled, staring uncomfortably at the floor.

Maya squeezed my hand, forcing me to look into her solemn gray eyes. "I feel that way, too. Cass has this whole thing about growing up and getting things over with. I think that was her mentality. I can't speak for Adrian. All I can say is if you just want to make out with him, go for it. But if you want a boyfriend or something . . ."

"Honestly, I have no clue what I want."

We sat in silence until she snatched the wine and hopped to her feet. "Boys are buzzkills," she declared. "Fuck love, let's dance!"

She ran to the stereo, cranking the Ramones, and we danced drunkenly around the room. Maya grabbed me by the arms so we could bounce up and down and shriek to each other that we wanted to be sedated, but she caught me right as I was bringing the bottle to my lips. Wine sloshed out, splashing across my face, temporarily coloring my pale blue bangs purple. We both cackled hysterically and Maya stumbled to the stereo to stop the music. I wiped wine out of my eyes, smearing my makeup. Then I looked down at my drenched T-shirt.

"Shit, you're soaked. We have to find you something else to wear," Maya exclaimed, hurrying to her closet. She began throwing shirts and skirts and dresses on the bed. "Hey, let's get dressed up! We could be twins," she suggested, indicating a vintage black velvet dress with a frilly lace collar and a nearly identical red one. "Or do you want something that goes with that?" She pointed at a shrug made of black and silver netting that I was eyeing. "Here, try it on!"

She tugged at the thin flannel I wore over my T-shirt even though it was summer, freeing my left arm before I could stop her. Talk about a buzzkill.

"Oh, Kara!" Maya moaned pitifully. "What are you doing to yourself?"

She gaped at the red welts and scabs that stood out against my pale skin like the imposing bars of a jail cell. I scrambled to cover up, but Maya gripped my shirt in her fist. She stared a moment longer, asking, "Why?" before she let it fall like a curtain on the body-strewn stage after the last scene of a Shakespeare tragedy.

I sighed, fumbling for an answer. "It sounds stupid, but when I'm really upset I need the pain to remind me I'm alive. I have to let the hurt out or I can't even breathe."

Maya nodded and lowered herself onto her bed, seeming satisfied with my response, but she questioned meekly, "How?"

"How?" I repeated, pushing clothing aside and sinking beside her. "With a knife."

"No." Maya took a deep swig of wine, her intense, smoky eyes zeroing in on mine. "How do you make yourself stop? I wanted to bleed so bad when my mom killed herself, but I was afraid I'd never stop."

She ripped her gaze away and hugged her knees to her chest.

My jaw dropped. "Your mom . . ." I couldn't even repeat her sentence, it was so heartbreaking. She'd never mentioned her mother before except to say that she was Cass's mom's sister. I thought it a little strange, but always assumed there'd been an ugly divorce that no one wanted to talk about.

But suicide?

Maya clutched the neck of the wine bottle with two hands, like she wanted to strangle it for loosening her up enough to confess such a secret. "Yeah, I don't like to talk about it. But that's why we moved here. My dad thought that maybe my mom would have been happier before she died if she'd been closer to her family. So here we are, closer to her family without her. Don't ask me how that works."

"It's probably about as logical as my cutting." I forced an awkward laugh.

Maya echoed the hollow sound and said, "You know what's weird? That I just told you that and you didn't even ask. Christian's been hounding me about it for weeks. One day he told me that his mom died of cancer when he was two and asked me where my mom was. I said my story was a little different and I didn't want to talk about it. But he keeps bringing it up. Says if I ever want an 'actual relationship' with him that I'll have to tell him because he can't handle secrets."

"Do you want a relationship with him?"

"I want a friendship. I don't think I can fall in love. I loved my mom and trusted that she would always be there and then one morning . . ." Maya sniffed back tears and I put my arm around her. "I love my dad and my grandma, because I did before I learned how bad it hurts to lose someone you love, but I can't intentionally fall in love. I'm damaged goods, as my grandma would say. Christian deserves someone who's open and trusting. I can't open up to him about this. I don't want everyone knowing. I mean, look how long it took me to tell you and you're my best friend."

"I am?" I asked, surprised.

Maya laughed a true laugh that cleared the tears from her throat. "Of course you are, silly!" She rubbed her eyes with the back of her hand, smudging eyeliner everywhere. "Oops," she said as soon as she realized what she'd done. "I guess we both have to fix our makeup now."

I hugged her again, reassuring, "It's just us here. We can look like fools."

Maya smiled and slid out of my embrace. "You're right. It's just us and we have wine. We should be dancing and singing like fools, not crying." She walked over to the stereo, flipped through her records, and retrieved a forty-five in a yellowing sleeve. "My grandma's Peggy Lee record. I promised I'd play it for you some-day, didn't I?"

She'd taught me the lyrics to "Is That All There Is?" in chemis-try class. It was a song from the late sixties that her grandmother once taught her. Maya would randomly sing it while we were doing lab or at Scoville or drunk in the corner booth in Shelly's basement. I was eager to hear the original.

Maya carefully put the needle to the record. The speakers crackled and a piano played. She sat down in front of the ste-reo, facing me as she began to recite the first verse in a husky voice.

The verses were spoken word. They told the story of a girl's life through experiences that were supposed to be momentous: a house fire, going to the circus, falling in love. But the girl was always disappointed by her experiences. The chorus, which Maya had me sing with her, basically said that if all there is to life is disappointment, we should just dance and drink and have a ball.

Maya and I both liked that philosophy. We swayed dramat-ically as we sang the choruses, waving our empty bottles of wine. But when Maya reached the last verse, the part she al-ways recited with the most gusto, my whole body grew cold. What Maya'd shared about her mother put a whole new spin on the end of the song.

Maya closed her eyes as she murmured, "I know what you

must be saying to yourselves. If that's the way she feels about it, why doesn't she just end it all?"

Her eyelids snapped up as she broke into the final chorus, belting it out like Janis Joplin. Maya's voice filled the room and she didn't seem to notice that I'd stopped singing. I expected her to burst into tears when she finished, and I prepared to leap up and hug her.

Instead, Maya just laughed. "I love that song," she proclaimed with a grin before putting the Ramones back on.

3.

ADRIAN WOULD ALWAYS SAY THAT I came up with the idea to turn his scrapbook of newspaper articles about the darker side of suburbia into a script, but it wasn't really a stroke of brilliance, just a comment I happened to make at Scoville one afternoon.

I'd been avoiding Adrian at the park all week because I was still grappling with how I felt about him. Should I try to be his friend? His make-out partner? Would I end up getting hurt if my feelings grew more serious? But on Friday, Maya and Christian disappeared to have another one of their friends-versus-more-than-friends debates. This meant I could spend my afternoon alone watching Liam skate by the statue or I could join Adrian, Quentin, and Cass at the bottom of the hill. I decided that spending more time with Adrian might help me figure things out.

Adrian had the notebook on his lap when I approached, so I asked if I could look at it again as an excuse to sit down beside him. He reminded me that I couldn't read the ballads until I wrote my own, but the five-subject notebook was half filled with newspaper clippings, so I had plenty of interesting reading.

After learning how a bunch of moms in suburban California were lobbying to put all the local sex offenders on an island,

I remarked under my breath, "Rapist Island, *that* would make quite a movie."

Adrian jumped to his combat-booted feet, declaring me a genius. "Kara, that's a great idea. We should write a script out of all these articles!"

"I was just talking to myself," I mumbled, but I celebrated on the inside, thrilled to have impressed him again. Besides, school had been out for two weeks, and sitting around smoking cigarettes and the occasional bowl at Scoville was already starting to get boring. Writing a script would make for an interesting summer project.

Adrian led us to the library across the street from the park to look for books on screenwriting and to a store to pick up another notebook. We returned to Scoville and I quickly familiarized myself with screenwriting format while Adrian culled his notebook for the perfect story. He went with a football game where a girl had actually gotten beheaded when the bleachers collapsed.

"Start with the head," Adrian instructed me, "that's a strong image."

```
EXT. PRESENT-DAY HIGH SCHOOL FOOTBALL
FIELD—NIGHT

JANET DAWSON, perky, blond, sixteen-year-
old head cheerleader for LINCOLN PRAIRIE
HIGH SCHOOL ushers the rest of the squad
away from the rickety wooden bleach-
ers that have just collapsed into rub-
ble. People, some injured, stand in small
groups nearby.
                    JANET
                (shrieking)
                Oh my god!
```

```
A  brown,  ponytailed  head  sits  severed
from  its  body  among  the  splintered  wood
and  dust,  its  face  frozen  in  shock.
```

Adrian read what I wrote, affirming, "That's *awesome*!"

Quentin flipped through articles, his black braids falling in his face. "Next maybe we can do date rape at an out-of-control party. That's a suburban classic."

Cass contemplated Quentin's suggestion, exhaling from her cigarette. "It is, but we need to think about how to tie all these incidents together into one story. Are the kids who were at this football game really going to go to a party after they just witnessed a girl getting beheaded?"

"Sure they would," Adrian insisted. "It's the suburbs, the land of ignoring your problems. And that's exactly what we want to illustrate in this script."

Cass inclined her head in agreement and recommended to Quentin, "Look for the one that happened in Minnesota. That was particularly violent."

—=≈{ }≈=—

We had fun that afternoon, but I was surprised when Adrian pulled me aside before I left Scoville and said, "So, there's this new place to see punk shows. A bowling alley in Logan Square, the Fireside. Wanna go see some bands with us tonight?"

Even though Adrian had both of his hands on my shoulders when he asked me and he stood close enough that if he lowered his head six inches he'd be kissing me, I knew this was not a date. He'd said "us," meaning Quentin and Cass, too.

I wanted to become closer friends with the three of them and I always wanted to see some bands, so I said yes. For purely non-crush-related reasons. I mean, would I have brought my little brother along otherwise?

4.

THE FIRESIDE BOWL WAS A SIGHT to behold. Giant, tacky red-and-white tiles covered the side of the building. A large red bowling pin loomed above the doorway, stating redundantly, "Bowling," and though it was probably secured well, the threat of it crashing down seemed imminent, due to the worn state of the establishment.

I'm sure many a driver innocently cruising down Fullerton before a show at the Fireside wondered why droves of scruffy kids with colorful Mohawks and liberty spikes were lining up to go bowling. You didn't get advance tickets to Fireside concerts, you just showed up. If the band was popular, you showed up really early, claiming your spot on the grubby concrete outside of the venue, which you would trade in for your place right in front of the band. If you got there early enough, you would probably see the band unloading their equipment while you waited in line outside. There was no stage entrance, no backstage, absolutely no border between audience and band. It was the way a punk show should be.

Adrian, Quentin, Cass, Liam, and I passed beneath the huge bowling pin, paid our five bucks, got our hands marked so that supposedly we couldn't drink—Adrian had a beer in his mitts within minutes—and emerged into the bowling alley. It was still a functional bowling alley. The bands played on a small platform next to the first two lanes and sometimes people bowled at the other end while the show went on.

Adrian led me toward the ball return between lanes four and five, helped me up, and then climbed beside me. We stood there with our feet uncomfortably hovering over the gap where the balls usually rested. We held hands the whole time. At first, I thought it was because I kept wobbling, my toes and heels the only things that had something solid to rest on, but he didn't let go once I gained balance. He held my hand and swigged from his illegal beer and occasionally shouted something into Quentin's ear. Much like with the kiss on the head, I didn't know what to make of Adrian's gesture. Excitement would bubble inside of me for a moment, but then I'd hear Maya say, *"Adrian doesn't do serious."* Instead of analyzing the situation, I forced myself to focus on the concert.

Cass and Liam left us right away, pushing their way into the pit. I watched them more than I watched the bands. Cass's dreads wriggled like snakes and Liam's skinny body collided with the shoulders and elbows of bigger, burlier guys.

Eventually, as much as I enjoyed having my hand in Adrian's, I wanted to be out in the middle of it all. I nudged Adrian in the side and he leaned down so I could shout into his ear. "I'm gonna go in the pit!"

He shouted back, "You're gonna go in the pit?"

I nodded enthusiastically.

Psyched by my decision, he turned to Quentin and shouted, "Pit!"

But Quentin shook his head and remained perched on the ball return, his toes tapping along with the beat.

Adrian jumped down and held his hand out to me. I steadied myself on his strong forearm as I leapt to the sticky floor. Then I led the way, shoving through the crowd to the place where it was most frenzied.

I'd been in my share of mosh pits by then; a good thing, because this one was by far the most intense. If I didn't know how to keep my balance, I'd have been flying around like a balloon that somebody had suddenly let the air out of. I lost Adrian to the tornado of people almost immediately (though I did see Cass fly by in a flash like the lady on the bicycle in *The Wizard of Oz*). I fell to the ground twice and got helped up by strangers. There were enough girls and nicer boys in the pit on that occasion. A few weeks later, I would learn the hard way not to expect to be helped up at a hardcore punk show when the pit is all boys with bulging biceps and shaved heads. I acquired a split lip that night, but on our first outing to the Fireside, I came out merely bruised.

After the last song, we hit up a diner a few blocks away. Adrian continued to hold my hand beneath the table, so I knew what happened at the show wasn't a fluke. Post-nourishment, we headed to Shelly's even though it was after one a.m.

A smattering of people passed a bowl around on the front porch. Harlan remained ever observant despite his heavy pot handicap. If my brother or Cass noticed my and Adrian's hand-holding, they'd shrugged it off, but Harlan was on it.

"I knew you guys would hook up!"

My cheeks started to get hot, but they quickly grew cold again when Adrian dismissed Harlan's remark. "I have no idea what you're talking about," he said with an inscrutable expression. But then he asked me if I wanted to see if there was any beer left inside. Since Quentin and Cass didn't follow us, I knew something was up.

When we found the keg bone-dry, I grabbed two shot glasses from the bar, told Adrian, "I know where there's vodka," and led him up to Shelly's bedroom.

Adrian leaned against Shelly's bed. After I produced the bottle of vodka from underneath it, he grinned at me. "What do we do now? Pillow fight?" He grabbed a lacy pillow from the bed, smacking me lightly in the leg with it. "Truth or dare?"

"What do you think this is, a slumber party?"

He smirked suggestively. "Maybe."

Wow, I'd figured maybe we'd talk about what was going on between us once we were alone, but maybe he just wanted to make out. Not entirely sure where I stood with that, I uncapped the bottle of Absolut and said, "Okay. Truth or dare?"

"Dare," Adrian answered automatically.

"Umm . . ." I perused the room for inspiration. At a loss, I sat on the floor across from him and pushed the bottle his way. "Do three shots. Right in a row. No chaser."

When Adrian rolled his eyes I remembered how wasted he'd been the first time we met. Obviously this would be no problem for him. He did the shots without so much as flinching. Completely sober, he stared into my eyes. "Truth or dare?"

Knowing I wouldn't get off nearly as easily, I quickly replied, "Truth."

All he asked with a simple smile was, "Did you have a good time tonight?"

"Yeah, I'm just bruised as hell." I rubbed my left shoulder and arm. His hand followed my path, lingering on my forearm. His touch sizzled. "Is that it? That's all you wanna know?"

"Do I get a part two?"

"I guess." I snagged the bottle of vodka and did two quick shots, wincing from the burn.

"Pain relief?" he quipped.

"Yeah," I lied. Truthfully, I was trying to quell my anticipation. I wanted to touch him like he'd touched me, maybe even kiss him, but I didn't have the guts to do it. I really hoped his next question would involve asking me out.

But consistently unpredictable, Adrian's hand dove under the thin fabric of my long-sleeved shirt and grazed the raised red lines beneath. "Why do you do it?" His voice was low, inappropriately seductive.

I jerked my arm away. "That's none of your damn business. If that's your question, I'll take a dare instead."

"Fine." He rocked himself forward and pressed his lips against mine. Hard. His tongue probed my mouth. His teeth scraped my bottom lip. All very intentional. All very good. I was truly breathless when he pulled back and sat cross-legged in front of me, nothing touching but our kneecaps.

I blinked for a moment and repressed an urge to stammer. This was a test. I needed to act as cool as he did. "Your turn. Truth or dare."

He nodded, obviously impressed by my recovery. "Truth."

This time my gaze fell upon his arms. I gestured at the "Thrown" tattoo on his right forearm and then the "Away" on his left. "What's it mean and where'd you get it?"

"That's two questions."

"You asked two questions."

"You didn't answer one."

"I took the dare instead," I pointed out, offended.

"Was that a dare?" he retorted, mock offended.

"Fine. Tell me the story behind the tattoo and I'll answer *your* second question."

Adrian inclined his head slightly. "Deal. I'll even tell you the real story, what I wrote in the notebook. My ballad, as you would call it.

"I got the tattoo in New Orleans. I went down there last year." He inhaled sharply through his nose and pushed his long hair over his shoulders. "I had a big blowout with my parents. My *adoptive* parents. They kicked me out, so I went to where I was born to try to find my real parents."

"Did you?"

Adrian didn't answer directly. "I got 'Thrown Away' tattooed because nobody wants me. Not the people who conceived me and not the people who worked so hard to get their white American baby. 'Cause those are the hardest kind to get, you know." He flashed a sarcastic, game-show-host grin. "The tattoo is a reminder that even though nobody wants me, I'm fuckin' here anyway."

He looked at me expectantly; time to keep up my end of the bargain. I didn't have a grand story like his. I discovered cutting through becoming blood sisters with Stacey, sure, but that was so cliché and really had nothing to do with why I kept doing it.

I glanced at my left arm, visualizing all the little lines that crisscrossed my skin beneath my sleeve. "Maybe I should get a tattoo instead. I just don't have words or an image to express the feelings I'm trying to release yet. Sometimes I hope the scars will form letters and spell it out."

"I know." He nodded and tapped the thick, black *a* in the middle of "Away." I saw faint lines like a fragile web behind the tattoo, hidden by the prominence of the dark ink.

"You did it, too?"

"Still do sometimes."

I was awed into silence, relating to this boy on a level I'd never dreamed possible.

"A lot of people do it," Adrian said.

Thinking of the last person I'd told about cutting, I replied, "Not Maya."

"If she doesn't, she wishes she could or she's got something else she does to cope." It was a bizarre gift he had, zoning in on the ugly truths people couldn't admit. "Cass does it," he informed me. Maya hadn't told me that, but they kept family matters private. Adrian brought me into his tightly knit group when he added, "Quentin, too. That's why you're one of us."

A blood bond without the ritual Stacey and I performed.

"And because you're smart as hell and you can write. First

your theory about ballads. Then the script you started today, wow." Adrian's eyes shone like a proud parent's, but the devilish gleam broke through. He raised the stakes, surprising me like he had throughout our game of truth or dare. "That's why you're my girl," he said with the slightest curl to his lips, so I couldn't gauge the emotion behind his smile.

I didn't know if he meant I was his girlfriend or I was his friend who he identified with or what. But I decided I didn't care and kissed him again. I liked kissing him. I decided that I would spend my summer with Adrian, going to shows, writing the "Stories of Suburbia" script, and, most important, kissing.

The Ballad of a Throwaway:
Adrian Matthews

"We are the sons of no one, bastards of young."

—*The Replacements*

December 1993

EVERYONE WANTS TO KNOW THE STORY BEHIND the tattoo. It's pretty hard to miss. Huge black letters down my forearms. Capital T-H-R-O-W-N on my right arm and A-W-A-Y down the left. In that fancy Old English scrawl, like all the rappers and the big skinhead dudes at hardcore shows get.

I say, you know how people got tattooed in concentration camps? It's kinda like that. This will always remind me that I survived the suburbs.

It's a shitty and un-PC thing to say, I know, but my shrink didn't label me a sociopath for nothing. And if I'm not saying something like that I'm making up a story:

I got it because my best friend and I got jumped. They shot us both for our sneakers and threw us in a Dumpster. I survived. He didn't.

I got it because my father flew into a rage about a golf game and came home so pissed that he threw me off a balcony.

I got it because my parents threw me out and I moved in with my mother's best friend. She's my sugar mama. It says "Picked Up" on my ass cheeks.

I got it because I'm a Dumpster baby. You know, a chick on the cheerleading squad got knocked up, had me in the bathroom stall during prom, and tossed me out with the trash.

I like good stories. That's why I started to collect them. The newspaper clippings, my friends' stories. The stories of suburbia, there's some great ones, huh? I like to think my own story is a combination of the last two. Minus the sleeping-with-my-mom's-best-friend and the thrown-in-the-trash parts. And I guess it's about time I told it.

My parents and I have had a hard time getting along since the beginning. My adoptive parents, I mean. Apparently, they brought me home when I was six months old and I cried for the next six months. Of course, I didn't even find out I was adopted until sixth grade. I learned it in typical suburban fashion: at the shrink's.

I'd been forced to start seeing the shrink the year before because I was LD/BD/ADD—you name it, if it ends with a D for disorder, I got it. On the plus side, my whacked-out brain chemistry is how I met my best friend, Quentin. We were always in the principal's office for acting out in class and the two of us started doing drugs together when we were eight. The legal ones: Ritalin, Adderall, Dexadrine. We traded them like baseball cards and took more than our prescribed dosages.

Anyway, my parents told the shrink I was adopted and he decided they should let me in on the secret, so we had our first and only family session. Suspicious, I went in with my arms crossed and parked myself on a chair instead of with them on the couch. Dad just sat there while Mom clasped and unclasped her manicured hands and smiled her fake-ass smile. "You were born in New Orleans," she began. I arched my eyebrows, but quickly settled back into a poker face.

Mom and Dad spent a couple years doing all they could to combine their own genes, and when that failed, my barren mother window-shopped for babies like she'd once shopped for shoes. They'd scoured the country from New York to San Diego, but none of the babies were good enough.

"Then we found you." My mom squeezed her eyes shut, clasped her hands tighter, and I almost expected her to click her heels together three times like she was fuckin' Dorothy trying to go home. She even resembled Judy Garland with the perfect coif of dark hair and the sparkle in her eyes masking the doped-up sheen. I'd always thought I'd inherited that hair from her, but apparently not. My hair had drawn her to me, though. "You were perfect, with that head full of big brown curls and the most soulful eyes I've ever seen." Yep, "soulful eyes," like a goddamn puppy dog. My mom, creative as a stick.

As I listened to her, one thought played on a loop, *These people aren't my parents, that's why I'm nothing like them*. This was both liberating and frustrating because, well, who the hell *were* my parents? But by the end of the session, I was still too overwhelmed to ask. The shrink prescribed drugs and regular individual visits, more of the same. I did those things when I felt like it. Collecting the articles for my suburban scrapbook became my form of therapy.

We had an assignment the first day of seventh grade where our social studies teacher handed out a stack of newspapers and told us we had half the period to find an article that interested us. Then we'd explain how it affected our lives. I found something in the *Chicago Tribune* about a fourteen-year-old girl who tossed her baby in the Dumpster after giving birth and went back to her honors English class. I carefully ripped it out and was the first to raise my hand when Mr. Baldwin asked who was ready to present. I summarized for the class, being sure to mention the gory details, like the bloody mess in the bathroom. I said, So that relates to me 'cause I'm adopted and that's probably what my birth mother did to me when I was a baby.

Jaws dropped. Mr. Baldwin had been warned in advance about me, like all of my teachers had been, so he took me outside and asked in a concerned voice if I'd taken my meds that day. When I claimed that I didn't remember, he sent me off to the school shrink with a hall pass, but I just walked straight out of school with the article folded up in my back pocket. I eventually taped it into a fat, red, five-subject notebook that was meant for math homework. I'm sure the shrink would call creating the book a "meaningful act," but everyone was so concerned about me ditching class, drinking, doing drugs, the typical crap, that I never got around to telling anyone but my friends about my opus to suburbia.

I didn't ask for the real deal about where I came from until the beginning of junior year of high school, when my parents and I had our biggest blowout.

I dropped out of school today, I informed them at dinner while Dad scooped mashed potatoes onto his plate. The blue bowl smashed on the ice white ceramic tile. Dad finally lost it.

Up until that point, he'd lectured me, grounded me, and despite my every defiance kept his cool like a champion chess player. But that night the face that was tanned by weekly golf games turned purple and everything he'd wanted to say came out. "No son of mine," he growled.

Technically, I'm not.

Dad turned on my dazed mother. "You were the one who wanted this." *This* meaning the adoption. *This* meaning *me*. "I told you that with somebody else's kid there would be no predicting." Yep, that was Dad, the accountant, a genius at logic, numbers, variables, and graphs. The more he spoke, the more I knew he'd always been distant not because I didn't enjoy golf or math homework or anything he liked, but because I wasn't his own flesh and blood. He made it clear he hadn't been the one who picked me out or even wanted me. "We knew nothing about how they treated him in the first six months of his life."

Mom objected, "Wait! You said you knew they treated him well. He was your friend's daughter's kid."

"Not 'friend,' an old business associate. I never claimed to know about his personal life. You just had to have a baby . . ."

I couldn't believe they were talking about me like I was a dog that turned out not to be pedigreed. I wasn't their troubled kid who they loved and wanted to care for. I was the poorly trained poodle who kept shitting on the carpet. Dad probably wished he could put me to sleep. I hated him so much. I imagined that he and his "business associate" had stolen me from my real mom. She probably missed me. She probably actually *wanted* me.

It was my turn to break a dish. Lots of them. I threw things off the table, demanding, Who are my real parents? Where are they? Tell me now. Tell me right fucking now.

Mom and Dad watched in horror as dishes, sloppy potatoes, dry meat, and slimy gravy hit the pristine floor. Mom fretted over how long it would take to clean up, and Dad shouted about how much it would cost to replace all this crap.

And when the fight was over, the kitchen totally trashed along with any family bond the three of us had ever shared, the guy who raised me told me to get out, that I couldn't come back until I followed *his* rules and went back to school and therapy. But in my mind, I'd won the argument, because when I threatened to start on the wedding china, the woman who raised me ran to her bedroom and came back with a page from her address book. My real mother's info.

But I wouldn't even see what the inside of her house looked like. I made a fifteen-hour, NoDoz-fueled drive down I-55 to stand on her porch—if a house with columns like a Roman palace has something as lowly as a porch—and wasn't even invited inside.

When I arrived in the Garden District of New Orleans, I took one look at the mansion and figured it had to belong to my mother's parents—my stodgy grandparents who had brokered the deal with the people who raised me.

I figured they'd direct me to a graveyard and tell me I'd gotten my self-destructive genes from my real mom. She was a drug addict, that's why my brain chemistry was out of whack. Or maybe she'd killed herself after they made her give me up.

If she wasn't dead, she'd probably been disowned. In the five years since I'd found out she existed, I'd attributed everything about myself to her. I didn't fit in with my middle-class, suburban classmates and, in my mind, she hadn't either. I made weird collages and scrapbooks, so she had to be an artist of some sort.

I never expected her to come to the door of a palatial mansion, summoned by a maid, no less, completely comfortable with what wasn't just suburban housewifery but filthy, fuckin' old-money rich. She carried herself like a little girl taught to walk with a book on her head. She'd perfected the patronizing smile meant for the help. She dressed high fashion, gave no hint she was hiding anything like tattoos or piercings or suicide scars or stretch marks from some illegitimate birth sixteen years earlier.

The only thing I recognized of myself in her was the shape and shade of the brown eyes I saw in the mirror every day. And Pseudo-Mom must have been wrong about them being soulful, because Bio-Mom's were completely soulless.

She looked at me, this kid with rumpled, unwashed hair, bloodshot eyes, and stained, torn clothing, like I was dogshit on the bottom of her pricey shoes.

Even though my own emotions were rioting, I had to mess with this woman's world. She was the kind of chick I did that to, whether it was throwing fruit at her BMW or stealing her checkbook and buying more crap I didn't need.

I'm Adrian. I'm the kid you gave up, I told her.

She didn't blink for about a minute, but that was her only indication of emotion. Maybe we had the medication thing in common, too. Finally she asked, "What are you doing here?"

I retorted angrily, What do you think? I wanted to know who my real parents are.

She did the long blink thing again—I didn't come to think of her as Bio-Mom just because of biology; she acted like a bionic woman. "Your real parents raised you."

No.

We would have remained there, holding an intense staring contest as the humidity in the air built, but a shuffling sound came from the house and then the shrill voice of a little girl. "Mommy, it's time to ride bikes!"

Bio-Mom looked trapped. She called, "Just a minute, Lily!" and closed the big, oak door, stepping onto the porch with me.

Concern flooded Bio-Mom's face. "You have to go home," she whispered sharply. "You can't be here. I have a life." She glanced back at the door, obviously worried that Lily might manage to heft it open.

I see that, I said bitterly, enraged that she'd cast me off because I'd come at an inconvenient time and then started a new family without any remorse.

Seeming to sense what I was thinking—maybe possessing some motherly intuition after all—her voice broke slightly when she told me, "I tried to keep you. It wasn't your fault. I was a sixteen-year-old rich girl who'd never dealt with any responsibility in her life and you cried all the time. I couldn't handle the crying."

I glared at her and spat, I suppose *Lily* never cried.

"Not like you did. I don't know why . . . I guess you knew how I felt . . ." She shifted from foot to foot, shorter than me even in her heels, and she broke our gaze to look over her shoulder at the door once more, cocking her ear for sounds coming from behind it.

I was ready to walk off then, but I realized I had one last hope. There was one more person I might identify with. My father, I asked. Can you tell me where he is?

This question finally destroyed her medicated mask, but somehow her tears didn't smear her perfectly applied makeup. "It was a crazy time when you were born. It was the end of the seventies. We were bored, we had money, coke was big. I was a different person. We were all different people. Someday you'll grow up. You'll grow up and you'll realize everyone does stupid things when they are young and everyone makes mistakes. But you'll be able to fix them like I was. I know you have good parents. My parents picked good parents for you."

Yeah, obviously they're great, seeing as I'm here, looking for you, I snapped.

"They're good people. They'll help you find your way," she continued to babble. Every word was so superficial. Basically she was saying: *"You can fuck up when your parents have money. That's why I gave you to someone with money. 'Cause inevitably you'd be fucked-up like me."* I didn't want to hear it.

My father, I repeated.

She sighed heavily. "I don't know. Maybe he's my husband. I always told him that he was your dad, but I've always wondered . . . I've always known," she corrected, after another over-the-shoulder glance confirmed we still had privacy, "it was his best friend, Joe." Her eyes got shiny but not tearful. "Joe died a couple of years ago in the Middle East during the Gulf War. We all got our lives together after you. I went to college. Alex and Joe joined the army. Alex became a doctor when he got out and Joe stayed in, went special operations. We got our lives together. I have a life." She turned her body away from mine, back toward the door, where the kid she wanted waited for her.

There was nothing she could give me, so I gave her and the big house the cold shoulder and descended the steps.

"Adrian," she said, and it hung in the air, which smelled thick and green like the Mississippi. I looked back but knew right away she wasn't going to hug me or try to comfort me, because she already had her hand on the brass doorknob. She simply justified herself one last time: "You'll grow up and understand someday."

I felt numb until I got to my car and then I was more pissed than I had ever been in my life. I would not fucking "grow up" and suddenly adapt. I didn't fit anywhere and I never would. Maybe that was why I'd entered the world screaming my head off.

I drove aimlessly around New Orleans for a long time because I couldn't go back to Chicago; no one wanted me there either. I decided I was on my own and would see what New Orleans had to offer before heading off to the next town.

I snorted smack for the first time off a tarot card at a fortune-telling table in Jackson Square. Jess, a Goth girl with purple eyeliner and crimped hair, charged me less for the drugs than she charged the tourists to predict their future. She took me back to the ramshackle apartment she shared with a bunch of punks, and when we got naked on her futon mattress I saw the tattoos of flowers on her hips, angel wings on her shoulder blades, and big, blue stars on her inner thighs. She told me she'd gotten the angel wings when she'd decided to run away from home. Wanting something to commemorate my journey, I murmured, I need a tattoo.

So Jess took me to her tattoo artist, who worked out of a shack in the swamps outside New Orleans. With a heavy Creole accent he asked, "Eighteen?"

Tomorrow, I lied, even though I wouldn't even be seventeen for another week.

A heavyset man with yellowing eyes and midnight-dark skin, he said, "Good. If you ain't eighteen and you get tattoo, you be in and out of jail the rest of you life."

I thought he was confused, meaning he'd get arrested if I wasn't eighteen, but then I realized that raised in the swamps, this guy probably really had the powers of prediction that Minneapolis native Jess faked to earn her living.

I'd been in New Orleans for two weeks and would have stayed forever, but I called Quentin the next day and asked him to come down 'cause things were never as cool without him. He said he was too broke, but if I came back home, I could stay with him, which I did until his parents got sick of me.

I went home to my fake mom's fake tears after a month of being on the run.

When Pseudo-Dad saw my arms, he asked, "What the hell did you do?"

I got it so I don't just grow up one day and forget who I am.

He rolled his eyes and took me straight to the shrink, who recommended more meds, family therapy, institutionalization if need be. But I do what I want.

The one good thing about coming from no one is there's no one to answer to.

5.

I NEVER INTENDED TO SAY "I LOVE you" to Adrian. My parents had rendered that phrase meaningless. I remembered how they kissed every morning before work while Liam and I sat at the kitchen table eating cereal. "I love you" was like a duet:

"I love you."

"I love you, too."

Who sang the first line and who chimed in with the second varied. Maybe it had alternated on a daily basis.

When my dad left, he took all my childish, romantic notions of Prince Charming with him. I had no interest in suffering from a broken heart like my mother did. Especially since according to the newspaper articles we used as fodder for our "Stories of Suburbia" script, broken hearts resulted in murder/suicides, a riot at a prom in Connecticut, and a hostage situation at a Taco Bell in a sleepy suburb of Cincinnati.

I convinced myself that what Adrian and I had was based entirely on our hormones. We made out. Everywhere. In the grass at Scoville Park, under trees, on benches, beneath the metal stage that had been set up for a lame folk concert series. In Adrian's car. In other people's bedrooms. In sticky vinyl booths at every diner in town. Up against the wall in the girls' bathroom of the Fireside Bowl. It went on for the rest of June, and all of July and August. Kissing Adrian made my summer fly by.

But Adrian never called me his girlfriend. We never had anything that resembled a standard date, unless you counted coffee and cigarettes at Denny's followed by sneaking into a movie. And we never had a song. For me, the girl who loved ballads, that should have been a biggie. But I told myself that I didn't care, that this was exactly how I wanted it. Sometimes when Adrian smiled at me a certain way after a marathon make-out session, or when he took my hand while we sped down Lake Shore Drive alone in his car, I felt a twinge of definite emotion, but I didn't acknowledge it until a rather bizarre conversation with Cass in early September.

It was a Friday, the end of our first week of school. When I got to Scoville, I saw Cass sitting alone on the brown, wooden sculpture across from the park entrance. I left Quentin and Adrian by the pay phone and went to her. Hoisting myself up beside her, I lit a cigarette and gestured at the piece of paper she held. "What's that?"

Cass handed me a flyer for the show at Shelly's house. Since it was Labor Day weekend, Shelly would be hosting her usual Friday shindig and this thing on Saturday. In an effort to make it more like a real concert, she had booked bands from a few different suburbs: Dirt Lip, a punk band from Berwyn; Baby Killer, metal from River Grove; and Svengoolie Is for Lovers, Craig's new band. Over the summer, when it became clear that Wes wasn't returning, the remaining members of Symbiotic went their separate ways. Quentin gave up music for the "Stories of Suburbia" script, and Christian devoted his time to skating and his on-again, off-again relationship with Maya.

Wes had become more of a myth than a person. People told stories like "Remember that time he stole all the Christmas lawn ornaments in north Oak Park and arranged them on the high school football field?" But no one seemed to hold out hope for his return anymore. Except Cass.

She took the flyer back, studying it, her long dreads hanging in her face. "Wes promised he'd come home for this, maybe sing a few songs with Craig. Symbiotic always played these parties."

"I'm sorry," I said, gently stroking her back. I felt awful for her. Wes had canceled at the last minute again. He'd just gotten an apartment in L.A. and claimed he couldn't afford the time off work.

"I know I should be happy for him because he's sober and doing well and stuff, but . . ." Cass stopped midthought. She chewed on her lower lip and pointed across the park toward the war monument. "Is that north?"

"Yeah . . ."

She drummed her fingers against the wood we sat upon. "I'm thinking of running away to Canada, there can't be border patrol, like, all along the border, there has to be little sections where you could just walk across a field and be in Canada."

Cass said all of this without taking a breath. The mile-a-minute rant from out of nowhere made me suspicious. When she turned to me and I caught a glimpse of her eyes, caramel irises swallowed by her black pupils, my suspicions were confirmed. "You're tripping, aren't you?"

Cass applauded. "I have been since Wes called last weekend. You're the first to notice."

"Jesus, Cass," I marveled. I was still afraid to try acid. I'd heard too many urban legends. Like the kid who thought he was an ice-cream cone slowly melting to death. In my mind, acid equaled psychotic breakdown. But Cass never freaked out. On the contrary, she took acid to remain calm.

"So wanna go to Canada with me?" she proposed with a grin. Even though I was totally sober, I considered it for a minute, but before I could say anything, Cass said, "You're right. It's probably a bad idea. And we'd miss our boyfriends."

"Adrian's not my boyfriend," I replied hastily. "We're just . . . I don't know."

Cass's head bobbed like one of those bobble-head dogs that people put in the rear windows of their cars. "Yeah, no one *dates* Adrian. I didn't *date* Adrian. We did lose our virginity together at a party at my house when I was a freshman, though."

I choked on my cigarette smoke. "I heard that."

She studied me with a small smile before sharing, "I haven't slept with Quentin. Yet. I want to be in love this time and I'm not quite there. Almost." She nonchalantly traced a heart in the dust on the slab of wood in front of us.

I shook my head, stunned by her confession. "You're very honest when you're tripping."

"I'm always honest. I'm subtly blunt when I'm sober, but not so subtle when I'm tripping. In case you're wondering about me and Adrian, which you are, we both wanted to get it over with, so we did. I hope for your sake he's better in bed, because I don't think he lasted five minutes," Cass stated, straight-faced.

Christ, acid made people weird.

"That's too much information, but actually Adrian and I haven't slept together."

It was Cass's turn to cough. "You haven't?"

"It's almost happened, but then we go back to kissing." I stared sheepishly at the dirty toe of my sneaker as I spoke. "I want to do it. I mean, I think he's hot. I like making out with him. But he always stops at a certain point. I don't know, he probably knows I've never done it and it's, like, too big of commitment for him or something." I X'ed out Cass's dusty heart sketch.

Cass snorted. "Sex? A commitment for Adrian? I don't think so." She whistled long and low. "Shit, I don't know if you're in love with him, but he's definitely in love with you."

"What?" I stuttered. I was talking about sex, not love. My hormones made sense to me. My emotions were a completely different story. Falling in love with someone sounded terrifying. "Falling" implied losing control; it implied landing badly and hurting yourself. I locked my emotions away because I feared getting hurt. However, if Adrian had feelings for me, maybe I could allow mine to surface. I tried to get Cass to elaborate. "That makes no sense. If he . . . you know, felt *that* way . . . wouldn't sleeping with me be a part of it?"

Cass twisted a dread around her finger as she explained, "Adrian's told me that he doesn't respect any of the girls he's slept with except for me. If he respects you, he loves you. Wow, and I thought a leopard couldn't change its spots."

"Did you get that one from Maya?" I joked nervously, still trying to figure out this love thing. *Does Adrian love me? Do I love him?*

"Maya and her grandma's sayings. They're contagious."

The sculpture shook as Adrian jumped up onto it behind us. He nudged me in the butt with his boot. "I'm bored. Wanna leave?"

I craned my neck to watch him stretch his arms overhead. His T-shirt rode up, revealing a flat expanse of bare skin with a light dusting of butterscotch-colored hairs, and the top of his blue boxers rising above his belted jeans. It made my stomach flip-flop—*Was that love or hormones?*—but I had friend duty. I'd allowed the silly talk about Adrian and sex and love to distract me. My head snapped back to Cass.

She was already waving me away. "Go, don't worry about me. I'm not really going to Canada. I'll see you tomorrow or whenever the hell the stupid show is."

Adrian jumped down before reaching backward for me. "It's tomorrow and you should lay off the acid," he remarked, muffled by the cigarette chomped between his teeth.

"Thanks for noticing!" Cass called cheerily after us.

When we got to Adrian's car, I asked, "Where are we going?"

"My house. My dad's at work and my mom always goes shopping on Friday afternoons."

I'd never been to Adrian's before. He lived on the far north side, on a street that only existed with its particular name for two blocks. My mom joked that the people who lived along it were so rich they'd paid to get it specially renamed. Adrian's foreboding house was massive. Might have been one of those "painted ladies" if it had been painted colorfully instead of dark gray.

He parked in the driveway, hoisted himself onto the hood of his car, and pushed open a bedroom window. "I forgot my keys," he explained, gesturing for me to follow.

I hopped gingerly onto the car and tumbled through the blue drapes directly onto a queen-size bed, which Adrian was at the head of, grasping for a nearby lamp. Illuminated, his room was a total sty. The floor covered in clothing and papers. The dark blue walls spray-painted with phrases and crude drawings. It looked like the inside of an abandoned building used as a squat. "Whoa," I said.

He shrugged like he had to explain the situation. "I'm not here very much. You're the only one who's seen this place besides Quentin."

"Really?" *If I'm in the same category as Quentin, maybe he does love me,* I thought. Still gaping at his graffitied walls, I mumbled, "You come and go as you please. You trash the place. Your parents let you do whatever—"

Adrian silenced my words and thoughts with a kiss. We thrashed around, ended up on the floor, crunching bits of newspaper beneath our backs. My heart pounded as his lips skimmed my neck and his teeth scraped my lips, gnawing them in that way that felt so sexy. His tongue battled with mine and his fingers tangled in my hair. We kissed and clawed and touched each other everywhere. I breathlessly told him, "Don't stop this time," and he just smiled. We probably would have done it—I saw a box of condoms among the rubble—but then I ruined everything.

Half naked on his filthy bedroom floor, I stared at Adrian as he playfully bit at the soft skin of my bare belly. I had a real-ization as he dragged his lips back up toward mine. I loved his mouth, his tattoos, his wild, brown eyes and even crazier tawny curls. I loved his honesty and how he used it to create the "Stories of Suburbia" project. I loved the sense of freedom he oozed. And most of all, I loved how he made me feel like I was just as free and brave and honest and beautiful as he was. It all added up. Before his lips met mine again, I found myself saying, "I love you."

Adrian blinked several times, but did not reply.

Embarrassed, I brought my mouth to his, trying to kiss him and regain the moment, but our teeth collided awkwardly. Then something even worse happened. A deep voice called Adrian's name and Adrian rolled off of me, flinging a dirty T-shirt across my bare chest.

I managed to get it on—inside out and backward—before the door flew open, revealing Adrian's dad: short, paunchy, and blond, the opposite of his son.

Adrian stood between the two of us, still shirtless, having chosen to put on his jeans instead, but his father didn't acknowl-edge his state of undress or toss a glance at me, half hidden behind Adrian's legs. "If you're home, you know what you are agreeing to," his dad said ominously.

"No, I'm not home. I'm just getting stuff." Adrian picked up a couple of CDs, and then casually pulled a T-shirt over his head.

I scrambled for the thin flannel I wore to hide my scabby arms. Though it seemed like I was invisible to Adrian's father, I turned around to zip my jeans, and wrapped my bra up in my own T-shirt as soon as I found them. I shoved my clothes into my backpack, reddening with shame that no one noticed.

Adrian yanked me past his dad as soon as I slipped into my sneakers.

"They kicked me out a week ago," he said dismissively as he started his car. "If I go home, I have to go back to school, go to therapy, all this bullshit."

I nodded numbly. "That sucks." All I could think about was that he still hadn't returned my "I love you."

He sped down a side street, staring straight ahead as he spoke. "I'm going to get Quentin from Scoville. I'll drop you off at home first."

Great, I'd said "I love you," and now he didn't want to hang out anymore.

"If we go to Shelly's tonight, I'll call you, but I don't think we're going since we'll be there tomorrow." He broke the distance between us, reaching, I thought, for my hand, but instead his fingers found the volume knob on the stereo. He turned the music up and leaned away from me again, not speaking the rest of the way to my house.

I looked out my window and thought of an article I'd just adapted for our screenplay. In Omaha, Nebraska, a teenage couple had been poised to have sex when the guy's dad walked in, but they'd been more startled than Adrian and I and they were doing some kinky knife-play thing, so the guy ended up accidentally slitting the girl's throat. It seemed a lot worse than my situation, but when Adrian dropped me off, kissing me lightning fast and leaving without a word, I actually wished our near-coital experience had ended in my death, too.

6.

A DRIAN HADN'T JUST REJECTED ME, HE'D left me without something to do on a Friday night for the first time since April. I entered my house in a daze, wandering toward the kitchen. Other than grabbing a banana when I woke up or chips to satisfy a late-night stoned craving, I hadn't eaten at home since June. Mom had insisted on having family dinners after Dad moved out, but her tendency to burst into tears before the food was dished out put a damper on things. Liam and I stopped coming home for dinner and eventually Mom stopped leaving us notes about the leftovers, let alone expecting us.

Sometimes, while I scarfed down fries and coffee at a diner, I thought about Mom. In my mind, she remained the weeping woman I just couldn't deal with. So I was surprised to see her reading the paper peacefully as she ate. I should have realized that almost three months had passed since my parents split, and if I'd had time to fall in love, she'd had time to mend her broken heart.

She caught sight of me hovering in the doorway and her face brightened. "I didn't know you'd be home. I can cook you something."

I practically had to leap in front of the refrigerator to prevent her from springing into action. "I'm not hungry."

A crestfallen expression dimmed her features. "You're just passing through, huh? I haven't seen you and Liam all summer."

I expected her to study me critically. Notice that my hair smelled like cigarette smoke and maybe like pot, too, and that hickeys peeked out from the collar of my T-shirt, which didn't even belong to me and was on inside out and backward. But she didn't see any of that. She wasn't blatantly ignoring it like Adrian's dad had; she was just too distracted by her own pain. She stared blindly past me, as if trying to project images of Liam and my father beside me, and murmured, "I miss my family. I should have focused on my kids instead of my heartbreak."

Mothers. They're so good at guilt. I'd been planning to retreat to my room and seek the solace of my knife (not that Adrian would acknowledge new cuts, let alone feel bad if he saw them), but instead I took the seat beside her, my old spot. She glanced suggestively from her food to my mouth, so I indulged her by eating the rest of her pasta.

But when she asked, "What have you been doing this summer?" I fell back into the old dinnertime routine and shrugged listlessly.

"Hanging out."

"Oh." She looked disappointed again. As I swallowed my last noodle, she pushed the paper napkins toward me in the bulky, poorly painted clay napkin holder that Liam had made for her in third grade. It was one of the things Dad had packed away when he remodeled. Even though Liam and I hadn't been around to appreciate it, Mom had put some effort into restoring our house from the empty shell my father had abandoned. *God, I'm a shitty daughter.*

"Actually, I do have something to show you," I told her, opening my backpack. "We're taking these newspaper articles about weird events and turning them into a screenplay." I displayed the notebook proudly, but when she reached for it, I said, "I don't know, Mom. It's kind of dark . . ."

"Well, maybe since the separation, I've been kind of dark."

I noticed a cynical glint in her eye that I didn't recognize—not on her, at least. I'd seen it in the mirror plenty of times. "Okay," I agreed. "Maybe you want the scene where the wife kills the workaholic husband by burning down his office." I flipped to the page and pushed the notebook her way.

She laughed wryly. "Did you write this one for me?"

```
INT. THE WATSONS' KITCHEN—NIGHT

MARGARET WATSON is a harried woman who
juggles motherhood and career. Her long
hair is always slipping out of place. Her
suit is worn because she chose to buy new
clothes for her kids instead. She's just
saved dinner from burning on the stove, but
her husband, MARK WATSON, hasn't answered
her calls to come downstairs for it.
```

I'd been writing from a newspaper article about something that had happened in suburban Maryland, but I could have been describing my own mother—well, until Margaret sends her kids to the neighbor's house, siphons gasoline from her car, and brings that up to her husband along with his plate of food.

Mom read eagerly, the same way she'd devoured my creative writing assignments in grade school. Except back then I'd written about princesses and aliens, nothing that hit close to home. When Mom glanced up from the notebook, she smiled, but in a forced way that made the lines near the corners of her eyes and lips prominent. Her sadness had aged her. "Guess this could've been me, huh?"

"I don't know," I replied softly.

"I keep going over the end of the marriage in my mind, trying to figure out what I could've done. But somewhere along the line he stopped loving me. You can't make someone love you."

I couldn't look at her, not because of the tears welling up in her green eyes, but because it reminded me of what had happened with Adrian, and I felt on the verge of crying myself. Fortunately, Liam chose that moment to slam through the back door, skateboard in hand. Any trace of sorrow on Mom's face disappeared. Her wide grin made her cheeks look fuller, hiding those worry lines. She clapped her hands, gleefully declaring, "Both of my kids in the same room with me!"

Liam responded as I had, guiltily hugging her as he lowered himself into the chair that had always been Dad's.

Mom passed my notebook Liam's way. "Look at this. Your sister is going to be a big-time screenwriter someday."

"Yeah?" Liam smirked at me and I knew he was repressing a remark about how stoned I usually was when I wrote in that thing.

"Yeah. And I would know. I saw a lot of movies this summer. It's actually more comfortable than you'd think going to the movies by yourself."

Liam's face faltered a little bit when she said that. To keep the conversation from getting depressing, I asked, "What did you see, Mom?"

"Well, I saw one that you guys probably did. *The Crow*?"

"No shit?" Liam exclaimed, but when Mom glowered at him, he corrected himself. "No way. Did you like it?"

"It was a little violent for my taste, but I liked it."

Mom asked Liam what he'd been up to and he showed off some skateboard tricks right there in the kitchen. Mom didn't care if the wheels scuffed the tiles. Our house felt like a home for the first time since Dad had remodeled the place and made it silent and sterile. It wasn't until Mom got up from her chair, announcing she was going to bed, that I glanced at the clock above the kitchen sink. It was nearly midnight.

I sighed, remembering my previous predicament. "I guess Adrian's not gonna call," I mumbled to Liam.

"Oh no," Liam mocked, fluttering his lashes. Studying him, I realized how much he'd changed from the previous summer when we'd sat at Lollapalooza and daydreamed about the kind of friends we had now. His thin face seemed older than fourteen, his green eyes drained of their innocence.

I snapped, "Why do you have to be so bitter? You sound like . . ." I wanted to say he sounded like Adrian, but I didn't know if that was how Adrian felt. He hadn't even bothered to tell me that much.

"Like a product of divorce?" Liam challenged with raised eyebrows, and gestured in the direction Mom had disappeared in. "Most marriages don't last, some teenage fling definitely won't. Love is a delusion. Where do you end up? Going to the movies alone and telling yourself it's fun? I don't want to end up like that. And neither do you. That's why you and Adrian are no strings attached, right?"

"Yeah," I lied. But there was no lying to my brother.

Liam's palms thudded against the table. "Kara . . ."

I wrapped my arms tightly around my chest, dipping my face toward Adrian's dirty T-shirt, taking in his scent: Winston cigarettes and the air that blows in through an open car window on Lake Shore Drive. "I told him I loved him, he didn't say anything back, and we didn't hang out tonight for the first time in weeks." Tears spilled down my cheeks.

Liam reached across the table and wiped them away with two fingers. His gesture was gentle but firm, as was his voice. "Adrian is not the kind of person you should fall in love with."

I batted his hands away and retorted sarcastically, "Why? 'Cause love is a delusion?"

Liam shook his head and slid into the seat Mom had vacated beside me. "You know Adrian's reputation, right?"

"How many girls do Jessica and Mary say he's slept with?"

"It's not about gossip. Did you see how Adrian acted before he was with you?"

"The key word is 'before.' And Cass knows Adrian well. She told me that he views me differently than other girls. I think she's right," I said smugly, omitting the part about Cass being on acid when we discussed it.

"I hope so. I want you to be happy, Kara. Just be careful. You don't need any more hurt in your life. And if he hurts you—"

The phone rang, interrupting Liam. I dashed over to the kitchen counter to grab it before the sound woke Mom.

"Kara," Adrian exhaled seductively. "I'm bored as shit and everyone's going to bed already. Wanna go for a drive?"

"Where are you?"

"Quentin's. But he's zonked, man." Adrian chuckled low and lazy, clearly stoned off his ass.

"It's late," I told him curtly.

"I know. I should've called earlier." He sighed. "Sorry about that and . . ."

I didn't breathe, waiting for him to finish his sentence with a response to those damned three words I'd said earlier. But he took so long to speak I thought we'd gotten disconnected. "Adrian?"

"Huh? Oh. I'm sorry I didn't call earlier. I missed you tonight. You sure you don't want to hang out?"

I did. More than anything. Especially after the "I missed you" comment. But I glanced at my brother, who was flipping through my script, pretending not to pay attention. I had to prove to Liam that I could take care of myself. And, for my own sake, I had to gain control over my emotions. So I told Adrian no, that I'd see him tomorrow, and hung up.

Without looking up from the notebook, Liam finished what he'd been saying before the phone rang. "If he hurts you, I'll kill him."

His display of protectiveness coaxed a smile from me, and I went over to ruffle his intentionally disheveled auburn hair. Feeling less vulnerable after turning Adrian down, I said, "Don't worry, he won't."

7.

WHEN ADRIAN PICKED ME UP ON Saturday evening to go to Shelly's, he kissed me with the usual zeal, but continued to ignore the unspoken words between us. I tried to forget them, too, and just enjoy the concert.

Shelly's basement was twice as packed as normal, teeming with all the outsider types from our high school plus a bunch from other towns. The sprawling room was arranged slightly differently. The pool table had been moved to a corner; drums, amps, and microphones were set up in the table's usual spot in front of the bar. The kegs—four instead of the usual two—were at the back of the basement, the space between them and the makeshift stage cleared out to allow plenty of room for dancing. I noted that Shelly had put the kegs in front of the big-screen TV as a protective barrier. If things got wild it would happen away from the beer; no one wanted to put the alcohol supply at risk.

I stood toward the back of the basement with Quentin, Cass, and Adrian as we watched the first two bands. Both of them filled Shelly's house with an ear-throbbing wall of sound that ended with a garbled thank-you and equipment being hastily shuffled out through the basement door beside the bar.

By the time Craig's band finally came on, I had a killer headache, which only grew worse as the band played. Adrian insisted we go up front for the performance. This meant standing directly in front of the squalling amplifiers for half an hour. Svengoolie Is for Lovers was "experimental noise rock." Adrian and Quentin attempted to mosh anyway. Cass stood beside me, swaying to the music she heard in her own head.

She was tripping peacefully as usual until the set ended and the last of the equipment was carried out. "What happens now?" she asked me.

"Well, Harlan's DJ'ing—"

"No, Wes should be here," she said, panicking. "Where's Wes? Where is he?" With that, she bolted for the basement door.

"Quentin!" I shouted, pulling him from a conversation with Adrian and Craig. "Cass" was all I had to say and he took off after her in hot pursuit.

I trailed him halfway through Shelly's dusky backyard, habitually rubbing the little cuts on my left forearm. Then I stopped, calling to Quentin, "I'll get Maya!"

But when I whirled around I found myself facing Jessica, who informed me, "Maya's out front breaking up with Christian for the fiftieth time. I wouldn't disturb them."

"Cass is Maya's cousin. I'm sure she won't mind," I replied icily.

Before I could walk away, Jessica grabbed my wrist, her envy-colored eyes narrowed and cruel. "I thought you might want to know what your boyfriend was up to last night."

When I tore her fingers off of me, she combed them through her short, black locks. I glared at her. "If you're talking about Adrian, we don't use those terms."

Jessica sighed patronizingly. "That works out nicely for him. But I feel sorry for you."

"What the hell is that supposed to mean?"

"I saw Adrian here last night," she purred. "He was with

Quentin and Viv. The three of them were snorting heroin and Viv and Adrian were making out."

Viv, the purpled-haired girl. And I remembered how stoned Adrian sounded on the phone when he'd called. I felt like I'd swallowed several razor blades, but managed to play it off, telling Jessica, "Like I said, Adrian and I aren't an official thing."

On cue, Adrian emerged from the basement and Jessica fled like the rat she was.

"What's her problem?" Adrian asked.

I studied him. Searching for traces of Viv. Or evidence of heroin. Or a sign that he cared at all that I'd told him I loved him.

"Nothing," I lied. "I'm going after Cass. She's been doing acid for a week straight. I think she's pretty messed up about Wes not coming home again."

He stared meaningfully into my eyes. "Kara, sometimes people just need space to get their head on straight."

"O-kaaay . . ." I let the word ring out, waiting for him to bring up what happened between us yesterday. I wrapped my arms around myself, bracing for the blow. He'd admit to the things Jessica accused him of, excuse his actions as an attempt to "get his head on straight," and I'd have to decide if I could forgive him.

But instead, Adrian pulled a joint from behind his ear and said, "Let's get high and let everyone figure out their own shit."

I shook my head, not even sure how to begin to respond to that. But before I could, a voice filtered down from the back porch: "Kara-leeeena! We're at the same party!"

Stacey. I hadn't seen her since the beginning of the summer when I'd called her in desperate need of some pot and a friend soon after my dad moved out. She'd slept over that night and we'd promised to spend more time together, but neither of us had followed through. We had separate lives and were part of completely different scenes. While I went to punk shows at the

Fireside, Stacey went to the Thirsty Whale, a suburban club with huge murals of Sebastian Bach and Axl Rose painted on the side of the building. Hair metal was still alive and well at the Whale and Stacey played the role of groupie.

Dressed in a denim miniskirt and a tight baby tee that read "Thank You For Pot Smoking," Stacey hung on the arm of a lanky guy with stringy black hair. She introduced him as "Todd, you know, the singer from Baby Killer, the second band tonight."

Oh yes, I thought, *Baby Killer, the band that sounded even worse than their name.* I forced a smile and said hi to Todd as I hugged Stacey and told her, "I'd love to hang out, but I have to check on a friend."

Stacey clung to me as I tried to pull away, whimpering, "No, Kara. We're at the same party. You're like . . ." She blinked, obviously drunk, but also struggling to see me in the context of my new life. "Look at you!" She pinched my cheek hard, beaming like a proud aunt. "You're partying. You're with a guy." Stacey gave Adrian an exaggerated wink and then glowered at him, shaking her fist over my shoulder. "This girl is my best friend ever and if you hurt her, I'll kick your ass!" Stacey was like the embarrassing drunk aunt who reeked of cheap beer and Marlboros.

Adrian chuckled. "You're Kara's best friend?" He flashed the joint at her. "Wanna smoke up with us?"

"Hell yeah!" Stacey exclaimed, linking her left elbow with mine and her right with Adrian's. "Come on, Todd!" she barked.

I tried once more to disentangle myself from her. "Stace, I'd love to, but my friend Cass just ran out of here upset and—"

Adrian leaned forward, looking past Stacey. "Quentin went after her. She'll be fine."

"Yeah, relax, Kara," Stacey insisted, tightening her grip on my arm. "I haven't seen you all summer. We need to hang out and this party's just getting started. Ooops!" Stacey stumbled and

Adrian and I barely managed to prevent her from falling down the basement stairs. "See," she hiccupped. "I'm the friend who needs you right now."

So I sighed and went along with them to a far corner of Shelly's basement. I figured that after Stacey smoked the one joint, she'd be ready for Todd to carry her out and drive her home and then I'd look for Cass. But Stacey had an amazing constitution. After she smoked the joint and cashed a bowl Todd had, she leapt to her feet, bouncing to the beat of the electro tunes Harlan spun. "Wanna dance with me, Kara?"

The pot combined with the beer I drank earlier left me feeling woozy. I waved her away, saying I didn't feel like standing up. She and Todd disappeared into the masses.

Adrian lifted his arm, his leather jacket creaking, and put it around me. He began to kiss the nape of my neck and it felt good despite my lingering doubts about him. But when I heard Quentin's voice, I immediately broke out of Adrian's embrace.

"Is Cass okay?" I asked.

Quentin slid down onto the floor beside me. "Yeah, she'd just been awake for too long. She's sleeping now."

"Told ya she'd be fine," Adrian murmured, nibbling on my earlobe.

I halfheartedly batted him away and leaned my head back against the leather couch behind us. Now that I knew Cass was okay, I just wanted to go to sleep.

Quentin asked Adrian, "You got some more weed, man?"

"Naw." Adrian's lips brushed my neck again. I turned my face toward his, allowing him to kiss me.

Quentin loudly dumped the contents of his backpack onto the basement floor. He discovered two pills and swallowed them, declaring, "Mmm, NoDoz!"

He quickly became manic, using some Wite-Out that he'd found in his bag to paint words on the black tile floor.

"Shelly's gonna kill you," Adrian said, dragging me onto the couch.

"No, she won't. Words are art," Quentin replied, pushing his braids out of his face.

I rested my head on Adrian's chest, closing my eyes.

Next thing I knew, the basement was silent and completely empty. Quentin stood over me, the floor in front of him covered in phrases, some big, some small, like:

icicle

she's staring like an epic

and he wears evasive conspiracy eyes

"Shelly likes it, Adrian," he annouced proudly.

Adrian peeled an eye open. "Good."

I asked groggily, "What time is it?"

"Three. Shelly said we could sleep over. She said we could watch TV if we wanted." Quentin looked longingly at the nearby big screen.

"Sleep, dude," Adrian groaned.

Quentin bounced from foot to foot. "Okay, I'll watch the TV upstairs. And maybe work on the script. Kara, can I take the notebooks from your backpack?"

"Sure, if you turn the lights off on your way upstairs."

The lights went out and I started to drift again, but after a couple of minutes of restless twitching, Adrian slipped out from under me and onto the floor.

"I'm not feeling that pot anymore," he explained, reaching into his pocket.

I yawned and stretched. "I'm not either, but let's just go to sleep."

"I wanna feel good as I go to sleep." He poured powder from a small vial onto the black tiles beside Quentin's Wite-Out masterpiece, chopping two lines with a razor blade he kept in his wallet. "Want some?"

I sat up and pulled my knees to my chest, peering over his shoulder. "Heroin." It was more of a statement than a question. It made at least part of Jessica's story true.

Adrian didn't answer, just offered me a rolled dollar bill.

Staring at the pale brown lines, I felt fascinated and frightened at the same time because heroin brought two words to mind: numb and dead. If Adrian had been making out with Viv like Jessica said, I really wanted to be numb. But I could cut to achieve that and I knew how to control cutting. I wouldn't accidentally slip and kill myself. With heroin, however, the boundary between numb and dead was easy to inadvertently cross.

I shook my head to decline. Adrian shrugged and snorted both lines. He put his supplies away and snapped the stereo back on, filling the room with the loud, angry sounds of Nine Inch Nails.

He returned to the couch and tugged me on top of him like I was a blanket. Wrapping his hands around the back of my head, he brought my mouth to his. I could taste something vaguely chemical in his kisses and found myself seeking the flavor with my tongue. Adrian's hands crept up my shirt, but after a couple minutes, he pulled his lips away from mine and settled his head against the couch. The ends of his soft brown hair tickled my collarbone as I placed my head on his chest. His palm rested across my back. His breathing became slow and even.

I tried to relax, but couldn't. I stared through the glass-block window above the bar across the room and watched the sky go from black to dirty shades of gray. I wanted to get up and turn off the music, but the thought of removing Adrian's hand from my body scared me. It seemed permanent. I waited for the CD to end, but someone had mercilessly put it on repeat.

Eventually Jessica's words rushed back into my ears. This

whole thing was too complicated, getting attached to a person, worrying if he was as attached to you.

I gently slid out from under Adrian's hand and it rested on his stomach right beneath where I'd been. Like I'd never existed. I paused to study him. His sharp cheekbones and the way his lip curled up on the right prevented him from looking innocent even in sleep. I whispered "I love you" into his ear, figuring it was a safe thing to say if the other person was sleeping and never actually heard it, particularly safe if you were leaving and never intended to say it again. I left Adrian sleeping to Trent Reznor's anguished screams.

Quentin sat on the living room couch with our script on his lap. When I lowered myself beside him, he looked at me, blue eyes wide. "What's wrong?"

"Couldn't sleep."

"What's wrong?" he repeated, gaze penetrating me like Adrian's always did.

I fiddled with a loose string on my jeans. "Did you guys come here last night?"

"We were wandering. We didn't even mean to. We just . . . I don't know why he keeps you at a distance sometimes."

"Because you've been doing heroin?"

Quentin wrinkled his brow, frowning. "He tell you that?"

"No, I watched him do it before he fell asleep. How long has he been using?" A sliver of pain worked its way into my voice.

Quentin stared at the black-and-white movie on TV as he said, "You know me and Adrian, always searching for the best buzz."

"What about Viv? Were you guys with her last night?"

He didn't answer.

Rage stirred within me, but I ran my fingernails over the scabs beneath my left sleeve. "Did he kiss her?" My tone was neutral, numb.

Quentin quickly glanced at me. I could have sworn I saw tears in the corners of his eyes. "Kara, no one means anything to Adrian but you."

"And you." I kissed Quentin on the forehead as I rose from the couch. "Thanks for telling me the truth."

"You're leaving us, aren't you?" he asked softly.

I couldn't bring myself to face him. I just whispered "See you later," and headed out into the bleak dawn.

OCTOBER 1994–JANUARY 1995

(FIRST SEMESTER OF JUNIOR YEAR)

"Sweet little girl, I wanna be your boyfriend."
—*The Ramones*

1.

WHEN I LEFT ADRIAN, I PROMISED myself I would never even think about falling in love again. And for the first month of my junior year, I did a pretty good job keeping myself distracted. At Scoville, I spent the majority of my time with Liam, Maya, and Christian. After their fight on Labor Day, Maya and Christian finally decided that they were better off as friends. There was some tension at first, but eventually that dissipated, and it was just me and my best friend and my brother and his best friend. Life was simple and comfortable. I felt at peace for the first time since the divorce.

Then one afternoon in October while we watched Liam and Christian skate, Maya dropped a bombshell.

"I was on the phone with Christian for three hours last night," she confided.

"Oh?" I arched my eyebrows. "Thinking of giving him another chance?"

She shook her head adamantly. "No. I'm not capable of being more than friends with him. The whole not-wanting-to-talk-about-my-mom thing is too much of an issue," she reminded me. "Actually"—her lips curled into a devilish grin—"we were talking about you."

"Me?"

Maya's eyes danced. "Christian's been pining for you. Apparently he was worried I'd be upset about it, but I think it's perfect. You're my girl best friend; he's my guy best friend. I told him I'd give you his number and that if you hadn't given up on men, maybe you'd call."

"What? You're trying to set us up?" I sputtered, horrified. So horrified I was blushing. Had she known I once had a crush on him back when I'd visited Scoville with Stacey?

"Christian's a really sweet guy, Kara," Maya said, growing serious. "And you deserve a guy like that after the crap Adrian put you through."

"Adrian didn't put me through anything. We had a fling and the fling is over," I snapped defensively. It was easier to pretend I hadn't had any real feelings for him. "And I'm not interested in getting involved with anyone right now, particularly not your ex."

"I don't even consider Christian my ex. We're friends. That's really all we ever were. And I want him to be happy. You guys would make each other happy."

I studied her intently, searching for signs that her smile was forced or she hid deeper emotions about Christian, but she seemed genuinely enthusiastic about pairing the two of us up. Regardless, I maintained, "No. Relationships are messy. I don't want one."

"Just call him. Get to know him a little bit." Before I could object, Maya whipped out the black Sharpie she used to draw pictures on her jeans. She grabbed my right arm (knowing it wasn't the one covered in scabs and scars), flipped it over, wrenched up my sleeve, and scrawled Christian's number in huge print.

But that night when I sat down on my bed with the phone, rolled up my sleeve, and prepared to dial, the ink on my forearm reminded me of Adrian's tattoos. It'd been a month and a half since I'd left him and I hated having random thoughts about him, especially since he didn't appear to be thinking of me at all.

It seemed that Adrian knew things were over between us when he woke up and I wasn't there. He'd actually disappeared for a month right after Labor Day. I didn't know if he'd run off to New Orleans again or to find Wes in L.A. or if he was just holed up somewhere doing heroin. Those were the popular theories that circulated, but with Adrian anything was possible. After he reappeared, he avoided me. I knew why I wasn't speaking to him anymore, but I wondered why he'd let me go so easily.

The conclusion I came to was that he hadn't called or even waved to me at the park for the same reason he'd never officially asked me to go out with him: I meant nothing to him.

Was I seriously going to put myself through that again with a different guy?

I tugged my sleeve over Christian's number and was placing the phone on the floor when it suddenly rang. Spooked, I dropped it, but managed to recover and grab the receiver.

"Kara?"

I recognized Christian's slightly cocky tone, but played dumb. "Who's this?"

"Christian. But I'm not calling for Liam, I'm calling for you," he added quickly.

"That's funny, Maya gave me your number and I was considering calling you."

"Yeah? Great minds think alike, I guess. How are you doing?"

"Okay."

At first, my awkwardness from early high school resurfaced and I could barely muster one-word responses to his questions. After all, I was talking to the cute boy from the Amoco station that I'd crushed on before I regularly hung out at Scoville Park. But then I reminded myself that I'd changed drastically in the past six months. The girl I'd been wouldn't even recognize me. I had friends. I'd sort of been in a relationship. I could handle a conversation with Christian.

Once I regained my confidence, Christian and I talked until three a.m. I untangled all the necklaces I was wearing and painted my nails while we conversed. He fixed and ate a turkey sandwich. We both took our phones to our windows so we could smoke. He heard the music playing in my room and guessed, "Bad Religion?"

I told him ding, ding, ding, he'd won a brand-new convertible and wasn't he excited. He told me no because his dad had one in their garage. "Midlife crisis?" I asked.

"For the past fifteen years," he replied wryly. He moved closer to his speakers and asked me, "Can you name that band?"

I guessed Pavement and was informed I'd won an all-expenses-paid trip to Florida. I told him that I was thrilled because I'd never been. Every year, my parents promised we'd be able to afford Disney World soon, but now I was too old and they were divorced.

Toward the end, I agreed to hang out with Christian that coming Saturday afternoon while he watched his five-year-old sister. I knew he and I had chemistry. I knew "watching his sister" meant that while she napped or whatever, we'd make out. I was resigned to it. I would just let it be physical, not emotional, because that was how these things worked. Then, as the conversation wound down, he surprised me.

"I didn't like the way Adrian treated you. He uses girls. I'm not like that and I definitely wouldn't do that to you."

"What do you mean?" I stammered. For the first time that night, my fingers danced over my scabby arm.

"I mean . . ." Christian faltered slightly, his words losing that characteristic swagger as he rushed them out of his mouth. "Kara, would you go out with me?"

After Adrian, it seemed so official and almost embarrassing, like a throwback to the fifties, when a guy gives a girl his class ring and they go steady. After Adrian, it should have meant the world to me. But I couldn't let it. "I don't know . . ."

"You aren't still with Adrian, are you?"

"No!" I snapped. Then my voice grew softer. "It's got nothing to do with Adrian. It's just me. Since my parents got divorced. Or maybe before that, watching them fake it. It got to me or something . . ." I trailed off. I'd never talked to Adrian about those feelings.

Christian's voice was comforting. "It's okay. I know exactly what you mean. Seeing my dad's relationships with women makes a good relationship seem impossible. And when your parents let you down, it's hard to trust anyone. But please, say you'll still come over Saturday. As a friend."

"Okay," I agreed.

2.

CHRISTIAN'S SISTER, NAOMI, ANSWERED THE DOOR wearing a pink dress made of polyester nightgown material and a plastic tiara in her blond hair. She stared at me, then turned to her brother and declared, "She is pretty as a fairy-tale princess!"

I wondered if there was a new Disney movie out that I didn't know about where the princess had turquoise bangs and wore ripped jeans and lots of eyeliner. Regardless, I thanked Naomi, adding, "I think you make a better princess than I do, though."

She beamed before informing me solemnly, "My brother likes you a lot."

Christian's face glowed redder than his hair and he laughed nervously. "That's the last time I confide in a five-year-old."

I blushed as well, but couldn't help smiling when Naomi protested, "Why?"

Christian shook his head and took Naomi's hand, guiding her away from the door. "Why don't you let Kara in and change out of your Halloween costume so we can go to the park?"

Naomi clapped enthusiastically, crowing, "The park! The park!" She ran a few laps around the living room like an excited puppy before skidding off in the direction of her bedroom.

"I should follow and make sure she picks something appropriate." Christian smiled at me and jerked his head toward the couch. "Have a seat."

I sat, but my eyes roamed the living room. It felt about as welcoming as a dentist's office. The decor looked like it'd come straight out of a magazine: expensive leather couch, glass coffee table—clearly not the place where Naomi regularly spent her time. Kids seemed like an afterthought to Christian's dad. He only had one photograph of each child, the most recent school picture, and probably updated the same frame on a yearly basis. There were no family shots, no pictures of Christian and Naomi as infants like the ones that cluttered the mantel at my house.

I hadn't been allowing myself to think about my dad in the four months since he'd left—thinking of him meant I cared, and I didn't, dammit!—but seeing how Christian's dad decorated, I couldn't help but wonder what my father's apartment looked like. Every week he called and invited Liam and me over. We always refused. His apartment was probably sterile as an OR, and unless he'd slipped a few photos out of the family albums while packing, he didn't have a single picture of me or Liam.

Before I could get too depressed, Christian and Naomi reappeared.

Christian lived three blocks from Scoville, but for some reason, I never thought we'd go there. It was bizarre being in the one tiny corner of the park I rarely spent time in—the playground. I usually only ventured as far as the bathrooms, housed in a small brick building that separated the playground from the wide green lawn that I treated like my own backyard. And I'd smoked pot in those bathrooms . . . with Christian on a couple of occasions. Thinking of that as I tramped through the sand with Naomi, I felt guilty, but it soon passed. As the afternoon progressed, it felt like that had happened in a different lifetime, a different world.

I chased Naomi until I was out of breath. We went down the slides until my legs were sore from climbing the undersize ladder that led to them. We seesawed until my butt hurt and took turns jumping off the swing until my knees ached. Then I rested on a bench and watched Christian lazily push Naomi on a swing, both of them all smiles.

I saw exactly how different Christian was from Adrian. I couldn't imagine Adrian as a kid; I just saw him miniaturized in a child-size leather jacket, dwarfed by long brown hair, sitting on the other side of Scoville puffing away on a cigarette, a rotten apple at eight. But Christian transformed in my mind, despite the scruffy Manic Panic "Vampire Red" hair. I could picture him as a kindergartner, the same age as Naomi, with naturally blond hair like hers, but worn in a bowl cut that hung in his hazel eyes. I wanted to return to childhood with him, that carefree time when the world felt safe and simple. Forget making out, smoking, and doing drugs, we could play tag and tease each other about cooties and—

Naomi's squeaky, high-pitched voice broke into my fantasy. "Why doesn't Daddy ever take me to the park? Mommy says that Daddy loves his girlfriends more than us."

She was resting her face against the chain of her swing, trusting Christian to push her slowly and evenly. Christian coughed a smoker's cough and cleared his throat, eyes pointed at the statue where he and my brother usually ground concerns like this into the concrete with their skateboards.

"I'll tell Daddy to bring you here tomorrow," he said sweetly, without answering her question. He stopped the swing, ending our refreshingly innocent afternoon. "Naomi, you look cold and it's getting dark. Let's go."

Naomi slumped off the swing with a trembling lip. "I don't wanna!"

Christian suggested, "We can play Candy Land . . ."

Her mood swung like a pendulum. She was clapping and smiling again, asking, "Kara, do you want to? Kara, will you stay?"

"Sure." I let her tug me in the direction of her house.

If the park had tired her out at all, she didn't show it. She soldiered on, making it through several games of Candy Land (during which she cheated unabashedly), two slices of pizza, and halfway through a movie—she chose *Cinderella* after learning it had been my childhood favorite.

When Christian carried her upstairs at nine, he told me I could stop the tape, but I remained engrossed, watching Cinderella's fairy godmother magically prepare her for the ball. I reveled in my little-kid moment until Christian returned.

"I love Naomi to death," he said, "but I really need a cigarette. Wanna step outside?"

As much as I didn't want to be that girl again, I did crave a smoke. And I couldn't go back to being five or even twelve when I still believed in happily ever after. If I watched the end of *Cinderella*, my newfound cynicism would spoil my happy childhood memories. Maybe it had happened too fast or for all the wrong reasons, but I'd grown up. So I followed Christian to his backyard.

I hadn't brought a jacket and shivered slightly when we stepped into the cool October air. Christian's arm snaked around my waist, pulling me closer. "Cold?" he asked.

"No, just . . . adjusting." His scent enveloped me: smoke, sweat, and something sweet I couldn't quite place that made it different than Adrian's. As much as I hated it, I kept comparing everything about him to Adrian. Being close to Christian made my stomach somersault like it had with Adrian, but the ways Christian touched and looked at me were different, softer.

We sat on the swing set in the center of the backyard. Christian leaned over and lit my cigarette for me. He stretched his long legs out in front of him, glanced at how close his butt was to the ground, and shook his head.

"You've outgrown it," I commented.

"Nah, I've always been too big. This is Naomi's. My dad buys her stuff to make up for not spending time with her." Christian's smile disappeared when he mentioned his dad. He clenched his jaw and pressed his lips into a straight line, staring off into the distance like he had at the park.

In an effort to cheer him up, I taunted, "Did Naomi tire you out too much for one last competition? I let her win before, but I can definitely jump farther from a swing than anyone."

Christian brightened immediately. "You're on."

We dropped our barely smoked cigarettes and pushed off, kicking up dirt. I stared at the moon intently, pumping hard. I swung to the point where I could go no higher, the chains squeaking, my swing threatening to flip over the bar. Glancing at Christian, I grinned and let go. Skidding across the grass, I nearly crashed into the picnic table.

But I stood up straight and turned to face Christian. "I win."

"Oh yeah?" Christian leapt off his swing. He knocked into me when he landed, wrapping his arms around me so I wouldn't fall. "I demand a rematch."

"On what grounds?"

"On the grounds that I always win," Christian declared with a cocky smile.

I smiled back at him, but pulled out of his embrace. "You're pretty arrogant, you know that?"

Christian held on to my hand, still smirking. "But it amuses you, right?"

I shrugged, wandering toward his house.

He released my hand, but only let me get steps away before calling, "Hey, Kara, will you go out with me?"

My shoulders slumped. Mild flirtation I could handle, I was even finding it fun, but I still couldn't do this dating thing. "No," I said quietly, all the playfulness drained from my voice. "I just can't."

I headed toward the front gate, prepared to leave, but he grabbed my hand once more. "On what grounds?" he mimicked.

I shook my head.

"Listen, I told you the other night, Adrian is stupid for—"

"Adrian isn't and wasn't anything to me." I yanked my hand away and glared into Christian's eyes. "You don't really know me. We've had, what, like five conversations and you think you like me so much that you want to go out with me?"

Christian's confident grin faded completely. "We've had more than five conversations, Kara. I know you better than you think. I know who your favorite bands are . . ." I rolled my eyes. "No, listen," Christian continued, "I know you're too smart to be hanging out with all of us losers at Scoville Park. You're a genius according to Maya and you're writing a brilliant screenplay—"

"So you picked up a few things from my best friend. It doesn't count!" I snapped. The mention of the screenplay, which I'd given up when I left Adrian, since the notebooks and original idea were his, only served as a stinging reminder of why I shouldn't get involved with another guy. When we'd inevitably break up, I'd stand to lose more than just him.

"Kara, wait," Christian begged. "Please. I just want a chance to know you and make you happy—" The back gate slammed. We'd been so involved in our conversation that we hadn't heard the garage door.

"Hello?" a deep male voice called.

Christian's father strode over to us. He was well dressed, handsome in that rich-architect way—tan, buff, and clean-cut like a Ken doll. He extended his hand, introducing himself to me and chiding Christian for not doing so. His friendliness was slightly creepy, though. I could smell the whiskey on him and sensed that if I were five years older, he'd probably be checking out my boobs.

"You should go out now, have a good time," he suggested to Christian, patting him on the back. "I already had my fun." He smiled at me, all pearly white teeth. "A couple rounds of golf and beer does an old guy like me in. You'll need to be with Naomi tomorrow afternoon, though, Christian. I have to have lunch with Denise. She hates it when she doesn't get to see me all weekend."

Christian growled, "Forget Denise, your *daughter* hates it when she doesn't get to see you all weekend. You know, one of her two weekends a month."

"Naomi and I will watch cartoons in the morning, let you sleep in."

"She wants to go to the park with you. She misses you."

Christian's dad waved him off, fumbling for the back door. "Just go out and have a good time, Chris. Don't worry about it. Jesus."

Christian stormed off so fast that I had to jog to keep up with his long, sharp strides. Our moment from before his father showed up was forgotten.

"That's my asshole dad," he told me after we'd gone a block in silence. He lit a cigarette and exhaled hard.

"My dad's an asshole, too," I sympathized.

That's all that we said to each other until we got to Scoville, which, at night and without Naomi, had lost all its luster and magic. It was just the place we went because there was nowhere else. We passed the playground without even looking at it. Beneath the yellow lamplight, I saw Mary and Jessica sitting on the steps of the soldier statue. Christian stalked past them without a word. He did stop at the top of the hill when he noticed Liam and Maya sitting together in the grass. It didn't seem like a romantic thing, but their knees were touching and they whipped around simultaneously.

Seeing it was us, Maya visibly eased. "Oh, hey," she said.

"It's one of the last nice nights, huh? We didn't feel like being at home."

"We didn't either," Christian echoed, nodding hello at my brother as I shot Maya a quizzical look that she ignored.

"I was telling Liam that in Florida, at the beach, I could see the stars." Maya squinted like there might be something to see in the purplish black sky, but the streetlights kept it too bright.

"I was telling Maya that we should run away there." Liam snuck a glance at her out of the corner of his eye, appearing pleased that she did the same.

"Hey, it's warm there," Christian agreed.

Maya added, "I'd rather live on the beach than at a hotel." She'd been in Oak Park for nine months and work still wasn't finished on the house her dad had bought. I guess he wanted it perfect as possible to make up for her mom's absence.

Christian and I were lowering ourselves to the grass when Mary and Jessica strode down the path nearby. Mary loudly remarked, "Christian just wants Kara because she slept with Adrian. He likes her for the same reason he went out with Maya and Cass. She's a slut."

Jessica's shrill giggle filled the air.

Before Maya or I could respond, Christian darted through a flower bed. He grabbed Mary by the front of her shirt, his other fist raised. "Don't think I won't hit you because you're a girl," he growled maliciously.

"Christian . . ." Jessica pleaded. Her haughty smirk vanished, green eyes widening.

Christian ignored her. "Apologize to them right now!" he demanded of Mary.

Mary's lip was quivering, which made her underbite look more pronounced than usual. She whispered, "I'm sorry," staring down at Christian's hand, so close to her throat.

He dropped his fist but didn't release her. "No. Look them in the eye and say, 'I'm sorry, Kara, you aren't a slut.' 'I'm sorry, Maya, you aren't a slut.'"

Mary did as told and Christian let her go, muttering, "Don't lie about people I care about."

Watching Jessica and Mary jet down the path, Maya whistled, "Nice. She was cruisin' for a bruisin'." She laughed at her own cliché like always and her laughter made the situation funny, not scary.

There'd been a split second—somewhere between Mary's first apology and when Christian lowered his fist—that I thought *this has gone too far,* worrying that Christian might really lose his temper. But all he did was ask for an apology, and in the end, it didn't seem much different than the first day I met Maya when she defended me against Maggie Young's bitchy remark.

Liam and Maya high-fived Christian and so did I. I wasn't used to people standing up for me and I liked knowing that both Christian and Maya had my back.

3.

CHRISTIAN ASKED ME OUT A TOTAL of six times in two weeks.

"Why do you keep turning him down?" Maya asked as we sat on my bedroom floor sharing my full-length mirror to prepare for Shelly's Halloween party. I was going as Cinderella with a punk-rock twist and Cass and Maya were to be my decidedly non-Disney wicked stepsisters.

"I have a better question. What's going on with you and my brother? I'm not choosing sides when you two break up," I admonished sternly, reaching for the can of Aqua Net. Cinderella with a punk-rock twist meant that we'd spiked my black and blue hair.

Maya rolled her eyes. They were smeared with red lipliner, because in the un-Disneyfied Cinderella story the stepsisters' eyes are pecked out by pigeons. "We're not going to break up because we aren't really dating. We both think love is for suckers. We get along really well, so we're friends. And I know you'd rather not know this"—Maya playfully leaned out of slapping distance—"but Liam's a good kisser, so we make out on occasion. We're mutually exploring the sexual tension in the platonic male-female relationship. It's a social experiment. No one's going to get hurt."

I cringed and not just because of the word "sexual" being

applied to my little brother who'd only recently turned fifteen. "Wasn't I already a victim of that social experiment? Why not trust my results?"

"Oh, Kara." Maya met my gaze in the mirror, her fake-bloodied eyes brimming with sympathy. "That's why you keep turning Christian down, isn't it? Trust me, he's the complete opposite of Adrian."

"It has nothing to do with Adrian," I huffed, turning my attention back to my hair.

Maya sighed, but let it go. She grabbed the phone from my bed to page Cass again. We'd been waiting over an hour for her. The full impact of our costumes would be lost if we arrived at Shelly's minus one wicked stepsister.

Finally, Cass returned a page. Maya answered, but I knew Cass wasn't coming once I heard Maya remind her to pour fake blood in her shoes because she was supposed to be the stepsister that cut her heels off to bag Prince Charming.

Maya hung up as I put on the combat boots she'd lent me. They were already covered in doodles she'd painted in Wite-Out, so she'd added GLASS on one steel-toe and SLIPPERS on the other. Maya smiled at her own handiwork, but then she pouted and said, "Cass isn't coming. And she's tripping again."

"So," I said with a shrug. Initially, I'd been alarmed by how much acid Cass dropped, but since no one else seemed concerned, I deluded myself into thinking it was no worse than smoking pot. Besides, hallucinogens and pills were gaining favor among our friends. Shelly's parties had come to center more around drugs than kegs.

"But now she can't partake in the Halloween treat I got for the three of us." Maya extended her hand, revealing three tiny blue pills. You could have mistaken them for something innocent like Advil if you didn't notice the Buddha stamped on them.

"Is that ecstasy?" I asked in an awestruck whisper. I'd never done it before, but Maya had a couple of times in Florida and swore it was the happiest drug on the planet.

"Yeah, and who's gonna take the third pill now? We don't have enough for both Christian and Liam, and I bet Harlan sold the rest of his supply."

"Liam won't take it. He thinks anything besides pot is a hard drug. He got pissed at me this summer for trying the Tylenol with codeine that Harlan got from his dentist."

"Okay, well, Christian'll take it. I just didn't want to leave anyone out. Ready to go?" She paused in front of the mirror to admire her baby-shit-green dress that some evil bride had once tortured her bridesmaid into wearing. I smoothed the strapless periwinkle number I'd found at the same thrift store and we were off.

Harlan had definitely sold a lot of ecstasy. There was way more dancing going on at Shelly's than usual. Normally, people filled the couches along the wall or stood around talking in the space that Shelly cleared in the center of the room. That night the basement had morphed into a minirave. Colored lights spilled across the shiny black floor and the flashing strobe made it look like everyone moved in slow motion. Costumed kids danced like charmed snakes to the throbbing techno that Harlan spun. He had quite the setup on the card table in front of the big-screen TV. The simple stereo system had evolved into a DJ booth complete with turntables. He'd financed it by selling acid, X, and other pharmaceuticals—real stuff to his friends and fake versions to the jocks who'd become Deadheads over the summer.

Liam and Christian, who'd been too cool to dress up in costumes and hated electronic music, led Maya and me to our usual spot, the corner booth on the side of the basement opposite the dance floor. This was fine with me for about twenty minutes. Then the X kicked in and I had an overwhelming need to dance.

My most likely partner, Maya, had disappeared with Liam to search for Cass, so I jumped up and extended my hand to Christian. "Dance with me!"

He grinned, but stubbornly slouched against the booth. "I don't dance to techno."

"Me neither, but tonight we should."

I led the way to the dance floor, Christian trailing me. I was shocked at how liquidy my limbs felt, how naturally I moved to the kind of music I usually hated.

Christian only swayed slightly, holding my hand and spinning me so that the tulle skirt of my costume ballooned outward. Entranced, he murmured, "I think I'm starting to like this music because it makes you even more beautiful."

"I like it, too." I let go of his hand and danced in front of him. People whirled around nearby, occasionally colliding with us and setting off a tingly ecstasy wave that made me giggle.

Christian laughed, too. His fingertips fluttered against my hip-bones, guiding me closer to say, "You're the most beautiful girl in the world, you know that? Not just outside, but inside. I can see your kindness pouring out of you." He cupped my face in his palms. "I'm falling so hard for you."

"Yeah?" I couldn't say anything more. His hands sent a charge through my skin like a defibrillator, leaving me pleasantly warm and woozy.

"Yeah."

And then we were kissing. We kissed all the way upstairs to Shelly's room, where we collapsed onto her bed. The comforter felt fluffy as a cloud. The room glowed pale purple. It was like heaven. Kissing Christian was heaven.

I remembered my dress being slightly too big in the chest, so I pulled away, giggling, "Can you see my boobs?"

Christian raised his eyebrows and asked, "I don't know, *can I*?" His hand poised at the zipper on the side.

I would have slept with him. Then and there. At the very least, I could have said I did it for the first time on ecstasy. But then Maya burst into the room. "Sorry to interrupt, but you guys have got to help me. Cass is freaking out."

"Jesus Christ!" Christian exclaimed, completely caught off guard by Maya's entrance. He sucked in air, centering himself. "No problem, we can help."

He picked up his T-shirt, which I didn't remember removing, but seeing the scratches and glittery lip gloss all over his chest, I assumed it was my doing. Fortunately, I'd managed to keep my ratty blue cardigan on over my costume. As usual, it hid the cuts and scars on my left arm—something I wouldn't have wanted to explain while rolling.

I held out my hand for Maya to help me up. "What should we do? Where is she?"

"The bathroom." Maya tugged me toward the end of the hall, where Liam paced outside the bathroom door.

Shelly's upstairs bathroom was definitely the worst possible place for an acid trip. Everything was pink from the mauve rug to the dusty rose tile; even the bathtub and sink were pale pink porcelain. Cass stood in front of the mirror, studying it so closely her nose nearly touched the glass. Her multicolored dreads stuck up every which way, like a crazed Medusa.

Maya stopped at the door to whisper her plan. "Kara should come with me. Christian and Liam, you guys check the bedrooms for Quentin, she keeps saying—"

"He died in his sleep!" Cass screamed.

Given a mission, my brother leapt into action, and Christian dutifully followed. Maya stepped into the bathroom, but I hovered in the doorway.

Cass stared into the mirror wearing the vacant expression of a mental patient. It was extremely unsettling. Maya lightly put her hand on Cass's shoulder, asking, "Cassie, how much acid did you take?"

Like a catatonic, Cass didn't blink, didn't speak. She tapped the mirror and recoiled as if shocked. Catching the reflection of me behind her, she turned. "You're a princess. I was supposed to dress up, too. Did I?"

She wore jeans and a baggy T-shirt instead of the hideous orange dress she'd purchased for her costume. I shook my head and Maya repeated, "Cassie, how much acid?"

Cass rubbed the tulle fabric of my dress between her fingers. "What? Oh. It wasn't kicking in after the first two hits so I took the rest of the ten-strip."

"All ten hits? The stuff that's been going around lately is triple-dipped!" Maya's eyes flooded with anxiety.

I gave Maya's hand a reassuring squeeze and stepped up. "Cass, do you want to go lie down in Shelly's room? The bed is like a cloud."

"I like clouds," Cass mused, but then she peeked back at the mirror. She rose on her toes and spun like a ballerina to face it. After communing with her makeup-smeared reflection for a moment, she slammed her palms against the vanity and shrieked, "No! This is the only place that's safe. People die in the bedroom. Quentin died, and Wes, he's dead, too!"

"Wes isn't dead, he's in California. And Quentin isn't either. Liam and Christian are going to find him," I told her calmly. The ecstasy prevented me from panicking. I'd never felt such inner peace. I just needed to transfer it to Cass somehow. I put my hand on her back, focusing my good vibes. My skin started to tingle, so I thought it was working, but Cass shook her head.

"Demons got him. I saw it. They took Wes first. Now Quentin. And they're turning me into a lunatic. Look at that lunatic in there!" She poked her mirror image's cheek, then gasped, clutching her own. "Ohhhh," she moaned, tears streaking her skin with more mascara. "I'm so fucked-up. I'm going crazy like my mother! And my brother is gone, gone, gone." She clutched at her dreads and pulled them across her face like a curtain.

I withdrew my hand from her because her fright was seeping into me and it made my bones ache. I glanced to Maya for help. Maya's fearless personality usually masked her tiny size, but overcome with worry, she shrunk into her ridiculous dress, fighting tears that threatened to douse her face with red eyeliner.

"Gone! Gone!" Cass screeched, convulsing like she was possessed. She flung herself into the small space between the toilet and the sink, still muttering about demons and death.

Maya started sobbing. Surrounded by all that hysteria, I might have lost it, too, but thankfully Liam returned.

He hung on to the frame of the door, afraid to enter, reporting, "Quentin's in the master bedroom. He's on something, but he's fine. I woke him up, but I couldn't get him out of bed."

"Okay." Maya took deep breaths, pressing Liam's hand in hers. "Thank you, now we just need to bring her to him." Liam and I both looked at Maya skeptically, but she blotted her face on the chartreuse skirt of her dress and knelt on the floor in front of her cousin. "Cass," she said like she'd never lost her cool, like she didn't look like an extra from *Carrie*. "Quentin's in the bedroom next door. Let's go see him."

Cass had been quietly rocking herself, but hearing her cousin's words, she exploded, "No!" Her arms and legs shot straight out in front of her to prevent Maya from getting closer. "It's a trick! This is the only safe place. The bedrooms are evil! That's where the demon took Quentin from me."

"Think acid instead of ecstasy," Maya mumbled to herself. She took hold of Cass's stiff hands and whipped out some drug logic. "Cassie, the mirror is what's evil. It makes you see bad things."

Cass's defensive posture softened. "You could be right about that."

"Of course I'm right," Maya encouraged. "The mirror is a trick. This whole room is an evil pink vortex. But the rest of the house is safe. Especially Shelly's dad's room, where Quentin is. Should we go see Quentin?"

Doubt draining from her eyes, Cass nodded emphatically. Maya and I helped her up and took her to the bedroom where Quentin sat in the center of a king-size bed, stretching his arms overhead like he'd just woken from a nap.

"Angel Quentin," Cass murmured, releasing me and Maya and rushing toward him. "It was horrible without you."

"Where'd you go?" he asked, drawing her close.

"I don't know, but I was very lost."

He lay back down, pulling her with him. "I thought we were talking. Then Liam woke me up . . ." he mumbled, sounding spacier than usual. Unlike Cass's eyes, which were all pupil, Quentin's blue irises had only a tiny speck of black in the center. His eyelids lowered over them like remote-controlled garage doors.

"I think he's on heroin," I whispered to Maya.

"Really?" She frowned. "That *is* a demon." She approached the bed, asking softly, "Cassie, are you okay?" and adding pointedly, "Quentin, are you?"

Cass's response was muffled, her face buried in the tangle of Quentin's braids and her own hair. "He's sleeping again." She flung her arm into the air, summoning us, "Come sleep, too."

We piled into the bed. I draped my arm across Maya to reach Cass, who held both of our hands. A pot or alcohol buzz might have been killed by the high emotions in the bathroom, but lying in the dark room, warmed by Maya's body, my sense of euphoria returned.

Out of the blue, Cass said, "I love him."

"What?" Maya asked groggily.

"Quentin. I love him."

"You got an ecstasy contact buzz?" Maya teased.

I propped myself up on my elbow because I wanted to see what real love looked like. Quentin was asleep. He and Cass curled toward each other, feet touching, backs rounded. Cass's head pressed against Quentin's chest and his lips brushed the top of her head like he was kissing her. The outlines of their bodies almost formed a heart. It was beautiful. I ached to find something like that. Damned ecstasy.

"No, I'm still tripping, but I'm in one of those lulls where I'm lucid," Cass explained. "Normally, I'd be looking for another hit right now. But I can't do that anymore." Her voice cracked, throat coating with tears. "Because I love him and I don't want us to screw it up and we are. I've been on acid for months now and in the meantime he got hooked on something way worse. I have to help him." She caressed his cheek gently, the way I wished someone would caress mine. Cass sighed, rolling onto her back and crying freely.

Maya sat up. "Cassie, are you okay?"

"I need Wes," she choked. "I can't take care of everyone like he did."

"Let's call Wes," Maya urged, stroking Cass's arm.

I watched Cass nod slowly and then I whispered to Maya, "I'll go find Christian and Liam, let you guys call Wes alone."

When I left the bedroom, Liam was nowhere to be seen, but Christian stood by the stairs, waiting for me. I tried to straighten the top of my dress without making too obvious an attempt to hide nonexistent cleavage from him. I felt like we'd been at a very bad prom and had no idea how to proceed.

Christian behaved just as awkwardly. He stammered, "What happened earlier . . ."

"The ecstasy," I said quickly. "It's the drug."

"Yeah, it is," he agreed, but he stepped forward. "Sometimes a drug like this brings out your true feelings, though." He squeezed my hand.

I squeezed back. It felt good. Not the same kind of crazed hormonal good as the kissing, but comforting good. I hadn't felt comforted in years and I needed it. I'd needed it when Stacey abandoned me, when my dad left, to get over Adrian . . .

Behind Christian, Adrian emerged from a bedroom, his curls disheveled, shirt on inside out. The purple-haired girl trailed after him. She giggled, grasping playfully for his belt, trying to reel him back. Until he caught sight of me, Adrian was smiling, too.

I wanted to punch him, not to mention kick that stupid purple-haired bitch's ass, but I forced my focus to remain on Christian, on the positive energy that was pouring from his hand into mine and on his suddenly nervous face. He said, "Kara, if I asked you to go out with me again . . ."

I managed to meet Christian's gaze and look at Adrian out of the corner of my eye. "I would say yes." Adrian stood right behind Christian as I repeated, louder, "Yes."

Christian pulled me into an embrace. He sighed with satisfaction and so did I as I watched Adrian shove the purple-haired girl's hand away from his waist. He shook his head at me, stomping loudly down the stairs.

"What did you expect?" I called after him.

"What?" Christian asked, clueless about Adrian's presence.

"Don't worry about it," I told him, snuggling closer to his chest, letting myself become absorbed in the glorious sensation of hugging. I lost myself in his arms for a long time, but then doubt pricked my brain. Had I said yes because this was what I wanted, because I yearned for the kind of love that I witnessed between Quentin and Cass? Or had I said yes to hurt Adrian? These worries seemed to literally scratch away inside my head and it made me squirmy.

Christian slid his hands down my shoulders. "Feeling okay?"

"It's been a weird night and I'm ready to get out of here. Why don't I find Liam? Then we'll see if Maya's ready to go."

"Why don't we both find Liam?"

"No," I said quickly. "You stay here so we can keep track of Maya."

"Okay." He kissed me. The gentle tease of his tongue against mine sent shivers down my back. I could find the love I was searching for with him. Definitely.

But for some reason, I went to find Adrian anyway.

I told myself I was looking for Liam, but I knew Liam would be out back, smoking pot with his skater buddies to chill after Cass's breakdown. Instead, I checked the front porch first—where Adrian always retreated when he wanted to be alone. And there he was, perched on the banister, huddled into his leather jacket, chain-smoking and flipping through his beloved notebook.

He was sulking and I felt smug. I'd had my revenge, now I could move on. Satisfied, I started to walk away, but Adrian's gruff voice stopped me.

"What are you doing with Christian, Kara?"

I turned around. Adrian's face was hidden by shadows, but his eyes glittered hard and judgmental. I crossed my arms tightly over my chest, feeling overexposed by my silly Halloween costume. Then I remembered that he had no right to be critical. "What were you doing with what's-her-name with the purple hair? Oh yeah, the same thing you were doing with her when we were still . . . whatever."

Adrian slid off the banister. I hated it, but my pulse quickened with each step he took toward me. He wore a remorseful expression. "You're right. I can't say anything. But don't hook up with him just to get back at me."

"I'm not. I don't use people like you do."

"I wasn't using you. You never said you wanted an exclusive thing. If you had . . ."

"What?" I raged. "I said I love you and you didn't respond. You took me home and went to a party and hooked up with someone else. What the hell was that?"

Adrian seemed momentarily stunned by my anger. Then he shrugged. The insolent shrug reserved for parents, teachers, and now me, the foolish girl who couldn't even technically call herself the ex-girlfriend. "I didn't know how to respond. You caught me off guard."

"So you made out with someone else to figure things out?"

Adrian took a slow drag from his cigarette. "No, I snorted smack to figure it out. Viv was there and things happened. I screwed up. I have a tendency to do that."

His nonchalance burned. A breeze swept across the porch and it didn't even chill me. The thing they don't tell you about ecstasy is that it doesn't just heighten the positive emotions. Anger, pure, venomous hatred, that gets magnified, too. Yelling at Adrian felt good. I realized that I never yelled, I cut and cried instead. When people hurt me, I hurt myself. Where was the logic in that? Especially when screaming clears your lungs, allows you to spit people's bile back at them. In that moment, screaming at Adrian felt better than kissing Christian had earlier. It felt better than kissing Adrian ever had. So I let Adrian have it.

"Well, I lied when I said I love you. You tricked me! You're incapable of love. All you do is hurt people! Like your supposed best friend, Quentin, who you got hooked on heroin. Did you know he nodded off and Cass thought he was dead and totally freaked out? Where were you? Screwing some slut? You don't deserve them and you don't deserve me either!"

A faint whoop trickled through the door behind me, and though it sounded too distant to be coming from someone who'd actually heard me, I took it as a sign of support. Even though Adrian towered over me by half a foot, I felt taller than him, especially as his gaze dropped to the scuffed toes of his boots.

Adrian exhaled cigarette smoke that floated past my ear. I tried not to think about how it had come from his mouth and how his lips had once felt grazing my earlobe. "You're right. You deserve the best. I just don't want to see you get hurt."

That shattered whatever hold he still had over me. "Aw," I mocked, "you don't? Well, it's a little too late for that, thanks to you."

I stomped my combat boot down on top of his, which felt good, even though I'm sure it didn't hurt him. Not physically. But when I walked off into the house, into Christian's arms, I knew that I'd left Adrian as devastated as he'd once left me.

4.

WHEN I'D FOLLOWED MAYA INTO SCOVILLE Park in April, I wanted "a life" in the typical teenage sense, meaning people to socialize with. I thought there were certain things I was supposed to be doing at sixteen to make my youth worthwhile. So I did stupid shit like set fires, go to parties, get drunk and high, and make out with boys who were incapable of connecting on any emotional level.

I'd been doing that for almost seven months and then, the morning after Shelly's Halloween party, I awoke to the realization that it wasn't really working out for me. My make-out sessions hadn't stopped me from feeling lonely late at night. Drugs and alcohol hadn't curbed my desire to cut my skin. Having a ton of friends and acquaintances hadn't kept my family from falling apart. My "life" wasn't making me happy.

Shit, Maya had warned me that the comedown from ecstasy would be harsh, but I didn't think I'd wake up the next day feeling like life was devoid of all meaning.

To add to my insurmountable list of problems, there was Christian. Why had I agreed to go out with him? I did not do well with those who possessed the Y chromosome. I had daddy issues, a spotty track record as a big sister, and then . . . Adrian.

I groaned, jerked the covers over my head, and planned to

stay in bed for eternity. But the smell of pancakes eventually lured me out of my cocoon.

When I noticed that she'd already vacated the My Little Pony sleeping bag she'd crashed on, I figured Maya was responsible for the breakfast odor. After all, Mom was out at Sunday brunch, a new post-divorce tradition with the friends she'd paid too little attention to while married. Liam never rolled out of bed before noon on the weekend, not to mention he hardly knew how to make toast. But the cook turned out to be someone I hadn't considered.

Halfway down the stairs, I ran into Christian, who carried a steaming plate of pancakes. He was dressed in a ridiculously frilly apron of my mother's and, god knew where he found it, the goofy chef's hat Dad wore when he barbecued. Considering my raw, chemically induced emotional state, the sight of the hat nearly triggered a crying jag, but perched atop Christian's red tangle of hair, it was too cute.

"I was going to surprise you with breakfast in bed," he said, but then he gestured with a spatula for me to follow. "Come join the rest of the family."

He led me to the kitchen. Dad would have freaked at the sight of it coated in flour, batter, and grease, but I thought it smelled good and felt warm, and it was filled with laughter like a kitchen should be. Liam and Maya sat beside each other at the table, giggling uncontrollably, obviously in the midst of a food fight. Liam had chocolate smudged on his face and Maya had powdered sugar in her hair.

Christian chided, "Can't leave you two alone for a minute. You're worse than my little sister."

He set my plate down in the place across from Liam, but I stood there blinking at the three of them. "Did you guys, like, wake up and start drinking or something?" I glanced around for liquor, hoping they'd left some for me.

Maya rolled her eyes. "Naw, silly. It's too early for that. We're having good old-fashioned sober fun."

"Cooking?" I asked incredulously.

"Yeah." She grinned. "I came downstairs and Christian had already started on the pancakes, so I joined in. We were both excited 'cause I live in a hotel and he lives in a bachelor pad, so we aren't used to a stocked kitchen. I found chocolate chips to make the pancakes tastier and your mom's aprons to make things more festive." She gestured to Christian's frills and Liam's green apron, which proclaimed "Kiss the Cook."

"They even dug out Dad's old hat, but when Christian wears it, he doesn't burn everything." Liam smirked, mentioning my father without a trace of bitterness for the first time in forever.

Christian carried his own plate to the table and sat down across from Maya. I cocked my head in his direction. "You cook?"

"My stepmother taught me a thing or two. And like Maya said, I live in a bachelor pad, so I have to fend for myself."

I studied Christian intently, ignoring the absurd apron and hat and trying to figure out who the hell he was. So many ingredients went into his personality. His usual cocky front that had sparked my early crush on him: the torn jeans, faded ironic T-shirts, and sheaf of messy red hair that hung in impish eyes. The defensive side that emerged when he felt like someone had betrayed his friends: the way he'd freaked out on Mary for insulting me and Maya. Then his softer side: he'd consoled my brother, a kid he hardly knew, during his worst moment; he regularly doted on his sister; and that morning, he'd transformed his little group of friends from broken homes into a family. Adrian had been mysterious, but Christian was complex and genuine. He was sensitive like me—the cocky front and defensive behavior, his way of protecting himself. Unlike with Adrian, I really understood where Christian was coming from.

Christian also had a sense of humor. He flicked a warm, gooey chocolate chip at my nose and asked, "Why don't you just sit down and try it?"

He indicated my food, but when I said "Okay, I will," I meant I'd disregard my ecstasy comedown-fueled worries and try him, a real relationship, and a new life that might actually contain the substance I needed.

5.

A WEEK AFTER HALLOWEEN, CHRISTIAN AND I were making out in his bedroom. He peeled off my cardigan right away. After ten more hot-and-heavy minutes, his hand roamed beneath the long-sleeved thermal I'd layered under my T-shirt. The idea of Christian seeing me in nothing but a bra was not nearly as intimidating as being forced to expose my left arm. I wanted to kiss, not discuss cutting.

I wrestled Christian off of me and sat up, hands poised at the bottom of my shirts, trying to indicate, *Okay, I'll take off mine while you take off yours.* I figured that while his shirt was over his face, I'd lean on my left arm to hide it. But Christian's eyes were on me, probably thinking I meant to do some sexy striptease. So I took the shirts off as fast as I could and flung my arms around him, hoping he wouldn't notice the scabs and scars.

"Whoa." Christian grabbed my left wrist and held my arm out between us. My cheeks burned in humiliation, so I turned away, but his soft voice compelled me to glance back. "Why do you hurt yourself?"

I could actually see tears welling up in his eyes. This extremely sensitive reaction was not on the list of what I'd anticipated. I'd expected him to be uncomfortable and I'd be blasé and tell him to ignore it, which he eagerly would. Or maybe he'd be judgmental and then I'd leave because obviously we weren't compatible. And, of course, deep down, I hoped he did it, too, and we'd share a mutual understanding like Adrian and I had.

I glanced down at the little red lines in various stages of healing and stammered, "I don't know. I just do it when things upset me. My family. School. Life." I cradled my naked arm against my chest.

Christian reached for it again, but stopped himself, fingers dangling in midair. "Why don't you talk to someone about what upsets you instead?"

My laugh sounded jagged and brittle as my scabs looked. "Who wants to listen to my petty problems? Everyone has them. I don't want to be the one who whines and complains."

"Maybe everyone would have fewer problems if they talked about them." Christian forced me to meet his eyes. His fingers stretched toward my wrist, gently caressing the unmarred skin near my hand. "Please call me before you cut. I'll listen."

I'll listen. Those two simple words spoken with sincerity summed up what I'd been seeking at Scoville Park. If I had someone who would listen and understand, I wouldn't have to cut. I mean, I never had to before Stacey bailed on me, right?

And for the next couple weeks, I didn't cut. Then again, I didn't have the urge.

6.

I KNEW THE FIRST THANKSGIVING WITHOUT DAD was going to be rough. Whenever we followed our usual traditions, his empty chair taunted us, conspicuous as a nasty lesion on someone's face. And then Dad tried to invite Liam and me for Thanksgiving at his apartment.

Before Thanksgiving, Dad called once a week, inviting us over. We always hung up on him, like Liam was about to one night in mid-November, but this time Dad managed to spit out a few sentences first.

Liam responded, "Fine. Do that. See if we care!" He clicked the cordless phone off and threw it across my bedroom into a pile of laundry.

"What was that about?" I asked as he slumped against my bed.

"Dad said if we weren't going to spend Thanksgiving with him, he was going to Wisconsin to be with his *family*."

Liam might have been summarizing. To be fair, Dad might have asked first, might have begged that we finally come to his place, but all I got was that succinct little sentence that ended with the word "family" and did not refer to us. And, meeting Liam's glare, I knew he was thinking the same thing I was: *Dad gave up*.

Yes, we'd pushed him as far away as we possibly could for the past six months, but he was our dad and he'd broken up our family. He was supposed to let us be pissed for as long as we needed to be and welcome us back with open arms when we were ready. Instead, he'd decided that if we were going to snub him, he'd snub back.

When I told Mom, she decided, "Let's do something fun for Thanksgiving. We'll go for sushi. We never got to eat it enough because your dad hated it."

Since I'd rather do anything besides stare at Dad's empty spot while choking down mashed potatoes, it seemed like a good idea. Perhaps it could've become a positive new tradition if Mom hadn't gotten a little too enthusiastic and drank way too much sake.

"This is fucked-up," Liam grumbled as Mom used us like crutches to get to her bedroom. He helped her into bed, but when she started to whimper about how she hadn't wanted things to be like this, crying about "till death do us part" like she had during her worst moments following Dad's departure, Liam bailed, heading to Maya's.

I wished I could have gone with him. Reassuring the waiter that I was old enough to drive us home had been pathetic, but lying in Mom's bed, listening to her intoxicated, completely in-appropriate ramblings while she suffocated me against her chest like a teddy bear?

Her worst revelation: "Your father isn't capable of love, I'm afraid he doesn't even really love you."

Thanks for destroying what was left of my childhood there, Mom.

She took it back right away, patting my head and slurring, "No. He loves you. Just not me. He wasn't capable of loving me. Try to find a man capable of loving you, Kara, but don't be shocked if ya fail. A good man is hard to find. Most'a them are liars. They convince ya to trust them, then *boom!* They leave. And what did your trust earn? Two kids and the bills for a house he remodeled in a way you didn't even like."

I really tried to be patient with her. To Mom's credit, until this moment, she'd managed to survive the divorce without getting completely annihilated in front of her kids. I doubted I would've been as strong. But I also wasn't strong enough to handle her rant about love and trust.

After ten minutes, I slunk out of her bone-crushing embrace, placed a trash can beside her bed in case she needed to barf, and left her mumbling, "Men lie and they leave."

I ran to my bedroom and flung myself on the bed, jamming my face into a pillow to smother the memories that Mom's diatribe had brought to the surface. Like the day Dad taught me to ride a bike without training wheels. I'd fallen and scraped my knee; not horribly, but at six the sight of blood made me scream.

"I'm hurt! I'm hurt!" I'd howled at Dad. "You let me go! You can't let go until I'm ready!"

"Shh, Kara," he'd soothed while carefully bandaging my knee. After he'd fixed me up, he urged me to try again.

"You can't let go before I'm ready," I insisted. "And you have to promise that I won't get hurt."

He'd affectionately stroked my hair, fingers gently detangling it. "I promise not to let go before you say you're ready. I can't promise that you won't get hurt, but if that happens I'll be right here to make it all better."

I pounded my fists against my mattress and screeched into the pillow, "I'm hurt! I'm hurt and you're not here, fucker!" I sobbed so hard I started to hyperventilate. Rolling over on my back so I could breathe, I whimpered, "Make it stop hurting." I repeated those words over and over until I had the strength to sit up and strip off my sweater. I had to deal with the pain by myself and there was only one way I knew how.

Just glimpsing my arm eased the pressure in my chest and slowed my tears. It was mostly healed, the freshest cut three weeks old.

I pictured the gentle look in Christian's hazel eyes when he'd said "I'll listen." But his eyes blurred into my father's. They were the same color, after all, and Dad had looked at me that way, too, and said similar things.

The words Mom had been muttering as I snuck out of her room echoed in my ears: "*Men lie and they leave.*" I saw a slide-show of moments of betrayal as I fumbled in my nightstand drawer for my knife. Adrian kissing me, then kissing Viv. Dad trying to tell me he loved me with the keys to his U-Haul truck in hand.

Christian will cheat or break promises, too, I thought. Before I could visualize his lips locking with someone else's, I slashed blindly at my forearm.

Once.

Twice.

I sighed deeply.

Numbness.

Relief.

Then I looked down at the large gashes flanking the blue vein that ran from wrist to elbow. I'd never cut vertically before. That was suicidal and my cutting had never been about dying. Was it now? Should it be?

I touched the slash on the left. It had split some of my newest scars in two. I liked the fresh pink scars better than the white ones. The white ones reminded me how long I'd been cutting. The pink ones were reminiscent of unmarred newborn babies and made me think I had a chance to be innocent, to heal.

I almost had, but here I was bleeding again.

As the blood oozed between my fingertips, soundless sobs shook my body. My arm would never heal. The pain would never stop. Everyone would always lie to me and leave. If that was life, why live it? I placed the tip of the blade to the center of my wrist, on the spot where all the veins that branched out into my hand came together and met the artery that traveled up my arm.

The phone rang, startling me so badly that I dropped the knife. I sat frozen through three rings, trying to decide if I should answer or kill myself.

Finally, I picked up, whispering hello. Christian's voice rushed into my ears. Normal, friendly words reminding me that someone out there cared. "Hey, what's up? Happy Thanksgiving! Done with sushi? How was it?"

I stared at my wrist and decided not to tell him I'd cut because he'd probably be really disappointed in me. I pulled a towel over my arm, blotting the blood and hiding the wounds because *I* was really disappointed in me. "Well, according to my drunk mother, my dad doesn't love me. So much for a new family tradition."

"That sounds pretty bad. At least my dad doesn't try to cover up the fact that Thanksgiving is just a day he gets off from work to drink with his buddies."

"You didn't even have dinner?" I asked, horrified.

"I ate pizza. Dad'll be back in a few hours, totally wasted, or maybe he'll end up at some chick's house. Holidays make people so lonely."

I glanced around my empty bedroom, the rock stars on my posters the only thing keeping me company. "I'm lonely."

"Wanna come over?"

So I went over.

And I lost my virginity.

I hadn't planned for it to be that way. I mean, virginity-losing is a pretty memorable thing and I didn't particularly want to remember it every year when I sat down with the family to celebrate genocide over turkey and mashed potatoes. But, as has been made obvious by numerous TV shows and coming-of-age movies, plotting out your own deflowering rarely works. It tends to happen spontaneously when the circumstances present themselves.

Christian and I had come to the same place Adrian and I had been at a few months before. Sex was the next logical step in the path we were on.

Adrian was the main reason why losing my virginity wasn't a big deal to me. I'd mentally prepared for it to happen with him, and then it hadn't. By the time it happened with Christian it was—no pun intended—anticlimactic. Not to say that Christian was horrible or anything, but I think I had the standard teenage girl experience: a little bit of pain, a lot of wondering if *this* was how *it* was supposed to feel, and then it ended in approximately ten minutes.

The awkward exchange of "Do you want to?" and "Is this okay?" before sex and the even more humiliating finding of the condom is a blur in my mind. The actual physical feelings would be forgotten after more sexual experiences, and the emotions weren't nearly as strong as the ones about my family that I was trying to escape.

Certain things were memorable. Images flash through my mind, censoring out the sex like a PG-13 movie.

He had *Star Wars* sheets, super old ones from his childhood. They were so worn in some spots that they'd become translucent, like when greasy French fries soak through a white paper bag. But they were also extremely soft.

And of course I noticed the music. Mark Arm from Mudhoney crooned, "Sweet young thing ain't sweet no more" over fuzzed-out guitars. Kind of fitting, though it wasn't like sex suddenly made me more grown-up than I was forced to be earlier that day when I lugged my drunk mother out of the sushi place.

On a more romantic note, I'll never forget how Christian and

I both kept opening our eyes while we kissed. We did it at the same time, so our gazes met and then we laughed in this cute, embarrassed way. I got uncharacteristically caught up in the sweetness of it all, just wanting to cling to him. I became aware of the way parts of our bodies fit together like puzzle pieces. He was the right height so that my head fit snuggly beneath his chin; the right weight so that he didn't crush me, but his hip bones didn't jut out and bruise mine. Fingers interlocked. Toes curled and touched. Hair fanned out on the pillow, his bright red, mine pale blue, together purple. Even the satisfied sigh he emitted as he rolled off of me at the end almost matched my own.

But then, as my heart rate slowed, I started to feel insecure. I realized that I was naked, sweaty, and it couldn't possibly be pretty. Flat on my back, my arms and legs at crooked angles, I resembled a chalk outline of a dead body on the mattress. Christian's arm was splayed across my stomach, weighing me down. I snuck a peek to my right and saw his eyes were closed. At least he wasn't studying me, but then I wondered what would happen next. Would he fall asleep like guys always did on TV?

I wished he had, because when he opened his eyes, his face suddenly darkened. He lifted his hand from its sweaty place on my belly and pointed accusatorily at my left arm. "What the hell did you do?"

I'd forgotten all about the cuts and apparently he hadn't noticed them in the heat of the moment. I flipped my arm over, pressing my palm into the mattress. The blood pulsed beneath my new wounds, the confrontation triggering my urge to cut again.

"I had a bad day, you know that."

"I thought you weren't going to do *that* anymore," he said through gritted teeth.

"Do we have to talk about it? Adrian just ignored it, why can't you?" I sat up, wrapped myself in a sheet, and scooted toward the foot of the bed.

Christian viciously dug his fingers into my shoulder, forcing me to face him. "I'm not Adrian," he growled.

I shrugged him off and rose to sort out my clothes. I shimmied into my underwear with my back to Christian. "I know you're not. But in this case I wish you were a little bit more like him."

Christian punched the mattress and I spun around, startled. He'd put his boxers and T-shirt on and sat at the head of the bed, glowering at me. "Why can't you just forget that asshole and be with someone who actually cares about you? I don't know how he could just fuck you and ignore that you were obviously in pain!" He gestured at my arm, which I'd hidden beneath my cardigan. I was fully dressed and ready to walk out on him. But then . . . "I'm falling in love with you so I can't just pretend those cuts aren't there."

"You're what?"

"I care . . ."

"But you also said . . ."

Christian extended his arms toward me. I rounded the bed tentatively and let him take my hands. "I'm falling in love with you. Does that surprise you? I wouldn't have slept with you if I wasn't." His cheeks reddened and he added almost inaudibly, "That was my first time."

Suddenly I understood how shocked Adrian had felt when I'd told him I loved him. I liked Christian a lot and he got my hormones raging, but love? Unable to respond to that part of his statement, I murmured, "That was my first time, too."

My confession threw Christian for as big of a loop as his use of the L-word had thrown me. "But Adrian . . . didn't you . . ."

"Oh, did you believe what Mary said about me being a slut? Thanks!" I spat, dropping his hands and surveying the floor for my shoes.

"I never thought you were a slut!" Christian objected as he reached for me again. "I'm sorry. I guess we should have talked about this before just . . . doing it. But it's a big deal. We can't let it end like this. We shouldn't fight. Here." He scooted over to the side of the bed I'd been occupying and patted the space beside him. "Please lie down."

Even though I was thoroughly confused, I stretched out on my back and he—rather ridiculously, since we were both fully clothed—pulled a blanket over us. He hugged me and said, "I really am falling in love with you. I'm not just saying that 'cause, you know . . ."

As he tenderly stroked my hair, I remembered my mother's words about finding a guy who was capable of loving me. Adrian couldn't, but Christian could. Christian was right; I should stop dwelling on the bad guy and give the good guy a chance. I rolled over to face him. "I think I'm falling in love with you, too." Maybe it wasn't entirely true, but I was sure it would be in due time. Besides, I knew how much it hurt not to hear it back.

Christian smiled, pulling me closer so that my head rested just below his chin. "I've been trying to find a girl like you since I was eleven."

"Puberty?" I joked, trying to lighten things.

"No." He kissed the top of my head. "Five years ago yesterday, on the eve of my first real family Thanksgiving with a mom, a dad, and a little sister, my stepmom, Claire, got a letter from this chick my dad was screwing behind her back. She took Naomi and left us that night."

I felt tears trickling into my hair and squeezed Christian hard, encouraging him to keep talking.

He took a deep breath and continued. "Claire tried to explain things before she left. She didn't want me to hate my dad, so she told me this whole story about how my dad was a womanizer because the only woman he'd ever loved was my mom, who died when I was a baby. Claire even told me where my dad kept this ring he'd given my mom back in high school. A promise ring. The next day, I stole it from my dad's nightstand so I'd have it when I found the perfect girl. I've been looking for her ever since."

Christian released me, pulling back to dry his tears and lowering his head onto the pillow beside mine. He bit his lip. "I guess that sounds stupid, huh?"

"No." I smiled and caressed his damp cheek. "It's a sweet story. What does the ring look like? Can I see it?"

He shook his head. "You'll see it if you're the right girl. I think you are, but I have to totally trust you first. Claire left my dad because of his secrets and lies. I don't wanna get hurt like she did. That's why Maya and I couldn't be together. She kept secrets."

I nodded, recognizing why he'd flipped out when he saw my arm. "It's why you don't like my cuts, right?"

"They represent things you won't talk about with me."

"I will from now on," I vowed.

"Good," he said. "And I just told you my biggest secret, so now everything is out in the open between us."

I snuggled against his chest. "I like that. It makes me feel safe."

"You'll always feel safe with me," he promised, tightening his grip on me.

The Ballad of a Hopeless Romantic: Christian Garrickson

> "Raised by my dad, girl of the day
> He was my man, that was the way."
>
> —*Red Hot Chili Peppers*

November 1993

THANKSGIVING DAY 1989, MY DAD GAVE ME some unsolicited advice about girls: "Don't date chicks with small tits. They'll blackmail you into paying for plastic surgery."

I was eleven.

He'd been out drinking because my stepmother, Claire, had just left him. Not because he wouldn't pay for *her* boob job. No, Dad slept with a twenty-two-year-old intern and apparently she was in the market for some fake double D's. When Dad didn't pay up, she wrote a tell-all letter to Claire.

Dad was a god to me when I was little. I was two when my mom died of cancer, so he was all I had. Whenever people asked me what I wanted to be when I grew up, I said, "My dad." I bragged about his cool job, pointing out buildings in the Chicago skyline and saying, "My dad designed that one."

He worked long hours, but made sure to be home when I went to bed every night so he could remind me that I was his "best buddy." And unlike other dads with good-paying jobs, since mine actually liked his, he didn't look old and stressed-out and he still had all his hair, so he landed hot chicks. According to him, that was very important. Personally, I wished he'd find someone to settle down with. I wanted a real family. A dad instead of a buddy. A mom to give stuff to on Mother's Day instead of a grave to visit.

Finally, when I was in third grade, Claire entered our lives.

On the outside, Claire resembled every other woman my dad dated: a blond at least five years his junior who could have stepped straight out of the Victoria's Secret catalog. But whereas those other chicks fawned over Dad's salary, Claire thought the best thing about him was me. She felt sorry that I didn't have a mom and insisted that a lot of their dates be kid-friendly. We went to Kiddieland and Cubs games and all the museums downtown. Needless to say, I was impressed. Dad was, too. He said a woman who treated his son like her own was a woman worth marrying. So he did.

Right before I started sixth grade, my sister, Naomi, was born. Maybe other eleven-year-olds would have been annoyed with a new sibling, babysitting duty and all of that, but I was thrilled. The first time I held Naomi, all tiny, pink, squirmy, and perfect, I realized I finally had the complete family I'd always wanted.

Three months later, Dad fucked everything up.

If there was one thing in my life that I could do over again, I would have forgotten to bring the mail in on Wednesday, November 22, 1989. I always brought the mail in when I got home from school and handed it to Claire. But that day I wish I'd been so excited about Thanksgiving, my first holiday as a part of a genuine, all-American family of four, that I'd just left the mail in the box for Dad to get. He would have recognized the intern's handwriting on the seemingly important envelope from his office and thrown it away. Instead, Claire opened it.

The rosy, new-mother glow to her cheeks faded and she went straight for the phone and called my father, demanding he come home. When he walked in, Claire ordered, "Christian, go to your room. Put Naomi down for a nap in there. Your dad and I have to talk."

They didn't talk. They screamed and stomped around upstairs for three hours. Even with Naomi's nonstop shrieking, I heard all about the dirty stuff Dad had been doing with some barely legal for more than a year.

When things finally got quiet and Naomi buried her exhausted, red face against my shoulder, I opened my bedroom door to find Claire standing outside of it.

Whenever I think about Claire, one of two images comes to mind. I either see her on the day she joined my family or the day she abandoned it. On her wedding day, she was perfect. Could've been one of those fresh-faced, blond brides on the cover of a wedding magazine. But after that blowout with my father, Claire was a completely different person. Her hair stuck to her skin with snot. Her face was splotchy and I noticed wrinkles near the corners of her mouth and eyes that I hadn't seen before.

"Christian, I'm sorry," Claire whispered in a raw voice, like an old woman with emphysema, and she collapsed against me, momentarily as weak as someone that sick. She hugged me tight and took Naomi from my arms in the process. She cradled her daughter, rubbing her downy head. As we sat on my bed, Claire took my hand and asked, "Did you hear everything?"

I nodded, waiting for her to explain it away like a bad dream.

Claire sighed and rolled her reddened eyes heavenward, blinking back tears. "I'm really sorry about that. Your father . . . he's the only family you had for the longest time and he loves you so much. I don't want you thinking bad things about him. That's not right. What happened between him and me is between him and me. You and Naomi"—she paused to kiss Naomi's cheek—"you guys are innocent."

I stared at her like she was speaking in tongues, because to my eleven-year-old ears she was. In my mind, she was my mom and the only thing I wanted to hear from her was "It'll be okay." I kept waiting for it, but she just babbled about how my dad was my family, acting like he was my *only* family, and I was not about to go back to that again.

Finally, I spoke up. "*We're* a family and things will be fine and tomorrow we'll have turkey . . ."

A flustered laugh leaked from Claire's lips and she covered her mouth to excuse it. Tears dangled from her long eyelashes. "Oh, Chris." She searched for the right words, surprising me with, "What has your dad told you about your mother?"

I shook my head, confused. I hadn't heard *her* come into the argument.

"Your mother was the love of your father's life. They fell in love when they were sixteen and if she hadn't died, they would've lived happily ever after and you would've had twenty sisters and brothers." Looking out the window, perhaps seeing my mother's ghost, Claire smiled and I was completely mystified. To this day, I still don't understand women's logic. How can they smile at somebody else's story when their own fairy tale is falling to pieces around them?

"My mother died," I said bluntly, trying to bring Claire back to earth. "And my dad met you."

Claire's gaze shifted from the window back to my face. "Yes, your mother died. And your dad never got over it. He still has some of her things in a cigar box in his nightstand. He has her wedding ring, but more important than that he has the promise ring he gave her back in high school. It's not this big diamond." She gestured to the band that I was glad to see still occupying her ring finger. "But it was worth a million times more because when your dad gave your mom that ring, he promised to be true to her and her alone. And he's kept that promise. She was the only one who he could ever be faithful to."

I finally saw how this connected back to Dad's cheating. I tried to comfort Claire, pulling my hand out of her grip and patting her shoulder. "But you're my mom now." I reached for Naomi, who had her fingers shoved into her mouth, peacefully asleep in Claire's arms. "And we're a family and my dad loves you and things are gonna be okay."

"Chris, you're such a hopeless romantic." Claire sniffled. "One day you're going to grow up and meet a beautiful girl. You'll give her that ring your daddy gave your mom and nothing will screw it up. You'll get your perfect family then, baby, I promise you. As long as you two can trust each other it will all work out." She rose shakily to her feet.

Panic seized me. "Where are you going?"

She didn't have to answer. When she opened my bedroom door, I saw what she'd left just outside. Two big suitcases loomed, packed in such a rush that I could see the tiny purple sleeve of one of Naomi's shirts sticking out.

"No! You can't leave. Don't take my family!" I charged past Claire, heaving my shoulders into the door, blocking her way out.

Naomi started to cry again and Claire rocked her. "Christian, please open the door," she requested calmly. "I'm not leaving you. You can see me and Naomi whenever you want, you just can't come with us."

"That's leaving! You can't leave!"

Claire reached for the doorknob and that was when I snapped and started hitting her.

Wait, that sounds really horrible, and it was, but you have to understand I was a little kid who'd been told he was losing everything. I wasn't hitting Claire, the woman I thought of as my mother, I was fighting for my family. And really, I just flailed at her stomach. It was still slightly padded by the weight she'd gained with Naomi, and it felt like hitting an overstuffed pillow. But then, I lost further control of my hands and slapped Claire across the face, leaving a red mark on her pasty cheek and causing her head to ricochet against Naomi's. It sounded like the first break of the balls in a pool game, and that awful noise brought me back to reality.

Claire stood strong, seemingly unhurt. I guess my fists weren't as powerful as they felt. But I dropped to my knees and curled into a ball, feeling like I was about to puke. "I'm sorry," I cried over and over again.

I prayed for Claire to bend down and hug me, comfort me like she did Naomi. I could hear her murmuring, "It's all right, baby. It's all right," as she massaged Naomi's sore head. Claire didn't touch me, though, but as she opened the door, nudging me slightly so she and my sister could slip out, she said very clearly, "Christian, it's not your fault."

It was my father's fault. I knew that. He'd broken Claire's heart, broken our home, and broken me so badly that I'd lost control and taken my anger out on Claire instead of him.

I avoided Dad the next day—the Thanksgiving that was supposed to be my first with a real family—until he gave up on getting his "buddy" to talk to him and went out drinking. Then I went upstairs and rifled through his nightstand to find the one pure thing left in my house: the ring Claire had mentioned.

I had it in my pocket while Dad slurred his messed-up speech about chicks with small tits. I rubbed the ring between my fingers, the simple gold band smooth except for the front of it, where two gems were set—my parents' birthstones. Pretending the ring was like a magic lamp, and Claire the genie inside of it, I tried to hear her whispers about true love over Dad's ugly words.

I keep the ring in my nightstand now. Dad hasn't even noticed it's gone. When I'm really lonely and wishing more than anything that Claire and Naomi still lived with us, I get the ring out and remember what Claire told me before she left. About how somewhere out there I'll find a girl I can trust completely, someone worthy of my mother's ring, and then I won't be alone anymore.

I know it's weird, a guy my age looking for that instead of just wanting to get laid. I sound like a hopeless romantic like Claire said. But really I'm afraid that if I don't find that girl, I'll turn out like my dad, and he's the last person on earth I want to be.

7.

"**IS YOUR MOM AS HUNGOVER AS** my dad this morning?" Christian joked between bites of his Grand Slam.

We'd met up for brunch at Punk Rock Denny's the day after Thanksgiving.

Punk Rock Denny's was a regular Denny's, but for some reason, the one in Oak Park employed mostly punks and skinheads, hence the nickname. The staff was very cool, letting us take over the smoking section for hours on end and only charging us for half of what we ordered. It was our cold-weather hangout. Once November hit, everyone stopped going to Scoville. Winter arrives fast in Chicago. One day all the leaves fall and next thing you know everything is blanketed in snow. It hadn't snowed yet, though, so Liam had run off to the park to skate first thing in the morning. I didn't blame him.

"Facing my mom today was really awkward," I told Christian as I pushed my plate away and lit a cigarette. "She kept apologizing and offering to make breakfast, but I could tell that would make her puke. I made her toast and reassured her that she was a good mom, so she'd stop beating herself up. I'm glad she's not normally a big drinker because I don't know how I'd deal with her morning-after remorse all the time. Now I know where I get it, though," I added with a wry laugh. "Every time I get too drunk or high, I wake up hating myself."

Christian leaned across the table and asked in a concerned whisper, "You didn't wake up regretting things this morning, did you?"

I reached for his hand, shaking my head. "Not the things we did. The thing *I* did before that . . ." I pointed at my left arm with my cigarette and sighed. "Waking up with cuts is worse than waking up hungover. I don't cut because it's fun. I always tell myself I won't do it again. This morning when I saw those cuts, I was so pissed at myself that I wanted to cut again. It's a fucked-up cycle."

"You didn't cut, though, did you?" Christian squeezed my hand so tightly my fingers throbbed.

"No."

"Good." He released his grip and kissed my fingers. The sweet gesture made me smile. "I don't want you to cut anymore. I want you to call me or Maya. Or think about Florida and how we're all gonna live on the beach as soon as we finish high school."

"As soon as Liam finishes high school," I corrected. Ever since the night that Christian and I had bumped into Liam and Maya at Scoville when they were talking about running away to Florida, it had become our group fantasy. Whenever things were rough for one of us, we'd talk about the house on the beach that we'd escape to one day. Liam was two years younger than the rest of us, so we always reassured him that we wouldn't leave him behind like Wes had done to Maya and Cass.

"Maybe we can kidnap Liam and homeschool him or something," Christian suggested with a grin. His gaze drifted over my head, so I turned to see my brother and Maya approaching.

Liam nodded earnestly. "I'm all for that. Get me out of Oak Park as soon as possible, please." He and Christian slapped hands.

Christian stood so Liam and Maya could take his side of the booth and he could sit beside me. When he wrapped his arm around me and I leaned my head on his shoulder, Maya exclaimed, "Aw! Now why are you two extra cute today?"

My face flushed and Christian cleared his throat. I threw my lighter at Maya, hissing, "Shut up!" and indicating Liam. Fortunately, he was too engrossed in the menu to notice Maya's teasing. I really doubted that he wanted to think about his sister sleeping with his best friend.

Of course Maya knew. I'd called her first thing in the morning and told her about it. I'd omitted the part about the cutting and the fight over Adrian. I wanted to forget that had happened. I wanted to fall in love with Christian. I wanted to be that girl he'd been looking for since the night his stepmom left.

I'd explained to Maya, "I never wanted to be a party girl. I just wanted good friends and the John Cusack movie boyfriend."

"Christian is totally the John Cusack movie boyfriend," Maya'd agreed. "And I bet he's gonna give you that ring for Christmas."

8.

CHRISTIAN INVITED ME TO HIS HOUSE on Christmas Eve to exchange presents. We sat beneath the Christmas tree in his living room. It didn't matter that the tree was fake, prelit like something you'd find in a mall, because Christian looked so genuine when he handed me a little box with shaking hands.

My hands were just as unsteady as I pulled the top off to reveal his mother's ring, a gold band with his parents' birthstones, garnet and sapphire. "Oh my god, are you sure you want to give this to me?" I gasped.

It had been exactly one month since we'd slept together for the first time. In that month the following things had occurred:

I hadn't cut myself. Not once. The week before Christmas had been hard because I was preparing for another Thanksgiving disaster. Mom promised that we'd have a peaceful day at my grandma's, though, and Christian talked me through all of my anxiety.

We stopped going to parties. The weekend after Thanksgiving, Christian suggested to me, Maya, and Liam that we skip Shelly's for a concert at the Fireside. That became our new routine on the weekends.

Aside from Maya and me sneaking the occasional drink in the Denny's bathroom and Liam's pot habit, we remained sober. As far as I was concerned, my make-out sessions with Christian provided a much better buzz.

Christian and I slept together five times. We didn't fight afterward at all. In fact, after the third time, Christian cupped my face in his hands and said, "There's no falling anymore, Kara. I'm definitely in love with you."

He repeated that again after insisting that he wanted me to have his mother's ring. "You deserve it. Won't you let me put it on?" he asked with a soft smile. Since Christian knew I hated wearing things on my fingers, he'd strung the ring on a delicate gold chain.

I glanced down at all the crap that crowded my neck. Was I really going to let beautiful jewelry mix in with beads, guitar picks, plastic hearts, and silver pot leaves?

"Wait," I told him. "I want to take all of this off first."

"You sure?"

He knew that those necklaces were my security blanket. Before the cutting, I'd had them to play with when I was upset. Now I wouldn't have scars to pick at or necklaces to nervously twist. I'd be putting all my trust in Christian. But that's what his giving the ring to me was all about. He was saying he trusted me one hundred percent and I should do the same. I nodded slowly.

He scooted closer to help me disentangle all of my necklaces. Ten minutes later, he finally closed the clasp on my new necklace. He opened his mouth to say "I love you," but I put my fingers to his lips.

He'd said "I love you" at least thirty times to me over the past few weeks. I always parroted it back, but worried that I hadn't really meant it. I wanted to say it first to prove to myself that I did. I kissed Christian gently and whispered "I love you" as I pulled away. And I meant it. I really did. He made me happy, he made me healthy.

But I hadn't forgotten about Adrian.

9.

ADRIAN'S FAVORITE DINER WAS A TWENTY-FOUR-HOUR dive in Forest Park called Ambrosia's. I hadn't been there since I'd stopped hanging out with him. Everyone else preferred Punk Rock Denny's because of the waitstaff, or Jedi's Garden because they gave you a bread basket even if you only ordered coffee. Ambrosia's was seedy and depressing by comparison.

The only other person I knew who loved it was Maya. She said it had character. She adored the multitiered, spinning display case that housed the desserts and provided some of the only light in the place. She also swore it was mob-run because this beefy Sicilian guy always stood at the back with his arms crossed. She nicknamed him Al after Al Capone. It was the place to take Maya if you needed to make her smile.

Maya called me at ten on Christmas night in desperate need of cheering up.

"I hate Christmas," she said, sulking. "The house is finished. That was my present. My dad took me over there and we had this fancy dinner in a big empty dining room. I mean, there was all this new furniture, but the house *feels* empty. He says it'll be better once my stuff is there, but . . ." I heard her swallow a sob.

"Oh, Maya, I'm sorry." I tried to highlight the positive. "It'll be nice to get out of the hotel after a year, though."

"No," she choked. "At the hotel I could pretend it was temporary. That eventually we'd go back to Florida and my mom would be there. Now I have to face reality. How am I gonna do that, Kara?"

Christian or Liam would have been better at consoling her with the right words, but she still hadn't told either of them about her mother. It was up to me to lift her spirits. "You'll face it at Ambrosia's with lemon meringue pie and rice pudding." Our favorite desserts. "And if that doesn't work, we'll hire Al to torch the new house."

That coaxed a laugh from her. "You think they're open on Christmas?"

"They never close," I assured her. "I'll pick you up in fifteen minutes?"

"Sure," she agreed. "But can we talk about things besides my mom?"

So when we arrived at mostly empty Ambrosia's, we discussed my Christmas instead of hers. Of course, the primary focus was the ring from Christian. Maya practically unzipped my coat for me so she could get a peek at it.

"It looks beautiful on you!" she exclaimed, sliding into her seat.

"You obviously knew he was giving it to me."

"Who do you think helped him pick out the chain?"

"Well, you should have warned me to get him something nicer than a couple of CDs. I felt kinda stupid," I said, turning over my coffee cup. The unoccupied waitress immediately filled it. Maya and I paused our conversation to order our desserts: rice pudding for me and lemon meringue pie for her.

When the waitress shuffled off to the kitchen, Maya told me, "Christian was afraid you wouldn't be surprised at all because he'd told you about the ring before."

"Yeah, but I didn't think he would give it to me after we'd been dating, like, two months. It's a big deal."

"It is." Maya nodded. "He really loves you."

I smiled and kept one hand on the ring as we ate and talked about everything except Maya's new house. Then Adrian walked in with a guy and a chick I didn't recognize. They took the booth by the rotating dessert display. I let go of the ring and my palm thudded to the tabletop.

Maya followed my gaze. She shook her head, said "Ignore him," and continued to talk about the skateboarding lessons that Liam had promised her as part of her Christmas present. I'd stopped listening. Eventually Maya waved her hand in front of my face. "Kara, you're staring."

"I'm not staring. I'm glowering." I narrowed my eyes further to emphasize this.

"You're staring and he's going to notice and think you want him to come over and talk to you." Maya stabbed her lemon meringue pie a little harder than necessary, but the clang of fork against plate didn't cause my ruthless glare to waver.

"No, he's not." Maya and I sat in the booth closest to the darkened banquet area. Adrian might have spotted us if he'd looked to his right when he came in, but he hadn't. "Who are those people? Did he ditch Cass and Quentin?"

"Why do you care? You ditched him and you're happier now, aren't you?"

Guiltily, my fingers fluttered to Christian's ring again. "Yeah, but I still wonder who those people are."

Maya shrugged, but her curiosity got the best of her and she glanced over her shoulder. "Harlan introduced me to that guy once. He's a dealer. No shock there."

"Really? But Harlan's just into hallucinogens. So he's an acid dealer, right?"

"Kara, who cares!" Maya slammed her fork down so hard that the meringue on her pie wobbled and I was forced to give her my full attention. "He's your ex," she growled. "And now you're with someone who cares about you in ways Adrian wasn't even capable of. Forget about him."

I hung my head in shame. "You're right."

For the next hour, I kept my eyes on Maya and my focus on our conversation, but when we were exiting the restaurant, Adrian finally noticed us. "Kara," he called.

I should've ignored him and kept walking, but I couldn't help it. I turned and said, "Oh, hey," like I'd just spotted him.

"Come here a sec."

Maya dramatically cleared her throat, but I pretended not to hear and took a few steps in Adrian's direction.

He asked, "You gonna be at Shelly's for New Year's Eve? Cass complains that she only gets to see you in gym class now. Everyone misses you."

I fought off a huge grin. I'd been telling myself that I didn't need parties or a gaggle of friends, but hearing that they missed me made me miss them, too. Not to mention the implication that Adrian missed me. I managed to keep my expression and tone cool when I said "I'll probably be there."

The corners of Adrian's lips curved slightly. "See ya then."

I followed Maya outside, but she headed in the direction opposite the parking lot. I grabbed her wrist. "Whoa, where are you going?"

She wrenched out of my grip, snapping, "I'll walk home, thanks."

"Why?"

Maya whirled around, cheeks blazing. "You're my best friend, but Christian's a really good friend, too. He gave you his heart last night and you're flirting with your ex? I thought you were better than that!"

"What? I wasn't flirting. I exchanged two sentences with the guy. And yeah, we have a history, but friendship was part of that history. Adrian understood me in ways no one else has. If I want to be friends with him—"

"How do you think that would make Christian feel?" Maya interrupted viciously. "Do you ever think about other people, Kara? Or only yourself?"

I shook my head slowly, angry tears forming in my eyes. "All of my friendships matter to me, Maya. And you know why? Because before I met you, I had one friend. *One*. You probably don't know what that's like because you have no trouble making friends. You're not shy. You walk into a room and everyone wants to know you. But I'm the wallflower, the girl no one notices or cares about. It felt good to know that Adrian and my other friends miss me and I'm looking forward to seeing them on New Year's. If you and Christian can't understand that . . ."

Maya apologetically reached for my hand. "I understand. I haven't always had a ton of friends either. When I left Florida I didn't have anyone."

"Seriously?" I asked, shocked because I'd watched Maya easily befriend so many people over the past year. But suddenly I realized that when Maya talked about missing Florida, the only things she mentioned were the beach and her grandmother.

Maya's gaze dropped to her feet and she scraped snow off one boot with the other. "It's a long story and I don't really want to talk about it any more than I want to talk about my mom." She exhaled, her breath hanging in the air like smoke, and looked up again. "Sorry I snapped at you. It's just Adrian . . . well, my grandmother would say he's the fox that could charm the chickens right out of their coop." Maya squeezed my hand between hers. "I've seen him hurt you before, Kara, and I don't want that to happen again because this time it would hurt Christian, too."

"I won't let that happen," I promised.

"Thanks."

Maya smiled and threw her arm around my shoulders. My words reassured her enough that she allowed me to drive her home, but didn't keep her from airing her concerns to others, namely my brother.

10.

LIAM APPROACHED ME AT SHELLY'S NEW Year's Eve party after I'd polished off an entire bottle of champagne. Christian had gone to find another one and I was in the midst of a drunken debate with Gonzo about the superiority of champagne (my side) versus beer (his side) when Liam interrupted, "Sis, take a walk with me?"

"Will there be a joint involved?"

"Naturally," Liam said, flashing his laid-back stoner grin.

So I thought nothing of his request and instructed Gonzo, "Tell Christian to wait here for me. I'll be back in time for the kiss at midnight. Then you and I will settle this debate."

Liam and I trekked down Shelly's block through the freshly fallen snow, passing the joint back and forth. I found that pot plus champagne equaled dizzy—a good dizzy, an it's-New-Year's-and-it's-snowing-and-this-is-how-it-should-be dizzy. But Liam was introspective as usual.

He exhaled a long, dragonlike stream of pot smoke through his nose and said, "What a year, huh? Last New Year's it was just you and me watching Nirvana on *Live and Loud* on MTV. I think we went to bed before Mom and Dad even came home."

I nabbed the joint. "Yeah, Kurt Cobain was alive, Mom and Dad were on a date, and we were friendless. I guess at least the last thing changed for the better."

"It changed for the better in a big way." Liam faced me, his eyes startlingly green. "With you, Christian, and Maya, not only do I have real friends for the first time ever, I feel like I have a real family for the first time in years."

I nodded and took another quick drag from the joint before handing it back.

"Christian's really good for you," Liam continued. "You're acting like the sister I haven't seen since Stacey moved. It's the kind of happiness you deserve. Happiness I knew Adrian would never be able to give to you." He picked up his pace and sharply turned the corner.

I cut across someone's crunchy, snow-dusted lawn to catch him. "Wait, what does Adrian have to do with this?"

Liam continued to walk swiftly, speaking over his shoulder, his words as cold as the snowflakes that blew into my face. "Maya told me about your run-in with him at Ambrosia's on Christmas."

I grabbed Liam by the crook of his arm, forcing him to stop. "My 'run-in'?" Anger tinged my voice. "We talked for a second about this party. Where I haven't even seen or spoken to him, might I add. Why the hell was Maya bringing it up? And why isn't she here saying it to my face?"

"Because she wasn't feeling well, so she went home. But she asked me to keep an eye on you and Adrian tonight because she was concerned, and honestly, so am I. I watch people closely. Maybe it comes from being the outsider all these years, I don't know. I hate doing it. I hate seeing things before people see them for themselves. Like the divorce."

"Liam, this isn't—"

He stomped his foot. "I've watched you and I see how even though Christian's at your side, you're always looking around for someone else. We walk into a diner, a show at the Fireside, anyplace Adrian might be and you're looking for him. And then Maya told me about how you were so concerned about Adrian at Ambrosia's. Neither of us want to see you or Christian get hurt. If Adrian's the one you want to be with—and I have a feeling that even though he's no good for you, he is—you need to figure it out. Because you, Christian, and Maya are the only people in the world I care about and if everything gets messed up"—he anxiously ran his fingers through his unruly strawberry blond hair—"I couldn't deal with it. It would be like the divorce all over again."

My fingers fell to the ring around my neck and I shook my head, afraid of failing at my one shot at well-adjusted happiness. "I don't want to mess things up. I wouldn't be able to deal with it either." I took a deep breath, hoping it would sober me, but it didn't. A million different emotions swirled and the pot-champagne high made them difficult to sort out. Good dizzy was turning into nauseous, confused dizzy.

"I'm sorry," I whimpered, "I'm so wasted right now and I can't handle this . . ." I glanced over my shoulder toward Shelly's house. "Christian's probably looking for us."

"Go find him, then. I'm going to check on Maya after I finish this." Liam brought the joint to his lips, but before he inhaled, he added, "Kara, if you aren't in love with Christian, break up with him. It'll hurt, but not as bad as it would if you cheat on him. Christian's my best friend. Don't break his heart."

With the weight of more responsibility than I could handle resting on my shoulders, I stumbled back to Shelly's. Suddenly my relationship wasn't just about my happiness but my brother's, too. I couldn't let Liam down. I *wouldn't* let him down. I was with Christian and I was happy. Wasn't I?

I probably should have gone home to sober up and think everything through. Instead, I decided to run from my feelings like always. So I headed in the direction of more liquor and ran smack into Adrian alone on the front porch.

He leaned against the railing, watching the snow fall while quietly smoking a cigarette and swigging from a bottle of champagne. He didn't seem particularly startled when I staggered up the steps, my untied combat boots thumping gracelessly against the wood. Adrian was never fazed by anything; I could have shown up screaming, holding a bloody kitchen knife and he wouldn't have blinked.

However, I was thrown off by running into him right after my conversation with Liam. Was this a sign of some sort? I froze on the top step, staring until he finally broke the silence with a simple "Hey."

I blurted, "I'm looking for Christian."

"Haven't seen him."

Unsure of what to do next, I stood there until a noise from inside the house brought me back to reality. The collective shout of a countdown: "Ten, nine, eight . . ."

Adrian rolled his eyes and slurped champagne. He offered me the bottle as the crowd inside shouted "Happy New Year!" I accepted and took a long, slow drink because that's what you do on New Year's, you drink champagne. But when I handed it back to Adrian, he pulled me toward him and kissed me hard on the mouth before I could even swallow. Champagne dribbled down both of our faces.

"What the hell?" I wrenched away from him, stumbling up the last step, closer to the safety of the front door.

He shrugged. "That's what you do at midnight. You kiss someone."

"Yeah, someone you love!" I objected, wiping my sticky mouth.

"Don't you love me, Kara?"

This was like a scene in our "Stories of Suburbia" script. He played the role of Bad Rebel Boy, loafing on the front porch in his black leather jacket, waiting to pounce on me, Good Girl Gone Awry, so that he could lead me further astray and fuck with my head.

And now it was time for me to have the big flashback. I saw a summer night, me in his bedroom for the first and only time. My fingers tangled in his brown curls. The two of us stripping down. Me, stripped. Stripped of every single inhibition when I looked at him and said the "I love you" that he threw back in my face.

I spun out of the flashback, drunk and angry. "Don't! Just don't."

If this was part of our script, something horrific would've happened at that moment: a car driven by another drunk teenager would careen out of control on the slippery street, skid across the snowy lawn, and hurdle into the porch, killing us.

But my life was not the "Stories of Suburbia" script; it was more akin to a teenage soap opera à la *Beverly Hills, 90210*. Instead of the car wreck, Christian walked outside.

"What's going on here?" he asked in a low, vacant voice.

I whirled around. "I was looking for you."

"But you found Adrian and kissed him."

"He kissed me!" I protested.

Adrian shrugged and swigged champagne like the whole situation bored the hell out of him. This really irritated Christian.

"She's my girlfriend, you know. *You* lost her."

Adrian didn't respond, but Christian seethed. He yanked me through the front door. "We need to talk."

I tripped up the stairs after him toward that atrocious pink bathroom where Cass had her acid freakout.

We passed a blur of faces. Mary and Jessica grinned wickedly at me, misinterpreting the way Christian dragged me by the wrist and I whined his name.

"Oooh, passion," Jessica snickered.

"Whore," Mary spat callously as Christian slammed the bathroom door.

"What's going on with you and Adrian?" he snarled, releasing my wrist with such force that I lost balance and crashed into the vanity, bruising my left forearm.

"I bumped into him accidentally." I grasped for Christian, trying to steady myself.

"Accidentally?" he scoffed, pushing me away.

I plummeted into a seated position on the toilet. The fuzzy pink cover did not cushion my fall. "Why are you freaking out?" I grumbled, rubbing my sore tailbone.

"Because I watched my father ruin every relationship he's ever been in by cheating and I hate cheaters!" Christian jabbed his forefinger into the ring that hung from my neck, pressing so it dug into my collarbone. "I love you! I trusted you!" he screamed in my face, beer breath blasting into my nasal passages. He removed his finger from the ring and pointed over his shoulder, indicating Jessica and Mary outside the door. "Are you a whore like they say you are?"

The rosy room spun and I wanted out. I didn't have to take his shit. I stood dizzily, groping for the doorknob behind him. "So what if I am?"

Christian blocked the door. "Say you're not."

"Let me out."

Suddenly, he twisted me around, ramming my back into the door. His palms pounded against my clavicle, thumbs digging into the base of my throat. I coughed and sputtered, barely able to breathe. As I struggled against him, his mother's ring swung back and forth on its chain. His hands crushed it into my chest again and again.

"Say you're not . . . say you're not . . ." he repeated as I tugged on his arms, trying to tell him that I couldn't say anything while being choked.

Rage contorted Christian's face into something completely unrecognizable—all flared nostrils, angry red skin, and gnashing teeth. *Demon*, I thought. *The pot and champagne have conjured Cass's acid demons.*

I caught a glimpse of myself in the mirror: black eye makeup smeared down my cheeks, making me look crazed, like Cass had. Except my face was as pink as the bathroom walls. Pink going purple because the demon in Christian's clothes continued to throttle me.

Finally he finished his sentence, screaming, "Say you're not in love with Adrian!" and releasing my neck so I could answer.

"I'm not," I gasped. "I'm not."

The demon dropped me to my knees so violently that they bruised despite the mauve bathroom rug. Then he was gone.

I crawled to the toilet, hugged the bowl, and puked. Afterward, I pressed my cheek against its cool, pink porcelain lip.

That did not really happen.

I flung myself into the small space between the toilet and sink like Cass had done to escape her demons.

That was not Christian.

I put my finger through the ring that still dangled around my neck and held it up. I focused on the way the stones sparkled and thought about Christian's soft smile under the Christmas lights when he'd given it to me.

He wouldn't do this. He didn't do this.

I rose shakily and stood in front of the mirror. I wet a Kleenex and wiped away my makeup.

This is a bad dream or a bad trip or something. Just blot it out.

So I went back to the party and drank until everything went black.

11.

I AWOKE WITH A THROBBING HEADACHE ON New Year's Day. Pot, champagne, beer, and a couple shots of god knows what—not a good combination. It hurt so badly that it momentarily overpowered all other pain. Then the awareness sunk in that every inch of me ached. The memory of *why* I ached followed.

Though much of my evening was lost in a murky fog, my conversation with Liam and encounter with Adrian stood out, and a blinding spotlight shone on my fight in the bathroom with Christian. Every word, every detail illuminated, as impossible to ignore as the irksome beam of sunlight that had battled its way through the slats of my blinds to wake me that morning. I wanted nothing more than to go back to sleep, nothing more than to forget, but I couldn't.

I sat at the edge of my bed in a T-shirt and boxers—a shirt and boxers I'd stolen from Christian, no less—and scoured my body for bruises. Red and purple splotched across my left wrist and forearm, forcing me to recall the way Christian had dragged me into the bathroom. A large, oblong mark ran along the top of my tailbone from when he'd thrown me down on the closed toilet. I stripped off my T-shirt and examined further using the nearby full-length mirror. Most dramatically marred was the stretch across my chest where his mother's ring had left six bruises.

I studied them for a long time—observing that they looked like hickeys, marks of love, not violence—before turning my attention to my arms.

The bruises there formed a camouflage over my pink scars. I hadn't cut since Thanksgiving; it seemed pathetic, but it was the longest I'd ever gone. And I'd done it because of Christian, because he'd been so caring. I still couldn't equate Demon Christian of the night before with the Christian who had comforted me so many times. How could he have possibly hurt me like this?

I numbly pressed on the bruises, poking harder and harder. Bruises were different than cutting, less satisfying because my blood was trapped beneath my skin. But cutting on top of the bruises didn't seem smart. The bruises had their advantage; I'd have them for a while and could make myself hurt just by touching them. I had a feeling that I'd want to make myself hurt a lot.

I traced my very first scar. The Stacey scar. I wondered how she'd rung in the New Year. Had her boyfriends ever done anything like this and what would she do if they did? I longed for Stacey for the first time in almost a year, since I'd met Maya. I wondered if a boy was going to come between Maya and me now. Would Maya still care so much about Christian if she knew what he'd done to me? Could I still care about him after what he'd done?

A moment from the very end of the night flashed into my mind. A slow dance to a fast song amid the thinning crowd in Shelly's basement. It must have been around four a.m. and I was completely blitzed. Christian murmured words that sounded gentle, like the Christian I was used to, but I couldn't actually understand him over the music. I heard "Adrian" and "flipped out" and "not me" and "we're both sorry, right?"

I told him, "The ring, it hurt me," pointing at my chest.

He held me closer, shielding me from view as he put two

fingers inside the collar of my shirt and pulled it down a few inches. He quickly released the fabric and kissed my neck, little nibbles that I'd taken as apologies. He looked into my eyes and swore, "Never again. Let's forget this happened."

Drunk, I'd agreed.

Sober, I had to think about what I was doing and why.

Part of me wanted to call Stacey and pick up where we left off in eighth grade, maybe even transfer to her school and pretend none of this had happened. But Stacey had her life now. She'd had it before I'd even gotten my own. And now my life was intertwined with Christian's, Maya's, and Liam's. They were like my family. Was I ready to lose two families in one year?

Liam had given me an out the night before, telling me I could choose Adrian. It seemed like both he and Maya expected me to do that. But I remembered what Maya screamed at me after we'd run into Adrian at Ambrosia's: *Do you ever think about other people, Kara? Or only yourself?*

And I remembered the look in Liam's eyes when he told me that Christian and Maya were the only true friends he'd ever had. He'd pleaded with me not to break Christian's heart, but he was actually asking for me not to break his.

I was determined not to, so I buried what happened on New Year's Eve. I would pretend none of it occurred and everything would go back to normal.

Somehow.

12.

SCHOOL STARTED AGAIN IMMEDIATELY AFTER NEW Year's, the last week of classes before finals. I played sick for the first three days, buying myself time to recover physically and emotionally. It was one thing to tell myself to pretend my fight with Christian had never happened, another to actually do it. Mom insisted I return to school on Thursday, reminding me how disappointed she'd been with the C's on my last report card. She wanted me as prepared as possible for my finals.

One "final" I definitely wouldn't be passing was swimming. I had no desire to swim midwinter as it was, but with five-day-old bruises to conceal, wearing a bathing suit—even the conservatively cut, sixties-style numbers the school issued—was exceedingly inconvenient. I'd take an F if I had to and reassure Mom that gym grades didn't count toward your GPA. I couldn't risk exposing my bruises, especially since Cass was in my class.

We were required to change into our gym uniforms when opting out of swimming. As I painstakingly tugged my navy blue shirt over my long underwear, the bruises on my chest aching when I lifted my arms, Cass approached. She looked as ridiculous as everyone in the standard mauve swimming getup, maybe more so because the color pink made her so uncomfortable she walked around stiff as a bodybuilder.

Cass raised her eyebrows, asking, "Not swimming the day of the final?"

"I've been out sick. Still not well enough," I replied in a scratchy whisper, faking a sore throat.

"That's why you haven't been returning my phone calls?"

Her tone was suspicious, but I ignored it and rose to help her with her hair like I always did. Cass's dreadlocks hung halfway down her back, a nightmare for her to cram into a swimming cap. As I twisted sections of hair into small buns, I explained, "I haven't really been able to talk on the phone. Not even to Christian."

It was true; I'd pretended to be sleeping whenever he called and insisted to Liam that neither Christian nor Maya should come over because I felt so crappy.

Cass cut right to the chase, as was her nature. "Well, I was calling because I was worried. What happened with you and Christian on New Year's? I saw him take you upstairs. I had to herd Mary and Jessica away from the bathroom. I think they were about to put their plastic cups to the door to listen."

I forced a sickly sounding chuckle, but gave myself away by nervously dropping her half-coiled hair. "You didn't stand out there and listen, did you?"

"No, I just hung around to see if you were okay. You don't remember us talking after you came out? You were a little incoherent. Also a little tearstained." Concern peppered her voice.

I searched the haze for my encounter with her. Had she been right outside the door? In Shelly's room, where I'd retreated for shots? In the basement, where I'd danced around with my second bottle of champagne? Most important, what lie had I told her?

"Honestly, I don't remember. Didn't I explain then? I can barely talk now," I croaked, pointing at my throat.

"You just said Christian took you in there to puke. But I talked to Adrian later and he said Christian dragged you off after seeing the two of you together. Did you and Christian fight over that?"

I hurriedly rewound her hair. "Yeah, kind of. But it wasn't a big deal."

As I snapped the bathing cap over Cass's head, my shirtsleeve slipped upward, exposing my bruised skin. She snatched my wrist and held it between us. "That's a big deal."

I tore my arm away, surveying for potential gapers, but everyone was too busy concealing their own bodily imperfections as they changed. "It's not a big deal."

"Kara, if Christian's doing this to you . . ."

"He's not." I refused to meet Cass's eyes, turning back to my locker as I lied, "I slipped in the snow, landed on my wrist."

"Are you sure that's what happened?" Cass addressed me calmly, too much like someone with an agenda, fishing for details.

I spun around, abandoning the sore-throat act to retort, "Are you Jessica now? On the hunt for gossip? Or did Adrian put you up to this? Well, you can tell him that Christian and I are fine. He's *not* going to come between us."

"Kara, I was just worried about you," Cass said, looking as serious as someone in a bathing suit and cap could. "I don't give a shit about your relationship with Adrian. I thought I heard you and Christian fighting in the bathroom and now you have this bruised wrist—"

"Christian and I are fine. Maybe you didn't see us dancing together at the end of the night. But we were. Everything's fine."

Cass persisted, reaching for my wrist again and asking, "When did you slip?"

"Just drop it!" I screeched. I'd spent three days in bed trying to get my act together, so I could smile at Christian and kiss him and hold his hand like I would have to at lunch the next period. If Cass made me relive New Year's Eve, it would all fall apart. "Don't you have a drug-addicted boyfriend and a crazy mom to deal with? Don't invent problems for me just to escape your own." I shoved Cass away, pushing a little harder than I intended, causing her to bang her shoulder into the lockers.

Two girls who wore their hair in matching, expertly disheveled buns stared at us as they exited the locker room. "Wow, and I thought *you* had issues," one joked to the other.

Tears burned in Cass's brown eyes and I knew it wasn't because of her shoulder. She shook off that injury, winding her arm around like she was about to throw a softball . . . or punch me, which I definitely would have deserved. I'd gone too far, hurting her terribly in my attempt to protect myself.

"I'm sorry," I whispered, but Cass had already started walking away, trying to look dignified in her pink suit with three dreadlocks still hanging out of her cap.

I watched her go, then changed back in to my regular clothes, went to the nurse's office, and asked to be sent home.

13.

RETURNED TO SCHOOL FOR MY FIRST full day on Friday—full except for gym class. Unable to face Cass, I hid in the girls' bathroom. Aside from that, I robotically went through the motions of my usual routine.

I held Christian's hand in the halls and kissed him as we parted for class. I did it quickly with my eyes partially open, so I wouldn't imagine his hands at my throat. His touch was gentle as it had always been, though. His fingers delicately grazed the small of my back when he pulled out my chair at our lunch table or opened the car door for me as we left school.

He drove us to Punk Rock Denny's and I watched Maya and Liam in the rearview mirror. Maya smiled and Liam laughed hysterically as Christian did an imitation of a teacher we all loathed. I realized that no one in my family had ever been able to make Liam laugh that way. *That's why you have to make things with Christian work,* I reminded myself.

We took our regular booth in the smokiest part of the smoking section. I sat beside Christian and forced myself not to flinch when he draped his arm across my shoulders. We smoked and drank coffee for a few hours before putting in our customary dinner order: burgers for Maya and Christian, Grand Slam for Liam, and fries and a side salad for me. We talked about the usual things as we ate—how much school sucked or whatever band ruled. My participation was minimal, but no one seemed concerned, probably attributing it to me being "sick."

After dinner, Christian brought up Florida. He was the most obsessed with the escaping-to-Florida fantasy, always planning exactly how it could be pulled off. "We should skip finals and go to Florida," he said. "We could live on the beach and I could play guitar for spare change. Liam could do skate tricks and Maya could draw pictures."

I waited for him to mention what I could do, but he didn't, so I piped up, "What would I do to make money, give blow jobs in the changing rooms on the beach?"

This brought the light conversation to a grinding halt. I'd meant it as a joke, but hadn't been able to pull it off because I pictured Christian blocking the bathroom door, drunkenly demanding, *Are you a whore like they say you are?*

Christian's head swiveled toward me in slow motion. When our eyes met, I could tell he was remembering the same moment. He laughed awkwardly and said, "That's funny, Kara."

An uncomfortable silence descended. Maya nodded at me and then jerked her chin in the direction of the bathroom. *Yes,* I thought, *time for drinks. That will help me regroup.* When Maya and I were bored at Denny's we locked ourselves in the handicap stall and passed a fifth of whiskey or tequila or whatever Maya had in her bag until things got fun again.

This time, things did not get fun again.

I rested my butt on the toilet paper dispenser attached to the tiled wall. She leaned against the tan divider that separated our stall from the next. There wasn't much space between us—enough for a wheelchair to fit through—but we could've been in different rooms. We didn't speak, didn't look at each other, our fingers didn't even touch as we handed off the bottle of whiskey. I focused on consuming the right amount—enough to block the memories so I could do a better job of acting normal, but not too much. I couldn't risk getting wasted and losing my cool.

Little did I know, Maya was fortifying herself for a confrontation. As I brought the bottle to my lips for my fourth and final swig, she caustically remarked, "I don't know if you said the blow-job thing to test Christian, but he's forgiven you for what you did on New Year's. If you love him anywhere near as much as he loves you, just let it go and move on."

I spit whiskey into the toilet. "He's forgiven *me* for what *I* did. What did he say happened?"

Maya met my gaze, her gunmetal gray eyes cold. "You don't even remember? He said you were fucked-up, but wow."

"What did he say?" I reiterated through tightly clenched teeth. Had I dreamt the part where Christian said to forget everything that had happened? Was I wrong to assume that he meant it would stay between us?

"He said that he caught you on the front porch making out with Adrian at midnight. He pulled you away and brought you upstairs."

I didn't remember being "brought." I remembered being dragged. I touched my left wrist, digging into the bruises. Should I show them to Maya? But she explained them away with her next sentence.

"He said you were majorly wasted, stumbling up the stairs. He practically had to drag you . . ."

Not practically. I closed my eyes, remembering being thrown into the bathroom. The bruises on my tailbone. I lifted the back of my shirt. Ready to turn and show her.

"You were falling all over the place, really banging yourself up. He worried that Adrian had given you something a lot stronger than booze. He tried to ask you what was going on and you showed him these hickeys all over your chest."

My eyes shot open. Maya's face was twisted in disgust like

someone had forced her to eat shit. She grabbed the bottle of whiskey from my fist, glaring at me while she drank.

"Not hickeys . . . and that was later when we danced," I stammered, remembering how he held me close and peered down my shirt. Yes, those marks had looked like hickeys. I'd noticed that myself the next day, but he knew. "He knew—"

She interrupted, "I know. You danced at the end of the night and you promised him never again. You guys decided to forget it had happened. He loves you so much and just wanted to forgive you . . ."

I slammed my head backward against the tile, trying to destroy the memory of the soft look in Christian's eyes when *he'd* said to *me, "Never again. Let's forget this happened."*

I hit my head again, cursing myself for being so stupid. Christian had known it would come out. And while I was trying to pull myself together so I could fake it for the sake of our friends, our makeshift little family, he was covering his ass so that when everything fell apart, *I* would be the one to lose them. I angrily snatched the whiskey from Maya, demanding, "When did he tell you this?" before taking a swig.

"I stopped by to see him on New Year's Day. I knew that Liam had talked to you about Adrian and was worried that you might break up with Christian—"

"Whoa!" I exclaimed. "Why didn't you call me?"

Maya wrenched the bottle back. "Because you weren't the one getting hurt."

"Oh my god." I started to cackle. "Oh my god."

"But before I could even explain to Christian why I was there, he burst into tears and told me about your fight and how determined he was to stay with you." Maya mimicked Christian: "'I love her so much, Maya. She's the only girl in the world for me.'" She pounded her fist against the stall wall, shaking it. "Why would you throw away love like that for someone like Adrian,

Kara? And if you're going to, just break up with Christian instead of faking sick to go off and do heroin with Adrian!"

"What? Where'd you get that idea?"

"Oh, come on! You're asleep every time we call. More like strung out . . ."

I couldn't believe it. I'd been in bed trying to get strong, to get past this for Liam and Maya, and I'd played right into Christian's hands. I pushed myself off the wall, fumbling for the lock on the stall door. "You're right. I'll go break up with good, honorable Christian. And then I'm off to get high with Adrian. That's what I do."

"Kara." Maya's voice softened. I felt her hand on my shoulder. "Please, I want to help you. I don't want to see you become a drug addict."

I turned back to her, sobbing. "I'm not a drug addict!" I took a deep breath, hoping desperately that despite being fed Christian's lies for six days, she'd believe me. "Christian really hurt me on New Year's Eve. Like *hurt me* hurt me. These are not hickeys." I yanked my shirt down to the top of my bra, revealing the stretch of bruises across my chest.

Maya's face froze in an expression I would have expected from a disapproving parent: her lips tightened into a straight line, brow wrinkled, eyes dark. She quickly knocked my hands away so the bruises were hidden once more. "That is seriously fucked-up, Kara. You're accusing Christian of abusing you? He would never hurt anyone. Especially not you, he loves you."

My mouth dropped open. "Maya, he tried to choke me. Remember that night in Scoville when he grabbed Mary? It was like that, but worse because I have this stupid ring around my neck." I pounded it against my chest to demonstrate how the bruises formed. Pain rippled through me, but I didn't wince. Pain gave me the strength to do what I should have done on New Year's Eve.

I put my thumb through the ring and tugged, snapping the thin gold chain. The chain skidded across the bathroom floor and I stomped on it as I stormed out, Maya trailing me.

Our booth was just a few feet away from the bathroom. I marched up to Christian and whipped the ring at his chest, snarling, "You can have this back. Give it to Maya. She loves you so much she doesn't care what you do. Even to her best friend."

Then I fled Denny's like I'd doused it with gasoline and lit a match. Running as fast as I could in case someone snapped out of shock and followed me, I zigzagged through slushy alleys and side streets. Since I had nowhere else to go, I decided to head to Shelly's, get really wasted, and forget everything.

Bull's-eye on the intoxicated part—when I snuck in through Shelly's back door, I found her and Harlan in the kitchen setting out Jell-O shots—but so much for forgetting my situation.

"Hey, sexy," Harlan purred. "Where's Maya and the boys?"

"I didn't know Jell-O came in purple," I said, ignoring his question and slurping one of the wiggly, delicious creations.

"Grape," Shelly told me, tucking her blond curls behind her ears. "Harlan made those. I made these." She handed me a bright green shot the unnatural color of Harlan's recently dyed hair. "Apple," she added as I swallowed it.

"Purple's stronger." I commandeered three grape shots.

"Are the others still at Denny's or something?" Harlan was so persistent, practically as gossipy as Jessica and Mary.

"Mmm-hmm," I agreed through another shot. After all, they probably still were. With the other two shots tucked firmly in my fists, I disappeared to the basement before Harlan could point out how weird it was that I'd arrived alone.

The outlook for avoiding interrogation downstairs was equally grim. It was only seven thirty, too early to be crowded, but everyone I didn't want to see had already arrived. I spotted Adrian sitting with Quentin on a corner couch. Jessica and Mary stood at the foot of the stairs, waiting for boys to throw themselves at or girls to torture.

"What, no entourage tonight, Kara?" Jessica snarked.

"She doesn't have an entourage," Mary corrected. "She's just Christian's groupie."

It took all my willpower not to pound her for that. Fortunately for her, I had my hands full of shots. I strode with determination toward the source of more alcohol and found to my delight that Gonzo, lumberjack-size king of small talk, was stationed by the keg. I said hello and he poured me a beer, immediately launching into a theory about how all the early settlers in America were crazy because of this mold that grew on their bread.

"These Puritans were, like, trippin' their faces off every day when they ate!" he informed me, gesticulating wildly with his gargantuan hands.

"Cool." I nodded, relieved that this conversation would not lead to any questions about where my "entourage" was.

After three beers and four shots, I continued to chat with Gonzo about absolutely nothing and Shelly's basement filled to the usual Friday-night capacity. Even though I stood near the keg, no one bothered me because Gonzo held my rapt attention.

Then, out of the corner of my eye, I saw Harlan descending the basement stairs. He wobbled with each step, ready to pitch forward and fall. I shoved my beer into Gonzo's hand and took off toward Harlan.

Guiding him the rest of the way down, I asked, "Dude, how many shots did you do?"

"I don't think it's the shots," he slurred with a woozy smile. "Vicodin. Shelly told her doctor she gets bad cramps to get it.

Good stuff. Better than codeine. Want some?" He fumbled in the pockets of his oversize jeans.

"No, I don't think so." The way I felt that evening made it tempting, but staggering, cross-eyed, unable-to-control-his-own-spit Harlan lessened the Vicodin-alcohol appeal.

His eyes suddenly widened. "Uhhmagawd!" His excitement was clear even though his words weren't. He rubbed his lips back and forth in an attempt to wake them up. Somehow it worked and he became easier to understand. "I forgot to show you something. I dyed my pubes green to match my hair!"

Before I could emit an oh-no sound of distress, his hand moved from pocket to fly and he shoved his shiny maroon boxers down to reveal the top of his crop. His pubes were indeed fluorescent green.

"Okay, I saw. Zip it up!" I squeezed my eyes shut, gesturing at his fly. But, problematically, I wasn't the only one who saw. We were near enough to the dance floor to have one of the roving lights shine on us at the worst possible moment. Conversations and dancing stopped.

Normally, it wouldn't have mattered. Everyone would have gone back to their business, writing it off as just another weird event at one of Shelly's parties: "Remember that time Harlan flashed Kara . . ." Maybe Mary and Jessica would have recast things: "Kara almost gave Harlan a blow job in front of everyone." But no one else would have interpreted it that way.

No one but Christian.

He, Maya, and Liam happened to come down the stairs at precisely the wrong time. Before I could even open my eyes to make sure Harlan had zipped, Christian's voice boomed in my ear. "What the hell? Are you so pissed at me that you're gonna play with his dick in public?"

Harlan said, "No, dude, I was just showing her my pubes." Before he could ask Christian if he wanted to see and subsequently get himself killed, Maya yanked Harlan out of the way. She did not return to rescue me.

Christian's face reddened like dangerously hot coal and his eyes locked on mine. I shook my head and veered for the stairs. "Fuck you. This has nothing to do with you," I snapped, not even interested in explaining the situation. Just being in Shelly's house with him made my bruises throb.

Christian, big and menacing as a bull, slid to the side, blocking my exit. "This has everything to do with me. You can't just mess around with Harlan in front of everyone, it makes us both look like fools."

"Why?" I scoffed. "I'm not *your* girlfriend anymore. Remember?"

I stretched the collar of my T-shirt down to the top of my bra, clearly revealing my bruises. Well, it was clear to Christian, anyway. I glanced around the room, noting the bewildered expressions of everyone else. Harlan squinted, confused, in my direction. Maya knew from a distance what I was showing off and was stone-faced, as she'd been in the bathroom. Mary and Jessica animatedly whispered to each other. Then my gaze drifted to the top of the stairs, where I saw Liam staring, appalled. I quickly released my shirt. No one was close enough to tell that I was bruised. I just looked crazy or slutty or both.

"I. Apologized. To. You." Christian gnashed his teeth between each word.

He spoke softly, trying to keep our conversation private, but I shouted, "I think I made it pretty damn clear at Denny's that I couldn't accept your apology!" I took another step in the direction of the stairs. I had to get up there and explain this whole thing to my brother, who wore that same numb-but-about-to-freak expression as when my parents announced their divorce.

Like my partner in a violent dance, Christian wrenched me toward him, pinning my left arm to his chest. Glaring down his nose at me, he snarled, "You and I are not done."

"Yes, we are!" As much as it hurt, I jerked my wrist from his grip, twisting out of the left sleeve of my cardigan. Nodding down at my bruised arm, I loudly declared, "See why!" so that all people pretending to ignore our little lover's quarrel would take notice.

"Kara, let's not make a scene here." Christian tried to shove my bare arm back into its sleeve. "I wish you wouldn't hurt your-self like you do . . ."

"Like *I* do?" I shouted indignantly.

Mary and Jessica had edged closer for gossip's sake, but now that she could see my bruises, Mary sided with me. "Christian, she obviously couldn't have done that to herself—"

"Back off, Mary!" Christian growled.

"Why don't you back the fuck off, Christian?" A low, rumbling voice came from behind me. Adrian stalked over from the couch he'd been occupying. He withdrew the butterfly knife he always carried from his pocket and flicked it open.

Christian's teeth ground together like his jaw was being tightened with a screwdriver. "What, so you can have her? You caused this whole situation."

"I'm not a possession and this has nothing to do with Adrian!" I seethed, still struggling to get loose.

Adrian took long strides, but didn't quicken his pace. "I don't really give a shit what the situation is, but if you've still got your hands on her when I get over there I'll cut them off."

Christian's hold slackened and he took off up the stairs. I swept my sweater around me and leaned against the railing, breathing deeply.

Adrian cackled. "That kid has always been the biggest wuss."

Mary snapped at him. "Shut up, this isn't some tough-guy contest. Kara's upset."

I felt an unfamiliar hand on my shoulder. Mary's gaze probed mine when I looked up. I shirked her off. "Don't try to be nice to me. You've never been nice to me!"

Mary's hands shot up in surrender. "Fine, whatever!" She stomped upstairs, Jessica following, riding Mary's coattails for once.

I hadn't meant to shout at Mary. She'd fallen victim to Christian's temper before, too. If anyone knew how I felt, it was her. My bitterness was really aimed at Maya. Where the hell *was* my supposed best friend? Why was one of our enemies defending me instead? I looked around the room for Maya, but she'd disappeared. Worried, I glanced at the top of the stairs, trying to locate Liam, knowing I really needed to explain everything to him, but he'd also gone. Probably with Christian.

"Great," I mumbled. I wanted another shot or preferably a shot*gun*. My roaming eyes finally landed on Adrian, who'd remained beside me, and I must have been wearing the most pathetic expression, because next thing I knew he had his arms around me.

He wove his fingers in the back of my short hair. "I'll kill him if you want me to."

The dam burst. Tears dripped down my face and into Adrian's long curls. "I just wanna forget him," I whimpered.

"Okay. Let's get out of here, then." His husky voice reminded me of last summer. Before Christian.

"Yeah, let's do that."

"I missed you," Adrian whispered as we started upstairs.

I took hold of his hand. "I missed you more."

He wrapped his arm protectively around me, guiding me toward the front door.

Christian stood at the shadowed far end of the porch. I intended to hold my head high as we descended to the sidewalk, but found I couldn't look at him. I folded inward against Adrian's chest and felt his mouth brush the top of my head. Maybe

I appreciated his gentleness. Maybe I did it out of reflex. But when Adrian and I reached his car, we were kissing. I couldn't even feel the eyes from the porch that weighed on us. It was so easy to slip back into old patterns.

==≍{ }≍==

Adrian took me to his house and I leaned against the headboard of his bed as he lit our second bowl. We sat facing each other, knee-to-knee, like we had at Shelly's the night we'd first kissed. The pot rushed directly to my head, reinstating the powerful buzz I had going before Christian showed up. I'd intended to calm down and go looking for Liam, but getting high felt so good.

However, as I got more stoned, Adrian acted more sober. "Seriously, Kara," he said, "I hope I didn't cause this whole mess."

I waved his comment away with a thick cloud of smoke. "I don't want to talk about Christian." The alcohol-pot combination made me bold. I leaned forward, nesting my hand in the hair at the nape of his neck. "I want to be with you. Pretend he never happened." I kissed Adrian powerfully.

"Kara, it doesn't work like that . . ." he objected, though he couldn't help but kiss me back. I pushed him down against the bed, my fingernails scratching his stomach, pulling his shirt off. He ran his fingernails across my stomach as well and slowly lifted my shirt over my head. Then he saw the bruises across my chest and froze.

"Jesus Christ. He did this?"

"Doesn't matter." I tugged my jeans past my hips. "He doesn't exist."

Adrian clamped his hands over mine, stopping me from undressing. "Yes, he does, Kara."

I sat up. "So what? Now *you* don't even want me? I thought you'd sleep with any chick with a pulse."

Hurt filled Adrian's brown eyes and he rolled over, reaching for our shirts. "I do want you. I've wanted you for months." He met my gaze again and said firmly, "But I'm not going to take advantage of you and hurt you worse."

I snatched my T-shirt from him. "No one could hurt me worse than he did or than you did the last time around."

"Kara . . ."

"Don't. I'm leaving." I attempted to thrust my shaking arms through my shirt, but was sobbing so hard that I couldn't. When Adrian tried to help, I shrieked, "I can dress myself. I'm not a god-damn child!" and pushed him away, bashing my elbow against the lamp on his nightstand in the process. "Ow! Goddammit!"

I shoved the lamp to the floor, my lip curling in satisfaction when it broke.

Adrian chuckled. "Did that feel good? Here." He grabbed an empty beer bottle from his windowsill. "Throw it." He egged me on, eyes glittering. "Trash the whole damn room if it will make you feel better. I'll help. No one's home to stop us." He took an-other beer bottle and tossed it at the mirror above his dresser. Shards went flying everywhere. "Your turn."

Before long, we'd heaved his dresser onto its side, yanked his mattress off his bed, and stomped the lamp to pieces. I went to overturn his nightstand, but he stopped me. "Nah, don't do that."

"Why not?" My cheeks were flushed; my whole body quiv-ered, savoring the adrenaline rush.

Adrian shrugged. "My drugs are in there."

"Oh yeah? Whatcha got?" I opened the drawer. He tried to slam it shut, but my hands were already inside. I extracted a vial filled with brown powder. "What's this?"

"It's not for you." Adrian plucked it from my fingertips and squirreled it away in his pocket.

"Hey! What are you doing? I thought we were having fun."

"I'm protecting you."

"Where the hell were you last weekend? Or in September?" I spat. "No one was protecting me then and now there's nothing left worth protecting."

Guilt washed across his face. "That's not true—"

"It's heroin, isn't it?" I reached greedily into his pocket.

"Kara . . ." But he didn't try hard enough to stop me and I got hold of the vial.

"You're not going to turn me down twice in one day, Adrian." I rummaged through his nightstand, emerging with a cigar box. Along with his pot paraphernalia, it contained a razor blade and a straw. Jackpot.

As Adrian protested, "Kara, don't do that!" I spilled out a line and snorted, just like I'd seen him do in September. It barely burned my nose. I did another one. A rush of warmth swam through my bloodstream. Soon I felt like I was flying. Everything was beautiful and light. The world turned blue and then gold. I'd never felt so high before and I loved it.

Adrian stroked my cheek and ran his finger down the bridge of my nose. "My girl." He sighed and murmured sadly, "I shouldn't have let you do this."

Shaking off his remorse, he cut three lines for himself and did them in quick succession, like he did the shots at Shelly's the night of our first kiss. He hefted the mattress back onto the bed frame and we collapsed onto it. Adrian's eyes closed slowly and reopened, glazed.

"Wow, heroin . . ." I said.

"Heroin for my heroine."

I moved my heavy limbs against his dark blue sheets; it felt like I was floating peacefully in a cool river. Adrian and I started to kiss, then forgot about it. He laughed and said something, but I couldn't hear him. My head emptied of all thoughts. I couldn't even remember Christian's face. Heroin hadn't just paused the movie that had been repeating in my brain since New Year's, it took it off the reel and burned it. All that was left was the blank screen. White noise drowned out everything. My eyes were open, but I couldn't see. It felt so good not to see.

——=≡( )=—=——

Some time later, Quentin pushed open Adrian's bedroom door and quickly shut it behind him. He didn't seem to notice the mess and the overturned furniture, his eyes locked on me, lying on the floor next to Adrian.

"Kara," he whispered, kneeling beside me.

My head lolled toward his voice. "Quentin."

Adrian propped himself up on his elbows. "Want a line?" He indicated the half-empty vial that sat atop the cigar box near our feet.

Quentin pocketed it, reprimanding, "You shouldn't have done this with her." He glanced over his shoulder, pale blue eyes filled with panic. "This does not look good."

"You saw what happened with Christian at that party. If she needs to escape, I'm gonna let her. She's—"

Pounding on the door and an angry voice: "Is my sister in there with him or what?"

Liam.

I sat up straight, gripping my head with both hands. "Oh shit!"

"They waited for you at Shelly's. When you didn't come back they asked me to bring them here," Quentin explained, wringing his hands.

"Who's 'they'?" Adrian demanded.

Before Quentin could answer, Liam shoved the door open. Maya stood behind him. I craned my neck, looking for Christian, but fortunately he wasn't there. That was the only good thing about the situation.

Liam stalked into the room. His gaze flitted across the mess but lingered longest on Adrian, then the cigar box, then me. "It's all true," he murmured. "Adrian. Heroin." He glared into my eyes, though I had a hard time focusing on his.

Adrian stumbled to his feet. "Dude, don't get the wrong idea."

Liam gritted his teeth. "Don't fucking talk to me."

Maya stepped between them, hands on her hips. "You need to leave the room," she instructed Adrian, her voice low and cold. Nodding in Quentin's direction, she added, "You, too. This is between the three of us."

Diminutive as she was, Maya commanded respect. "Okay," Quentin agreed quickly, grabbing Adrian by the arm.

"If you upset her," Adrian warned, jabbing his finger in my brother's face.

Liam snorted. "If *I* upset *her*?" He approached the spot where I sat, kicking things out of his path. Looming over me, arms crossed, he asked Maya, "It's all true, isn't it? Everything Christian told us at Denny's after she left."

I struggled to stand, fiercely shaking my head. "No! Are you going to listen to my side of the story or are you going to ignore me like Maya did?"

"I wanted to hear your side of the story, Kara!" Liam shouted. "I didn't believe Christian at first. I made them go to Shelly's to look for you. Then there you were, wasted, fondling Harlan . . ."

My head still bobbed from when I'd been shaking no the first time. "I was not!"

"And you flash your damn hickeys at Christian."

"They aren't hickeys!" My fingers fluttered to the neckline of my shirt, but Liam slapped his hand over mine to stop me.

"I don't want to see. Just like I didn't want to see you kiss Adrian from the porch."

"You saw that? I was looking for you."

Liam tugged at his spiked hair. "You obviously didn't look too hard. I just went outside for some air and you walked right past me. You left without me *again*." His body twitched violently like he was going into a seizure. I tried to touch his arm, but he swatted me away. "First you ditch me at Denny's without any explanation. Then you don't even bother to try to talk to me before you run off with Adrian."

"Liam, I'm sorry. I wasn't thinking—"

"Damn right you weren't! You never think of me. You're so goddamn selfish!" He stopped and took a deep breath. His tone grew calm and even. "When I saw you kiss Adrian, everything Christian said seemed true. But I still wanted to believe in you. Christian tried to convince me to leave after you did. He said, 'She's going to do heroin with him, Liam. She's not coming back for you.' But I was convinced you wouldn't ditch me. So, instead of comforting my best friend, I waited at Shelly's for you for *two* hours."

Tears streamed down my cheeks. "I'm sorry, Liam. I just . . . I lost track of time."

"How did you lose track of time and forget about me?" he demanded.

"I don't know."

"I know." Liam's voice was cold and he shook his head in disgust. "You're on heroin. Everything Christian said about you was true."

"No, not everything is true. Let's talk about New Year's Eve . . ." I trailed off, desperate to organize my thoughts. Despite the grave situation, I was having a hard time staying awake. I fought to keep my droopy lids from closing.

Liam grabbed my face and forced my eyelids open with two fingers, screeching, "You're on heroin!" He released me and stomped over to Adrian's cigar box. The razor blade and straw still sat on top of it along with a thin dusting of brown powder.

Liam held it out in front of me. "You think I don't know what this is? Stop lying!"

"Okay," I sobbed. "I snorted heroin. But only for the first time. Only because of what Christian did . . ."

Pure hatred filled Liam's eyes and he launched the cigar box across the room. It crashed into a wall, contents spilling everywhere, mixing with the rest of the rubble. "Liar! I won't listen to your selfish crap anymore. Fuckin' junkie," he spat, and stormed out of the room.

I collapsed to the floor, crying and rocking myself, mumbling, "Just once. One mistake. Because of Christian."

Momentarily, the room was silent except for the sound of my sobs. When feet crunched through the mess I looked up, expecting Adrian. But it was Maya. I'd completely forgotten about her. She'd let my brother have his say and now it was her turn.

She squatted beside me, crying as hard as I was, her face a mess of black eye makeup. "I wanted to believe you. I mean, I couldn't believe Christian would hurt you like that," she stammered. "But I thought maybe there was a misunderstanding. Maybe since you were wasted, you got confused and thought Christian was trying to hurt you when he was really trying to help you."

I wiped my nose on the back of my hand and told her, "I'm not confused."

"No, you're not." Maya sniffed and dabbed her eyes. She got to her feet, towering over me. "You're using heroin and you'll say anything to cover it up."

She headed for the door. I pushed myself onto my hands and knees, trying to go after her. Not able to move fast enough, I shouted, "Why are you listening to Christian instead of me?"

Maya turned back. She bit her lip and whispered, "I don't have to listen to anyone. All I have to do is look at you. Sober up, Kara. So that someday your brother and I can forgive you."

"No!" I screamed as she shut the door. "You didn't believe me and I will never forgive you!"

⸺⸺≺ }≻≈⸺

Adrian reentered his room moments after Maya left. I was curled in a ball on his bed beneath his comforter. He peeled the blanket back and asked, "What can I do?"

"Let me sleep," I insisted.

Adrian did as instructed and I fell into a dreamless slumber while he and Quentin rummaged around, recovering the contents of the cigar box.

⸺⸺≺ }≻≈⸺

I awoke just before dawn. Blinking in the bleak gray light that crept in through the crack in Adrian's dark blue drapes, I needed a moment to realize where I was. Adrian slept on his back beside me. Quentin slept huddled in a sheet on the floor near the bed. I spotted the cigar box on Adrian's nightstand and carefully climbed over Adrian to reach it. Tucking the box under my arm, I sidestepped Quentin and tiptoed to the center of the room, to the spot where I'd been when I screamed at Maya that I would never forgive her.

I should've woken Adrian and asked him to take me home to see my brother. I should've apologized to Liam and forced him to listen to my side of the story.

Or I should've woken Quentin and asked him to take me to Cass. I should've begged her forgiveness for the incident in the locker room, told her she was right about Christian, and asked her to talk to Maya with me.

But six days before, I'd awoken bruised and hungover and I'd buried all of my feelings in an attempt to do the right thing, to protect Liam and Maya, to hold our fragile group together. I'd failed and I didn't have the strength to try again.

I opened the cigar box and took out the razor blade. I studied my arm, the bruises that had started to fade near my wrist. I could cut over those or I could cut higher up where my skin was unmarred aside from old scars. I remembered the rush that cutting provided, but I also thought about the way my arm ached afterward. Hadn't I felt enough pain?

Heroin, on the other hand, had been completely painless and it obliterated every thought, every memory. Maya's plea to get sober rang in my ears, but I couldn't. Last weekend, I'd fought demons for them. I'd lost. Now I needed relief.

I rifled through the cigar box again for that little vial. It was nearly empty, but there was enough for two lines. I poured the powder out on top of the box, cut the lines as precisely as I would if I were carving them into my own skin, and snorted.

I deserved this oblivion, this total numbness. At least for a little while. Once I felt strong again, I'd stop and get Maya and Liam back.

CHORUS

JANUARY–JUNE 1995

(SECOND SEMESTER OF JUNIOR YEAR)

"Why can't we not be sober?
I just want to start this over."
—*Tool*

1.

THE FOLLOWING FRIDAY, I WOKE UP late for school as usual and found a note taped to the kitchen counter that read: "Liam and Kara— You're having dinner at your father's house Saturday night at six. No buts . . . Love, Mom."

It was the end of finals week. They'd announced the divorce right after finals in June. What would the big news be this time? My first instinct was to ask Liam what he thought, but of course he hadn't spoken to me all week.

So after I took my last test, I trekked to Adrian's. I'd gone to his house every day after school that week. His parents were on a cruise, so Adrian, Quentin, and I had the place to ourselves to snort lines and write the "Stories of Suburbia" screenplay. I'd been surprised to discover that though they'd continued to gather newspaper articles, work on the script had ceased when I stopped hanging out with them.

"You were the best screenwriter out of the four of us," Adrian told me with a grin. "Cass is pretty good, but not as good as you."

I'd been nervous about running into Cass because I hadn't seen her since our fight, but she never showed at Adrian's. When I asked Quentin about her, he said, "She's studying. She's taking the school thing really seriously lately."

Adrian, on the other hand, had stopped going to school again. He'd decided it was pointless since he wasn't going to graduate with his class at the end of the year. When I got to his house at noon, he answered the door groggily.

"Time to wake up and listen to me complain about my life," I announced, pushing through the door and heading for his bedroom.

Our relationship was different this time around because my attitude had changed so much after what happened with Christian. I could take Adrian or leave him and he knew it, so instead of being elusive like before, he offered himself for the taking.

I plopped down on Adrian's bed. Covered with rumpled blue sheets, naked pillows whose pillowcases were stuck between the mattress and the wall, and a gray comforter splotched with ink stains, it was still the neatest spot in the room. He'd never bothered to pick up after our ransacking. A new layer of crumpled notebook paper, scattered newspapers, and dirty clothing covered the things we'd smashed on the floor.

Adrian stood in the center of the room, rubbing his tattooed arms. He took off the Dead Kennedys shirt he'd been wearing for the past three days and switched it out for a Naked Raygun shirt, revealing his defined torso for a split second. I felt a twinge of desire, but it was nothing like my swooning moments of the past, even though he still looked as good. Better even. He was a little leaner, his cheekbones slightly more prominent. His hair and the stubble on his face were scragglier than usual. Maybe this was evidence of increased drug use, but if so, he wore it well.

Adrian grabbed his cigarettes and an ashtray off the windowsill and joined me in bed. I chain-smoked my way through three cigarettes, ranting about the note, ending with "So what do you think it means? I bet they're getting back together before the divorce is finalized. They were so horrible together. God, they're stupid."

Adrian plucked my cigarette from my hand before the smoldering filter could burn me. "Yeah, parents suck," he agreed, offering me another smoke and lighting it for me. Then something happened that had never happened before: Adrian opened up to me without me asking. "Want to know what mine did last fall?"

Realizing that he meant the period of time right after I left him, when he disappeared for a month, curiosity overwhelmed me. "Yeah."

"Remember how the one time I brought you here, my dad came barging in and said I couldn't be here unless I followed their rules?"

I nodded.

"Yeah, well, I was fine with that. I had friends' couches to crash on. I had a car to sleep in when I wore out my welcome. Then, the morning I woke up and found you gone, I found my car gone, too. I walked home and didn't see it in the driveway, so I looked in the garage. My dad had cleaned it out just so he could lock up my car. Needless to say, I was pissed. So I put my fist through one of the windows." Adrian mimicked a sharp jab, then his left hand cascaded down his right arm, illustrating "Blood. Lots of it. My parents came running out and I stood there like a crazed beast, screaming, 'Gimme my fucking car!' And my mom cried about how bad I was bleeding.

"And my dad said"—Adrian took on a gruff monotone—"'Adrian, the car is ours. You can't have it until you get some help.' I said fuck that and put my fist through another window. Of course my asshole dad called the cops, so I took off, all bloody and everything." Adrian stubbed out his smoke.

"Where did you go?"

"I wandered the city for a few days. The Blue Line runs all night, you know, so I slept on the train. I spent a lot of time by the lake, got high with strangers in every neighborhood in Chicago. It's a beautiful city." He smiled.

"I know." I thought of the way the lights blurred against the lake when we sped along Lake Shore Drive in his car.

"But I had glass in my arm and the wound was getting infected, so I had to come home." Adrian shrugged nonchalantly, but I gaped at the thick scars on his right wrist, noticing them for the first time. "As soon as I walked in, my dad called the cops again. I didn't go to jail or anything. My parents checked me into a psych hospital."

"Really?" I asked, horrified.

Adrian grinned darkly. "I'm a sociopathic drug addict. But I'm also really good at playing the game. I was out in twenty-eight days and now"—he reached for the cigar box he kept his stash in—"back to old patterns. My parents don't care as long as it's not in their face. That's the point of my story, Kara," he said wisely as he spilled heroin onto the slick, razor-scarred top of the cigar box. "Parents are surface level. If yours get back together, it's an appearance thing. Don't trick yourself into believing otherwise, and get the hell out of there as fast as you can. Okay?"

He chopped two thick lines with a razor blade and handed me the straw.

"Okay." I snorted my line.

After he snorted his, we settled under the covers of his queen-size bed. We drifted off for a while, and when I came to Adrian was talking. His voice sounded distant and delayed, like he was calling from another country and the connection was bad. "I really want to apologize for how things ended between us. I'm glad we're getting a second chance. I . . ." He nodded off for a moment before picking up midsentence. " . . . really fucked up. You were the first girl who actually mattered and it scared the shit out of me. That's why I couldn't sleep with you or, you know, say . . ."

"I love you?" I finished his sentence, hoping he'd repeat my words.

He didn't take that particular second chance, though. He cleared his throat. It was like telephone lines crackling; suddenly our connection was clear. His voice grew louder and he spoke at a normal pace. "When you left I realized that you were the only girl I'd ever given a shit about. I never had girlfriends because I never clicked with anyone like that. I had friends and I had chicks I hooked up with. Then there was you and you were both and it confused me." He laughed and it sounded strange, like an echo from somewhere else. "I'm a sociopath, remember. I don't understand human interaction."

I laughed and it sounded just as strange, like it came from another room or another time or maybe it was left over from last summer. Lots of things were left over from last summer. Like kisses. My lips found Adrian's and when we kissed, it felt raw and pink like the thick scars on his wrist. I pulled back, let my head drop against his shoulder, and drifted off for a while.

Then we were kissing again and it felt better this time, like drinking cold water. I drank for a long, long time. His hands started to explore my skin and vice versa, but his touch felt like sandpaper and his skin like a rocky beach with all the scars and the bumpy tattoos. I imagined mine felt the same. So I let go of him and curled into a drug haze.

I awakened to the sound of him chopping more lines and sat up to snort another. Then came more cool-water kisses and this time touching each other felt smooth like wet pebbles. Adrian pulled the gray blanket over our heads. I felt safe, enveloped by a cloudy sky. I got naked under the comforter and so did he.

Sex with Adrian for the first time was gentle, painless because of the drug, but there was none of the wild passion that fueled our make-out sessions in the past. Heroin made it all about sensation and less about emotion. We wouldn't sleep together often, but when we did I was high; it was the only way I could do it without remembering Christian.

That particular night was a blur of me and Adrian nodding in and out, waking up to kiss and do more lines. My first heroin binge. At one point, I called my mom to tell her I was sleeping over at Shelly's. I stayed in Adrian's room until six the next evening. Then he dropped me off at my dad's apartment, which was a block away from Scoville Park. Time to face reality.

Dad's place was sparsely decorated without so much as a photograph on the fridge. In the kitchen, Liam stared at the wood grain of the table, refusing to look at Dad or me. I felt momentarily guilty about sleeping with Adrian and about the line I'd snorted before I left his house, certain my brother could sense these things, but as I sat down beside him, I caught a whiff of pot smoke in his tangled, unwashed hair. I wasn't the only one who'd walked into the situation with drug-induced armor.

Even though Dad offered to take them, neither Liam nor I removed our coats. Gesturing to the empty table, I said, "I thought we were having dinner."

Dad cleared his throat nervously. "I thought we'd go out together."

I looked up at him. He seemed to have gotten smaller, skinnier in the past seven months. His closely shaven hair was graying faster and thinning at the top. His hazel eyes had lost their sheen, looked more sunken and beady. Without Mom and the two of us, he'd lost his luster. He'd gone from being my overworked but loveable daddy to an old man. That's why he wanted us back, I assumed. And this dinner would be to celebrate it. Mom would be waiting at the restaurant, smiling.

Dad asked, "Can I get either of you something to drink?"

He pulled a beer from the fridge for himself, so I requested, "Vodka and 7UP?"

"Not funny, Kara," he replied with a grimace.

Dad sat down, took a deep breath, put his palms flat against the table, and then clasped them together. Jesus, how nervous did his own children make him? Just because he'd left us for a few months? Surely, he thought we'd be thrilled by his news and revert to our giddy little-kid selves, who adored him. Why was he so freaked?

After a long pause that made me think he was nodding out on heroin, too, he finally said, "So, I got a promotion." He droned about the details for a while. Money. Blah-blah-blah. I waited for the part where he had the revelation about wanting to be a family again, but it never came. Instead, I suddenly tuned in to the words "moving" and "Wisconsin." The next full sentence I heard twisted a knife in my guts. "Your mother said to tell you both that you have the option to come with me or to stay."

Liam stood up and launched Dad's beer across the room, the glass smashing against the white cabinets. "You're abandoning us again?" he raged. "First you move out. Then Kara betrays me, and now you abandon us again." He stared at us for the first time, jade eyes murderous. "Fuck both of you." Then he took off for the door.

Dad stood there openmouthed and I snapped, "Don't worry, I'll go after him. But no, obviously neither of us wants to move to Wisconsin with you."

It was the divorce announcement all over again. I chased Liam to Scoville Park like I had then, but now he hated me as much as he hated our father. I screamed his name three times before he finally whirled around in the center of the frozen hill and screamed back, "What the hell do you want?"

I rushed over to him, panting as I said, "I didn't betray you. At least I didn't mean to. And we need to stick together now."

"Wasn't it Christian who suggested that last summer?" Liam crossed his arms over his chest and glared into my eyes. "When you betrayed him, you betrayed me."

"This isn't about Christian. This is about our family—"

"Christian and Maya are more of a family to me than you, Mom, and Dad have ever been!"

"I'm sorry." I winced, blinking back tears and begging, "Please tell me how I can help you."

"Give me all your money so I can get the hell out of here," he demanded, extending a cold, bare palm.

I laughed uncomfortably. "We can't really run away."

"Who said anything about 'we'?" Liam growled, shoving his hand into the pocket of his winter coat. "Just leave me alone. That's what you're good at. I don't want to talk to you any more than I want to talk to Dad."

Before he could stomp off, I grabbed his sleeve. "You aren't really going to run away, are you?"

Liam wriggled out of my grip. "I'm surprised you aren't running away right now. To Adrian. To you know . . ." He put his finger to his nose, holding one nostril closed and pretending to snort a line. "Go get high, sis. I'm fine." He took off down the hill before I could stop him.

"Liam, I'm going home," I shouted after him. "I'll be there all night. Just knock on my door if you want to talk!"

And I did exactly that. I went home, stayed sober, resisted any urge to call or go see Adrian and waited up for Liam. I did not want to let him down again. But he never came to me.

In the morning, Mom woke me up screaming that Liam and her car were gone.

2.

WHEN I CALLED ADRIAN IN HYSTERICS to tell him my brother was missing, he told me, "Cass's freaking out because her cousin took off last night, too."

"Can you please bring Cass over here?" I asked, knowing that my mother wouldn't let me out of her sight.

After what I'd said to Cass the last time I'd seen her, I half expected her to punch me. Instead, she hugged me. "They're out there with Christian, aren't they?" she whispered as we embraced.

I nodded, tears streaking my face.

"You think they'll go to California, to Wes?" Cass asked hopefully as she wiped away her own tears.

"No, I think they'll go to Florida."

And that's what we told the cops. Cass and I faced that interrogation together. Normally, we wouldn't rat out our friends, but we were too worried.

We spent the afternoon huddled together on my front steps, chain-smoking in the cold. Despite the weather, it reminded me of last spring when I sat with Cass on Shelly's porch while she wished for Wes's return, dropping acid to numb herself. Now I was the one with the chemical escape.

I snorted only one line, just enough to stay calm without getting sleepy. Mostly, I resorted to my old method of anxiety relief. First, I straddled the toilet and used the razor blade to cut a line of powder on top of the tank. Then, as the drugs soothed my brain, I rolled up my sleeve and drew the blade across my forearm. The bleeding slowed my racing heart.

Cass slept over and after we turned out the light, I confided, "I can't lose my brother. I don't know how you live without Wes."

"Well, I know he's safe and healthy where he is and at least I had Maya," she murmured from the floor beside my bed.

"Neither of them should be out there with Christian." I started to cry, but tried not to let it into my voice. "I should have made them understand what he's really like. If anything happens . . ."

I heard the swish of sleeping-bag material and Cass was in the bed beside me, teetering on the edge until I scooted back to give her more space. She said, "If anything happens, I'll never forgive myself. I saw what Christian did to you, but I let you push me away. I should have gone to Maya. I should have actually done something. Instead, I threw myself into schoolwork because I couldn't deal with your problems or with Adrian and Quentin using as much as they have been. I'm supposed to watch over you guys. I promised Wes that I would."

I heard her sniff and took her hand. "You can't take care of everyone. Sometimes you have to take care of yourself," I reassured her, trying to assuage my own guilt as much as I was hers.

She squeezed my palm and we fell asleep in my bed, holding hands.

3.

A WEEK PASSED BEFORE THE COPS FOUND my mom's car in a beach town near Fort Lauderdale and brought Liam, Maya, and Christian back to Oak Park.

My brother arrived home in handcuffs with a big, purplish bruise across the left side of his face. He'd gotten into a scuffle on the beach, but since the police hadn't picked him up until after the fight, they couldn't charge him. My mom didn't press charges over the stolen car either because she was so relieved to see him. I listened from upstairs as she and Dad both wept and screamed at Liam before confining him to his room. I desperately wanted to see if he was okay, but Liam slammed his door without stopping at mine, so I assumed he still wasn't speaking to me.

Hurt, I pulled out the Altoids box that I stored heroin in and did a line. I zoned and woke to a knock that I recognized as Liam's. I shoved the box under my pillow as Liam shut the door behind himself and sat down at the edge of my bed opposite me.

"Hey," I said.

"Hey," he replied. There was nothing for an awkward moment until he said, "I'm sorry. I was wrong about you and . . ." He grimaced as he spat the name. "Christian."

I sat up from my nest of pillows and leaned toward him. "If you want to talk . . ."

"I don't," he snapped.

"Sorry."

"No, I'm sorry." His voice softened. He studied my face for so long it made me uncomfortable. His gaze flitted from my bangs, which were stringy and greenish since I hadn't bothered to touch up the blue in three weeks, to my chapped lips to the bags under my eyes. "You are using heroin, though, aren't you?"

There was no tone of judgment in his voice, but I stiffened and didn't respond.

"Let me try some," he pleaded, his eyes growing huge. "Pot, it's just not enough anymore . . ."

And I felt the same tug-of-war Adrian must have. Because you know that even though you do it and you like it and it feels good, it's a bad drug. You know that even though you say you aren't a junkie, you were hooked from the first taste. And you don't want someone you love to get into something so bad. But I knew Liam had been through something worse: Christian. Though Liam refused to talk about it, I was sure Christian was the one who'd bruised his face. I knew how badly Liam needed to feel good.

I unearthed the Altoids box and reached for the hand mirror on my nightstand. I shook brown powder out of a plastic baggie, divided it into lines, and handed my little brother a rolled dollar bill.

I only let him do one line and he was fine for about fifteen minutes. Then he curled up at the foot of my bed, moaning that he felt like he was going to throw up. I put my Strawberry Shortcake trash can on the floor next to him and he puked into it repeatedly, looking how I must have when I was eight, had the stomach flu, and vomited into that very trash can for a day straight. I'd heard that most people puked their first time on heroin and I'd given Liam such a tiny amount, I knew he wasn't OD'ing. Still, I fought off my own drug haze to keep watch over him.

"I'm never doing this shit again," he swore, wiping bile from the corners of his lips. "This sucks."

Heroin had never made me sick, so I couldn't agree, but I was pleased he felt that way. I didn't care enough about myself to stop using, but I cared enough about Liam not to want him to start.

That night I couldn't fall asleep until Liam did. I awoke the next morning to find him sobered up and staring at me. He said, "I wanted to repeat that I'm sorry I didn't believe you about Christian."

I propped myself up on my elbow. "Why do you believe me now?"

"I don't want to talk about it. I just wanted to apologize again."

And with that, he smiled sadly and left the room.

The Ballad of Fallen Idols:
Liam McNaughton

"And the lonely voice of youth cries, 'What is Truth?'"

—*Johnny Cash*

April 1995

ALL MY HEROES LET ME DOWN.

It started in third grade with Johnny Cash. He'd been my idol since I was four, so naturally when we were assigned an oral report on the person who influenced us most, I picked Johnny. I even sang "Walk the Line" a cappella in hopes of impressing Lizzie Jordan, the most beautiful girl in our class.

The room filled with snickering before I got to the chorus. Lizzie laughed loudest of all. "Now we know why he dresses like such a weirdo," she told the girl next to her. I should've known from her New Kids on the Block lunch box that she wouldn't appreciate the Man in Black. I ran to the bathroom in tears, wishing I'd played it safe and picked Ozzie Guillen, my favorite guy on the White Sox. All the other boys had picked either baseball players or their dads.

I don't know if I ever considered my dad a hero. I can't remember worshiping him that much because he was barely around. Kara tells all these stories where he's the center of the universe, but in my mind she was the brightest star.

My first memory is literally looking up to her. I was probably about three, just waking up from a nap, and Kara hovered over my bed, waiting for me. "What do you want to do, Liam?" she asked, eyes glowing with the possibilities. Back then, we did everything together. She read to me and taught me to read. She sang to me and listened to me sing. She came up with elaborate imaginary games: we looked for gold in the Old West, flew spaceships thousands of years into the future, and had our own band in the present day.

My sister mattered more than my mother, father, and Johnny Cash combined. She also let me down worse than any of them. Part of the reason I didn't concern myself with making friends when we moved to the suburbs was that I thought she'd always be there. Then she met Stacey and ditched me. I was hesitant to trust her when we got close again two years ago. But at least she brought me into her world at Scoville Park.

We weren't as tight as I wished we could be at times, like when my parents split up. I really needed Kara then, but she was focused on Adrian. Fortunately—or unfortunately, depending on how you look at it now—I found someone new to lean on . . . well, to the extent that guys lean on each other. Christian and I skateboarded, listened to music, and remarked every once in a while about how our families sucked. But I looked up to him like I had Kara. I listened to his stories about how we'd leave Oak Park one day. I believed in him. He became the brother I'd sometimes wished I could trade my sister in for.

Then he started dating Kara. A little awkward, but it was cool at first. I liked having a group of friends that felt like a family. I liked having my sister around on a regular basis. Until she screwed everything up.

Kara tried to reach out when our dad abandoned us yet again. But I just couldn't trust her. Whenever anything bad went down, it seemed like she took care of herself first and came back for me later. Christian, on the other hand, had always been there for me.

When I told him about my dad's impending move and how I just wanted to be a million miles away from my family, he said, "Let's do it." He said he couldn't steal his dad's car because his dad loved that thing more than him, so we took my mom's. We swung by Maya's and told her we were finally leaving for Florida and asked her if she wanted to come.

She took one look at the big house that she and her dad had just moved into and said, "Yeah, I can't stand this place. Let's go."

Honestly, I wouldn't have left without her. I'd gotten kind of attached.

I always developed crushes on my sister's friends: apple-scented Stacey with her big blue eyes that stated up front, "I'm trouble," and smoky Cass, whose thick dreads reminded me of Bob Marley. But Maya, she was my sister's prettiest friend by far. She smelled like the ocean, sounded like the South, and looked like Kate Moss with curves and bloodred hair. More important, Maya and I connected the first time we really talked.

It was a Saturday night at Scoville when Kara was off hanging out with Christian and his little sister. I sat at the foot of the soldier statue, smoking up when Maya walked by. I nodded hello at her and she laughed and asked, "Is that dinner?"

"I guess."

"Can I have a bite?"

I shrugged and extended the joint, trying not to act as awkward as I felt with this gorgeous girl standing over me, gleaming beneath the shitty street-lamp that made everyone else look nicotine-stained. I stared at her knee, which peeked out from her ripped, doodle-covered jeans. She had one freckle on each side of her kneecap, perfectly symmetrical, like eyes. I pointed this out to her, immediately feeling like an idiot for making such a stupid stoner observation aloud.

But Maya grinned and exclaimed, "You noticed, too!" She plopped down beside me and bent her knee, swinging her lower leg. "I pretend my calf is an elephant's trunk." She giggled to herself and handed me the joint, which tasted like Dr Pepper—the flavor of her ChapStick.

I relaxed, realizing that pretty as she was, you didn't have to play cool with her. She was the kind of girl you could really laugh with. We smoked a couple joints and did exactly that, examining the patterns our freckles formed, discussing other goofy theories we'd had since we were kids, and eventually exchanging stories from childhood.

We'd moved to the grass so that Maya could stretch out and she told me about her days on the beach in Florida. "I spent all my time with this little boy, Taylor Williams. When I was eight, my grandmother declared that he and I were soul mates and we'd grow up and live happily ever after. So I tried kissing him once at a bonfire, but our lips were both chapped and we pulled away at the same time, going, 'Ewww!' Before we grew out of that cooties phase, his family moved to Sarasota."

"Maybe you'll find each other again if you're soul mates."

Maya shook her head. "I don't believe in that crap."

"I don't either. My sister says the divorce has made me cynical." I rolled my eyes.

"Your sister's a romantic. That's why I set her up with Christian. He needs someone who believes in love. And Kara needs someone she can trust, who won't hurt her like Adrian did."

"But didn't you and Christian sort of have a thing this summer?"

Maya laughed and sat up to look at me. "Christian wanted love and trust. I just wanted to kiss. I can't handle that other crap. After all, someday I'm gonna run away back to Florida and live on the beach, where I can see stars instead of city lights. What about you?"

It would have been the perfect moment to kiss her, but Christian and Kara arrived. Maya and I did kiss a couple days later when we went for what was supposed to be a short walk at lunch and ended up two miles away at Thatcher Woods. And eventually, even though I told Maya I didn't believe in love, even though we weren't officially a couple, I fell in love with her. Not Johnny Cash–June Carter love, but when we were on someone's couch or in a booth at Denny's and she'd stretch out with her head in my lap, staring up at me as she talked, she was my favorite person in the world.

Maya got a little weird sometimes, like she had these fits of sadness and didn't want to talk to anyone, even me. But I figured it was a girl thing; my sister was like that. After Kara and Christian broke up, Maya was particularly quiet and moody, but we all were because Kara had betrayed us.

I thought things would get better in Florida. The two-day drive down there was fun, full of that sense of freedom we'd always talked about. Then we got to Fort Lauderdale where it was unseasonably cold, not "sunny and green green green with palm trees and eighty-degree weather even at Christmas sometimes" like Maya promised. And we were broke because all our money had gone to gas, and spare-changing on the beach wasn't very profitable. Worst of all, Maya sunk into an inexplicable depression. She cried herself to sleep in the backseat of the car three nights in a row, refusing to let either of us comfort her.

Christian, who was already freaking out that we were broke and nothing was going the way it was supposed to, grew increasingly frustrated with Maya. On the fourth afternoon, he took our last ten bucks and said he was going to get us dinner. He disappeared for three hours. I waited on the beach with Maya, who wasn't even talking anymore, and worried that Christian had ditched me with no cash, a car that was out of gas, and a catatonic who I couldn't even really call my girlfriend.

Finally, he came down the beach with a bag of McDonald's and three large drinks. The sun setting at his back cast an orangish red glow around him, making him look heaven-sent, which it kind of felt like he was, at least for the moment.

He put the food down in front of us, and then he opened his coat and said to Maya, "If this doesn't cheer you up, nothing will." He pulled out a big bottle of Jack Daniel's and a carton of Winstons. He looked to me, reached behind his ear, and withdrew a skinny joint. "I met some punk kids in town," he explained. "Stole them some whiskey and cigarettes, too, and they gave me this in exchange."

"Thanks, man," I said.

"Thanks, Christian," Maya echoed in a soft, rusty-sounding voice.

He smiled at her. "Good, you're talking. Now start drinking and get happy, okay? 'Cause tonight we have the kind of fun we always talked about having when we got to Florida."

Maya nodded and took a shot of Jack straight from the bottle.

"That's my girl." Christian quickly drank his pop halfway down and filled his cup back up with whiskey.

I lit the joint, but since it was thin and there were three of us smoking, it went pretty quick. Even though I preferred pot to alcohol, I started drinking Jack and Coke, too.

Everything was fun and games for about two hours. Even Maya was telling stories, laughing, and joking like usual. Christian and I started horsing around. We ran down to the edge of the water, daring each other to go in. After about ten minutes, I realized Maya wasn't with us.

"Hey, where'd Maya go?"

"Shit," Christian said.

We wandered up and down the beach, calling her name, but didn't see her anywhere. It had grown dark, particularly by the water's edge because the light from the streetlamps that lined the road didn't stretch that far.

I panicked. "We're never going to find her!"

Christian put his hand on my shoulder. "It's going to be okay, Liam. Just give me a second. Let me think." He took two long swigs from the nearly-empty Jack Daniel's bottle. "You go check the car. I'll keep searching the beach. We'll meet back at the spot where we ate dinner in twenty minutes."

I nodded and took off in the direction of the car, believing it would be okay because Christian said so, trusting him in a way I'd never even trusted my own dad.

We'd parked about three blocks from the beach. I ran as fast as I could, slowing only when I started to feel queasy. The whiskey-pot-McDonald's combination was not settling well. I felt sicker still when I got to the street where we'd left the car and saw flashing lights: a tow truck and two cop cars.

Shit. We hadn't had a chance to switch out the license plates as planned. No doubt my mom had reported the car stolen and me missing. The police would be looking for us. I fought off my nausea and sped back the way I'd come. I had to find Christian and Maya. We had to get the hell out of town.

Approaching the beach, I noticed a faint glow coming from the window of the bathroom where we washed up in the mornings. The building was closed for the season, but Christian had managed to bust the padlock off the door to the men's room. I hurried toward it, hoping Maya was inside.

She was, but Christian had found her first.

Before I reached the door, I heard Christian screaming at her, "What the fuck is wrong with you? Stop moping around like someone died. If you've got a problem, then talk about it!"

Maya shouted back, "Someone did fucking die, okay? My mom killed herself. That's the family secret. That's why I left Florida. And being back here is making me relive it all over again. Are you happy? Now let me go!"

"Seriously? That's all? You broke up with me because you couldn't tell me *that*?"

I stormed through the bathroom door and found Maya struggling in Christian's grip. He'd hoisted her up the same way I'd seen him lift his little sister, taking hold beneath her armpits. But he'd always tossed Naomi in the air, making her giggle. Instead, he'd slammed Maya against the wall and pinned her there, her feet dangling two inches above the cement floor. Maya helplessly flailed her fists into Christian's arms. She was pink-faced and sobbing, the dark makeup she so carefully applied each morning streaking her cheeks like skid marks leading up to a bad accident.

"Let go of her!" I exclaimed, charging Christian the way football players did when trying to knock an opponent off balance. My right shoulder caught him in the ribs, forcing him to release Maya. Even though Christian was slightly bigger than me, I had rage on my side. I moved like a snow plow, shoving him across the room and pinning him against the opposite wall.

Palms firmly planted against Christian's chest, I looked over my shoulder at Maya. She'd sunk to the floor and wrapped her arms around her shins. She stared unblinking at Christian and me with her lips slightly parted, like she was about to speak. But when I asked, "Maya, are you okay?" she didn't respond.

I turned back to Christian, pressing him harder against the tile wall. "Why the fuck did you flip out on her? She was obviously upset, why'd you go and make it worse?"

Christian ignored me, speaking to Maya instead. "Why didn't you tell me about your mom? My mom died, too. I understand. If you'd just told me about it months ago, none of this would have happened. Kara never would have happened. I loved you, Maya. I always loved you."

Christian was obviously drunk. There were telltale red splotches on his cheeks and his eyes were bloodshot. But for him to profess his love to the girl I was with, right after he'd attacked her, no less . . . Before I could organize my feelings of betrayal into words, Maya started to laugh.

I looked over my shoulder again, watching her rise shakily to her feet. "You love me?" She chuckled without opening her mouth; it sounded kind of like a growl and kind of like a sob. "You love me and you did this?" Maya pointed to her left cheek; the rest of her face had gone pale while it remained pink.

My head whipped back to Christian. "Did you fucking hit her?"

Before he could respond, Maya tossed out another accusation. A worse one. "You did this to Kara, too, didn't you?" The acoustics of the bathroom amplified her angry whisper. She repeated, "Didn't you?" and it echoed, bouncing off the walls, the urinal and bathroom stall to my left, and the mirror that hung above the sink to my right. It wouldn't stop echoing in my brain for weeks.

"What?" I murmured in shock. My grasp on Christian loosened. I held him with one hand, turning sideways to look at Maya.

She walked woodenly toward Christian and me, massaging her chest and shoulders where Christian's hands had been. She fixed her gray eyes on Christian. They looked as cold as the ocean that we could hear pounding against the shore outside. "Kara showed me the marks on her chest before she ran out of Denny's that night. She told me they were bruises, but I didn't believe her because you told me they were hickeys. I told her Christian would never hurt someone he loved. But if you loved me . . ."

As Maya trailed off, I whirled on Christian, clenching my free hand in a fist. "Did you hit my sister?"

He just stared at Maya over my shoulder, slack-jawed.

Maya continued, speaking in a monotone, punctuated with that strange laugh that sounded more like a cry. "She said you'd grabbed her like you had Mary at the park last fall. I laughed when you grabbed Mary like that. I thought you were cool for defending us. I thought Mary was getting what she deserved for talking shit about Kara and me. But Kara didn't deserve to get choked. I don't care what she did. She didn't deserve what you did to her. What we did by leaving her . . ."

What we did. I pictured my sister collapsing on the messy floor of Adrian's room after I dismissed her as a lying junkie. *"Just once,"* she'd cried out. *"Because of Christian."* But I'd ignored her.

Christian's angry snarl snapped me out of the memory. "Kara did deserve what she got. She's a lying, cheating, junkie whore!"

I swung for his jaw, screaming, "She started using because of you!"

He ducked my punch and shoved me backward. I collided with Maya, who caught herself by grabbing the sink basin. Before Christian could open the bathroom door, I regained my footing and leapt at him. We tumbled to the floor, narrowly avoiding cracking our heads against the urinal. I rolled on top of Christian, punching him in the face three times, blood splattering from his lip and nose.

I bellowed, "I hate you!" though I hated myself as much as I hated him. I'd walked out on Kara, thinking she deserved it for all the times she'd let me down. "She didn't deserve it!"

"Stop it!" Maya shouted, and when I turned blindly to look at her, Christian caught me square in the cheek.

We flipped over: him on top, me scrambling backward, protecting my head by sliding it under the toilet stall wall. Before he could pull me out, Maya screamed "Stop!" again and glass shattered. Christian flattened himself on top of me for a moment, but as soon as the last shard clinked to the cement, he pushed himself up and took off out the door.

I turned over on my stomach and wiggled out from under the stall wall. Maya was huddled beneath the sink, holding the broken neck of the Jack Daniel's bottle. She'd smashed it against the mirror, leaving a big dent in the center surrounded by a web of cracked glass ready to fall into the sink above her head. I dropped to the floor and dragged her out, ignoring the glass that dug into my knees.

After I pulled Maya from the bathroom, I studied her in the light that leaked through the door. There were scratches on her hands, but I didn't see blood anywhere else. "Are you okay?"

"Forget about me," she urged. "Go after Christian. He has the car keys. You can't let him take the car."

I started laughing then, so hard I bent over to brace myself against my knees to catch my breath.

"It's not funny," Maya sobbed. "I can't be here anymore. With the memories of my mom and now this."

I stopped laughing as quickly as I'd started and stood up, drawing her into my arms. "I'm so sorry about your mom. I wish you'd felt comfortable enough to tell me . . ."

Maya went stiff and jerked herself out of my embrace. "You should hate me for not telling you about Kara."

I shook my head, reaching for her hand. "Christian had us all fooled. But he's going to get what's coming to him." I pointed toward the street. "There are cops at the car. They caught us and I was upset, but now I'm glad. We're going to go up there and tell them how he attacked you—"

"No!" Maya interrupted, stubbornly crossing her arms over her chest. "I deserve what happened because I let him hurt my best friend."

"Maya, he fooled us. And now he's going to pay for what he did to both of you—"

"No! Stop defending me, Liam. You of all people shouldn't defend me. Do you know why Christian had me fooled? Because I was in love with him! I watched all those sweet things he did for your sister and I wondered why I ever let him go."

"But—"

I wanted to tell Maya that I loved her, but she silenced me. "Don't. It's time to go home and apologize to Kara. It's over."

She meant "We're over," whatever we'd been in the first place. My first instinct was to run into the bathroom and cry the way I had when Lizzie Jordan laughed at my attempt to serenade her in third grade. But this pain was too crippling.

"No, Maya," I moaned.

"Shh." She put her fingers against my lips. Even though the air around us smelled like the ocean, her usual scent, all I could smell was whiskey. The stench of it made my stomach churn. I pushed Maya out of the way and dropped to my knees, retching.

I was still puking in the sand when the cops came. It was just like a Johnny Cash song: prison-bound after abandoning my sister, losing my woman, and being betrayed by my best friend. Christian had destroyed the closest thing I'd had to a real family in years.

Of course, I only spent one night in jail before they sent me home. I didn't sleep, because every time I closed my eyes, I saw Christian pinning a girl to a wall, sometimes Maya, sometimes Kara. When I got home, I tried to blot it out the way my sister did, with heroin, but that just made me throw up like I did on the beach. I like the drugs that keep me awake instead, so I don't have to dream about Florida or Christian or anything he did.

Even though I don't want to remember Christian, I also know I shouldn't forget what his betrayal taught me. So I ripped down the *Gleaming the Cube* movie poster that hung over the head of my bed; Christian had given it to me because we both loved that eighties skater flick.

Scrawled in its place next to my poster of the Man in Black sneering and flipping off the world is a list I wrote in red Sharpie: *"Addiction. Selfishness. Violence. No heroes."* My reminders that I'm through believing in anyone besides myself.

4.

MAYA AND LIAM WERE BOTH GROUNDED for three months. By the time they could leave the house for anything other than school, May approached and it was warm enough to hang out in Scoville Park again.

The group dynamics at Scoville had changed completely since I'd started going there a year ago. The original group of nine kids who Liam, Maya, and I befriended had splintered. Of course, things were in flux when we met them. Jessica and Mary had been spreading rumors about Cass. Everyone missed Wes. It seemed like he'd been the glue holding them together, and once they realized he wasn't returning from California, everyone went their separate ways.

Our circle at the center of the park shrunk. I expected Craig to join Adrian, Quentin, Cass, Maya, and me, but instead, he, Jessica, and Mary sat with his new bandmates. At least Craig still came to Shelly's parties and was friendly with everyone.

Christian, on the other hand, stayed away from us and we acted like he didn't exist. Though Maya and Liam still weren't talking about what happened in Florida, everyone seemed to know that Christian was the one to shun. He and my brother had both returned with bruised faces, but Christian looked a lot worse. His lip was split, his nose was broken, and a blood vessel in his eye had burst, leaving a red spot that didn't disappear for over a month. Everyone thought of Liam as a peaceful pothead, so if he'd flipped out on Christian, Christian must have done something unforgivable.

Even though Christian still came to the park to skate, he left whenever Liam approached the statue. Christian no longer had any male friends; he hung out, creepily, with the freshman girls who came to the park to flirt with guys. They were like little alternative cheerleaders with belly button and nose piercings, black or blue fingernail polish, bleached or Manic Panic–ed hair, baby-doll T-shirts, and plaid minibackpacks that they carried their cigarettes and flasks in.

These girls were all in love with my brother, too, but even though Liam still skated sometimes, he snubbed Christian and all his girlfriends. He'd shifted groups, too, having bonded with Harlan, Shelly, and a couple other ravers in gym class. I teased him that his pants were getting bigger every day. He'd also dyed his hair blue like Harlan's, and instead of keeping the punky spikes he'd once had, he was letting it grow into minidreadlocks. I barged into his room the day I heard techno blaring.

He just smiled. "Do some ecstasy. You'll get it."

"I have and I still don't get it." Quietly, I was pleased that he'd stayed away from heroin as promised. E and acid were harder than pot, but definitely preferable to heroin when my little brother was concerned.

Whatever had happened in Florida had messed up Liam and Maya's relationship as well. They were cordial to each other, but the two of them never hung out together anymore. At first I thought it was because they were both grounded, but it continued when their paths crossed at parties or the park.

I didn't ask about it. Part of me was still angry at both of them for not taking my side over Christian's in the first place. I found it easier to forgive my brother because I hadn't forced my side of the story on him, but Maya had ignored the truth. That ate away at me.

A couple days after she returned from Florida, Maya had called and apologized to me in the same vague way Liam had. "I was wrong about Christian and you. Dead wrong and I'm sorry," she told me, but she wouldn't reveal how she'd come to that conclusion. When I asked, she said, "My dad's yelling at me to get off the phone. I'm supposed to be grounded."

She and I had an uneasy truce, but our friendship wasn't the same. When we spent time together outside of the park, we watched movies or listened to music—activities that disguised the lack of conversation. I even stopped having her put colors in my bangs, just leaving them blond, because it was too awkward to sit in silence while she did it.

My unspoken anger prevented me from opening up to her. And Maya had come back from Florida a completely different person. Mousiness replaced her flamboyance. She stopped wearing makeup and let the red in her hair fade. Instead of bouncing around, singing, and sharing her latest social experiment with everyone, she quietly doodled in her sketchbook, often wearing headphones so no one would approach her. But I didn't question it or worry about her; I figured it was her penance for not believing me from the beginning.

Well, that and I didn't really worry about anyone because I was on heroin.

The afternoons that we spent at Scoville were painfully sober because Cass was around. She hadn't lectured me about heroin, but she'd laid into Quentin and Adrian often enough that they avoided using in front of her. Because of this, I enjoyed the days when Cass went home to study, and Quentin, Adrian, and I could go to Adrian's, get high, and work on the "Stories of Suburbia" project.

The five-subject, spiral-bound notebook had gotten huge as

a pregnant woman at the end of her eighth month. We visited libraries and newsstands and collected stacks of newspapers. One afternoon, Quentin found an article about a beautiful island off the coast of Florida plagued by drug addiction. Several teenagers from a seemingly perfect community had overdosed within weeks of one another.

"That'll never be us," Adrian said as he taped it into the book. "Gotta be a junkie to OD."

Even though the three of us snorted smack at least once a day on weekdays and binged like crazy on weekends, we didn't believe we were addicts. After all, we were functional. We had a goal that had nothing to do with drugs: writing a screenplay.

But as the original "Stories of Suburbia" notebook grew, our separate screenplay notebook languished. We were having trouble developing a central story. Finally, Adrian had a revelation on a dreary Friday while we went through newspapers in his bedroom.

He found an article in our town's paper and tapped the page frantically, exclaiming, "Hey, this is about us!"

Quentin and I looked up, shocked, thinking we'd been unknowingly caught for some petty crime. But Adrian pointed to the headline, "Local Teens Seek Their Fix Across the Border."

The picture below the headline was from the inside of an SUV where shadowy figures in the front seat stared out at a brick apartment complex. The "border" the article referred to was that magical line down the middle of Austin Boulevard that separated Oak Park from the West Side of Chicago. The "fix" was heroin. And Adrian said it was "about us" because he and Quentin did go to some undisclosed location just inside the city limits to buy.

Adrian eagerly tore the article out of the paper and plastered it down with scotch tape in his original notebook. Then he declared, "I know what the problem with our screenplay is." He snatched the screenplay notebook from my lap and began ripping out all the pages we'd—mostly I'd—written.

"What the hell are you doing?" I panicked, reaching for my precious work. He tossed the empty notebook back at me and started flipping through the original "Stories of Suburbia" notebook, tearing out most of its pages. He was more careful with those, I noticed, stacking them on the floor beside him.

Adrian left the handwritten pages and some small police blotter clippings alone. "Our story is too big," he explained. "We have the beheading at the football game. The birth at prom. The mom setting her husband on fire. The party scene, but they're all different characters and they don't connect because they *aren't* really connected. Each one could be a crappy TV movie and I don't want to write a crappy TV movie, I want to write something real." Adrian indicated one of the handwritten pages. "I'm keeping our stories and our crimes in here 'cause those are real. We'll use those." He turned to the last page of the notebook and slapped the heroin article. "And this will be our opening scene. Us buying drugs in the city."

Catching on to his idea and enthusiasm, I wrote in the screenplay notebook:

EXT. CITY APARTMENT BUILDING—NIGHT

I stopped. "I don't know how to write this. You guys never take me."

Adrian shrugged and glanced at the digital alarm clock that sat on its side on the floor. "I guess we'll have to, then. We're about to meet our guy to get stuff before Shelly's party anyway."

Quentin's face fell at that suggestion. "No, Adrian," he said, soft but firm, "she can't go."

"Why?" I objected, sick of being ditched whenever they went to buy.

Quentin's ice blue eyes seared into mine. "Because it's not a movie, it's real and it's not safe."

His warning instilled more curiosity than fear, so I was pleased when Adrian overruled him, saying, "Writers need experience. She can come."

Twenty minutes later, I was in the backseat of Adrian's car, cruising across the invisible border to Chicago. Up front, Quentin mumbled to Adrian, "What are we getting tonight, anyway?"

"I think he's got China white, man."

"Seriously? We're actually gonna get to try that shit?" Quentin grinned and sung along a bit louder with the Screeching Weasel song, "Hey Suburbia," that played on the car stereo.

I knew exactly what they were talking about. A year ago, I'd never paid for drugs, smoking pot only when someone had it to share, and I never thought about where it came from. Now I spent all the money I had on drugs, and thanks to Adrian, I had encyclopedic knowledge about the origin of heroin. The West Coast got their heroin from Mexico, made up of mostly black tar, which wreaks havoc on your veins, and some brown powder. The East Coast and the South generally got their heroin from South America and it was white, but not China white, a very particular, very powerful kind of heroin from Asia. Due to its central location in the country and because it served as a distribution hub for the rest of the Midwest, Chicago had a unique heroin market. Most of it came from South America, but you could get heroin from Mexico and Asia, too. If our guy had China white, we'd hit the jackpot.

I stared out the window, taking in my surroundings. Even though we were barely a mile from my house and the streets had the same names, everything was different. Instead of seeing women in their thirties pushing strollers and stopping in front of an art gallery to gaze at the pictures, I spotted girls younger than me pushing strollers, stopped by a group of older guys who were gathered in front of a liquor store.

As we slowed in front of a seemingly abandoned building, Adrian snapped, "Kara, don't fucking look around!"

"What?" I asked, oblivious.

Quentin reached around from the passenger's seat to shove my head between my knees. My stomach leapt into my throat as I waited to hear bullets striking the car or something. Quentin chastised me, "You don't want to see anybody do anything and you don't want anybody to *think* you saw them doing anything." It was the only time he'd ever spoken to me sharply and he immediately apologized. "I'm sorry," he said quietly, "but keep your head down."

I did as told, my thoughts returning to the division between this part of the city and us. Here we were: three white spoiled-brat suburban kids in a Honda, there to buy drugs. How fucking cliché. I guess gawking out the window did make me look like an idiot tourist or something, though I felt just as stupid with my head in my lap. Not to mention there was really no point in me going along because I didn't observe anything to write about.

Adrian left the car running and went inside somewhere. Quentin kept singing along to the stereo, which was how I knew how long it took: two and a half punk songs, or five minutes. Adrian got back in the car and started driving again, mumbling at Quentin to keep an eye out for cops. Eventually, he told me I could sit up, but I looked straight ahead until we crossed Austin and were a few blocks into Oak Park.

Instead of being excited by our drug pickup like I'd thought I'd be, I felt nauseous and disgusted by my own ignorance. I was glad we had heroin and were going to a party in a few hours, so I could forget about it.

———⋘⋙———

When we got to Shelly's, I opted to chill on the couch in her living room alone instead of braving the basement. I'd snorted a few lines of China white and it definitely felt stronger. I wanted to zone quietly and enjoy the buzz. But right as I achieved a blissful, half-passed-out state, warm hands clapped over my closed eyes and the shriek of "Kara-leeena, guess who!" jarred me awake.

Stacey leapt over the back of the couch as my thick tongue struggled to sound out her name. "Stahhh . . . Stay . . . Stacey?"

She threw her arms around me and smothered me in her dark hair, which still smelled mostly the same, like that apple conditioner she always used, but with a hint of patchouli underneath. She pushed me away, her hands still gripping my shoulders, so we could study each other. She was the same old Stacey, but she'd ditched the trashy outfits she'd taken to wearing when she'd started chasing boys freshman year and replaced them with a Grateful Dead T-shirt and hemp necklaces.

Despite her latest makeover, her personality remained intact. "Where the hell have you been, bitch?"

"Um, right here?" I blinked, still very dazed. "Where have you been?"

"With Jason." She pointed behind us at a guy with a long, sun-bleached ponytail, stoned green eyes, and an obscene number of hemp necklaces. He waved.

"Hi, Jason. Didn't we smoke pot together once?" I asked, vaguely remembering him from the park the previous summer.

"Probably." He shrugged, smiling. "Adrian used to sell to me."

"We need to catch up!" Stacey insisted, shaking both of my hands. "Have you lost weight? Your face seems skinnier. Jason, can you get us some beers? And a Coke for Kara 'cause she looks like she's falling asleep. Have you been partying hard, girl?"

As Jason strutted off to the keg, I admitted, "Yeah, I'm here, like, every weekend. What about you? I haven't seen you in months."

"I've been dating Jason the whole time," Stacey said proudly. "We haven't been around because this is a high school party. Jason's not in high school. He's got an apartment. I'm over there a lot."

She launched into the story of her life since we'd last spoken in the fall. She elaborated on Jason, telling me how nice and laid-back he was. She went on forever, playing up how cool his apartment was and playing down that he paid for it by selling pot. She also told me the names of all of his fish before she asked, "So, what have you been up to?"

I didn't want to talk about Christian so I told her about Adrian, referring to him as my boyfriend for the first time and acting like I'd been seeing him all along even though the night she'd met him was the night I'd walked away from him. I also neglected to mention the heroin, enthusing about the screenplay instead.

"Awesome! You're writing a movie? My best friend's gonna be famous!"

I grinned, more at her still calling me her best friend than her saying I was going to be famous.

"Can I see the notebook? Can I write my story in it?" she asked, blue eyes wide.

I took it out of my backpack, warning, "You have to write yours before you can read anything."

She snatched it from my hands and gestured at Jason, who'd shown up with our beers midway through my explanation of the script/scrapbook project. "That's fine, get to know him."

Jason and I made small talk, mostly about his fish, while Stacey wrote. I sipped from my beer, but didn't really drink it. I wanted another line pretty badly and was about to excuse myself to the bathroom when Cass appeared.

"Can I talk to you, Kara?" Both her voice and her expression were flat. Not good.

"Uhh . . ."

I looked to Stacey, hoping to be rescued, but she was so into her writing that she didn't even raise her head. She waved me away, saying, "I'll find you when I'm done."

So I trudged upstairs to Shelly's bedroom with Cass. She half closed the door and then glared at me with her arms crossed over her chest. "What the hell is going on with you?"

Damn, I wanted a line. I shook my head. "What are you talking about?"

Cass set her jaw hard. "Heroin. You do a little bit, fine, it's your deal. I had my acid phase, I can't judge. But you and Quentin are doing way too much. And now you're going with them to buy?"

"Where'd you hear that?" I tried to look shocked, hoping it was from Jessica or Mary so I could easily deny it.

"Straight from the horse's mouth. Quentin doesn't know what he's saying sometimes when he's high."

"Well, if he doesn't know what he's saying—"

"Don't fucking lie to me!" Cass thundered like an angry drill sergeant.

"Don't fucking yell at me. You aren't my mom."

Cass seemed near tears as she twisted her dreads around her fingers. "Since Wes left I've tried to look out for everyone, but I can't handle it anymore! You and Quentin have a serious drug problem. Maya's been weird since she ran away and I need you to help me with her, but instead you're high all the time."

"I am not."

"Yes, you are. You think it's not noticeable, but everyone knows, Kara. They may not see how often you're high, but I do and it's out of control. Adrian got Quentin sucked into this and now you—"

"Don't blame Adrian for what Quentin and I do. Adrian's not forcing us to do anything. If you and Quentin have problems—"

Cass flailed her arms wildly. "This whole goddamn town is on drugs and it's not okay anymore! It's not pot and acid and beer. I'm not saying those things are good. But Kara, shit, Adrian and Quentin are *shooting up*. You know that, right?"

A chill ran through me. I was doing drugs with them, how could I not know that? "That's bullshit."

She flared her nostrils, clearly trying to suppress the urge to slap me. "No, it's not. And you should also know that your brother's smoking crystal with Shelly and Harlan."

"What?" I exploded. "Now I know you're lying!"

"Go find him," she challenged. "Look in the garage. You'll notice right away that the smell of the smoke isn't like pot."

"Shut up!" I shrieked. I didn't need this. I needed a line. And who cared what Cass would say about it? I didn't need her or Maya. My old best friend had resurfaced.

As if on cue, Stacey walked in. She looked at us warily and asked, "Um, should I come back?"

Cass stalked past her. "No, I was just leaving."

Stacey watched her go, then blinked twice and said, "Didn't we shoplift with that chick once?"

"Yeah—"

Glass shattered in the next room. I heard Adrian scream "Fuck!" and when I reached the bedroom door, I caught a glimpse of him fleeing the bathroom.

He nearly knocked Cass over as he hurtled down the stairs. She clung to the railing, but recovered quickly and made it to that hellish pink bathroom before I could.

I didn't see what was inside right away because she blocked the doorway, eyeliner coursing down her cheeks in black rivulets. "Call 911 now!" she hollered at me.

"What hap—"

Cass dropped to her hands and knees, revealing Quentin slumped between the toilet and the sink with a belt around his arm. His face rested on the fluffy toilet lid cover; Quentin was naturally pale, but against the pink his skin appeared stark white. Even his lips, which were partially open, looked colorless. Cass sat him up straight and gently but firmly slapped his cheeks. When his eyes didn't flutter open, I started to hyperventilate. Cass turned to me and screeched, "911!"

I ran for the phone in Shelly's room, collapsing to my knees in the center of the floor to dial. When the operator picked up, I breathlessly rattled off Shelly's address and "I need an ambulance now!"

"What's your emergency?" the woman asked, sounding so calm I wondered if I was speaking to a recording.

"My friend overdosed." I shuddered as Cass shouted Quentin's name over and over, growing louder and increasingly hysterical.

"Do you know what he took?" the robotic voice questioned.

"Help!" Cass wailed. "Help!"

"We need that ambulance now!" I insisted, digging my fingernails into Shelly's carpet.

"It's been dispatched, but the more information I can provide, the more prepared the EMTs can be."

I tore out pieces of pale blue carpet, picturing the studded belt around Quentin's skinny arm. "Heroin," I sobbed. "He shot China white heroin."

After the operator said something about the ambulance being a few minutes away, I dropped the phone, scrambled to my feet, and rushed back to the bathroom.

As word filtered downstairs that the cops were coming, everyone—literally *everyone*, even Shelly—fled except for Maya, who'd been sitting on the front porch smoking a cigarette by herself when Adrian came flying out of the house like he was on fire.

Maya hurried upstairs, fighting the current of kids streaming outside. We met at the bathroom door and found Cass hugging Quentin. She'd stopped screaming. Instead, she repeated, "No, you have to wake up. No, no, no," in a ragged whisper.

I clung to the door frame, taking in the details of the scene.

There was a spoon and a lighter sitting beside the shell-shaped soap dish on the sink. The needle lay on the shaggy mauve rug near the shower. Apparently Adrian had yanked it out of Quentin's arm during his attempt to revive him. Then he'd bashed his fist into the mirror. Shards of it were scattered in the sink, across the floor, and even on Quentin's lap.

Maya and I knelt on the broken glass, trying to pull Cass off of Quentin so we could attempt to resuscitate him. But Cass had already felt for Quentin's pulse, and unable to find it or feel him breathing, she knew. Just *knew*.

Quentin was gone. He had died before Adrian even walked in on him.

5.

I'D LOST THE "STORIES OF SUBURBIA" notebook in the shuffle at Shelly's, but I still saved all the articles about Quentin. The story of his OD made the *Chicago Tribune* and got a whole spread in the local paper: front-page article, follow-ups, editorials, and letters to the editor from angry parents who wanted to know how the hell high school kids were getting heroin (apparently they hadn't seen the article on page three the prior week) and how these parties had been going on under the police department's nose. In full-on suburban witch-hunt mode, they cried out for criminal charges against Shelly's dad for negligence and felony penalties for various drugs (heroin and pot) and paraphernalia (pipes for smoking both marijuana and methamphetamine) found in his house.

Since Shelly's dad was a lawyer, he got out unscathed, but he sent Shelly to rehab and then boarding school, because obviously, spending less time with his daughter was the solution. And I'm sure the people who cried out against him were the same kind of parents whose kids fended for themselves every day after school while they pulled long hours. Maya normally would have told us that her grandma always said, "People who live in glass houses shouldn't throw stones," but she hardly tossed clichés around with her usual panache anymore.

Even though Cass raised concerns about Maya not even five minutes before we found Quentin dead, now Maya and I worried over Cass instead. After all, there wasn't much worse than finding your boyfriend dead of an overdose.

There was no obituary in the slew of articles about Quentin. Quentin's mom made a statement that her son was "a nice, quiet boy who'd never done something like shoot heroin before." She knew that wasn't true, everyone did, because the medical examiner's report estimated he had been shooting up for two months. The papers were nice enough not to contradict Quentin's mother, though. They also cited all funeral services as private. Presumably, Quentin's family didn't want media or Quentin's weirdo friends reminding them of who their son had been toward the end.

But Maya insisted that Cass needed to say good-bye. She left a message for Quentin's mother using the sugary, southern politeness she'd learned from her grandmother: "Ma'am, I know you're going through a lot, but your son had a girlfriend who loves him very much. She's my cousin and I'm calling because she's too broken up to talk right now. If you could please call me back with information about the wake so I could help her say good-bye to your sweet boy, I would really appreciate it."

Maybe it was the tearfulness in Maya's voice or the way she called Quentin a sweet boy, but Quentin's mother did call back. She simply asked that we didn't bring too many people, vehemently singling out Adrian as uninvited. Not that we knew where he was. No one had been able to find him since the night Quentin died. Not even the cops.

We saw a completely different side of Quentin in the pictures of him as a child arranged at the front of the funeral home. I'd thought he'd been born with that inky black hair, since it suited him so well, but he was blond as could be as an infant in his crib.

"He's so sunny," Maya murmured, touching a photo of six-year-old Quentin building sandcastles on a beach. "Reminds me of Taylor Williams."

"Who?" I whispered.

She cracked a smile for the first time in weeks. "Just a li'l boy I knew back in Florida."

Scanning the funeral home, where everyone was at least twice our age, I felt out of place and inappropriately dressed. Maya and I both wore vintage finery. Her dress was black velvet even though it was a warm spring day, mine was too lacy to be formal, and they both were too short. But those were the kinds of dresses we had. Cass didn't own any. She looked like a frumpy housewife with dreadlocks, expressionless and stiff in the shapeless, ankle-length black dress Maya had found for her at the thrift store.

I glanced back at the door wishing we could leave, but Cass stared straight ahead at the open casket.

Maya took a deep breath. "Sure you're ready?"

Cass nodded sharply.

So Maya led her toward it while I lingered momentarily in front of the pictures. There was only one that included Adrian. I was surprised they hadn't cut him out, but you could barely tell it was him, his eyes shaded and scruffy brown hair disguised by a blue baseball cap. He and Quentin wore matching Little League uniforms, Adrian tossing a ball, Quentin swinging a bat. They had to be about nine.

Soon after that, the pictures changed. In his seventh-grade photo, Quentin had the black hair; beginnings of short braids stuck up from his head like inch-long wires. Aside from a shot of a stoned-looking, teenage Quentin standing beside a Christmas tree with his arms crossed, there were only school pictures from junior high forward, each with Quentin's braids grown longer. The photo montage ended abruptly when Quentin stopped going to picture day sophomore year.

The last image I saw of Quentin was the one I didn't want to see. I treaded slowly down the aisle toward the casket, which Maya and Cass now stood beside. Inside lay the most unfamiliar Quentin of all, dressed in a suit, cheeks drowned in fake color, and hair chopped military short to remove all of the braids and most of the black dye.

This is not my friend. My friend is not dead, I told myself.

But as I denied, Cass came to terms. She cried for the first time since she found him. She cried as she bent down to kiss his cold face. She cried as we walked to our seats in the back of the room. She cried as she listened to Quentin's father call his son "a smart boy who fought to overcome a learning disability and became an avid reader, a Little League champ, and winner of the sixth-grade science fair." He stopped at the point the candid photographs had, when Quentin suddenly became the person he didn't know.

I realized that it would be the same way if my parents had to eulogize me. It was probably the same for any teenager, but most of us would grow up and eventually allow more photo opportunities at college graduations and weddings. Quentin wouldn't have that chance. That's when his death finally hit me and I started to cry. Knowing that I had a chance and would probably screw it up made me sob harder.

Cass stood. "Quentin," she sniffled, voice cracking for a moment before she took a deep breath and gained her usual tough-girl poise. "Quentin and I . . . we've been together for over a year now and we've been friends a long, long time. He was the kindest . . ." She stopped to breathe again. "He was loyal to his friends, and he was the best thing in my life. He made me a better person. I just wish he . . ." She blinked, taking in the eyes of all Quentin's relatives around her. "He was wickedly intelligent. He knew more about philosophy than anyone. His poetry and other writing . . . well, he did great things. And I loved him." She groped for me and Maya on either side of her and we eased her into her seat.

"That was real good," Maya assured her as the last relative rose to speak. Cass stared straight ahead at the casket and nodded, crying silently again.

Between the service and the trip to the cemetery, I excused myself to the bathroom supposedly to fix my makeup, which I did, but I also poured the last of my heroin onto the corner of the sink and snorted it. It wasn't nearly enough to make me as numb as I wanted to be when they put Quentin in the ground, but I'd been rationing what little I had for a week, using only every now and then to take the edge off. I think Maya knew what I'd been doing because she wore a tight-lipped frown when I got into the car.

At the cemetery, I kept looking for Adrian, figuring he would find out where Quentin was and risk arrest to say good-bye. I never saw him, though, and we were among the last to leave. Cass got on her knees and patted the fresh mound of dirt, murmuring, "Bye, Q. I love you. I won't ever forget."

When she stood up and dusted the dirt off, she thanked Maya. "You were right. I needed to say good-bye." She glanced at me, too. "Thank you both for taking care of me. I need a little time alone now."

And that was it. Not to say she was instantly better, but she was ready to grieve without using us as training wheels.

I wish I could have been as strong as she was and grieved without my personal crutch.

I went two days without getting high. Two unbearable, awful days. I threw up in the mornings and had chills all night. When I managed to sleep, I had nightmares of Quentin in his casket under six feet of dirt. He had the strange fake-tan makeup and the military haircut, but the studded belt was still wrapped around his skinny arm. Maggots ate away at the hole where the needle had been. I woke up sweating and screaming. I tried to cut myself, hoping it would soothe me, but I could barely control the knife with my shaking hand. When I finally cut, the sight of blood just made me feel sicker. I cradled my arm, crying. I wanted numbness, not pain.

I admitted to myself that I was an addict and would do anything for the drug. It was okay. I could do it for a little while longer because my friend had just died and my boyfriend had disappeared. I'd grieve, I'd be a junkie for a month or so, and then over the summer, I'd get my shit together and prepare for senior year. That excused what I was about to do.

The third day without heroin, I knocked on Liam's bedroom door. I heard him cough and scramble about, and then Harlan let me in.

"Hey, sexy," he purred. The purple circles under his eyes matched the shade of his hair.

My brother nonchalantly sat on his windowsill, smoking a newly lit cigarette. Three sticks of incense burned on his dresser, but it didn't cover up the acrid smell that definitely wasn't pot, more like burning bleach.

I gave Harlan air kisses, as was his new custom, and strolled over to Liam. I stared right into his bruised-looking eyes and told him, "I know you're smoking glass."

"Uhh," Liam blustered, but I held up my hand to stop him.

"I just want to know if your guy can get me heroin, too."

Harlan appeared behind me, hands on my shoulders, guiding me into a seated position at the foot of the bed so he could give me a massage. "My guy can get you anything you want." He smiled, flicking his tongue against my earlobe.

I swatted at him. "Harlan, you are so weird!"

But I pulled out three twenties and placed them on the bed beside him.

6.

CHICAGO'S BEST WEATHER FALLS IN EARLY June, when there aren't any more cold snaps and it isn't blazing hot yet. That's when I liked to spend all day at the park. One fine afternoon, I'd arrived at Scoville and retreated to the shade where Jason and Stacey were sitting on the brown wooden sculpture. We chatted for a while and then I needed a line, so I headed up the hill for the bathroom by the kiddie playground, locked the door, and snorted two off the toilet tank. I emerged feeling good and strutted back toward Stacey.

Maya suddenly appeared from behind a pine tree. At first I didn't recognize her; she'd dyed her hair jet-black like Quentin's had been.

I wrinkled my nose at her. "What did you do?"

"What the hell are you doing?" she spat.

"What are you talking about?"

"You're still doing heroin after it killed Quentin. Cassie's ignoring it because she can't bear to watch you. I was hoping you'd run out now that Adrian's gone . . ."

"Whoa!" I dramatically waved my arms. "I am not doing heroin. I was peeing. I've had a lot of iced tea today. Doesn't your grandma have a saying about iced tea and summertime?" I smiled, encouraging a change of subject.

But Maya's mood was as dark as her hair. "The tea's been making you rather sleepy lately. Drinking decaf?" She pointed a chipped fingernail so close to my face it made my eyes cross. "Not to mention your skin looks terrible, and what about the pinpoint pupils?"

I brushed her hand away like it was a mosquito. "Thanks for pointing out my acne. And it's sunny. Haven't you ever seen a cat's eyes when it's sunny?"

"You're not a goddamn cat, Kara! You're a junkie! Don't deny it!" she yelled, scattering birds from the nearby trees.

As I glanced around the park to see if Maya's shouting had drawn attention, I caught a glimpse of Christian grinding his skateboard against the statue while fourteen-year-old girls fawned over him.

When Maya turned her head to look at Christian, I smacked her across the face. "It's your fucking fault!" I snapped as she cradled her red cheek in shock. "Who denied things first? Who looked right at the bruises Christian gave me and said"—I rolled my eyes, adopting a falsely sweet tone—"'He would never hurt anyone!'"

Maya stopped rubbing her jaw and whispered, "I was wrong about that."

I shook my head and tried to stalk past her, but she grabbed me by the wrist.

"Wait, I have something for you." Maya brought the "Stories of Suburbia" notebook out of her bag. "I saw this when we were leaving Shelly's the night Quentin died. I grabbed it because I knew it was important to you and Cassie. I tried giving it to her, but she doesn't want it. Too much of a reminder of Quentin, I guess. I thought maybe you'd want it."

"Thanks," I replied icily, taking it from her.

Before I could walk away, she pleaded again, "No more heroin, Kara."

Still angry, I mocked her. "No more black hair dye, Maya. It makes your skin look sallow and you're not nearly as pretty."

I stormed down the hill, not knowing that those bitchy words would be the last I'd ever speak to Maya, that the unfamiliar black hair would be my last sight of her.

I wish I could rewind time and undo a lot of things: failing everything but English junior year, dating Christian, getting hooked on heroin, Liam's meth problem, Quentin's overdose. But that conversation with Maya is my biggest regret.

I'd never get a chance to apologize to her.

The next morning Maya's dad found her soaking in cold, bloody bathtub water with her wrists carved to hell.

7.

ACCORDING TO THE AUTOPSY, THE CAUSE of Maya's death was drowning. Before she slashed her wrists, she'd taken a handful of pain pills to ease what had to be unbearable pain, and a handful of sleeping pills to ensure she wouldn't wake up. She'd fallen asleep, slid into the pinkish bathwater, and suffocated there.

Maya's death was more gruesome than Quentin's, but it only appeared on page five of the local paper. I saved the article, but not in the "Stories of Suburbia" notebook. That remained in my backpack, where I'd stuffed it after Maya returned it to me.

Wes flew in from California for the funeral. It was the first time I'd seen him aside from the photographs that Cass and Maya had shown me. In those, he'd worn his hair in fuzzy dreadlocks that reached the bottoms of his ears, revealing the thick hoops in his earlobes. He also sported rings in his left eyebrow and right nostril. He'd been perpetually stoned in all of the photos, his bloodshot eyes in desperate need of Visine.

In person, he looked older, more mature. Escaping our hometown had clearly been good for him. He'd cleaned up while the rest of us hit rock bottom. He'd cropped his hair close to his head, leaving little more than black fuzz along his scalp. It revealed cheekbones that were sculpted, not hollowed out by drugs like my brother's. His chocolate eyes were remarkably clear, unlined, no purplish pillows beneath them like mine. He'd taken out all of his piercings, but when he rolled up his shirtsleeves tattoos of brightly colored swallows emerged.

Wes's old friends nodded at him, but kept their distance; the only person he spoke to was Cass. He put a strong arm around her and led her to the front of the church. The death of her cousin following so quickly on the heels of losing her boyfriend had made Cass look smaller, ashen. She only smiled when Wes mentioned that he'd talked their father into letting her spend the summer with him in California as long as she came home to finish out her senior year.

Watching them together made me wish I had an older brother. Cass leaned on Wes, letting him be her caretaker for once, while I tried my damnedest to care for Liam. I held his hand as we followed them to our seats. Big tears dripped from Liam's sleepless eyes and he kept sucking back snot or wiping it on his sleeve like a little kid. I hugged him against me through the service.

I went to the bathroom before we left church. But I didn't set up a line like I had after Quentin's memorial. I opened the Altoids box I had in my purse and flushed the heroin down the toilet.

As I watched it go, I addressed Maya. "I'm quitting. Like you asked me to last week. I'm really sorry I yelled at you like that. And slapped you. And made fun of your hair. I'm sorry . . ." I sobbed, squeezing my eyes shut and turning around, hoping that when I opened them, she'd be standing in front of me.

Of course she wasn't.

Liam clung to me at the grave site, but I felt really alone. My best friend was being put into the ground next to her mother. A few miles away, Quentin lay in another box. Cass was leaving for the summer. Adrian might never come back. I looked for him, hoping he'd show, but he didn't. A lot of other people did, though, because unlike with Quentin's funeral, the information was public. Harlan held hands with Shelly, who'd just gotten out of rehab. Harlan had dyed his hair black when he heard about Maya's suicide and cried inconsolably for an hour. Shelly wore a long, black sundress that Maya would have liked and had her thick, blond curls tamed into a braid down her back. She looked very sober; I hoped she'd be a good influence on Harlan and my brother before she left for boarding school. Craig, Mary, and Jessica stood at the back. I didn't have the energy to be angry at the two girls for coming when they'd been so hateful toward Maya; besides, they both wore expressions of remorse. If Christian had shown up, I would have freaked, but fortunately he stayed away.

Stacey and Jason didn't go because they didn't know Maya well enough, but after I returned home with Liam, Stacey called a few times. As evening approached and my craving for heroin increased, I finally picked up the phone because I wanted something to do to distract myself. Stacey sounded like she needed me and when she invited me to her mom's house instead of Jason's, I worried briefly that she'd broken up with him, and I really couldn't deal with consoling her over something as seemingly unimportant as that. But I borrowed my mom's car and drove into Berwyn.

Beth was at work, so we sat in the living room on the futon that doubled as Beth's bed and fired up a bowl, which I was grateful for, hoping the pot would temper my body's desire for heroin. I'd already started to get mild chills and shakes.

As Stacey exhaled, she said, "I guess you haven't read that ballad thingy I wrote in your notebook or you'd be lecturing me."

I wrinkled my brow, confused. "No, I haven't looked at it since Quentin . . ."

"I figured." She sighed heavily, relinquished the bowl to me, and stretched out on the mattress, staring up at the ceiling. Her hands slid over her stomach. "I'm pregnant, Karalina." She used my old nickname with a wry smile and turned her head to the side to look at me. "You're gonna be an aunt."

I coughed up pot smoke. "Wow." I took another hit and held it in for a moment before placing the pipe in an ashtray on a nearby table, out of her reach. "You're right, you can't have this."

She sighed again, pouting like a child. "I know. I have to quit today. This was the deadline. Jason and I said we would decide by tonight if we're keeping it or not. Actually, Jason said I should decide and he would support me either way. He's a good guy, Karalina." Her gaze drilled into the ceiling. "And he'll make a good dad. Even if I make a shitty mom."

I tried to keep emotion out of my voice—not hard because I didn't know what emotion to have. "So you're keeping it. The baby, I mean."

"Yeah." Stacey shrugged, dragging her shoulders up and down against the futon. "My mom kept me. I'd feel bad otherwise. But I'm gonna do it right. I'm gonna move in with him and get married. The whole"—she popped her lips open into an O and widened her eyes—"shebang."

I snuck a glance at her belly, which still looked flat beneath her T-shirt. "Is that what you want or do you want me to talk you out of it?"

She laughed. "No, that's what I'm doing. But I needed to tell my best friend before I told Jason and I wanted to smoke one last bowl with you for old time's sake." Stacey maneuvered into a cross-legged position and met my eyes, fat tears streaming down her cheeks as she blubbered. "I'm sorry I was a shitty blood sister and a shitty friend and I ditched you for boys, but now I'm pregnant and I'm sure that's not a surprise. Our teacher looked at me when she mentioned teen pregnancy during the sex lecture in sixth grade."

"Oh, Stace." I snorted. "She looked at you because you were passing me a note." I pulled her into my arms and let her cry. My face also grew damp as I told her, "And you don't have to apologize for being a shitty friend. I've been one, too. I could have talked to you and . . ." I choked back a sob as I mentally added, *I could have talked to Maya.*

Our cryfest lasted only a few minutes. Then Stacey sniffed back snot and asked me to relight the bowl. "One last time," she said.

Before we parted ways at her front door—she was heading to Jason's and I was heading home—she made me promise to read her ballad immediately. I dropped my mom's car off at home, grabbed my backpack, and walked the mile to Scoville Park.

I trekked up to the top of the hill and picked out a spot on the grass slightly east of the soldier statue, positioning myself beneath the yellow glow of a lamp so I could read easily. Stacey's entry should have been the last one, but the last handwritten pages were filled with Maya's careful script.

The Ballad of a Redhead: Maya Danner

> "If you live through this with me
> I swear that I will die for you."
>
> —*Hole*

June 1995

WORSE THINGS HAPPEN AT SEA. THAT'S WHAT my grandma always said when we had rotten luck. One of her many "wisdoms," her fancy name for her clichés. She reassured my mother with those words when the Thanksgiving turkey came out of the oven still frozen in the middle. She said it to my father on the side of the road when the tire of our rental car blew out on vacation in Arizona. She consoled me with that phrase freshman year when my best friend, Lori, told me she was never speaking to me again. Grandma stopped reciting that particular wisdom after my mother's suicide 'cause even though it happened on dry land, it seemed like nothing could be worse. But as it turned out, Grandma was right: the worst things do happen at sea, or near it at least.

That was one of the thoughts that ran through my head when Christian found me crying over my mother in that bathroom in Florida, picked me up, slapped me across the face, and pinned me to the wall to scream at me. It all happened so fast. Probably less than a minute went by before Liam busted in and pulled Christian off of me. Amazing how many thoughts I had in that brief moment. Now I know what they mean by the phrase "watching your life flash before your eyes."

In the same instant that I thought about Grandma's old saying, I also saw Kara standing in the bathroom stall at Denny's with the front of her shirt yanked down to reveal blue and yellow splotches on her chest. I heard her implore, "Christian *really hurt* me." But before I could relive the way I dismissed her claim—flash!—I was reliving how my friendship with Lori fell apart.

It was all because of Adam Irle, a junior that Lori had a huge crush on. He threw a party a month before prom and Lori insisted that we go and I talk to Adam to find out if he liked her. She thought it would be the best thing in the world to go to prom her freshman year. I didn't care about that kind of stuff. I was still a tomboy even though my body had betrayed me a year earlier and gotten all girly and curvy and people started calling me pretty instead of funny.

I was happy to help Lori out, but wasn't able to track down Adam that night until I was pretty wasted, and I guess when I asked him to go someplace quiet to talk, he thought I was coming on to him. He led me up to his bedroom and before I knew what was happening he had me pinned to his bed with his tongue down my throat and his hand down my pants. I hate to think what would have happened if Lori hadn't barged in, but part of me wishes she hadn't.

She dragged me outside and stood by disgusted as I puked in the oleander. I collapsed in the damp grass and tried to explain, "I didn't want that! Couldn't you tell by the way he was holding me down?"

Lori loomed over me, hands on her hips, and said, "Yeah, right! Like Adam would just attack you. He's a great guy. You're a traitor and a whore and I'll never forgive you for this!" Then she stormed out of my life forever.

I never bothered trying to explain what happened with Adam to anyone else. If Lori didn't believe me, it didn't matter. And Lori told everyone her version of the story. I went from being relatively popular to school tramp in a matter of days. But I didn't care about my reputation. I mourned the five years of friendship that Lori'd thrown away because it was easier to think I was a slut than that a guy she liked was scum.

So what's my excuse for doing almost exactly the same thing to Kara? I don't have a much better one than Lori did: I was in love with Christian even though I didn't fully realize it until I kissed him on New Year's Day.

Yeah, that's right. I'm the pot who called the kettle black, as my grandmother would say. I kissed Christian after lecturing Kara about pining for her ex. I betrayed her and I also betrayed her brother.

Liam, the beautiful boy I should have loved if I'd known what was good for me. Liam, as loyal as his Irish eyes were green. I can't even count the nights that he listened to me while we wandered the town, smoking cigarettes and shivering against the cold, midwestern winter wind. On New Year's Eve, I'd aired my concerns about Kara and Christian. After seeing the way Kara had reacted to Adrian at Ambrosia's on Christmas Day, I'd become convinced she was going to break Christian's heart. I worried about them so much that it made me physically ill and I left Liam to talk to his sister. He came over to check on me later and told me that he thought Kara would probably break up with Christian that very night.

So I went to see Christian first thing the next day. He was one of my best friends and I knew how heartbroken he was going to be.

Christian answered the door in his pajamas even though it was noon. He rubbed bleary, hungover eyes and I apologized, remembering that he'd probably been at Shelly's until dawn, drowning his sorrows if Kara dumped him.

Christian grabbed a couple Cokes for us and we went down to the basement. "What brings you by?" he asked as we settled on the couch.

"Actually, I wanted to talk about you and Kara. Did something happen between you guys last night?" I bit my lip nervously, not wanting to upset him.
He'd been acting so casual, maybe nothing had occurred.

Suddenly Christian burst into tears. "I caught her kissing Adrian at midnight,"
he sobbed. "We had this big fight in Shelly's bathroom, but by the end of the
night, we were dancing together. I love her so much, I can't let her go."

"Whoa, slow down." I scooted closer to him and took his hand. "Tell me
everything."

Christian sniffed. "Well, what did Kara tell you?"

"Nothing, but I've been worried that something might happen with
Adrian."

"Oh, okay." He leaned against me, putting his head on my shoulder. I
stroked his messy red hair as he told me the whole story—his version—
about Kara being wasted and falling all over the place, about the hickeys on
her chest.

By the time he finished, he was stretched out across my lap, using my
knees as a pillow. He started talking about all the things he'd done for Kara.
"She used to cut herself. Did you know that?"

I nodded.

"I've been helping her to stop, encouraging her to call one of us when
she's upset. Part of the reason I gave her my mother's ring was because I
was so proud that she hadn't cut in a month. I really wanted to help her get
healthy. But Adrian . . . I'm afraid he's getting her into heroin. I'm afraid she's
really going to self-destruct. I just want to take care of her and protect her. I
love her so much."

Christian's lip quivered and tears trickled down his cheeks, soaking the
ends of his hair. Kara was so lucky to have someone so devoted to her. I thought
about the way he'd defended her honor—defended both of us, really—when
Mary called us sluts in the park. I remembered how he'd anguished over
which chain to buy for the ring when we'd gone Christmas shopping together.
But his real gift to Kara had been the way he'd carefully watched over her

and encouraged her to heal. And she didn't appreciate it. She didn't want to heal; she wanted the false escape that Adrian provided. But I wanted to heal. I wanted to turn back time and tell Christian about my mother so he'd take care of me. I wanted . . .

I bent down, brushing my lips against Christian's.

He immediately rolled off of me, landing on the floor in front of the couch. He scrambled to his feet, stuttering, "I . . . I can't. I love Kara."

My hand flew to my mouth I wanted to cry and vomit like I had the night Lori found me with Adam Irle. I managed to stammer, "I didn't mean to . . ."

Christian walked me to the door and gave me one of those just-friends-pat-on-the-back hugs. "I won't say anything," he assured me. "Liam, Kara . . . I wouldn't want to hurt them."

So I trudged home in the gray, January cold, thinking Christian loved Kara. He would never hurt her. *I* would be more likely to do that.

And that's all I could think about when Kara showed me those bruises at Denny's. Kind, gentle Christian, he would never do that. It must have been a misunderstanding.

It wasn't until Christian had me pinned to the tile wall in the men's room in Florida that I realized it was all an act. Christian had burst into tears on New Year's Day because he thought he'd been caught, that I'd come to confront him about hurting Kara. When he realized I didn't know, he took advantage and put on a performance so powerful that I left thinking I'd taken advantage of him.

After the police brought us back from Florida, I tried to tell myself that it was over and Christian had lost. I mean, he'd lost all his friends, but then again, so had I. I'd watched Liam's heart break when I admitted that I'd loved Christian. I knew Kara would never truly forgive me and I didn't deserve to be forgiven. I was lucky she hadn't shunned me the way Lori did.

Worst of all, Christian found a way to torment me that no one knew about.

He stayed away from me—from all of us—in public, probably because he was afraid of Liam, but he used his little groupie girls to hurt me in the worst possible way. Two of them flounced past me when I was sitting alone in the cafeteria. One said loudly to the other, "That's the crazy redhead Christian dated last summer. Her mom killed herself, that's why she's totally nuts."

Rumors. The kind I'd tried to avoid by not telling anyone but Kara about my mother's death when I moved to Oak Park because I hadn't wanted to feel like I did during my last two months of high school in Florida. After my mom died, no one talked to me, like my bad luck was catching. Instead, the whole school scrutinized me from afar, waiting for me to snap like Mom had. Of course, Christian only had the ears of ten little freshman girls, but it was enough. I passed them in the hallways and watched them stare at me, giggle, and whisper. From time to time, I'd see Christian, too. If I was with other people, he'd ignore me, but if I was alone, he'd flash a smug sneer.

I never told anyone the details of my mom's death, not Kara, not even Cassie or Wes. If I talked about it, I'd visualize it and live that day all over again. But I guess I might as well write it all down now because thanks to Christian, it's been all I can think about for the past four months.

—=≡{ }≡=—

My mother killed herself the way most women attempt it, with pills, a cocktail of Prozac, Xanax, trazodone, and a bunch of similar drugs. She succeeded where most women fail 'cause she'd been planning it for years. She collected prescriptions, going to her shrink, saying she wasn't feeling so happy, was anxious, couldn't sleep, could she try this pill she'd heard about? She'd go back a couple months later, saying nope, that's not working, and her doctor would suggest something else. After she died we discovered that she'd squirreled away the leftover pills until she had a cornucopia of them. A pharmacopoeia.

And one night in October, she went to the bathroom and swallowed nearly a hundred of them. Then she crawled into bed beside my father like nothing was amiss. She even set her alarm, radio tuned to NPR, set to go off at 6:30 a.m.—fifteen minutes before my dad got up and thirty minutes before I did, so she could have coffee ready for him and breakfast for me. When it sounded, she always turned that alarm off lickety-split, so Dad didn't wake, but not *that* morning.

That morning I went into the kitchen and no one was there, so I ran to my parents' bedroom with an awful, sick, I'm-too-late feeling. I started crying before I even opened the door because I heard both of their clocks blaring, the steady fire-drill buzz of Dad's overpowering the soothing radio voices of Mom's. I found Dad hugging Mom to his chest. Her cold, dead body faced away from his 'cause she'd turned her back on him as she settled down to die. Turned her back on both of us.

That morning when Grandma came over, it was the first time I'd seen her without makeup. She always said it was the duty of a well-mannered woman to assure that no one ever saw her without her face. My grandmother had style, and not blue-haired old-lady style either. She covered the gray with her natural honey blond color and kept her short hair fashionably cut. She didn't wear a ton of makeup, but when she showed up without the usual mascara and pink hue to her cheeks, it was disconcerting. And even worse, when she tried to convince Dad to unclamp his arms from my dead mother and call the coroner, she seemed to have forgotten all of her wisdoms. She didn't have consoling words for either of us. Like everyone else, "I'm sorry" was all she could say.

Dad blamed himself. "She never was happy in Florida and I kept her here," he kept repeating in the days after she died. My parents met while attending school in Chicago, my mother's hometown, but when they married, Dad asked Mom to move just north of Fort Lauderdale where his mother lived.

And yes, my mom missed her sister, and for some reason, Chicago winters, but the truth of the matter is that my mother was never happy, period. She had sad genes. Her mother had 'em, her sister has 'em, and I've got 'em, too. They're buried deep down inside, waiting for the opportunity to strike. For my mother that time came when she had me. That was about a year after the move to Florida, which may be why my dad gets mixed up about when her sadness hit. Or else it's just easier to blame Florida than me.

My mom sunk into a depression right after I was born. She medicated heavily, but was always distant. That's why my grandmother was more of a mother to me than my mom. She taught me everything, how to use a sling-shot, how to walk in high heels, and most important, how to draw. And when Dad decided we were moving to Chicago after my mother's funeral, well, leaving Grandma was like facing death all over again.

Since my dad was convinced that my mother hated Florida, he'd had her buried at her family's plot in Chicago. On the plane, he told me he'd put in for a transfer to his company's Chicago office.

The day after we buried my mother, I dyed my hair red for the first time. Black would have been more mournful, but I needed red. You see, I decided then that if I was gonna kill myself, I'd do it the hard way, by slitting my veins open, and I'd do it in the bathtub 'cause I hear the warm water eases the pain a little bit. So I bought that red dye and when I got in the shower to rinse it out of my hair and it streamed down my body, I pretended it was blood. I even plugged the drain, let the tub fill, and sat with my eyes closed in the fake bloody water for an hour.

I returned to school the next day, where everyone gawked at me worse than they had the previous spring when Lori made me out to be the town whore. I hoped desperately that since something so awful had happened, Lori would finally let go of her grudge and be the friend I needed. But when I saw her in the hall, she turned to her new best friend and said, "Is Maya a freak or what? Her mom kills herself and she dyes her hair red? Instead of grieving, she's looking for attention."

I wasn't, but now I'm tired of the attention the red hair gets me. Those gossipy freshman girls call me "that redhead." My hair allows Christian to pick me out in a crowd. And I've lost so much in the past two years: Lori, Mom, Grandma, Kara, Liam. So today I dyed my hair black in an attempt to grieve properly for all of it. But it didn't work. Without my fake blood in the shower, I need the real thing.

I thought that maybe writing all of this down would make me feel better. Grandma always told me, "Secrets lead to sickness." She said they call it coming clean because secrets and lies make you dirty inside. I hoarded secrets like my mother hoarded pills and I ended up with just as deadly of a collection as she. I imagine that before she swallowed all those pills, she spread them out on the countertop and admired them. Maybe she meant to sweep them into the toilet and flush them away, but she didn't.

And neither can I.

Please don't feel guilty, Daddy, Grandma, Cass, Wes, Liam . . . especially not Kara. Don't blame yourself. Blame him. We've both been lost at sea since Christian happened to us. Please, Kara, swim to shore.

⸺⸢⸥⸺

When I looked up from the page, I realized I'd smeared the ink with my tears. I sobbed as I read, overcome with guilt, thinking if only I had opened the notebook as soon as she'd given it to me, I could have stopped her. But the last part made it clear that she'd decided to die when she'd written her ballad and her last sentence made me furious. How dare she ask me to keep swimming after she let herself drown?

I thrust the notebook into my backpack and started rifling through all of its compartments because I desperately needed a line. I hoped I'd forgotten a little baggie of heroin in there at some point.

I was so busy rummaging that I didn't hear the click of skateboard wheels coming down the sidewalk. I jumped when a familiar voice taunted, "Kara . . ."

Christian sneered at me in that smug way that Maya had written about, his hazel eyes blistering with scorn. He stepped on the end of his skateboard, snapping it into his open palm, and sauntered across the grass in his self-assured, snotty punk gait. He'd chopped off his hair—or probably had one of his little groupies do it for him—and all the red was gone. It was bleached to an obnoxious yellow and poorly spiked.

"You think you're so fuckin' tough, don't you?" I spat through my tears, whipping my backpack to the ground and getting to my feet, glaring at him. "So you've found me alone and you're gonna intimidate me, huh? Like you did to Maya?"

I flung myself at Christian, fists raised, railing, "You don't scare me. You're the weakest person I've ever met!"

Laughing, he deflected me with one arm like I was a beach ball. I probably would have swung at him again anyway, but I really lost it when I noticed he was wearing Maya's Ramones T-shirt. He'd always coveted it, so she'd lent it to him for a month as his Christmas present. Apparently he'd never returned it.

"You asshole!" I screamed. "You drove her to her death. You don't deserve anything of hers!"

I charged again, punching the air, swiping for his neck with my fingernails, and bringing one knee up, aiming for the prize. I was prepared to bite, claw, and crush his balls to get Maya's shirt.

But he lifted his skateboard like a shield and shoved me with it before I connected with skin, bone, or testicles. I landed on the grass so hard it knocked the wind out of me. As I gasped for breath, he fell on me with his full weight. I kicked. I uselessly pounded on his back. I rocked side to side, trying to dislodge him.

Then, suddenly, I was free. Christian was rolling down the hill with another boy, a blur of brown hair and tattooed fore-arms that I recognized as Adrian's. They stopped at the bottom with Adrian landing on top. Adrian's butterfly knife glinted in the light and slashed across Christian's cheek. Christian howled in pain, shoving Adrian with the same force he'd used on me, but Adrian only shifted to the side slightly. Christian struggled out from under him, holding his bloody cheek with both hands, and took off running.

I dropped my head and buried it in the grass. Within seconds, Adrian was at my side, pulling me into his lap, asking, "Did he hurt you? What can I do? Do you need to go to the hospital? Should I call someone?"

When I finally found my voice, I said, "Just get me high."

Never one to object to that proposal, Adrian helped me to my feet and down the hill toward the stage at the front of the park, which we'd smoked pot beneath the previous summer. I crawled under first. He pushed my backpack in after me and followed, his own backpack strapped to his back like a turtle shell.

Adrian withdrew his cigar box from his bag and asked, "You have anything to cut lines on?" I got out our old notebook and he tapped brown powder onto the cover without even looking at it. He cut two lines and handed me a straw. "They're both yours."

I snorted one right after the other and sat up slowly, eyes closed, savoring the numbness as it spread through my sinus cavities into my brain. When my eyelids fluttered open, I expected to see Adrian bent over the notebook, chopping more lines, but instead he had his belt off, wrapped around his left arm.

He concocted a mixture of powder with bottled water and cooked it in a bent, black spoon over the flame of his lighter. I told myself it smelled like it looked, molasses, or like poppy flowers on fire, but actually it stunk. Still, I watched him suck it up into the needle and said, "I want some."

"You've had some," Adrian replied through the belt clenched in his teeth.

"I want that."

"You can't have it." He flicked the vein that bulged above the first *A* in the "Away" tattoo.

"Christian wasn't the worst thing that happened to me today. I buried my best friend this morning." The words fell from my mouth tonelessly. I kept my eyes on that needle.

Adrian sighed, set the needle on the notebook next to the spoon, and got out another needle that was still in its plastic wrapper. He slid the belt off and handed it to me. "Find the arm with the bigger vein. Put this around it."

Suddenly, I was scared like when I got to the front of the line for a roller coaster. But I was determined to ride the ride. I needed a rush that would obliterate my memory of everything that had happened that day. "Are you going to inject me?"

Adrian shot some of the liquid from the first needle back into the spoon and filled the new needle. One needle was a quarter full, the other three-fourths. He held on to the needle with the smaller amount. "Yes."

I slid the belt around my right arm and tugged it tight. He tapped at the vein. I looked away until I felt the prick. I started to look back, but the shot hit me like a school bus, like snorting five lines at once. "Shit," I said, and immediately nodded off.

Adrian shook me awake, indicating I should follow him out from under the stage. We crawled halfway up the hill and settled in the grass with our heads resting on our backpacks. We had brief conversations, drifting in and out.

"Where have you been?" I asked him at one point.

"All over. Last night I slept on Quentin's grave." Adrian played with his own curls. "I loved him. He was my best friend."

I nodded off, woke up again, and squeezed Adrian's hand. When he didn't respond, I leaned over and kissed his dry lips. He blinked and I told him, "I missed you."

"I missed you, too." He seemed to drift off, but then he said, "Kara, I love you. I have for a year now."

I'd been waiting so long for those words I should have sprung up and done cartwheels across the park. My heart should have done cartwheels, at least, but I was so numb, I couldn't even feel my own joy. All I could do was snuggle into the crook of Adrian's arm and say, "I love you, too."

When I came to again, the park was drenched in sickly gray light. I blinked and took in my surroundings. Was it dawn? Shouldn't dawn make things look new and bright? Why was everything monochromatic? The grass, Adrian's hair, his skin—it all looked old and withered. Dying.

Shit.

Adrian's face seemed as white as Quentin's had been the night he died. I softly slapped Adrian's pasty cheeks, chanting, "Wake up, wake up, wake up!"

He didn't respond. My own shouts sounded far away, like hearing Cass scream at Quentin to wake up through the wall while I made the 911 call. No, I couldn't handle this. I couldn't lose Adrian and Maya in the same day.

Bile rose in my throat. I crawled a couple feet from Adrian to avoid puking on him. *We met when he was puking. This is sort of poetic,* I thought as I gagged. *Wait. Heroin doesn't make me throw up. I've taken too much. I'm overdosing.*

Panic. My skin flashed hot, then went clammy.

"Adrian, help!" I cried out. "Help, I think I'm dying."

He didn't hear me. Probably already dead.

And my vision was blurring, like looking out the window of the "L" as it hurtled at light speed into a subway tunnel. I buried my face in the brittle grass, narrowly missing my own vomit.

Please, Kara, swim to shore.

I thought I heard Maya actually speak those words and when I glanced up, I thought I saw her, sitting cross-legged on top of the metal stage. If I could get there. If I could reach her.

Swim, crawl, whatever it takes, I told myself. *Or you won't meet Stacey's baby. And Liam won't have anyone to hold on to at your funeral.*

But I only managed to drag myself about six feet before my limbs stopped working. I rolled onto my back, murmuring, "Liam, I'm sorry."

I felt myself sinking, sinking, sinking.

My heart slowed.

The world went black.

I opened my eyes again because I thought I heard Cass's voice. All the sounds were muffled, like listening to a TV three rooms away. The distant noise of passing cars was the first thing to become clear. People murmured but their words were indiscernible. I almost drifted off again, lulled by the traffic. Then Cass shouted at full volume.

"Fuck you, Kara, not you, too!"

I saw her tears. I saw the ambulance lights flashing. I saw my mother over Cass's shoulder. I wanted to tell them that I was okay, but Adrian's name slipped out.

Cass got pissed, started cursing him, and told me, "He left you here to die and saved his own ass. Just like with Quentin!"

"But I'm not dead. I'm not dead," I repeated, chuckling to myself.

I couldn't help laughing. My life was so fucked, I couldn't even just OD and die. I was going to survive and have to deal with all the losses and all the messes I'd made.

Laughing was the only thing I could do. I closed my eyes again and laughed. I laughed and laughed despite my aching, dry throat. I laughed as my mother and Cass cried over me. I laughed as the paramedics took me away.

GUITAR SOLO

AUGUST 1995

(SUMMER BEFORE SENIOR YEAR)

"If I could start again a million miles away
I would keep myself, I would find a way."
—*Nine Inch Nails*

1.

"**L**IAM, PLEASE LET ME IN," I begged, my damp cheek pressed to his bedroom door.

I'd been standing there for fifteen minutes. Dad emerged from my room, a crate of CDs in hand. He set it down and banged his fist against Liam's door.

"Let your sister in," Dad demanded in a booming voice. "We're leaving in five minutes and I don't want to waste time taking your door off the hinges."

"Thanks, Daddy," I whispered as he picked up the crate again and I heard Liam's lock unlatch.

"Sure, Kara," Dad replied. "I think this is the last of it, but double-check, okay?"

I nodded dutifully before opening Liam's door. My brother smoked on the windowsill, staring out at Dad's Corolla and the small U-Haul trailer attached to it containing my things.

"Thanks, Daddy," Liam mimicked as I approached.

"Liam, please—"

He cut me off with a cold glare. "Whatever. Here's your note-book. I assume that's why you're here."

The "Stories of Suburbia" notebook thudded against my chest and I hugged it to me before it could drop to the messy floor. When Liam had arrived at the hospital after my overdose,

I grabbed his hand and yanked him close, quietly instructing, "The notebook in my backpack. Get it and make sure no one reads it." Ensuring that no one violated my friends' ballads mattered more to me than anything in the world.

"Thanks for holding on to this for me." I stood a couple feet away from Liam, hesitant to get any closer.

"I shouldn't have," he snapped, "seeing as you're betraying me and Mom by moving to Wisconsin with that asshole."

"Mom wants me to go. She knows if I stay here I'll screw up again. And Dad's not an asshole. He's been coming in for therapy sessions with me twice a week and he's only going to be working part-time, so he can spend more time with me. If you come up Labor Day weekend, the three of us can go camping—"

"Shut up! You're betraying me!" Liam jabbed his cigarette at his bedroom wall where, beside his Johnny Cash poster and some other graffiti about not having heroes, he'd written "BE-TRAYER" in big, black capital letters, an arrow pointing toward my room. "You said you were just going to play the game in rehab, remember?"

That was what I'd vowed to do when my parents first checked me in to a private psych hospital to be treated for heroin addiction and self-injury. But on day nineteen of my sixty days, I'd realized that I actually had to stay sober. Even though my therapist, Dr. Larson, had urged me to tell my brother what I'd learned that day, I'd kept it to myself, convinced Liam would scoff at my epiphany. Now I had a choice: spill or leave with Liam hating me.

Nervously fingering the hem of my black baby-doll dress, I took two tentative steps toward the window. "Liam, there was this girl named Annie that I had group therapy with—"

"Dude, I don't want to hear it!" Liam clapped his hands over his ears. "I don't want to hear a single thing you have to say unless it's 'I'm not moving away.'"

Dropping my notebook, I wrenched Liam's hands off his ears and held them firmly between mine. "Annie. I thought she was the craziest one in the bunch because the rest of us were in there for drugs or drinking, but we were normal. Annie had some kind of breakdown. She didn't talk. She'd shaved her head and she had big bandages on her arms, 'cause she tried to slit her wrists or whatever."

Liam squirmed in my grip, freeing one hand, but he just used it to take his cigarette from his mouth. "Like Maya," he said softly.

"Like Maya," I repeated, kneeling in front of him, continuing to cling to his other hand. "But I didn't even think about that at first. I was minding my own business, just counting down the days till I got out. Then there was this group therapy session where Dr. Larson made me share. Remember how Mom brought me that newspaper clipping about Adrian?"

"Yeah."

"I had to pass that around. I was like, 'My boyfriend got arrested for breaking into a vet's office and stealing ketamine to sell at raves. He's doing nine months in County. My mom wanted me to see what path I was on.'" I rolled my eyes, demonstrating the attitude I'd had about sharing. "Some girl across the circle said, 'That's not the path *you* were on. You checked in here after a bad overdose, right? You keep using and you're gonna *die*.'"

"Whatever," Liam interrupted, fluttering his long lashes. "You never OD'd before you shot up."

"And that's exactly what I said. But then Annie spoke up for the first time."

I remembered the way her vacant eyes suddenly focused. They'd met mine as she whispered hoarsely, "You can't use heroin in moderation."

That was when I really studied her. The wispy red hair just beginning to grow back, the bandaged arms. My stomach turned when I realized, *That's how Maya's arms would have looked if she survived.*

I felt sicker still when Annie continued, "My older sister was like you. She OD'd and died the day after she left rehab. Two weeks later, I did this." Annie extended her arms, palms up, forcing me to stare at the white gauze taped around them, wrist to elbow.

While Dr. Larson encouraged Annie to share more, I recalled one of the last thoughts I'd had before passing out at Scoville Park: *Liam won't have anyone to hold on to at your funeral.*

"So what the hell did she say?" Liam demanded impatiently, releasing my hand and tapping his fingers against the windowsill.

"That her older sister OD'd on heroin and died." Feeling the tickle of tears in my nose, I bit my lip. "Annie tried to kill herself after her sister's funeral. I thought of you . . . I realized I have to stay sober for you, Liam."

"Wow. Thanks, Kara." Liam nodded, sounding sincere, but when he lifted his green eyes to meet mine they were filled with rage. "But that doesn't explain why the fuck you're leaving. If it's so important to be there for me, why are you abandoning me?"

"Because I have to stay sober."

Liam leapt off the windowsill, shoving me out of his way. He bounced up and down like an out-of-control marionette in the center of his room. "So go to fucking meetings! Isn't that what addicts like you do?"

Slowly rising to my feet, I studied him: his matted blue hair that hung to the bottom of his earlobes, the raccoon circles under his eyes, the huge jeans that hung off his wiry frame, and the twig-thin arms that poked out of his T-shirt. Instead of band shirts, he'd taken to wearing plain white tees and writing slogans on them in Sharpie. "Rehab Is for Quitters" was scrawled across his chest. "You're a drug addict, too, Liam," I said, picking up the "Stories of Suburbia" notebook again.

He rolled his eyes at me and ashed his cigarette on the carpet. "Whatever. I never OD'd. I never shot drugs—"

I clapped the notebook against my thigh, causing the flimsy material of my dress to billow. "You were going to bring me drugs in rehab!"

Liam had been allowed to see me alone for the first time on day forty. He played the sullen-teenager role so well that no one but me noticed he was using. I recognized the way he fidgeted in his seat. Everyone else was distracted by his sighs and eye rolls.

Without parents and a therapist present, Liam didn't work very hard to conceal his strung-out appearance. His shirt that day inexplicably read "Tiger" and his pants drooped farther off his skinny hips than usual, revealing way more of his plaid boxers than I wanted to see. He tugged the dirty jeans up, apologizing, "Sorry, they took my belt and my wallet chain, too. You're, like, on serious lockdown here. They practically body-cavity-searched me, but . . ." He leaned in and whispered, "Next time I'll bring you something, put it in plastic, and keep it under my tongue. Good plan?"

Closing my eyes to the memory, I sighed. "The day you offered to do that was the day I knew I had to move. Before that, whenever Mom, Dad, or Dr. Larson brought up going to Wisconsin, I told them that my friends I got high with were either in jail or dead, so I'd be fine staying in Oak Park."

"Oh, so now it's my fault that you're leaving?" Liam kicked a sneaker across the room. "Why didn't you just tell me that you didn't want drugs? I'll keep that shit away from you if that's what you want."

"Liam, I can't stay sober here and I can't be a good sister to you if I'm not sober." I shook my head sadly. "Look, I've talked to Cass about this. She was mad when Wes bailed at first, but when she got to California this summer and saw how good he was doing, she knew he did the right thing. She wishes I didn't have to move to Wisconsin, but she understands. And Stacey understands. Please, can't you try to understand?"

"No." Liam crossed his arms over his chest. "You've ditched me too many times."

"Okay," I stammered. "But can I at least have a hug?"

"You can have a hug when you're moving back home."

Tears dripped out of my eyes. "Fine," I murmured, and started to walk away. But then I remembered that he was a drug addict. Quentin had OD'd and died. I'd OD'd and almost died. And then there was Maya, whose death hadn't been drug related, but the last time we'd spoken, we'd fought and I couldn't worry about that happening again.

I spun around and enveloped Liam in an embrace before he knew what was happening. "Call me when you want help," I cried into his dirty hair.

He shoved me away. "Fuck you."

I dried my tears on the back of my hand before exiting Liam's room, then headed for the bathroom. I sat on the closed toilet and straightened the top of the spiral binding on the "Stories of Suburbia" notebook. Grazing my fingertip with it, I thought, *Not very sharp, but it'll have to do.*

Since I was wearing short sleeves and would probably be forced to do so from now on even in deepest winter, I flipped up my skirt, scratching my inner thigh with the metal wire until finally a teeny drop of blood. A wave of relief.

But shame followed immediately on its heels. "Fuck," I murmured. I'd been out of treatment for all of an hour and I'd already messed up.

Mom rapped on the door. "Kara, you okay in there?"

"Yes, I'll be out in a sec!" I hurriedly pressed a piece of toilet paper to my minuscule cut, tossed it in the toilet, and flushed.

One tiny setback, I assured myself. Dr. Larson had said cutting would be harder to kick than heroin because I could use almost anything to hurt myself. Obviously that was true, but I hoped that when I got out of Oak Park things would be less stressful. I also hoped my next good-bye would go more smoothly. At least Maya couldn't yell at me.

Dad had agreed to stop at Maya's grave before we left town and Mom offered to pick up anything I wanted to bring to Maya. I'm sure she was thinking flowers, but she'd gotten Winston cigarettes and red Manic Panic dye like I requested.

I placed those items on either side of the flat stone marker and sat down in front of it. Dad remained in the car, pretending to read a book and give me privacy, though he kept glancing over to make sure I didn't burn myself with my own cigarette.

"Sorry I haven't been to visit you lately, but I've been in rehab. I'm sober. And I learned to draw while I was in there." I laughed at myself, crying at the same time because I wanted to hear Maya's chuckle.

When I opened my sketchbook, I wanted her to come up behind me and point at my horrible sketch of a hissing cat and say, "You call that drawing?"

"Okay, I'm not very good. I don't have your talent," I said as if we were having a real conversation. "But I did spend all summer working on a picture for you."

I flipped to the back of the book and carefully tore out a sketch of Maya and me sitting on the bottom of a slide at the kiddie playground at Scoville. I'd drawn it all in dark pencil except for Maya's bright red hair and my blue bangs. My arms were flung outward, mouth open as I grinned and said, "Tada!" Maya's arms were wrapped around my waist, her lips smooshed against my cheek in a melodramatic kiss. I'd drawn it from a photo Liam had snapped. There was a brief period of time after Christian had taken me to the playground with his sister that I wanted to seesaw and slide while Christian and Liam skated. Maya had eagerly indulged me.

"Why'd you stop playing there?" Dr. Larson had asked when I showed him my sketch.

"Winter came. By the time it was warm enough again, I was a junkie."

Dr. Larson recited the words I'd inscribed on the bottom of the drawing: "'I wanna be a kid again. I wanna play in the park.' What does that mean?"

"They're lyrics from a Slapstick song, a local ska band that Maya loved to see live."

"Dr. Larson was obsessed with getting me to write instead of draw," I told Maya. "So whenever I did write something, he really read into it. I guess those lyrics did mean something, though. This is the way I wish our friendship could have been, just playing in the park. Forever."

Part of me wanted to collapse on her grave sobbing, but I knew that meant my dad would come and carry me to the car. I needed to leave with dignity, so I kept talking through my tears.

"I'm going away, so I can stay sober. Liam didn't understand, but I know you would've. And Cass will be back soon to visit you. While she was in California, she sent me all this information on USC's film program. I still really want to go to school for screenwriting. Learning to write screenplays is the one good thing that came out of this past year."

Dr. Larson had furrowed his bushy white eyebrows when I told him that I wanted to make film school my long-term goal. "But you refuse to write. You always insist on drawing." Sketching how we felt or writing unsent letters were the options we were given in treatment when we wanted to cut or use. I always did crappy drawings.

I explained it to Maya like I had Dr. Larson, "I don't write about real life anymore. I'm writing a screenplay about vampires. If I can't escape with drugs, I'll escape into imaginary worlds."

Maya, of course, said nothing. Though I kind of wished she would. I traced the letters on the small, flat marker. Maya Estelle Danner. Estelle was her grandmother's name. "I wish they'd inscribed one of your grandmother's sayings," I told Maya. "I miss them. They were good advice. What would you tell me now?"

Words Dr. Larson had often repeated echoed in my brain as I flipped through my sketchbook to a drawing I'd made following Liam's visit: *"You'll need to write and talk about real life someday, Kara."*

Immediately after Liam left, I'd knocked on Dr. Larson's door. As I sat down in the chair across from his desk, I informed him, "My brother should not be allowed to see me. He'll bring me heroin."

"Is your brother a drug user?" Dr. Larson had asked point-blank.

I couldn't bring myself to betray Liam. Not when I was about to hurt him so badly by moving away. He'd need an escape. *Cass did acid to cope with Wes leaving and she's fine,* I'd reassured myself as I lied: "No, Liam just has friends who deal."

But when I returned to my room, I crudely sketched a tombstone that read, "Here Lies Liam. It was all his sister's fault."

Looking up from the drawing, my whole body shook as I started to cry silently. The tips of my fingers traced Maya's middle name again. "Your grandmother would say, 'Secrets lead to sickness.'" It was the last "wisdom" Maya had shared in her ballad.

I kissed Maya's headstone and walked back to my dad's car. "I'm ready to go," I said in a scratchy whisper.

Handing him my sketchbook, I added, "But you and Mom should plan on getting Liam some help."

EPILOGUE (PART 2)

THE BALLAD OF THE STORY COLLECTION

> "One day there'll be a place for us
> One day I know there'll be a place called home."
>
> —*PJ Harvey*

December 1999

I**T TOOK FOUR YEARS FOR MY BROTHER** to accept that he needed help. During that time, I graduated from high school in Wisconsin and moved to California to pursue a degree in film at USC. Whenever I heard from Liam, I ended up in my therapist's office for an emergency session.

Sometimes Liam called when he was wasted and wanted someone to talk to. Mostly he called when he was broke. I'd refuse to wire cash to Chicago and he'd scream at me, but I never gave in. Finally, on a hot day in July just a few months before his twentieth birthday, I got the kind of phone call I'd hoped for:

"Kara, I'm flying into LAX tomorrow and I want you to pick me up and check me into rehab." With all the cigarettes and god knows what else he smoked, Liam finally had that Johnny Cash baritone he'd desired at age four. He also had a laugh that sounded like a cough. "Preferably one with hot celebrities."

I took a deep breath. "Does Mom know about this?"

He chuckled again. "Who do you think bought the plane ticket? I spent my last dollar on a speedball that landed me in the ER. Though at least I did my last shot in some Gold Coast high-rise. Where were you? Facedown in the dirt at Scoville Park?"

"Yeah, you're way classier than me, Liam," I replied sarcastically, writing down his flight information.

He'd already done a twenty-eight-day program in Chicago, but he knew if he was really going to get his act together, he'd have to get away from home like I had. He wanted my eagle eye on him after he did one more in-patient stint and then moved into what he termed "a very glamorous halfway house."

"After that, I want to go back to school," he told me as he paced around my Echo Park apartment, marveling at my view of palm trees while he chain-smoked. "I don't know if they'd let a loser high school dropout into USC, but maybe if I do time at community college first. Don't laugh, but I think I want to be a social worker. You know, help kids so they don't have to hit rock bottom like we did."

I pointed at him with my mouth open like I was about to laugh, but then I grinned. "I think that's awesome, Liam. You always did give good advice. If only I'd taken some of it." I sat down on my bed, encouraging, "Seriously, you'll get there. I got to film school, after all."

He stopped pacing and looked at me. His eyes were a little lined for his age, but at least the circles were gone. And he'd shaved off the dreads, reverting to the strawberry blond buzz cut he'd had as a kid. "You haven't slipped, not once?"

"I've done a pretty good job staying away from drugs. I drink occasionally. It's the cutting I couldn't give up for the longest time, but I haven't done it in over a year." I displayed my arms. White lines stood out against my tan skin, but there were no fresh pink scars there or on the tops of my legs or on my belly, where I'd continued to cut secretly through my sophomore year of college. "I was working a high-stress job this spring and I almost started up again. The important thing is to know your triggers. Also, you love your cocaine and that shit is everywhere here," I warned Liam.

Worry puckered his forehead as he plopped down beside me. "I know," he nodded gravely. "And I've already messed up this rehab thing twice. But that was when Mom made me go and when it was court-ordered. I didn't want to do it. Now I really do."

"Then you will do it and I'll help." I hugged him tight, pleased he didn't feel nearly as bony as he had when he was using.

Liam squeezed me back and reached for the ashtray on my nightstand. He noticed the ragged red notebook that sat on a stack of school books on the bottom shelf of a nearby bookcase. "Shit, you still have this thing?" He ran his fingers across the ransom-note lettering of "Stories of Suburbia" on the cover. "Did you read it?"

"Aside from Maya's entry, no. I'm not allowed because I never wrote in it."

"You *never* wrote in it?" he asked, appalled. "Even I wrote in it. You should write in it now so you can read it."

I took it away from him and stuffed it back on the shelf. "No, I'm not ready. Shrinks have been encouraging me to write about my feelings and memories of Oak Park for years, but I just can't. I don't see the point of reliving it."

Five months later, when Stacey convinced me to come home for the first time, Liam insisted on putting the notebook in my carry-on. "Maybe you'll write in it or at least let it remind you to stay out of trouble."

I read the entire notebook cover to cover on the plane. No, I didn't write in it first. I broke that rule because I'd realized it had only hurt everyone. If these were true ballads, they were meant to be sung. Maybe if I had heard Liam's or Maya's sad, truthful songs earlier, I could have helped them. Maybe we could have helped each other.

Liam's ballad ultimately did help me when I ran into Adrian at Stacey's. I thought about Liam, finally sober and ready to start his first semester of college. It would destroy him if I put one toe down the old path. I couldn't let him down again like I had when we were younger.

My slightly drunk, zigzagging journey through Oak Park with Stacey made me crave the good old days, but I didn't let myself forget that in the aftermath of those "good times" I'd lost two of my friends forever and almost lost my brother.

When I saw Adrian in Stacey's living room looking like he'd stepped straight out of 1995 with the long, tawny curls, the worn-in leather jacket, and tattooed skin scented like the air off Lake Michigan, my old feelings for him came rushing back. But Adrian and I smoked cigarettes and talked until dawn on Stacey's back porch, and that was as far as it went.

I showed him the notebook, too, and told him I read it.

"And you didn't write in it first? You broke the rules. I should keep it." He gave me one of his sly grins. "I've still got all the pages with the newspaper articles in a box in storage somewhere."

"Those aren't our stories, though. I got the better pages. Besides, I'm gonna write in it. If it's not too cold on New Year's, I'm going to go to Scoville and start writing."

Adrian took the notebook, flipping carefully through it with his cigarette-free hand. "You're going to spend New Year's at Scoville?" he asked incredulously.

"Yeah."

"The dawn of the new millennium, when Y2K hits and all the power goes out and the world falls into chaos, you're going to be at Scoville Park."

I hugged myself, shivering in the cold, and smiled. "Seems fitting, doesn't it?"

"I guess." Adrian grinned flirtatiously, his eyebrows arching over dangerous, dancing brown eyes. "But wouldn't you rather go to a party with me?"

"No."

"Show at the Fireside? The city's shutting it down soon. You might not get another chance."

"They've been saying that since we were in high school."

Adrian's smile grew widest of all when he said, "A hot night in my bed?"

"I thought you didn't have a bed because you just got out of jail."

He whistled long and low. "You really know how to reject a guy, don't you?" He tugged the collar of his coat down and pushed his long hair off his neck, indicating the ink on the left side of it. "You always liked my tattoos. Check out the latest?"

"If you're trying to get me to come close enough so you can kiss me, it's not going to work. And you shouldn't have gotten tattooed there. You'll never get a job."

Adrian shrugged. "The dude who tattooed me when I was sixteen told me that if I got that tattoo I'd be in and out of jail for the rest of my life and so far he's been right. Let him be."

I frowned. "You're better than that."

"Whatever, Ms. Straight-and-Narrow with her lip ring. I bet you have tattoos."

"I can take the lip ring out and none of my tattoos are in visible places. And no, that is not an invitation for you to see them," I added quickly because he'd already opened his mouth.

"I really fucked up when I lost you." Adrian grew somber, fingering a page in the notebook written in Quentin's handwriting. "And when I lost Quentin." He tapped his neck tattoo, fighting tears. "That's what I got here. Q for Quentin. Got it on the fourth anniversary of the day he died."

I breathed through my teeth, suppressing a sob. "I have an M with angel wings around it on my back. For Maya. My first tattoo. Got it a year after she died."

Adrian shut the notebook and stared at the cover for a minute. When he looked up at me his eyes were damp. "I haven't been to visit Quentin in too long. You wanna go with me? We can go see Maya, too."

That was the hardest invitation to turn down. I shook my head back and forth several times before I got the words out. "I'm going to do that while I'm here, but I'm sorry, I can't do it with you."

I was crying freely now, and so was Adrian. "Okay, I get that. I'm glad you and your brother got out, you know."

"I wish you would," I choked.

"Maybe. I'll call you if I do."

I knew that, as hard as I hoped, unlike Liam, he would never call. I recognized my own old cravings in his eyes. He couldn't deal with this. He needed a line, a pill, a needle, whatever it was he did now.

Adrian extended the notebook with a shaky hand, but before he let me take it, he asked, "You aren't gonna write on New Year's because you think the story you have to tell is what happened on New Year's five years ago, right?"

"You mean Christian?" It was the first time *that* name escaped my lips in ages.

Adrian inclined his head in a sharp nod.

"No. I don't think so. I don't know what I'm gonna write about yet."

"Good." Adrian relinquished the book. " 'Cause that's not your whole story. Not even close."

"I know."

Adrian rose to leave. He squeezed my hand as he passed, but didn't try to kiss me or hug me. He didn't even say good-bye. As his foot hit the first step, he turned and said, "Make it a movie like we planned, okay?"

I smiled over my shoulder.

"I'm serious, man. And I don't care who you get to play me, but you know when the screen goes black, before the closing credits, put that it's dedicated to Quentin."

I heard his voice falter, but his face was shrouded in darkness, so I couldn't see if he was crying again. Tears streamed down my cheeks as I added, "And Maya."

"And Maya," he echoed.

As I listened to him walk away, I pulled my knees up and hugged them, pressing the notebook between my thighs and chest. I let the tears fall hard. I let them freeze against my face in the cold. Then I had one more cigarette and I finally went inside.

I half expected Stacey to be waiting up for me when I tiptoed in at six a.m., but she wasn't. I packed the notebook away and tried to get comfortable on the couch underneath the blue plaid blanket that had been on Stacey's bed at her mom's house for years.

I couldn't sleep. The sky had started to lighten, so instead of being completely dark, the room had that sickly gray tinge to it that I associated with the night I OD'd. This brought on a wave of anxiety and I squeezed my eyes shut, trying to pretend I was in my bed in California, where it was only four and still dark, but that didn't help. Only one thing would.

I crept into the room next to the living room with my backpack. The light in there seemed brighter, safer, more blue than gray. It fell on a twin bed with a Winnie the Pooh blanket and cast an ethereal glow around Lina, highlighting the dark brown ringlets of hair that surrounded her head on her pillow, the tiny hand that hung down from the side of the bed, and her smooth, cherubic cheeks. Even in her sleep, Lina smiled, innocent and carefree as a child should be. I wanted to freeze time, so she could stay that happy forever, never have to face the troubles that her mother and I had.

Settling on the floor amid her scattered toys, I unzipped my backpack. I kept my gaze trained on Lina, making sure the sound didn't disturb her, but she proved to be a very heavy sleeper.

I took out the notebook and stared at it. I had to tell this story. For Lina. Because I couldn't stop time and she would grow up, but she didn't have to grow up too fast like Stacey and I did.

At first I still didn't know what to tell or how to tell it. There wasn't just one defining moment that I could sum up in five to ten painstaking handwritten pages like my friends had done. I couldn't just write about the fight I'd had with Christian on New Year's Eve or my overdose in Scoville Park. There was so much more.

Skimming my friends' stories again, I realized that their lives had been bigger than the tales they told, too. Cass was more than a girl who coped with her mom's mental illness and her brother's absence by doing acid. Adrian was more than a kid who felt abandoned by both his birth parents and his adoptive parents. And that's when I saw it: my story was the sum of all these parts.

I glanced at Lina again, reassuring myself of her deep sleep, and then I quietly ripped pages from the notebook. I removed each person's story, or ballad, as I dubbed them so long ago, and began to arrange them like puzzle pieces. I didn't put them in chronological order, but in the order in which they'd influenced my larger story. Next, I tore out blank pages of paper and placed them in between, marking the gaps I'd have to bridge with my memories. Each one could be its own ballad, some short as a punk anthem, some long as an epic song.

I took a cue from the movies, opening with a topographical view of Oak Park. I smiled as I imagined a camera focusing in on Scoville Park, the only place in my hometown that I would ever think of as home, as my stage to shine on, as mine.

AUTHOR'S NOTE

This book is a work of fiction. Oak Park is a real place and I did grow up there around the same time as my characters, but the story and all the people in it were born in my imagination.

Why did I write about a real place? Because I love reading about the Chicago area during different eras and wanted to capture my corner of Chicagoland in the era in which I came of age, the early nineties. The landscape is forever changing: the car spindle in Berwyn is gone, Ambrosia's has long since closed, the Fireside Bowl doesn't hold punk shows anymore, and even Scoville Park looks different. But now these places will always exist the way I remember them in this book.

For the sake of full disclosure, here's what I have in common with my main character: Kara is a year older than me. We both have hazel eyes, love PJ Harvey, root for the Chicago White Sox, and have a weakness for boys with tattoos. I have a younger brother, but he's nothing like Liam at all. My parents are divorced, but they divorced when I was older than Kara and they aren't really like Kara's parents. I did meet one of my best friends while shoplifting at North Riverside Mall. I've also known a few people who dyed their nether regions bizarre colors. But none of my friends were models for any of my characters.

On a more serious note, there was a real heroin problem in Oak Park when I was a teen. I was not addicted to heroin, but knew people who were. Like Kara, I struggled with self-injury while in high school and into my twenties. Both of these issues are close to my heart, so I want to provide you with resources in case you or your loved ones are coping with addiction, depression, or self-injury:

S.A.F.E. ALTERNATIVES: www.selfinjury.com;
1-800-DONTCUT

To Write Love on Her Arms: www.twloha.com

National Hopeline Network: www.hopeline.com;
1-800-SUICIDE

SAMHSA: findtreatment.samhsa.gov (substance abuse treatment facility locator)

The Addiction Project: www.hbo.com/addiction/

BALLADS OF

STEPHANIE KUEHNERT

READING GROUP GUIDE

DISCUSSION QUESTIONS

1. "The ballad of suburbia: give me loud to drown out the silence," Kara says as she bonds with Liam over live music. Silence is a major theme in the novel. Discuss the ways in which Kara and her friends cope with the silence. Why is it necessary for them to drown it out?

2. Kara and Maya's friendship is initially formed because they recognize each other's punk rock style. Identify some of the other moments where the main characters search for social and cultural markers on the road toward friendship and romantic interests. Do these initial and sometimes superficial connections often lead to lasting relationships? Why or why not?

3. Kara, Wes, and Liam move away from the "safety" of suburbia to heal. After Quentin's death, Kara says the parents are in "suburban witch-hunt mode." What does this imply about the conventional ideas about the suburbs? What does this say about the significance of appearances? Are appearances more important to the parents, or their children? In what ways?

4. Maya, Kara, Christian, and Liam all fantasize about escaping to Florida. Figuratively and literally, in what ways do the characters escape? What are they escaping from?

5. Scoville Park becomes everyone's stomping ground. What does Scoville Park represent? How does the perception of this place evolve from the beginning of the novel to the end?

6. In Adrian's ballad he writes, "The one good thing about coming from no one is there's no one to answer to." Does this account for Adrian's unattached behavior? Is this an excuse?

7. Many of the ballads are declarations of pain and quests for answers. Discuss the various characters before and after their ballads. Do you feel more sympathetic to the characters once you know their individual histories? Do you become more involved in who they are? Whose ballad would you have liked to read that wasn't included?

8. The teenage characters spend a lot of energy trying to avoid ending up like their parents. Do you think any of them succeed? Particularly in Maya's case, does attempting to run away from her mother's past cause her to run right into history?

9. Because much of the story is narrated by Kara and the ballads are first person accounts, the adults rarely seem relevant, and are mostly included as sources of pain. Do you think this portrayal of the parents is fair?

10. Compare Wes and Cass's relationship with Kara and Liam's. How do they mirror each other? How are they different?

11. Quentin's and Maya's deaths seem to add to the silence of suburbia. When Kara ODs and asks Liam to hold on to the notebook to protect her friends' ballads out of fear that the parents might read it, is she protecting her friends or only adding to the silence? Do you think the parents have a right to know? Did Kara make the right decision?

12. How is depression portrayed in the novel? How does it affect characters other than those who are directly dealing with it?

13. Kara expresses her difficulty making friends, saying "I can't get past the feeling that I don't belong." The mosh pit is portrayed as both a place of violence and camaraderie. What is the sig-

nificance of the mosh pit in the novel? What other places are similar? How does the mosh pit help Kara get over her crowd insecurities?

14. Both Stacey and Kara lose the presence of their fathers, physically and emotionally. Compare and contrast how that affects their own romantic relationships with men. Does one make better choices over the other?

A CHAT WITH THE AUTHOR

Q: The opening lines from the Smashing Pumpkins are really powerful. Why did you start there?

A: Simply because I think it's a beautiful song about Chicago. When
I moved away from Chicago and would go back home to visit,
that song would always pop into my head—even though I wasn't
born in Chicago, it's my home. Some of my memories of growing
up in the Chicago area are beautiful, some are painful, but it's my
place. I think that's how Kara feels, too, and the song just sums
those feelings up perfectly.

Q: Whose ballad is closest to your heart? Whose was most difficult
to write? Do you have a favorite?

A: I don't know which is closest to my heart; they all are to some degree. None of them directly relate to my life experiences, but I've
felt the emotions that each character is expressing at some point.
Adrian's ballad is my favorite. I love his voice and it was a nice
change of pace for me to write from a male POV. Though I loved
writing in Stacey's voice, too. Maya's and Christian's ballads were
the most difficult to write. Maya's ballad is a suicide note. It was
very complex. And Christian . . . he's an abuser. He lies to himself.
His view of the truth is skewed, so how is he going to be honest
in his ballad?

Q: Christian seems to be the "villain" of the novel. Is his name meant
to be ironic? Did you include his backstory to make him more

human? Are his mother's death and his stepmother's flight supposed to justify his violence toward women? And why is that coupled with the tenderness he shows his little sister?

A: Christian's backstory certainly does not justify or excuse his violent actions. I included his ballad for the same reason I included the others, because I believe, like Adrian does, that an event or series of events can shape who we become. Of course how we were raised comes into play as well and look how Christian's dad treats women. I don't think people are just evil or "villains" through and through. Real people are multidimensional and I strive to portray my characters that way. I know firsthand from volunteering with domestic violence survivors and surviving an abusive relationship myself that abusers like Christian are not mean all the time. They often do have a tender side like Christian with his sister. And yes, his name is meant to be ironic.

Q: Female friendships seem to be central in the novel (Mary and Jessica; Kara, Maya, and Cass; and Kara and Stacey). What are you ultimately saying about them?

A: Teenage female friendships fascinate me. They are so complicated. They can save a girl's life or they can destroy her. I've experienced each of these types of friendships. I've had the backstabbing/mean-girlfriend, the friend who is so dear, but you both have too many trust issues to open up, and the childhood friend from whom you grow apart. Ultimately, I guess I'm hoping that when I write about female friendships, it will help girls to examine their friendships, cherish and build the healthy ones, and escape the unhealthy.

Q: Did you pull from your own experiences to portray the early stages of Adrian and Kara's relationship?

A: Oh, god . . . Yeah, a little. I definitely had a couple of those we're-not-really-dating-but-we-kinda-are relationships. And of course I got attached like Kara did.

Q: How many ballads did you contemplate writing while you were trying to find the right lines for each character? Was it a difficult process? Can you share some lyrics that didn't make it into the final story?

A: Actually all the ballads that I planned to write made it into the book. I usually wrote a draft of the ballad before coming up with the lyrics. I'm constantly listening to music so if I heard a line that reminded me of a character, I'd write it down. Some, like Adrian's and Cass's, came to me right away, and I knew Liam's would be from a Johnny Cash song so I just listened to a lot of Johnny Cash. In the first draft, Maya's lyric was "She looks like a teenage anthem/She looks like she could have been happy in another life" by Everclear, but that song came out after Maya died. I think the Hole lyric suits her much better anyway. That was the toughest part, finding a lyric within the right time period by a band that the character would listen to.

Q: What type of research did you do to portray Kara's sensation of cutting? Was it difficult for you to get inside her head during those moments?

A: I didn't have to do research because I self-injured as a teenager. All I had to do was remember, but those are some rough memories. So in some ways it wasn't hard to get inside her head because I've been there, but in other ways, it was the hardest part about writing this book. It's a painful place to go. I haven't cut in eight years, but it's a lifelong addiction.

Q: How much of the novel, like ballads, is supposed to be didactic? What do you want your readers to take away from the novel, from the perceptions of suburbia?

A: I never go about writing a novel intending to teach a lesson or moral. It's always about the characters. I like to write about the kinds of characters that I wanted to read about as a teen, to tell stories that are underrepresented in literature. I wrote this book simply to give kids like my characters a voice. There is a perception of suburbia as perfect and safe, but there are broken homes and broken hearts everywhere. I think there is a tendency in our culture—maybe in suburbia especially—to ignore the elephant in the middle of the room. We don't talk about our problems. We don't always pay enough attention to what's going on with our kids and then are shocked when they OD on drugs or a school shooting happens. I didn't have a lesson in mind while writing this book. I just wrote it to break the silence.

Q: Writing is obviously important to you, but why do you make it central to the story? Does creating their own stories give the characters a sense of control? Is it supposed to be therapeutic?

A: I do believe it is therapeutic. It was for me and for many of my friends growing up. As a teenager, it is so hard to talk to anyone about your feelings, but if you don't work through them in some way, you can lose control of your life. This book is ultimately about breaking silence. Writing is the tool that these characters use to do that.

Q: Why did you end with Lina?

A: Because she is the future. She is the next generation; she is hope. I don't write stories with happily-ever-after endings—Maya and Quentin wouldn't have died if I did—but I do like to end on a hopeful note. Kara has been resistant to writing her ballad for years, but looking at Lina, she finally realizes why it is important to be open about the painful things in life. She's learned to break the silence. Hopefully, Lina will have a better life because of it.

Q: Do you have another book in the works?

A: Yes, I have a couple actually. One draws on my favorite Greek myth, the tale of Persephone, and continues to explore the dynamics of friendship between teenage girls. The other is my "bartender book." I've been a bartender for a few years and have collected some great material so I need to write a bartender character!

ENHANCE YOUR BOOK CLUB

1. Listen to your favorite song and create your own ballad. Or, write that ballad you thought was missing or rewrite the ballad of your favorite character.

2. Whether you're from the suburbs or the city, start your own collection of quirky newspaper clippings.

3. Visit the author's website at www.stephaniekuehnert.com and listen to the playlist she's made to go along with the novel. Try making your own mix CD out of the various songs and bands that are mentioned in *Ballads of Suburbia* to take with you to your next book club meeting. It'll set the mood—and keep your ears tuned to the lyrics to pick up some of the author's influences.